Broken Soul

"Steamy, violent, and hinting even more great things to come, *Broken Soul* is a series highlight. . . . Jane fans will be delighted." — All Things Urban Fantasy

"The story is fantastic, the action is intense, the romance sweet, and the characters seep into your soul. At the end of *Broken Soul*, I smiled, closed the book, and hugged it. I loved this one." — Vampire Book Club

"Intense action scenes, shocking revelations, and Machiavellian plotlines keep readers on their toes, though it's the steady world building and dynamic characterization that keep readers returning." — Smexy Books

Black Arts

"Faith Hunter returns with a bang. . . . [Her] mastery for writing suspense-filled chapters that keep the reader on pins and needles turning pages shines through." — SF Site

"*Black Arts* is possibly the best Jane Yellowrock book to date. With a perfect balance of action, relationships, magic, and healing, fans will love it, and new readers will get sucked in." — All Things Urban Fantasy

"An action-packed thriller. . . . Betrayal, deception, and heartbreak all lead the way in this roller-coaster ride of infinite proportions that will keep readers twisting and turning until the very last page." — Smexy Books

"A fascinating story [that] showcases Jane at both her most vulnerable and most kick-ass. Faith Hunter has outdone herself." — Fresh Fiction

Blood Trade

"In *Blood Trade* Jane comes back with a vengeance . . . a perfect blend of dark fantasy and mystery with a complex and tough vampire-killing heroine."

— All Things Urban Fantasy

continued . . .

"Faith Hunter's Jane Yellowrock series is a high-octane urban fantasy that follows its own rules and keeps you guessing until the very end." —Smexy Books

Death's Rival

"A thrilling mystery with epic action scenes and a kick-ass heroine with claws and fangs." —All Things Urban Fantasy

"Holy moly, this was an amazing read! Jane is the best urban fantasy heroine around. *Death's Rival* catapulted this series to the top of my must-buy list."—Night Owl Reviews

"A wild, danger-filled adventure. The world building includes a perfect blend of seductive romance, nail-biting action, intriguing characters, and betrayal from all sides."
—*RT Book Reviews*

Raven Cursed

"A lot of series seek to emulate Hunter's work, but few come close to capturing the essence of urban fantasy: the perfect blend of intriguing heroine, suspense, [and] fantasy with just enough romance." —SF Site

"A super thriller. . . . Fast-paced, *Raven Cursed* is an exhilarating paranormal whodunit with several thriller spins."
—Genre Go Round Reviews

Mercy Blade

"There was something about the Jane Yellowrock series that drew me in from the very beginning. . . . *Mercy Blade* is top-notch, a five-star book!" —Night Owl Reviews

"I was delighted to have the opportunity to read another Jane Yellowrock adventure. I was not disappointed but was somewhat overwhelmed by the obvious growth in Faith Hunter's writing skill." —*San Francisco Book Review*

"Faith Hunter has created one of my favorite characters ever. Jane Yellowrock is full of contradictions . . . highly recommended." —Fresh Fiction

Blood Cross

"Readers eager for the next book in Patricia Briggs's Mercy Thompson series may want to give Faith Hunter a try."
—*Library Journal*

"In a genre flooded with strong, sexy females, Jane Yellowrock is unique. . . . Her bold first-person narrative shows that she's one tough cookie but with a likable vulnerability . . . a pulse-pounding, page-turning adventure."
— *RT Book Reviews*

Skinwalker

"Seriously. Best urban fantasy I've read in years, possibly ever." — C. E. Murphy, author of *Shaman Rises*

"Stunning. . . . Plot and descriptions so vivid, they might as well be pictures or videos." — SF Site

"A fabulous tale with a heroine who clearly has the strength to stand on her own . . . a wonderfully detailed and fast-moving adventure that fills the pages with murder, mystery, and fascinating characters." — Darque Reviews

"A promising new series with a strong heroine. . . . Jane is smart, quick, witty." — Fresh Fiction

More Praise for
the Novels of Faith Hunter

"The world [Hunter] has created is unique and bleak . . . [an] exciting science fiction thriller."
— *Midwest Book Review*

"Entertaining . . . outstanding supporting characters. . . . The strong cliff-hanger of an ending bodes well for future adventures." — *Publishers Weekly*

"Hunter's distinctive future vision offers a fresh though dark glimpse into a newly made postapocalyptic world. Bold and imaginative in approach, with appealing characters and a suspense-filled story, this belongs in most fantasy collections." — *Library Journal*

"It's a pleasure to read this engaging tale about characters connected by strong bonds of friendship and family. Mixes romance, high fantasy, [and] apocalyptic and postapocalyptic adventure to good effect." — *Kirkus Reviews*

"Hunter's very professionally executed, tasty blend of dark fantasy, mystery, and romance should please fans of all three genres." — *Booklist*

ALSO BY FAITH HUNTER

The Jane Yellowrock Novels

The Rogue Mage Novels

DARK HEIR

A Jane Yellowrock Novel

Faith Hunter

A ROC BOOK

ROC
Published by the Penguin Group
Penguin Group (USA) LLC, 375 Hudson Street,
New York, New York 10014

USA | Canada | UK | Ireland | Australia | New Zealand | India | South Africa | China
penguin.com
A Penguin Random House Company

First published by Roc, an imprint of New American Library,
a division of Penguin Group (USA) LLC

First Printing, April 2015

ISBN 978-0-451-46596-2

Printed in the United States of America
10 9 8 7 6 5 4 3 2 1

To my Renaissance Man,
who can fix anything, who has an open mind-set,
a generous heart,
and who puts up with my still being
"such a strange little girl"

ACKNOWLEDGMENTS

Let's Talk Promotions at www.ltpromos.com for getting me where I am today.

Lucienne Diver of the Knight Agency for guiding my career, being an ear when I need advice, and working your fingers to the bone.

Isabel Farhi of Roc for keeping tabs on me through review time.

Eileen Chetti, copy editor, for the fine work at catching all the boo-boos!

Cliff Nielsen . . . for all the work and talent that goes into the covers.

Mindy Mymudes for beta reading. For being a fount of knowledge. For being a great friend.

Lee Williams Watts for being the best travel companion and assistant a girl can have!

Joy Robinson for holding my hand through two travel crises.

Beast Claws! Street team extraordinaire!

Poet and writer Sarah Spieth for giving me Jane's medicine bag. It is perfect!

Margot Dacunha for help on the French lines throughout the book.

Richard Copeland for gun stuff (all errors being mine, of course).

Mike Prater for letting me be a pest with the odd questions.

As always, a huge thank-you to Jessica Wade of Roc, the best editor I could have. You make me into a much better writer than I am capable of alone. I don't know how you keep the high quality up, book after book, especially now, with the Kicker kicking things around. You are extraordinary.

AUTHOR'S NOTE

Hi, all. I'd like to touch on a few ways in which Jane's world is different from ours. In *Dark Heir*:

The Coliseum Place Baptist Church burned in the aftermath of Hurricane Katrina. In reality, it was demolished after being burned, but in Jane's world it still stands, scorched but intact. It became, in Jane's world, sacred ground, but no longer a place of worship. There are small storefront churches everywhere in the South, offering sermons and worship in multiple languages and offering to help the community, just like The Church in this novel.

Tech: Inevitably, in a long-running series, technology will catch up with a writer and a character. In order to keep Jane and her world fresh and believable, I've tried to look ahead, into the future, to see what might be real in just a few years, and to incorporate that into the Yellowrock world. I hope I've been successful, but (ha-ha) only time will tell.

When it comes to guns: Jane is not a shooter, US military, or even a dedicated hunter. Unlike Eli, she doesn't think about guns and weapons in proper military vocabulary or formulas. She thinks "point and shoot" and prefers idiotproof weapons. Her terminology was created for that mind-set. I hope the military and shooters out there will remember that when they evaluate the weapons sequences.

Dark Heir is book nine of the Jane Yellowrock series. YOU, the Beast-fans, are the reason why. You have my "forever thanks"!

CHAPTER 1

Twist Your Lil' Bobblehead Right Off

I stood against the wall, nursing a busted knuckle, watching my sensei try to recover. Daniel held a black belt, second dan, in hapkido, had a black belt in tae kwon do, and a black belt in tai chi—the combat martial art, not the pretty forms that hippies and old people do on beaches at sunrise. (Not that I had anything against pretty martial arts, hippies, or old people. I'd outlived all of the people who were alive when I was born, so I was old. Real old.)

Daniel hadn't competed in years, however, believing that competition was for sissies and martial arts were for fighting and killing. He was probably a lot more dangerous than most people who did compete. And right now he was on his back on the practice mat, trying to figure out if his lungs still worked. It had been only about thirty seconds since I'd thrown him to the floor, knocking the breath out of him, but that can seem like a lot of time when you aren't breathing.

"I'm not kissing him," Eli Younger said, still gasping, sweat dripping off him onto the mat in little splats. My Beast and I had been sparring with both of them. Admittedly, it was a little too wound heavy to be just sparring, but testosterone and the urge to defeat the skinny girl were powerful motivators, keeping them coming back for more when they should have stayed down. And Beast had been having fun.

"Artificial respiration isn't technically kissing," I said, watching as Daniel fought back the natural panic of the air starved, arching his back, stretching his throat, trying to force open his airway.

"Still not kissing him. Sorry, bro," Eli said, toeing Daniel's shoulder. "Been nice knowin' you."

Daniel sucked in a breath that sounded like rubber bicycle tubing being stretched out by a couple of disgruntled sumo wrestlers. Strained. Very strained. Eli laughed. Faster than most humans can manage, Daniel whipped his arm around, his fist catching Eli on the outer knee joint. If Eli hadn't already been bending into the direction of the hit, his knee would have buckled and Eli would have needed a brace or vamp blood to heal. Daniel was powerful, even flat on his back.

As it was, the guys rolled across each other like high school wrestlers, but punching and stabbing with fingers, kneeing below the belt. They separated, rolled to their feet, and engaged again. All I needed was popcorn and a beer and it would have been perfect. Delighted to sit this one out, I slid down the wall to the wood floor, my sweaty back to the wall, knees bent in a half lotus, and relaxed. The guys were really going at it, fists, kicks, sweat flinging, with a little blood mixed in. I had to wonder if something was bothering them, because this was starting to look real.

My sensei's style was perfect for me, because I had always studied mixed disciplines and never went for any belt. I trained to stay alive, using a fast, violent amalgam of styles geared to the total annihilation of an attacker. My fighting style had best been described as dirty. Daniel and Eli, my partner in Yellowrock Securities, both fought dirty. I winced as Eli took a boxer's blow straight to his chin and wobbled on his feet. But either he recovered fast or it was only a feint, because he kicked out, catching Daniel in the solar plexus. In fighters' terms it wasn't a low blow, but since I had just hit Sensei there, it wasn't exactly sweet either.

Daniel skipped away, his breathing pained. I wondered whether he'd broken a rib.

The dojo was in the back room of a small jewelry store

on St. Louis Street, the store specializing in faceted gems, vintage styles and settings, and real antique pieces. The dojo was down a narrow service alley, thirty inches wide, damp, and dim, and was open to the public only after store hours. I was one of a select few students Daniel saw during the day. I had my own key.

Eli took a fast series of punches to the ribs, bounced off a white-painted wall across from me and into the mirrored back wall. Daniel nearly got his boy parts crushed by a kick, but he jumped back, caught one of Eli's ankles, and twisted it hard and fast, putting torqueing pressure on the knee. Eli was expecting the move and leaped off the floor into a twirl and kicked Daniel in the side of the neck with his other foot. They both went down. Daniel out for the count. Idiots. Eli was wheezing with pain. The hand he supported himself with had left a bloody print on the mirror.

The long room had hardwood floors, two white-painted walls—one now stained with blood—one mirrored wall (ditto), and one wall with French doors that looked out over a typical New Orleans–style enclosed courtyard planted with tropical and semitropical plants. Three cats, tails twitching, lounged on a low brick-stucco wall near the splashing fountain, which was designed in the fashion of a mountain stream, with the small pool at the bottom filled with plants. The cats, looking bored and hot, were watching the humans fight. The enclosed courtyard was surrounded by two- and three-story buildings and was overlooked by wrought-iron galleries dripping with potted vines and flowering plants. Sensei lived upstairs in one of the apartments, and he usually dropped down using a rappelling rope and climbing gear. I had a feeling he'd be going back up the hard way, one slow step at a time.

Since Daniel was rolling over, marginally awake, and it looked as if the fight was over, I shifted my weight and clapped slowly, the sound ringing brightly off the unadorned walls. "Danny boy, I think you got your butt beat," I said.

"Maybe." He winced as he rolled to his backside and stood upright, stretching muscles that had to have deep bruises. "But it took two of you. Tag team." Daniel was average height, had muscles like rolls of barbed wire and a face no one would remember for two seconds. A man no one would notice.

Silent, working out the kinks, he walked around the room, bare feet solid, body as balanced as a walking tree, looking Eli and me over, considering.

I grinned at my partner and said, "Yeah, but I'm still holding back. A lot."

"You are not holding back," Daniel said, disbelief etching his face. "Seriously? Still?"

"Bro, she is absolutely still holding back." Eli bent his injured knees, testing for damage that might need more than ice, elevation, anti-inflammatory meds, and time to heal. "When she really lets go, it's nothing like human speed or human strength. She'd twist your lil' bobblehead right off that skinny neck."

I managed to keep the discomfort off my face. I still wasn't used to part of the world knowing that I was a supernat, and was even less accustomed to hearing it spoken of like it was no big deal. It had been my secret for so long that it still *felt* like a big deal. But Eli was right. If I let go with Beast-strength and -speed, I could do some damage. Once he knew I'd been holding back, my training and sparring sessions with Daniel had changed. Now he pushed the normal human boundaries, trying to see what my limits were. There were two problems with that: I didn't really know what my boundaries were, especially with the newfound ability to fold or bubble time, and my limits seemed to be changing now that my Beast and I had soul-bonded.

Daniel tossed a dry towel to Eli and the two guys dried off, still trash-talking.

I ignored them and pushed off the floor to my feet, seeing my reflection in the long wall mirror. I was moving a little differently now, smoother, more catlike, limbs and joints and muscles rolling and balanced and effortless. It was freaky. In the last month or so, my eyes had started to glow more often as Beast stared out at the world through my vision. Again, freaky. I still had my long black hair, currently braided close to my head, and the copper skin of my tribe—*Chelokay*, or *Tsalagi*, the Cherokee. Also known as The People.

I caught a towel tossed my way and wiped down. Showers would have to wait until we got back to the house. The dojo wasn't set up for lockers and shower stalls.

Outside, the fountain tinkled in the enclosed courtyard.

A cat made a *mrowr* sound, probably telling Daniel that it was suppertime. Cats could be demanding that way. I know. My Beast is a mountain lion and she's big on being fed, though she prefers her food freshly caught and slaughtered by her killing teeth.

From the pile of gear on the floor, I heard both of our phones singing to us—both playing "Hit Me with Your Best Shot," by Pat Benatar. It was the ringtone for Alex, the other Younger brother, and the tech partner of Yellowrock Securities. If he was ringing both lines, this couldn't be good.

I bent and caught up both cells, underhand throwing Eli's to him and opening the Kevlar cover to mine. Eli said, "Go ahead."

"Get to suckhead HQ. Something's going down."

Eli and I grabbed up our gobags and trotted from the dojo, into the alley, moving fast. I gave a single wave to Daniel as the door shut behind me. I had a glimpse of Sensei, still standing against the wall, fists on his hips, looking better than Eli's opponents usually did. I knew he wanted to go with us—he had been hinting it—but dealing with vamps took practice and a lot of emotional and verbal restraint. I wasn't sure how restrained Daniel would be if a male vamp came on to him for dinner and a date. Vamps were a lot less reticent about sexual matters than most humans, and Daniel gave out strong, uncompromising hetero signals, a challenge to any vamp. Eli had quickly learned to fob them off with a laugh and a polite refusal, but Daniel struck me as the belt-him-first-and-stalk-away-mad-second kind. Which could get him dead, fast.

"You're on speaker," Eli said to Alex as the dojo door closed. "It's too early to be a vamp problem. An attacker would fry." I closed my cell and listened.

"Nothing on the outside cameras. It's inside. At the ballroom."

Vamps could maneuver inside most of vamp central, the windows being long and narrow and newly covered by electric shutters. I took a breath to speak and got a lungful of alley stink that was enough to bowl over an elephant. It smelled of urine—some of it not from cats—and all of it baking in the summer heat and humidity. I said, "Gimme details, because I'm not heading back to vamp HQ to settle a love spat or to get in the middle of a long-standing feud between vamp factions." There were too many vamps in the relatively small space, and there had been more than a few violent incidents. Vamp-on-vamp action was outside my job requirements as long as no humans got caught in the cross fire.

"Got nothing that makes sense," Alex said. "Still pulling up camera footage. But it's bloody and it's bigger than the usual fanghead altercation."

Still moving at speed, we emerged from the alley, clanged the gate shut, and made it to the SUV, with Eli beeping the vehicle open. The trapped heat exploded out. We opened all the doors to let it air, which gave us time to take in the scenery. Traffic clogged the streets in the French Quarter so badly that we might not be able to get out of the parking spot unless someone was looking for one and let us out so they could get in. It was bumper-to-bumper gridlock. I'd be glad when my Harley was repaired and I could again weave through the New Orleans traffic. "We're gonna hafta hoof it to HQ, Alex," Eli said, "but we're not going in wearing street clothes. We'll change here. Give us details as they firm."

"Copy. Better you than me in this heat, dude."

Eli got behind the wheel and synced up our cells to the vehicle. I took the backseat and started gearing up—leathers, weapons, boots. Not easy in the backseat of an overheated SUV with windows tinted vamp-black, even one as roomy as the brand-spanking-new one Leo had provided for my use. Eli turned on the cab lights and the AC, but it would take forever to cool off. I shook out a handful of baby powder and tossed the container to Eli, both of us liberally powdering down the sweat and sliding the leathers over our limbs as Alex began to give us the particulars.

"Looks like it started in the sub-four basement about three minutes ago. Two fangheads fighting over a human woman. She's hurt. Del sent down reinforcements, but they got caught up in it and now it's a brawl."

Eli spat a curse under his breath, sliding on his new, high-tech combat boots and yanking on the laces. He had a point. Injured humans meant we had no choice but to intervene.

"It's getting nasty. Sending you vid now."

On the SUV video screen, we had a clear view of a sub-four hallway and about ten vamps. It was a bloody mess, not abnormal for vamps fighting, but weird to be happening before dusk, when most older vamps were sleepy or sleeping, and the young ones were out cold, often unable to be roused.

"That looks wrong," I said of the fight. "But I'm not sure why." I checked the loads of my weapons and slid them into the oversized gobag. We were licensed to carry in Louisiana, but no one wanted to get detained if a hot, sweaty cop, stuck in traffic, saw us jog by.

"Yeah. They look . . . stumble-y. Like *Night of the Living Dead* but faster," Eli said.

"That's it. Vamps are graceful, and these are klutzes. I'm ready," I said, strapping on my thigh rig.

The SUV's engine went silent and we slid from the dark interior into the humidity. It was like being hit in the face with a soaking-wet, wrecking-ball-sized sponge. Eli beeped the SUV locked, and we reactivated our cells and started down the sidewalk, moving fast.

Holy crap. We had to *jog* in this heat?

As if reading my mind, Eli called back, "It'll put hair on your chest."

"That's what I'm afraid of." Inside me, Beast chuffed and sent an image of my half-Beast shape, covered in Beast pelt. I didn't have the breath to reply, not in this heat, and just kept jogging, the late-day summer sun like a steam torch on my exposed skin. I followed Eli down back alleys and, once, through a T-shirt and tourist-kitsch business, out the back, through the courtyard, into the back door of a restaurant, and out the front onto the street on the other side. No one stopped us, but I'd bet we'd end up on someone's YouTube channel somewhere.

To Alex, I said, "I know Del is in charge, but notify Bruiser that something's transpiring at HQ. Just in case."

"Copy," Alex said, his voice toneless enough to make my skin itch.

Bruiser was my . . . something. *Boyfriend* was too high school, *lover* was too sex-specific, *significant other* seemed more long-term and stable than what we might be starting to have. So *my something* was the best I could do. But he was also the former primo of the Master of the City of New Orleans, and Del, while capable, might need some backup. Informing him was not the same thing as calling for Bruiser's help like said high schooler. Or at least I didn't think it was. Having a "my something" wasn't exactly common for me.

We rounded the corner, approaching vamp central from an oblique angle, not one I took often. I needed to walk the area more. Next winter maybe. During a hard, cold rain.

The high brick fence that surrounded HQ was topped with coils of razor wire, and the heavy iron gate—replaced after it was damaged, not so long ago—looked fine, the central, circular drive empty of cars. Peaceful. Calm. But when I pulled on my Beast-hearing, I heard muted screams and the sound of gunfire. I sped up, moving from a jog to a sprint. "Gunfire," I reported.

"Roger that," Eli said, sounding calm, his breathing steady as he increased his speed to match mine. The former active-duty Ranger always sounded calm, though, so that wasn't such a big deal. "Alex?" he said. "Update."

"They broke the camera. Sorry, bro. Working now to integrate your new headsets into the system. Get ready to switch out."

"That might be the intent of the weird-looking fight," I said. "Taking us off-line and out of the intel so someone can do something they shouldn't."

"'Something they shouldn't' covers a lot of possibilities," Eli said.

"Is everything localized on sub-four?" I asked.

"Negative," Alex said. "As of right now, per the cameras, it's subsiding at the ballroom but spreading to sub-three and farther into sub-four."

"Crap on crackers," I said. But at least the violence wasn't on sub-five.

Chained in the lowest basement at vamp headquarters was one of the Sons of Darkness, one of the oldest vamps on earth, one of the founding fathers, as it was. His existence there had been a secret. Not so much now. Joses Bar-Judas was trouble of the worst vamp kind—a nearly immortal blood-drinker, but this one had the powers of a superhero and the morals of Torquemada and his merry band of torturers. If Joses ever got his sanity back and his body rehabbed, he'd be capable of doing anything a vamp could do but better and faster, and he would also be able to do witch magic—no telling what kind of witch magic, but I was betting on powerful and bloody.

During the decades that his presence as a prisoner was secret, Joses had been a useful captive for Clan Pellissier, his blood giving the Master of the City, Leo Pellissier, and his cronies special power and abilities. But with his status known, he made a formidable, dangerous pawn on the chessboard of vamp politics, especially with the European vamps wanting his return. And if Joses ever truly recovered, he'd be a deadly, psycho enemy. If this fight had been about him—somebody wanting to kidnap him or kill him or drink his potent blood—we would have been in trouble. The Son of Darkness was a power I had no way to gauge, evaluate, or fight against.

We rounded the corner and raced out of the blaring sun and under the porte cochere. Baby powder, the stink of our sweat, and the smell of vamp blood filled my nostrils. "Coms system is a go," Alex said.

Eli and I secured our official cells, slipped on the high-tech ear-protector headsets. They had been created for variable noise reduction during tactical ops, where situational awareness and interunit communication were equally important. In combat, soldiers wore helmets. We hadn't gotten that far along in personal protection yet. The new headsets had only recently replaced the earbuds we used to use and were tied into the coms system at vamp HQ and to Alex, so we could hear what we needed to hear and yet be protected from the worst of the ear damage of weapons fire. Over the new headset, I heard Derek Lee, Leo's other Enforcer, say, "... standard ammo. Continue to take the vampires down. Three-burst, midcenter shots. They'll heal. Do not—repeat, do *not*—target humans. If humans are involved, use any of the nonlethal compliance methods at your disposal. Repeat, nonlethal measures for humans."

"We're in," I said to Alex, who was still back at the house. Then, to the security people at HQ, I said, "This is Jane Yellowrock, We're under the porte cochere. Protocol Cowbird."

"Legs," Derek replied. "Protocol Cowbird affirmed."

Cowbirds left their eggs in other birds' nests instead of building ones of their own. The protocol named after them had been designed not for fighting off vamps from outside, but for dealing with problems already on the inside, for instance, like a nestling that wanted to take over from the rightful owners. "Update us."

"We've got fighting in the subbasements," Derek said. "Hostilities are under control at ballroom and on sub-three, but sub-four is still hostile. Elevator is stopped on top floor, on override, at my order. But conflict has spread through basement stairs. I have men there, but they're cut off from reinforcements. And this fight's not according to previous methodology. They're not moving at vamp speed."

"Copy." That was what I'd noted on the cameras earlier, the stumbling, zombie-dance motions, still faster than human, but not the smooth, gliding, faster-than-sight speed vamps can use. Not normal.

There was no one at the back entrance, and Eli stepped out, motioning me to trail him and take the left wall. He'd take the right. I nodded. He moved ahead, pressed his palm over the biometric reader, and dashed into the cool dark of the windowless, air-conditioned entrance. I followed. The doors whooshed shut behind us and I took cover behind the half wall I'd had built there for just this purpose; I blinked, waiting for my eyes to adjust. As soon as I could, I did a quick look-see and popped back behind the wall.

With the exception of Eli, standing behind a decorative fluted column, the back entrance was empty of people. The white marble flooring, with its new black and gray marble fleur-de-lis inlay, and the pristine white walls were empty of blood-and-gore spatter. Art from some of New Orleans' best painters over the last three centuries hung on the walls, hiding things Eli and I might need someday, in handy-dandy caches built into the walls. The stairs to the ballroom were just ahead, the door open and a light angling in. I raced from behind the wall to an angle where I could see up and down at the stairs landing.

"Not moving at vamp speed? Possible compulsion?" Eli asked, taking us back to the important parts.

Multiple three-bursts from automatic weapons fire erupted over the coms system. Over it all and up the elevator shaft also echoed the piercing wails of vamps dying, high-pitched and eardrum piercing. Eli ripped off his earpieces and left the headset hanging.

I yanked mine away and then stuck it back to hear Derek say, "Best guess. Things have been dicey ever since Adrianna got here."

Despite the heat, I was suddenly cold all over and swore silently to myself. "*Adrianna?* How many times do I have to kill her?" Adrianna had been on the losing side in multiple attempts to take over the position of Master of the City of New Orleans, and I'd staked her more than once in retribution. She was gorgeous, violent, and even more wacko than most vamps. I'd been paid for her head not so long ago, but for reasons that had never made sense, Leo had, once again, refused to kill Adrianna true-dead. "When did she get here?" I pulled a vamp-killer and a silver stake. No more Mr. Nice Guy. This time when I saw her, her head was gonna roll.

"Last night about eleven. Leo welcomed her and put her on sub-four in a room that used to belong to her and her scions."

"Stairs from sub-three opening into the closet? Lock on the outside? Everything falling off the walls? Everything rotten?" I asked.

"Stairs and lock, yes. Same room, but redecorated."

"So he knew she was coming," I spat. "He's known for a while."

"Best guess." Derek didn't sound happy about it. "I shoulda called," he added, a familiar ring of self-blame in his words, "I get that. But it looked like the usual vamp crazy shit."

"Language," Alex muttered, his voice tight as he monitored coms.

"Company," Eli said, his voice calm, cold, and uncompromising. His combat voice. He nodded to the elevator shaft.

"Fighting's supposed to be contained in the ballroom," I said.

"Yeah," Eli said, adjusting his weapons. "Funny how things change."

But the elevator wasn't moving, hadn't arrived. The doors opened slowly, an unbalanced, uneven motion, the way they'd move if hands forced them open instead of the electronics. Rather than the beautifully decorated, ice white and cream-of-tartar–toned elevator, we saw an empty shaft, black, dank, and dark.

From the shaft came the stink of vamp and human blood and the recorded strains of Chris LeDoux singing "This Cowboy's Hat." It was an odd combo. "Blood," I whispered, as air from the lower floors reached me. "Human and vamp. And . . . holy crap."

Something in my voice alerted Eli, because he switched weapons faster than I could follow and pulled up his small subgun loaded with silver ammo. A black form rose in the open shaft. Eli started firing, to heck with three-burst rounds. He shot in bursts of what sounded like ten rounds each before a short pause and a second burst. Eli emptied one mega-mag and slammed a fresh one home.

In the full second and a half that it took Eli to remove and replace the magazine, the form slithered/slid/floated/flew out of the shaft. So fast it looked feathery. Beast rammed into the front of my brain. As black as the unlit chute, as dark as a minion of hell, the *thing* crawled across the floor on all fours, moving like a centipede, feathery, fast, as graceful as an insect or a bird or . . . a lizard. That was it. Whipping and undulating like a hybrid of an insect and a lizard, its head and neck and limbs working together and yet totally separate to propel it forward.

In an act that I had never, ever wanted to experience again, Beast reached through me and brought up the Gray Between, the gray place my skinwalker energies were stored. *No,* I thought at her. She ignored me. Time slowed fractionally, then more. And again, to a consistency of tar, a hot, clinging thickness to the air. The *thing* was Joses Bar-Judas. A Son of Darkness. Leo's prisoner. Until now.

The last time I saw him, he had been a sack of bones hanging on the wall of the lowest subbasement, crucified there with silver spikes, held in place with silver chains and several pocket watches, each containing a piece of the iron spike of Golgotha. He had been a dried-out, leathery husk of a *thing,* nowhere near human, blackened all over, with insane, glittering black eyes. He'd also been overly chatty for a nutcase with a dried-out strip of jerky for a tongue. And I had thrown a silver knife into his throat to shut him up.

In hindsight I could see that might have been unwise.

CHAPTER 2

Warp My Sexual Development Forever

His black eyes settled on me and his mouth opened slowly, so slowly, to reveal a maw full of cracked and broken teeth, brown with age, and fangs like tusks in his upper and lower jaws. Even in the time bubble created by my Beast and me, Joses Bar-Judas could see me, see us. Power rippled across him, sparking white and black, colder than an arctic snow, hotter than volcanic ash falling from a flaming sky. The power didn't so much dance across his skin as sizzle. So unbelievably powerful. And that was new. That meant he'd fed, and well.

I didn't know how it had been arranged or carried out, but the fight among vamps on sub-three and -four had been a diversion. For this guy.

In the bubble that let me stand outside of time, he altered course, shifting trajectory fractionally, heading right for us. Eli was squeezing the trigger of the subgun. From inside the bubble I could see the silver-lead rounds leaving the muzzle of the gun, spiraling and twisting, half an inch at a time, a puff of black dust exploding out with each round. And Joses, a Son of Darkness, ducked to evade them. He was that fast.

Faster than HQ's ambient time, I unsheathed a silver-plated vamp-killer. Leaped forward, taking the time bubble with me, ducking beneath the rounds blasting forward and the hot brass discharging out to the side of Eli's gun. My right arm extended in front of me, point forward, more like the way one would use a sword than the way one would hold a knife in a knife fight. I heard the deep tones of a voice in my earpiece, the word so slow the sound was meaningless.

I pushed off with my toes, stretching into the lunge, feeling the new muscle memory of sword practice supporting my intent. Joses opened his fingers, exposing his hand. Around his neck was a gold chain, like a necklace, with red things dangling from it like rubies. On his wrist he wore a bracelet, half-hidden by the tatters of clothing, or maybe tatters of half-mummified flesh; it too was shiny gold.

My eyes latched onto his black ones, his desiccated lips moving. Shock thrummed through me like the single tone of a large bell, recently struck, vibrating, a pounding pulse of surprise.

As the vibrations hit me, I realized that the pulse wasn't just shock, but was part of the word I'd been hearing. Joses Bar-Judas was speaking that word. That *wyrd*. A spell of darkness encoded into a single word, the power released when it was spoken.

The first syllable slid along my blade, heating it red-hot. Before I could react to the heat starting to burn where I gripped the hilt, it rolled up my arm, singeing the leather, heating the silver-over-titanium chain links between the outer leather and the silk lining. Over my shoulder and neck. The *wyrd* of power slammed me in the face like a sledgehammer.

Even in the time bubble, I was knocked backward, hard, my head whipped forward and back, my arm shoved down. I struck the wall, spine and back of my head first, then my limbs, ricocheting. My whole body shuddered at the impact of the power.

The time bubble popped.

I was rammed down into the marble floor, feeling my whole body hit and bounce. Just before everything went dark, I saw Joses Bar-Judas skitter out the door. Into the dusky . . . sunlight.

         *   *   *

I woke slowly, with a headache pounding like I had been tucked into a fifty-five-gallon drum and someone was beating on it with a mallet. My gut was twisted, a gripping torture that felt as if I had swallowed a nest of live rattlesnakes and they were attacking me all at once. "Holy crap on crackers with . . ." I gagged, retched, doubled up on the floor, as my adnominal muscles contracted and my lungs forgot to breathe. The bout of pain and nausea lasted forever before it began to ease. After too long a time, I was able to force a hand between my chest and thighs and press against the knot that used to be my belly. I licked my lips, unable to think, and not remembering what I'd been saying.

"Jane?" The voice was tinny and far away. Oh yeah. Someone had been calling me.

I managed to inhale, my ribs protesting. Strongly. But the smells that hit my nose were of nitrocellulose, burned gunpowder, blood. Lots of blood. Battle. I had to get better, fast.

"Jane!" the tinny voice shouted.

I grunted. Managed to slit open my eyes. The light was blinding. I scrunched them shut and waited out a dozen of the painful mallet-pain-heartbeats. When the ache seemed to be abating, I tried opening them again. I was lying on a white marble floor, on my side, with my back against a gray-white wall and my head turned at a painful angle. Over me hung a painting, crooked on the wall. I blinked groggily at it to see a blond woman with grayish hazel green eyes, wearing some kind of gauzy evening gown, her shoulders bare, her décolletage mostly bare too. I knew her. Katie. Katie the vampire. I knew vampires. I *worked* for vampires. *Right.* And I was sick because Beast had taken over and forced me to fold time. At least this time when the bubble of time popped, I wasn't throwing up blood.

Using one hand and both feet, I shoved myself upright, to a sitting position, knees bent up to my chest. The other hand fell, limp, pain ripping up my arm as it landed on the floor. There were blisters on the hand, the kind you get if you accidently pour scalding-hot tea on yourself. I'd done that at my sensei's dojo when I was a kid. It had required a trip to the emergency room, but the blisters had healed really fast. Because I was a skinwalker. It was all coming back.

The hand hurt when I tried to open it, and I sucked air through my teeth as I released the thing I was holding. It clattered to the floor. It was a knife, scorched, ruined. The blade, once silver-plated steel, was warped, the edge wavy, the silver blackened where it had melted and formed runnels before cooling again. The leather-wrapped hilt was blackened except for the shape of my hand. A vamp-killer. I kill vampires. It's what I do. *Right.*

"Janie! Answer me or I'm calling the cops!"

The memories finally started moving, a slow cascade that morphed into an avalanche. Alex. Coms. Eli. Derek. Joses. *Holy crap. The Son of Darkness.*

I raised the unblistered hand and tucked the headset back in place in one ear. "I'm here, Alex," I whispered, my throat so dry it hurt to breathe. "How long have I been out?"

"Ninety-seven seconds out totally, another hundred forty getting your wits back." He cursed foully and didn't apologize for it, so I knew he was scared. The four minutes, plus or minus, didn't seem like a long time, but in battle that could feel like forever, especially to the people watching and not taking part, unable to help.

"Update," I said.

"Eli and Derek and three security guys are running through the Quarter, chasing a smoking fanghead-zombie thing. I guess no one told the zombie-vamp that the sun was up and he needed sunscreen." Alex made a sound that could have been an attempt at laughter but fell far short. His levity was a crack at sounding macho, when he was really in panic mode.

I decided to not respond to it, saying instead, "Tell them to be careful. Joses has a *wyrd* of power and he knows how to use it."

"I know." Alex's voice went grim. He sounded harder, older, than he had only this morning. "We all know. Debrief," he said, ready to catch me up to date on the missing four minutes. "Eli put a mag and a half into him as you went all Jedi knight and attacked. In the next half second, Joses used the spell on you. Eli jumped behind the half wall. He wasn't hit. Derek appeared from the hallway and filled the zombie with silver. He took a spell-hit too, but not near as strong as yours. He dropped back through the doorway and out of line of fire. Then Eli put nearly a full magazine into the zombie's back. The vamp didn't use the spell this time, but the rounds didn't even slow him down.

"He took off outside, leaving a trail of smoke. Eli and Derek's men followed. Derek, when he could stand again, pulled you against the wall, out of the way, and went after them." He took a breath that sounded suspiciously tearful. I didn't comment on it. Just waited.

"Jane?" Before I could reply, he went on, his distress deeper. "Next time there's trouble at an entrance, stay behind the damn wall. It was built to protect you from every single thing that hit you, vamps, magic—"

"Eli's okay," I said, softly.

"You don't know that. He isn't answering on coms."

"Oh," I said, understanding why he was so rattled. "He's probably busy," I said gently. "And he's off premises, so they'll be communicating by talkies or cell. And they probably haven't had time to sync their phones into your system." Then, to give him something to do, I said, "Tell me what's happening on the other floors."

He took another breath, this one more stable but still wet sounding. "Yeah. Okay. I'm monitoring coms from offsite, so I don't have access to the remote joystick for the dynamic cams. But on sub-three we have vamps feeding in the hallways. Just a word of warning—don't go down there. I had to turn off the video. I need to scrub my eyeballs with bleach. There's stuff happening down there that's gonna give me nightmares and warp my sexual development forever."

"Yeah. I'm real worried about that." *Not.*

"How bad are you hurt?" he asked. "Do you need to shift?"

I blinked and looked up. Right. He could see me on the security camera. *Beast?* I thought at her. She didn't reply, and I had to wonder if the blast of magic had hurt her. I shook my head to clear it and sought the Gray Between, the place where my skinwalker magics rested. And it wasn't there. I . . . couldn't sense it at all. Fear twisted through me like frozen barbed wire, burning where it touched.

Using the action to cover my reaction, I pushed myself to my knees, then to my feet, with my unblistered left hand. My gut was roiling, and I retched, the spasm making the pain worse for a terrifying space of time, but I didn't vomit blood. *Always look on the bright side.* I'd had a housemother who used to say that, at the children's home where I was raised. I wasn't sure how that related to the sickness I experienced after folding reality, but it wasn't bad advice. I might try it as soon as I could stand upright again. Walk again.

With the toe of my boot, I tapped the scorched vamp-killer. The blade shivered and split, sharp shards of steel flying up and tinkling down to the marble. With my left hand, I lifted my right arm against my waist, feeling blisters burst along my lower arm. The pain was like sliding my arm through burning cacti. It was all I could do to keep from screaming, but I held my breath until the agony eased, keeping silent for the Kid. Moisture leaked into the silk lining, feeling cold and slimy beneath the roasted leather.

Even though he was not yet of legal age, I knew better than to treat Alex like a child, and since I knew he could see my face, I answered honestly, "I've had better days. Continue." As Alex talked, I opened the med-pocket on the thigh rig and pulled out a roll of self-adhesive sticky bandage, fashioning a makeshift sling so I could keep the arm in place. The material was black, like my leathers. Eli liked military medical stuff, and so a lot of our medical gear was plain white, stark black, or army camo. In this case, the color would make my injured condition less of an issue until I could see to it.

"Sub-four floor is calming. Leo's there. He's pis— He's not happy. But he's not raging either. Wait. He's heading down."

"Down to sub-five?"

"Yeah. And cameras are off-line there. Working to get them back on system, which would be easier if I was there or if Angel Tit was on duty." Angel Tit was Derek's best coms and security guy, and we all worked well together, but he was out of town and new people meant less reliable help. "Leo's moving fast, Grégoire right behind. You better hurry." Grégoire was the best fighter the American Mithrans had and was utterly devoted to Leo. He was also Leo's right-hand boy toy.

Hurry. Right. "Keep me in the loop when you hear from Eli and Derek." The Kid grunted again, sounding remarkably like his big brother. I sheathed the stake I had dropped, unaware I had even drawn one in the fight, found a bottle of water in my gobag, and took a sip to moisten my throat. I wanted more but had discovered the hard way that anything on my cramping stomach made me throw up. A lot.

Recapping the bottle, I pulled a handgun, one with an ambidextrous grip, so I could hold it in my left. My injured right arm was now cradled against my belly so I wouldn't bump it on something and maybe pass out. Again.

With the elevator out, I wound my way up to and through the ballroom and out a set of stairs that led only up again, then around through the walls and back down. In the past few weeks, we had mapped most of the secret stairways, elevator shafts, and passages and installed electric lights with battery backup. They were low-maintenance, low-level illumination, in this case just tiny button lights down one side of the stairs, though some of the larger stairways had two sets of lights, one on either side of the casing.

Alex came back on, saying, "Police just got reports of, and I quote, 'a man on fire, running through the streets, being chased by gang members.' So I guess black guys have to be gang members, right?"

"Yeah," I said, my voice low so as not to carry as I made my way down and around and down again, to the landing at the bottom of sub-five, the fifth-floor subbasement. I smelled blood on the updrafting air, vamp and human, and lots of it. From sub-four I could hear sounds that let me know the vamps were getting happy and well fed. I adjusted the grip on the weapon and gasped when I joggled the right arm. Something was very wrong with that. Beast should have sent me some relief by now. I could hear her panting in the back of my mind, and I got an image of her lying on a rock floor, licking her paw pad. Right front limb, just like mine. Yeah. She was hurt, but I'd have to deal with that later. *Hang on, girl.*

"Jane?" Alex said again. "There are reports of a white wolf joining the chase with the gangbangers."

I hesitated an instant. A white wolf had to mean Brute. We hadn't seen him in weeks. So how did he know a vamp—that vamp—was free? Brute had bitten Joses Bar-Judas the last time I'd seen him, and when one supernat takes a bite out of another, anything might happen, maybe even some mystic mumbo-jumbo-tracking thingamajimmy. *Crap.* Something else to worry about later. My list was getting really long.

I succeeded in getting the pocket door on sub-five open, and light and my blood-scent flooded the darkness beyond, illuminating the clay floor and the bodies, their vampire and human blood a mixed stench that made my stomach roil again.

Leo was kneeling over them. He was vamped-out, three-inch fangs extended on the hinges in the roof of his mouth, his eyes like black pits in bloody sclera. Leo was scary, but after seeing the Son of Darkness in all his magnificent horror, Leo looked nearly human. I chuffed with pained laughter at the thought, and Leo whirled to me.

His nostrils flared and shrank, his lips pulled back, as he smelled/tasted me on the air. His shoulders lifted, his talons spreading, claw-like. "You are injured," he hissed. "I smell your blood, your burned flesh."

"You know, Leo, the last few minutes have really sucked. And if I have to fill you full of silver and then fight my way outta here, it's only gonna suck more. So how about you pull up your big-boy panties and let's see what's happened in this FUBARed afternoon."

Behind him, Leo's second-in-command, Grégoire, unsheathed his weapon, which was way more threatening and way less sexy than one might imagine. With two fastfast steps, Grégoire positioned himself between Leo and me, his sword pointed at my throat. I didn't take my eyes off the MOC.

Leo blinked. Blinked again. His fingers softened their positions, relaxing; his talons slid back into the sheaths across the tops of his fingers that hid them when he was faking human. His eyes bled slowly back to human, and something like humor entered his eyes. Leo opened his mouth, and the fangs snicked back on their hinges. "I assure you I do not wear big-boy panties, or panties at all, a fact I will gladly allow my Enforcer to investigate at some later time." He stood straight, losing that hulking-monster-in-a-dark-alley posture he'd been holding. And I saw that his hands, mouth, and jaw weren't bloody. He hadn't killed anyone. Yet.

Grégoire resheathed his sword and stepped to the side, his eyes taking in everything and everyone in the room. Vamps are hard to read at the best of times, but right now, Grégoire looked like stone, a fierce, furious, and oddly worried statue, some golden warrior carved by Michelangelo. He was sniffing, taking in the scents, and his scowl deepened as he moved around the perimeter of the room.

"Yeah. No, thanks. I'll take your word for it." I pointed the barrel at the bodies. "Who?"

"The fools who transgressed and betrayed me," Leo said.

Feeling a little safer, now that he sounded rational and Grégoire was otherwise engaged, I entered the room, leaving the door open. I had a flashlight, but no way was I putting the gun away just for some light. My eyes adjusted to the dark more slowly than usual, and I approached Leo with my body bladed, weapon down at my thigh, knowing that, injured and with Beast out of things for now, I was in no shape to fight my boss. If he went nutso, I'd have to shoot him. And run.

The two bodies I had seen from the doorway were lying on the clay flooring, positioned about ten feet out from the wall, one male, one female, both vamps, lying on their sides. The position was oddly familiar. Leo and Katie, his heir, had been positioned similarly last time I had been down there. This time, the female had curly red hair that fanned out on the clay floor, hair I remembered well. The vamps' bodies looked totally human, relaxed in sleep, until I got close enough to make out the small pool of blood beneath each head and the gleam of silver at each temple. I moved closer to make sure, because they looked so peaceful.

So did the pile of humans lying on the clay farther out, appearing well and truly dead, all of them relaxed and calm looking, not in postures of fighting. Just . . . asleep. Which was something I had seen once before, in photos down at NOPD. A whole unit of city cops had been taken down in an alley, not a shot fired, all of them drained dry by a master vamp with a gift for mind control. The humans had died happy, probably dreaming of being on a beach, sipping piña coladas, while a vampire-skinwalker monster drank them down and then ate their livers. It was why I'd been hired to come to New Orleans in the first place, to track down the vampire who had killed them. A vamp who had been a lot more than *just a vamp*.

Unlike the cops, however, these humans hadn't been eaten. "I have called for master Mithrans to turn them," Leo said to me, gesturing with his chin at the humans. "There is life enough in them to bring over." His voice sounded funny, not quite himself, as if he was holding something back, holding something in.

Before I could figure out what was going on with Leo, there were numerous pops as the air pressure changed, to reveal vamps bending over each human. Some were high-placed vamps, like Dominique, Grégoire's blond, beautiful heir, and some were low-placed ones, like Edmund Hartley, who was the vamp version of Leo's bond slave. There were humans to help, and a dizzying miasma of scents washed over me, bloody, peppery, papery, the herbal signatures of vamps under stress and the pheromones of humans holding down panic.

"They signed the papers?" I asked, meaning the contracts that humans signed when they became blood-servants, designating what was to happen if they were almost killed in service—whether they would be allowed to die or brought over.

"It is being dealt with," Leo said. Which didn't really answer my question, but whatever.

I toed a puddle of cooled metallic slag in the floor. It didn't move. I looked up to the wall where Joses had hung. And back to the dead vamps, putting the scenario together. "The vampires came down here, pulled the silver stakes out of his wrists and feet, and let him off the wall. At some point, the pocket watches you were using to control Joses were activated and used in some spell. The working melted them down to puddles of bubbling goo." I kicked another one of the disfigured, burned watches and chain with my boot, and it didn't move. They were all stuck to the floor, melted into the clay, which had to take some kinda heat.

"With his mind he trapped the humans they had brought to feed him and drank them down. Then, a little healed, he held the vamps still and drank *them* down. And then he stabbed his rescuers through the brains with the silver spikes and took off."

"Yesss." Leo's voice sounded ticked off again, that slithery dangerous tone vamps used when they wanted to remind you they were killers, at the top of the food chain. "You, my Enforcer, were supposed to keep my headquarters safe. You were supposed to keep my people safe. You were sup—"

"Stuff it, Leo. You were supposed to tell me when anything changed. Like Adrianna coming back. When did she show? Last night? Right. You didn't call. So don't blame me when you're playing vampire games and it comes back and bites you in the butt." I angled my body so he could see the gun, just in case my attitude was more than he wanted to put up with. Or maybe I should just throw up on him. That might keep him from attacking me. Toeing the female vamp, I said, "I'm taking her head this time. Gratis, since you already paid me. But you wanna tell me why she's still alive? Or was? And why you let her back in here?"

Leo looked around the room slowly, and though his shoulders didn't droop, it was obvious that he knew he'd screwed the pooch on this one. He frowned, a totally human frown, and said, "Rumors have persisted for many years that Adrianna had possession of objects of value to me—*les objets de puissance, les objets de magie.* I allowed her back, assured her of my good graces, and kept her under surveillance, with the intent to take *les objets de magie* from her."

Objects of power. Magical objects. Well. That was honest. For once. "She was Joses Bar-Judas' what? Sweetheart? Honeybunch? Snack cake?"

Leo smiled this time and drew in a breath that he didn't need. The last of his hostility drained away when he exhaled, so maybe breathing did play a part in vamp physiology, like releasing tension. What did I know? What did anyone know?

He took another breath to speak. "*Snack cake*, my Enforcer?" he asked, with heavy emphasis on the first two words. "No. She was his lover for a number of years. Some claim that she was present the night he disappeared, but she was with me that night, hoping to gain some favor. I don't remember now what she even wanted, what she bargained for."

Sex and blood for a favor. Got it. "Uh-huh. And the thing you wanted to take away from her? The thing you let her back inside HQ for? Did you get it?" I remembered the hints of gold at Joses' neck and wrist. "Or did the Son of Darkness get away with them too?"

"Or perhaps you took them from him," Leo said, his shoulders rising again, his pupils widening, his sclera going scarlet. Leo was over-reactionary tonight. That was interesting and dangerous. Very dangerous.

"I don't have anything except wounds," I snapped, as my intestines did a tight, breath-stealing curl. Gasping shallowly, smelling the stink of my burned skin, I said, "Joses was wearing things made of gold at his wrist and neck when he took off. You can check your surveillance footage."

Grégoire drifted to his master's side and placed two fingers to Leo's waist, a calming gesture. I toed Adrianna again, seeing abrasions around her neck where a necklace had been wrenched off. A similar rip in her flesh showed at her right wrist. "Necklace? Maybe bracelet of some kind, ones he ripped off of her? So I can guess that once word started to leak out that you held Joses prisoner, Adrianna— and probably the rest of the fanghead world—decided he should be free and that they should be the ones to do him that favor. Get on his good side. So she brought the magical mystery jewelry here to set him free and join him on his golden throne to take over the world, right? 'Cause that's what most evil villains want, though why anyone would want responsibility for this ball of dirt, I don't know."

Leo's shoulders slumped. He ran his fingers through his hair, holding the back of his skull with both hands as if trying to hold it together. He scrutinized each of the bodies for a moment, studying their faces. Their peaceful faces. "I have miscalculated," he said at length. "Badly." He dropped his hands slowly and looked into Grégoire's eyes, as if seeking comfort. "My people are in grave danger."

"Nous sommes tous bien, mon cœur. Il n'y a pas de raison de s'inquiéter." Which I thought a reassurance of some sort.

I decided Leo was in control enough for me to holster the gun, which I did before unlocking my knees and dropping them to the clay floor. With my good hand, I pried a pocket watch free. Clay, hardened into stone or brick, came with it. Holding my injured arm tight against me to prepare for the jar, I pulled a knife with a solid steel hilt and banged the butt on the watch until the half-melted lid cracked open.

Inside was the round iron disc, the magical part of the pocket watches, items that might—or might not—have been intended to alter time, to give the user a way to fold or bend time and reality, as I did, to give the user control over time, which translated to power over others. I hadn't really figured out much about them and had been hoping I'd never have to. But whatever spell they held, Joses had used it to help him get away. The iron disc looked different from the others I'd seen before. This one looked like someone had burnished it with a metal tool, then polished it with oil and a soft cloth, bringing all the brightness to the surface. It shimmered. I found another pocket watch and opened it the same way. Ditto on the iron disc. There were more, and I collected the discs from them too, holding them all in my good left palm. I shook them like one might shake dice at a craps table.

In an undamaged state, the discs were magnetic, attracting others like them, and if allowed into close proximity, they latched together into a single unit, seamless, becoming a solitary oversized disc. Like magic. These, not so much. They didn't react at all.

I remembered the way Joses had moved while I was in the bubble of time. Yeah. *Time.* That was part of the spell and part of what all the vamps wanted. If you could control time or act outside of it, you could do *anything.* And now Joses Bar-Judas had used a *wyrd* and parts of the iron from the spike of Golgotha to maneuver outside of time. And he also now knew I had the same ability, without the iron.

My life just kept getting better and better.

"My Enforcer?"

I dragged my thoughts back to Leo. "Yeah. Sorry." I shook the discs again and forced myself to my feet. "He used whatever spell was in the discs. They look inert. He got away. And he'll want revenge on you for holding him here for, what? Decades?"

"Yes."

"And he'll take it out on anyone he can get to, human or vamp."

"Yes. You are to find him and bring him to me. Alive."

I'll get right on that, I thought. "I understand my duties, Leo." Which didn't say that I'd do exactly what he wanted. No promises on Joses being undead when I brought him back. I pocketed the discs and tapped my mouthpiece. "Alex. How long on the cameras?"

"Back up and running. I didn't want to interrupt your tête-à-tête. Working now to find out if anything is left of the vid."

"Thanks. I want to know how the vamps got down here. Who's on coms upstairs? I need to talk to them, see footage."

"Collating footage now," Alex said. His tone implied that I was stepping on his toes, trying to tell him how to do his job. "Coms was supposed to be one of the new guys, name of Roman," he said, "but he called in sick. His mother had a heart cath today." I could tell I wasn't gonna like whatever he said next. "Vodka Martini was on coms today. He's dead, Jane. I have footage of Adrianna walking in and stabbing him in the spine at his shoulder blades. And feeding until his heart stopped."

Shock spiraled through me, combining with the nausea already curdling in my gut. Martini had been with us a long time, as long as I'd known Derek, and had just come back after rehab following an on-the-job injury. Graying hair, ready laugh. Good with coms. Steady, reliable. A nice man killed because Leo had kept Adrianna alive.

Steeling myself against my grief, I said, "Make sure Roman's mom really did have a heart cath. Make sure we know where he was all day. Make sure he didn't have a sudden need for money or favors. Get yourself some help either here or at the house. Angel Tit, if you can get him back. Get all the footage collated, all the subjects identified. I want a timeline of what happened here and I want it yesterday."

"Yes, ma'am," Alex said. From his tone I knew he was feeling the loss of Martini.

"Hang in there, Alex," I said softly. "Let me know when your brother checks back in."

"Roger that."

I snapped my coms unit off and turned to Leo. "Why did you let her back in? What did she have that you wanted?" When Leo hesitated, I added, "What magical toy did Joses Bar-Judas get away with, and how much trouble are we in because of it?"

Leo didn't answer. Disgusted, I pulled a vamp-killer and went to Adrianna. Still holding my injured arm close to me, I positioned the blade at what was left of Adrianna's throat and prepared to bear down. Any vamp killed and not beheaded stood a chance of rising, a revenant, a mindless, blood-hunting, killing machine. Any vamp killed and brain-poisoned with silver stood an even better chance.

Leo's hand landed on my forearm. "No, my Enforcer. You may not." Effortlessly, he lifted me and the blade up, and when I was standing, he removed the blade from my hand. Deftly, he resheathed it. "She may make a bargaining chip for the Son of Darkness, assuming that he recalls his affection for her when he regains his sanity. Dead, she is useless." At my expression—which couldn't have been pretty—Leo chuckled. "I will feed her and care for her in a scion lair. I will not let her starve or torture her with want. And I will personally make certain that her cage is secure."

"Sure you will. But, you see, it's a little late for promises, Leo." I pointed at the humans.

Leo frowned, but it was more a "waste of good food" and "more scions to chain and feed" expression than an expression of concern. I pulled a flash and went to the humans, who were being fed drops of blood by vamps, shining the light into each face. I knew two of them personally. Or I had. I tapped the mic. I gave Alex the names of the injured and dead. "Leo has decided to keep Adrianna alive," I said. He cursed. Again. I didn't respond; I must be getting used to the boys' language.

"If you're saving Adrianna, why not save him too?" I asked Leo, pointing at the other vamp.

The MOC shook his head. "He cannot be saved. He is not old enough to survive silver. He is true-dead and may rise as a revenant if you do not take his head."

I figured it was a blood-master thing. Leo knew when his people could be saved or not. To Alex, I added, "His name is Mario Esposito." Mario, a dark-skinned Italian vamp, had hit on me once, big-time. He had thought he was prettier and smoother than he really was, and I had used that to get something I wanted. I tried not to remember his mouth on my neck as I drew a vamp-killer. Efficiently, using the blade Leo had just put away, I cut through what was left of Mario's cervical spine. There wasn't enough blood left in him to spew, but the sound of the blade going through tissue was wet and sticky, followed by the harder, muted thumping and grating of steel on bone. The blade wasn't made for boning or jointing animals, but it did the job, eventually, leaving only the stink of vamp blood meeting silver on the air.

I wiped the blade on Mario's coat, noticing only now that it was white cloth with gold threads woven through it. Like, real cloth of gold. And Joses and I had ruined it with blood-stains. They'd never come out. A laugh tittered in the back of my throat but turned to a gasp when I stood and my jacket pulled on my injured arm. At least my stomach was feeling better. I no longer wanted to toss bloody cookies.

I tapped my mic and said, "We're gonna need lights and equipment."

"Roger that," Alex said. "Eli's on the way down."

I pretended not to hear the utter relief in his voice, that Eli was back. "Copy."

Ignoring me, Leo extended his talons toward Adrianna and pushed into the gore that was her head, gripping the blunt end of the huge silver stake buried deep in her temple. With a jerk, he pulled it out and threw it across the room, his tolerance of silver marking him stronger than most other vamps I knew. He scooped his arms beneath her and lifted Adrianna. From behind us, the other vamps, almost in unison, lifted their humans and popped away, moving like blurs up the staircase. Leo moved more sedately, away from the stairs, his bestie, Grégoire, on his heels. The elevator thumped and the doors opened.

Eli and Del stood there, Bruiser behind them, watching. Eli was holding a psy-meter, designed by the Psychometry Law Enforcement Division of Homeland Security for measuring ambient and active magical energy. I used to measure in at sixty-two. No telling what I measured now. I gave Eli a finger sign to wait and he offered back a truncated nod, understanding that until Leo departed, any measurement was void. I hadn't asked my partner how he managed to get one of the rare psychometers, which were exclusive to the use of law enforcement and military. Sometimes it was better not to know stuff.

Without a backward glance at me, Leo walked onto the elevator, the others moving out of his way. He left behind droplets of Adrianna's blood, and maybe a little bloody gray matter. I didn't look closely at Leo's trail. As he passed Adelaide, her eyes followed Leo, her face full of emotion, none of it good, none of it making sense. When the elevator door closed, Del moved quickly across the room and through the pocket door, up the stairs, as if chasing the vamps and their human burdens. She wasn't running, not exactly, but she wasn't taking her time either.

As she left, Bruiser approached, his eyes on me. At six-four, he was a tall man, even to me, topping my height by several inches. Looking every inch the Enforcer, the primo of a master vamp, neither of which he was anymore, he studied the room, the humans, the beheaded vamp, silent. But he took no command position, which felt so odd to me. He had always been Enforcer and primo, always in charge. Now he was Onorio and living off premises and . . . often in my bed, or I in his. But he never interfered when I was working, recognizing my authority as Leo's current, temporary, part-time Enforcer. Everything was all backward.

"Suggestions?" I asked.

"One or two," he said smoothly. "Over dinner, soon."

Which meant later, privately, and not for any listening ears at coms. I nodded. I needed to know what was wrong with Del. I needed to know about Adrianna. I needed to know a lot of stuff, and Bruiser hadn't been at his apartment last night, which meant he had stayed at HQ. I assumed. I didn't really know. And I was too chicken to ask, fearful of sounding like a lovesick schoolgirl, whining, *Where were you last night? You didn't answer my text. Were you with your old girlfriend?* Which I knew he wasn't, since his old girlfriend was Katie of Katie's Ladies, my former landlady, and Leo's heir. And Leo's lover. Vamp bed jumping was normally hard to keep up with, but Alex was currently handling the security cams and console for Katie's place of business, until we could train Deon, her chef, for that job. We had access to all the cameras, and Bruiser hadn't been there. Katie had been otherwise entertained last night. I tried to ignore my own relief at that. I trusted Bruiser. I did. But we hadn't established the boundaries of our relationship yet. I wasn't sure we really *had* a relationship yet.

Into my earpiece, I heard Alex ask, "Did I just see Leo carrying Adrianna, still with her head, up to his office?"

I nodded, then said, "Yeah. Creepy, I know. But he wants her alive."

"But she tried to *kill* you. More than *once*. She was a *pig*. And now she's a brain-dead pig. Hungry for a good meal of bacon and scrambled brains, anyone?"

I chuckled at the sophomoric humor, the laughter bumping my arm, the pain reverberating all through me. "Stop. Please. And follow Del on the cams. Tell me what's up with her."

"She took the stairs to Leo's office. She was standing in the hallway when he went past."

"And he didn't look at her."

"Correctomundo. A bad case of lovelorn, brokenhearted girl stuff?"

"Yeah." And something else to ask Bruiser. How to make Leo fall in love. I grinned, picturing his face when I asked.

CHAPTER 3

Not My First Time at This Rodeo, Sugar

I stood out of the way while Eli, stinking of sweaty leather and failed deodorant from his dual runs in the sun, took ambient magical readings. The psy-meter needle was every-where, flipping from one side—zero magical ambiance—to one hundred: redline magical activity or resonance. Most of the activity was on the wall where Joses had hung, crucified for a hundred years, give or take.

Yeah. Lots of magic juju, its distinctive pins-and-needles taint brushing my nose, as if trying to induce a sneeze, the stink of vamp and human blood, the reek of fear and anger. And if purpose had a scent, it too was part of the miasma of sub-five.

No one had said so, but I knew that Leo was in danger from this guy, a threat like I had never fought before and had no way to look up or research. And the world's best research guy, Reach, was gone, vanished in the wind. Not that I missed him, the two-faced, backstabbing bastard. But. I was still worried about him. How stupid was that?

No, there was no Reach with his in-depth database to

help me discover how Joses might intend to twist witch magic and vamp mojo together and turn them into a weapon, one served up with vengeance and a side dish of insanity. Alex was good. But he wasn't Reach. Or Reach before he'd been tortured by Satan's Three and gone on the run. Assuming all that story he'd given me was true. Which it might have been. Probably was. Reach had disappeared, gone off the grid. No one in the vamp-hunting community—which was small and growing smaller by the day—had heard from him.

When Eli finished measuring once, he did it all again, this time marking the measurements down on a tablet that was synced to Alex's console, like a map of magical stuff—substance and activity. Smart. If I hadn't been hurting so bad and fighting the need to hurl, I'd have applauded.

When he was done I let him come to me, and I looked over his work. "Deets and conclusions?" I asked.

"The Headless Wonder," he pointed at Mario, "has marginal amounts of magical residue on his clothes. His hands are suffused with it, and so is his right wrist."

I looked at Mario, remembering the egotistical guy who had thought I was coming on to him and slobbered all over me while I used him to get down the elevator. I wasn't proud of that, nor the "means to an end" mentality that had gone along with it. I bent and studied Mario's wrist, noting that the skin was abraded in a circular pattern. I imagined what Mario would do if someone had offered him a magical bracelet, and yeah, he'd have put it on. He wouldn't have been able to resist the urge. And the bracelet had left residue on his flesh.

Eli pocketed the tablet and went to the wall where Joses had hung. He pulled a packet of sterile gauze from a pocket in his pants that held medical supplies and opened the paper packet. With the roll of gauze, he scraped at some dried gunk left on the wall—blood, skin cells, gross fluids—and put the gauze back in the opened packet and into his gobag.

I grunted in approval. I should have thought about it and hadn't. Evidence gathering was my bag, not my partner's, but Eli had been studying the how-to of the PI business, saying he wanted to know everything about the business he had bought into. It had paid off.

"Mario and Adrianna brought something—or maybe more than one something—magical down to the basement,"

Eli said, his words echoing my own conclusions. "Using it, or them, and the humans, they freed Joses."

"Why the humans?" I asked.

Eli looked at me strangely. "Because the stakes are silver. And there's no device or cloth or gloves on the floor or on the vamps that they could have used. No claw hammer. No burned fingers. Hence, they had a human or humans to help."

"Oh. Yeah." Of course. Obvious. Except when pain was thrumming through your gut and brain, short-circuiting everything logical.

"You okay, Janie?" Eli asked.

Alex said over the headphones. "No. She's hurt. She did that thing again where time slows down for her, and she was nauseous from that, though she seems better now. From what I could make out in the vid, the spell hit her right hand first, and it's bandaged into a sling, so I'm guessing she has burns on her right hand and arm."

Eli closed the psy-meter, clamped it between his left arm and his body, and held out his right hand, a signal that demanded I let him see. The gestures were efficient and military. I just stared at his hand, the dark skin outlining the pale palm. "Jane?" he asked.

"I don't—" I stopped and blew at a strand of hair that had worked its way loose from the fighting queue I had braided this morning. It wanted to dangle in my face and tickle my nose. "I don't think I can."

Eli pulled something from a pocket, and I heard a click the same moment that a bright light landed on my hand, pressed against my waist. Eli said nothing, just studied the hand, all blistered and juicy and weeping flesh. "Second-degree burns. How far up does it go?"

"My shoulder? Maybe?"

Eli said, "Alex. If Edmund is still on premises, get him into a private room, with some human females to act as duennas. Send one of them down here to get Jane and escort her up as soon as everyone is assembled. It's daylight, so she can't shift into her cat and then shift back. She'd be stuck in Beast form until sunset. And Jane's waited a little too long to get the sleeve off. It's got to be cut off and it's going to be bad." He looked at me, his face lit from below. "You are an idiot."

"Um. Yeah. Okay." He was right. What could I say? Except, "My Beast is supposed to ease the pain. She hasn't. So maybe there's something wrong with her too."

He shook his head, confused. "Your Beast? Your skin-walker magic?"

Right. I hadn't told him *everything* about Beast, the other soul now twined with mine. I'd have to add a total soul-baring to my social calendar. A strange sound, like the first note of a shattered laugh, escaped my mouth before I pressed my lips together to hold it in. When the sound was under control and shoved down deep, I said, "For all intents and purposes, yeah."

"The spell that hurt your arm, you're saying it also hurt your magic?"

"Maybe. I don't know yet."

Eli tapped his mic. "Bro, I'm sure you're on top of it already, but if not, start a search of all the security cameras to see what the dead vamps brought down to the basement."

"Done it. Every single security camera they passed shows the same thing. Two vamps and ten humans walking into security, where they killed Martini. Then taking the stairs to the basements. They met another vamp on sub-four, female, wearing a scarlet cloak with a hood." And we didn't have sufficient cameras in sub-five yet. Of course. Dang it.

"A human female, blood-servant to Leo, named Zelda, is on the way down," Alex said. "Red hair, green eyes, freckles, five-five, one-sixty, all muscle and boobs."

As he finished the description, the elevator opened, and I realized that there had been no *ding*, no tone to tell us it was there. Curious. Useless, but curious. A woman stepped through the doors and paused, one hand holding the doors open. Eli looked from his tablet and the photo the Kid had sent. "Verified," he said into the mic. "Other female for the healing? Vamp?"

"A woman named Gretchen, who Janie calls Titan Two. And Edmund, because they *liiike* each other."

I narrowed my eyes at the insinuation and then remembered that there were security cameras in most rooms. The Kid may have seen a healing session with Edmund not so long ago, one in a small room off the locker room. *Great. Just freaking ducky.*

To me, Eli said, "Go," and pointed to the elevator.

Rather than deal with the problems in sub-five, I went.

Every step jarred my gut and my arm, as if knowing what was about to happen made everything infinitely worse. And since getting the leathers off was going to be way worse than Eli expected—because I would refuse to let them cut off my leathers—maybe my arm was indeed putting out caution alarms.

The elevator doors closed, leaving me in the tiny mobile room with Zelda. I turned off my headset and cleared my throat; she slanted a look up at me. "I only have two sets of fighting leathers, the fancy ones for when I officially act as Enforcer, and this set that I keep in the back of the SUV." She didn't reply, a look of polite inquiry on her face her only reaction. "I need more than one pair," I explained. "They're expensive and it takes time to get them made, time I may not have if I have to go after the thing from sub-five." When she looked confused, I said, "I'm trying to say that I don't want you to cut the sleeve. I can be healed of a wounded arm, but I can't do without the fighting leathers."

Persistently polite and reasonable sounding, she said, "Leathers are part of your expense account as part-time Enforcer and acting head of security. Why not order four or five sets?"

"Yeeeeah . . . ," I drew out the word. "About that. Allowing Leo to provide them for me is binding me to the MOC a little more closely than I want."

Puzzlement in her tone, she said, "It's common knowledge that you can't be bound. Our master tried and was not successful."

"That's not—" I stopped and looked up at the camera in the corner. There was a mic hidden in it, so whoever was on coms would hear, meaning Alex and a stranger, neither of whom I wanted in on my business. Zelda seemed to catch my discretionary look up and went silent. The elevator stopped and, without responding to her comment, I followed Zelda off the elevator to a floor and hallway I didn't go to often—the living quarters of the permanent staff.

One of the rooms was Del's, and I didn't so much remember which room that was as pick up her scent as we passed it. A scent of heartbreak clung to the air. Del was suffering as Leo's primo, and I had no idea how to help her through it. It was girly stuff, like love and blood-servant stuff. Binding stuff. Sex-with-vampire—*ick*—stuff.

Zelda paused outside a door and, her voice pitched low so only I would hear, said, "There is job-bound, there is emotion-bound, and there is blood-bound—all kinds of binding. Then there is stupid-bound. In this case, I think you're stupid-bound. Even I can smell your blood." She opened the door and entered the room, leaving me standing in the hallway with a frown pulling down on my face.

Stupid-bound? I looked at my hand. It was worse. It was gonna hurt like crazy to pull the sleeve off. And there was gonna be blood and that clear wound fluid—serous fluid, that was it—all over the inside silk. I'd never get the blood-scent out, and every vamp around would be able to smell me coming. She was right. I wasn't thinking clearly. *Stupid-bound*.

I stepped into the room and closed the door behind me. There were three people waiting in the room: Zelda, another human female whom I recognized as Titan Two . . . and the vamp I was expecting, Edmund Hartley. He was slight, quiet, watchful, and nondescript. A vamp no one would notice in a crowded room. But his history and personal experience said that he was much more than that.

The room smelled of vamp and blood and sex. It was an outer-wall room with a window, which was covered by steel, electronic blinds on the outside and a padded velvet board on the inside, and metal bands that secured the board in place, making it very hard to remove and endanger a sleeping vamp. It was a room for a low-level vamp because, even with the precautions, it was dangerous for vamps by day. Yet this room was clearly used as a lair, and by the scent, by Edmund. And Zelda. His sex and dinner partner. Edmund had fallen a long way from clan blood-master to slave, with an outer room at vamp HQ. I was still learning that story.

"Cut it off," I said to Zelda. "You're right." To Titan Two, I said, "There are plastic braces at the joints, silver-over-titanium chain link everywhere, and some Dyneema. It's gonna be hard to cut off."

Titan Two held up a pair of leather snips, a pair of metal snips, and a box cutter with a new-looking blade. "Not my first time at this rodeo, sugar," she said, trying a Texan accent and not making it work at all.

I sighed. "Yeah. Right." *Beast?* I thought. She still didn't answer. It occurred to me that since I had accepted the soul-binding between us, maybe what healed me healed her. *Vamp healing coming up. Hope you like Edmund.*

Beast chuffed back, the sound full of pain.

Getting the leathers off hurt. Hurt like I had never expected. It was a three-person job, Titan Two cutting and snipping, Zelda easing the leather back and ripping my damaged flesh off with it, and Edmund shedding his own blood and using his tongue to heal. Unlike other times I'd been vamp-healed, times when the wounding was finished and only needed vamp saliva and blood to make it feel all better and scar quickly, this time a rewounding was taking place at the same time as the healing, and the vamp saliva had no way to keep up with the pain. I screamed a few times. I cried all the way through, the nose-dribbling, sobbing, hiccupping, whining kinda crying. I smelled the stink of my burned and broken and torn flesh and the scent of my own blood and tears. It was ... bad. Really, really bad.

When it was over, I fell asleep, my body so full of endorphins, adrenaline breakdown products, and Edmund's saliva and blood that sleep was the only possible reaction. Only vaguely did I wake when someone bandaged my arm and later pulled a T-shirt over me. I knew by the smells that I wasn't in danger, and so couldn't bother to rouse myself before dreams smothered me back under.

The dream was an odd one, full of confusing images, of white and black wings and claws, as if a white bird and a black bird were fighting. Of rain and lightning and the sensation of being cold, so cold I knew I was dying. Of someone speaking Cherokee, the *Tsalagi* words for God, chanting, *"Yehowa, Edoda,"* words for Great Spirit. *"Unequa, adanvdo."* And *"Anidawehi,"* the word for angels. *"Yehowa. Edoda. Unequa. Adanvdo. Anidawehi. Unequa, anidawehi*—help me, accept me as sacrifice, or set me free."

I came to myself with a gasp of fear, lying in a bed, on clean sheets, still wearing my leather pants, my boots off, my upper body swaddled in a soft T-shirt that I recognized by feel and scent without having to open my eyes. The dream faded as the scents and sensations of the real world took over. The shirt was a fuzzy purple long-sleeved T with a colorful red-striped dragon on the front. It was my shirt, given to me by a vamp and a witch, with the power of healing woven into the fibers and into the dragon on the front. It was ugly, but the healing worked into it had lasted through several healings and repeated washing and drying. I loved this ugly shirt.

Edmund was cradled around me, his arms around my waist, which, with vamps, usually meant a need and request for sex, but he was so relaxed that he had to be sleeping. He sighed, relaxing further, a boneless slump, the breath telling me two things—he was asleep and probably dreaming of being human, and that he'd recently drunk fresh blood. It was Zelda's, and I smelled Zelda on the other side of him. *Oh goody. A ménage à trois sleepover.*

The light was dim, and even with my eyes still closed, my time sense told me that the sun was still up outside. The feeling of well-being and the lack of pain told me that I was safe. I had time to rest and to think and to put things together. And time to worry.

I had gotten used to Beast being able to mute my pain with her own body chemicals, so accustomed to it that I no longer thought about how often I drew on her gift. If the new soul-binding, the fighting ability, and the time-bending powers of our half-Beast form were gonna make it harder to deal with a purely human injury, that was a serious drawback, one I needed to figure into any future fighting circumstances, along with the gut-wrenching downtime required when I was forced to use the time-bending / reality-folding gift that was new to us.

Or maybe today's inability to use her pain-muting capacities was just because of the magical origin of the injury. I had to make time to meditate and check out Beast in my soul home. I could feel her there, and something wasn't right. But before I could concentrate on me, I had a list of Enforcer stuff and vamp-hunter stuff to do.

First was to talk to the priestesses and see how to track Joses Bar-Judas and how to kill him. I had a feeling he'd be leaving a swath of dead humans in his wake unless I got to him first.

Second was to figure out where Leo had taken Adrianna and make sure she wasn't going to cause problems on her own again. Second and a half was to find out what the magical jewelry that Mario and she had been wearing did, so I could counter it next time we met up. Third, once I had the Son of Darkness beheaded, was to research how she had known Joses Bar-Judas and make educated guesses on how Leo planned to use her brain-dead (hopefully) self.

Fourth was to check in on Del. Try a little girl talk.

Fifth was to talk to Jodi, my contact in the New Orleans Police Department. NOPD's woo-woo room might have records I hadn't found yet about Joses. Now that he was free and possibly a danger to the public, I needed to tell her about Joses and accept the figurative butt whupping I was likely to get for keeping his presence a secret. And ... injured humans. There had been injured humans in the basement, and it was unlikely that they all survived being turned. I was supposed to report dead humans to the local law, and I'd been too hurt to think clearly about that. Now I had no way to determine if there were dead humans or not. Leo would never tell me, nor would his people.

Satisfied that I had a plan of action, I opened my eyes to see that a dim light came from a small electric lamp on the bedside table, cast from some form of metal, old enough to have a patina of verdigris in shades of green and brown, topped by a square, buff-colored shade. It was elegant in ways I didn't usually appreciate, formed by an artist's hand in a stylized shape of a woman holding a child. It sat on a green-veined, marble-topped table with metal legs of the same style and material as the lamp. A gilded mirror hung over the fireplace, which was faced with more of the green-veined marble, as was the mantel. The walls were a green so pale that they looked almost white, but for the white-painted moldings at the ceiling, door, and floor, which contrasted brightly. The floors were wood, with rugs tossed here and there in black and greens and tiny spots of red, as if blood had splattered across them. Everything in sight was really expensive, even to my untrained eye.

The linens were shades of greens—natch—from emerald to fern to celery, and the bed itself was a humongous four-poster of black wood carved with vines and flowers. Two chairs nestled at a dainty, antique tea table were upholstered in pale, shimmery fabric that looked like silk. I didn't know much about furniture, but there was something that said this was stuff Edmund had brought with him into slavery to Leo. Master-vamp furniture. And that meant that Leo had allowed him to keep it. More secrets to discover about the vampire Edmund Hartley.

Carefully, I lifted Edmund's arm from my waist and slid to a sitting position on the edge of the bed. My right arm was bandaged and twinged with pain as I rose, like being stuck with tiny needles all over its skin, from fingertips to the middle of my back. I stretched it slowly, not liking the feel of the healed but still tender flesh, and gathered up my boots, spotting my cell in a boot bottom. I looked around for the rest of my clothing and weapons. Zilch. Somebody had made off with my stuff, hopefully to clean the body fluids off it.

However, my headset hung over the doorknob, and I carried what I had left from the room, to put on in the hallway. One-handed wasn't the easiest way to boot up and get into coms, but I managed it and turned on the set as I moved down the hallway in the direction of the elevator. "Jane Yellowrock here," I said into the mic. "Who's on at coms?"

"Juwan here, Legs. Good to hear you up and around."

I came to a quick stop in the hall and leaned against the wall. Juwan was the real-world name for one of Derek's men. He was a sharpshooter home between deployments when I first met Derek. I had ridden Bitsa, my Harley panhead, into the hood to get permission to hunt for a rogue vamp. Derek had come out to talk to me. Juwan had targeted me, a dead-on hit with a laser scope between my shoulder blades. I wasn't sure what a shooter was doing there, running security after a breach, but I'd find that out later. First, it was likely that I had to establish boundaries. Most of Derek's men seemed to need that from time to time, and with Juwan seeing me for the first time, wearing a fuzzy purple dragon T-shirt, I'd better start right away. "Twizzlers, Juwan," I said.

Twizzlers had been the code word Derek had used to make Juwan not shoot me. Juwan laughed, his voice mellow over the in-house coms channel. "You remember that, do you?"

"Hard to forget the moment when Uncle Sam's finest has the spot between your shoulder blades all lit up like Christmas lights. What did you have on me that night?"

"USMC M40A5."

The M40A5 was essentially an AK-47. "Ouch. That one mighta killed me."

Juwan laughed. "Yeah, maybe. I hear you're kinda hard to kill." Not happy that I was an ongoing topic of gossip, I grunted, and he went on. "Course, shootin' you from that angle and distance would likely have punched right through you and taken down one of Derek's other guys. He'da been pissed. Sorry. I hear you don't like the way marines talk."

He didn't sound sorry. He sounded challenging, the way men did when other men have built you up into something to be confronted and defeated. *Lucky me.* I might have to fight this guy someday soon. *Just not today, please,* I silently asked the ceiling. I stretched my hand and made a grip, the skin moving painfully beneath the sleeve and bandage, the muscles feeling tight. The entire arm was tender. But . . . I smiled and looked up, searching, knowing there had to be a camera on me somewhere. When I found it, I grinned into it, showing teeth. "You wanna make a big deal out of language, we can do that, Juwan. But understand. If you challenge me over something so stupid as polite conversation, when I beat your butt, it'll go on YouTube so all your marine buddies can see you get your backside handed to you by a skinny Cherokee chick."

Juwan laughed over the headset, the confident tone slowly changing to one less certain as he saw my expression over the security camera.

"Think about it." I pushed off the wall and continued down the hallway. "And while you're thinking, do a search of archived footage from the sparring room. Make sure you want to pursue this. Otherwise, we'll just let it go and pretend this little convo didn't happen."

"Yeah. Roger that."

I could hear little faint tappings, the sound of fingers on a touch screen. "Meanwhile, I need to know where the priestesses are. Are either of them on-site?"

"Yes, ma'am. Interesting that you asked. They turned off the system at thirteen hundred forty-two, when they entered the library on the floor where you are now. Take a left and a right, and you'll see the door. It's closed but not locked. They used the remote to turn on the gas logs."

Interesting that I asked? "Gotcha. Thanks."

"Welcome, Injun Princess. Anytime."

Still pondering the statement *Interesting that you asked*, I moved toward the library, deciding that the priestesses had probably told him to send me in the moment I woke up. Outside the library door I pulled my cell and flipped open the armored case. I texted Alex with, *Why Juwan in security? He alone?*

Instantly I got back the answer to the last question. *Angel with him. Out USMC. Hon. disch. Retraining for civilian life.* I interpreted the message to read that Juwan was out of the marines with an honorable discharge and starting a new life.

I sent back *K*, knocked on the door, and waited until I had permission to enter.

CHAPTER 4

I Am the Keeper

Sabina Delgado y Aguilera and Bethany Salazar y Medina sat together at the library table, in the afternoon, with the sun still up outside. There were no windows, so it wasn't a miracle, but seeing any vamp awake and active in daytime was enough of a rarity to throw me off my stride. A pile of old books, teapot wrapped in a quilted cozy, and teacups sat on the table between them. The aroma of tea mixed with the scent of old books, leather chairs, and wool from the carpet in a soothing fusion.

As I moved across the room, my fingers found my wounded arm, still feeling not quite right, the skin tender. Even after my nice rest, I wanted nothing more than to curl up with a cuppa and maybe a novel—not that I read books. Not ever. But the smell here made me want to try.

There were other cups on the table, and as I approached, Sabina placed one on a china saucer, the kind shaped to hold the cup secure and catch any minor spills. She placed it at an empty chair and poured tea into the cup. I guessed that was my invitation to join them.

I said, "Thanks," sat, and added cream and sugar to my tea. The spoon was sterling silver and tinkled as I stirred. I noted that the outclan priestesses were also using sterling, handling the silver as if they no longer had to worry about silver poisoning. I could count on my fingers the number of vamps who could do that without getting blistered, and have digits left over. I sipped and discovered that the tea was delicious. Not that I was surprised. Vamps spent money on the things they treasured.

"You are welcome in our house. We offer hospitality to you," Sabina said.

I was flying by the seat of my pants already and the vamp day hadn't even started, but I figured that the formulaic welcome meant they would let me keep my blood supply inside my skin. I dredged up the manners taught to me in the children's home where I was raised and said, "I am . . . honored for the hospitality and, uh, recognize the gift of it, and, um, thanks for the tea. Too. The tea also," I clarified. *Crap.* This was stupid. But I didn't say that aloud. I was learning. "It's . . . enchanting." *Could tea be enchanting?* I wondered. Poisoned, yes, but enchanting? I shook away the mental wanderings.

Sabina and Bethany were both nearly two thousand years old, belonged to no clan, and were the keepers of the holy relics. They were also the arbiters of most anything that Leo couldn't or didn't want to handle. And both were scary powerful. I was smart enough to know that being allowed to drink tea with them was intended to be a humongous honor, but all I could think was that they were about to put me in a bind, one way or another. I'd come in there to ask them how to track Joses Bar-Judas, per Leo's order, but I had a feeling they had agendas of their own.

"Have you seen the camera film of Leo after the Son of Darkness escaped?" Sabina asked, her nunlike, starched white gown rustling.

"No, ma'am. Should I?"

"Yes. Turn on your device and ask it be sent to you." She poured more tea for her and Bethany and sat back, looking relaxed. I hadn't had anything to eat since breakfast, and lunch was long past, and my stomach growled, deep and low. I pressed a hand there to keep it quiet. I had food to eat and stuff that needed doing, but if the priestesses wanted me there to watch video, that is where I'd be. Into my cell I texted to Alex, *Footage of Leo after Joses escaped? Send to me.* He sent back a *K*, and moments later, my cell tinkled with the incoming video.

I waited as the vid opened on my cell and clamped down on a gasp before it got free. The footage was of Leo, holding Gee DiMercy down in the hallway, surrounded by humans who looked like they were waiting on something. The humans looked jittery, uneasy. I didn't blame them. Leo wasn't being kind to Gee; there was no tenderness or laving with tongue to stop pain. Leo was savaging Gee's throat.

My own throat spasmed, shutting off air as remembered pain became real again. I clamped my good hand around my throat protectively as I watched. Over the vid, I heard Leo growl like a wild animal, a grizzly, deep and sonorous. This was violence far worse than what Leo had done to me. There wasn't going to be anything left of Gee DiMercy's throat. If he were human, he'd already be dead. I waited for a human to pull Leo off, to shout for help. That didn't happen. *Had Leo killed Gee?* Was I gonna have to watch that? The pain in my stomach ratcheted up a good six levels into an inferno.

What was Leo upset about? He had been fine when he left me, carrying Adrianna.

On the video, Gee's hands unexpectedly came up and encircled Leo's shoulders, patting him tenderly, the way a mother might a fractious baby. Leo's body went limp for a space of seconds, and then he pulled away, wiping Gee's blood from his mouth with a shaking hand. Gee's throat closed up, healing as I watched.

Leo looked better now. Calmer. So what was I seeing? Maybe what Gee had just done had calmed the savage beast? Something similar? Leo looked up at the humans and gestured for them to follow him, which they did, down the hallway. One was carrying Adrianna, who was still dripping blood and brains. That was gonna be hard to get out of the carpet. Brains were sticky and adhered to fibers.

There was a blink in the digital vid, and I was now seeing the camera down the hall from Leo's office. Three humans were stumbling along, all heavily blood-drunk and weak looking—anemic. I checked the time frame. Half an hour after Leo had bled Gee.

"Is Gee okay?" I asked.

"Our Misericord is well," Bethany said. "But he will not

remain well if the master of this city continues to drain him in anger."

"You must find the Son of Darkness and bring him back to us," Sabina said, echoing Leo's command.

"Once he is caught like a bird in a raptor's talons, we will remove his sacred blood to tame him and place him back upon the wall," Bethany said.

"And his blood will fill the holy relic for preservation," Sabina said, her voice carefully bland.

I stared back and forth between the two priestesses. Those statements were so confusing I had no idea where to go with any of the information contained in them. Their faces were expressionless and cool, as if the idea of starving a vampire into greater, but compliant, insanity and using him for their own ends was an acceptable practice. And I had no idea what the *holy relic* was, but chances were it wasn't anything to do with religion as I understood the word.

Humans had been researching ways to preserve vamp blood so they could test it for use in human medicines and drugs. So far, no go. Vamp blood decomposed quickly, no matter the preservative they tried, and even fresh, it didn't cure every human illness; some of them seemed impervious to vamp blood, unless the patient was turned. And even turned, they had to go through years of the devoveo—the madness of the turn—with no certainty of surviving physically or mentally intact. Vamp blood was no panacea, sometimes healing, sometimes not, which was why vamps still existed as free beings at all.

Vamp blood also made the drinker susceptible to the mind-warping abilities of the vamp he or she was drinking from. A few sips and the drinker would be willing to do anything the vamp said, including removing shackles and shooting guards. The addictive properties of vamp blood kept most powerful humans from becoming blood-servants or paying for the privilege of drinking it. Vamps made dangerous captives.

So vamps weren't being kept prisoner, or not openly, anyway, and drained of blood for sick humans to become healthy. But if human researchers ever discovered that there was a way to preserve vamp blood, there would be all-out war, as humans caught and shackled the vamps and drained them little by little for healing and cures and whatever else they could devise, all in the name of humanity and compassion. The relic, whatever it was, needed to remain secret.

Keeping my tone as grim as theirs, I said, "Preservation? Not supposed to be possible."

"Joses' blood is different," Sabina said, her dark eyes on her teacup. She sipped, her robes *shushing* in the quiet library as she lifted her arm. "It has been known to survive the test of time."

"We need his blood. It is necessary to bring my Leo to great power," Bethany added, also not meeting my gaze, but watching Sabina, a disturbing light in her eyes. Bethany wasn't always sane, even as vamps went, and the jewelry in her ears and twisted and knotted and braided into her hair caught the lamplight with shots of gold and the glint of rubies. "It is necessary to make him fierce and stalwart enough to defeat the Blood Challenge of the Son of Darkness, when our enemies come to us for war." She meant the other Son of Darkness, Joses' brother. The EuroVamps were already making plans to show up there. When they found final proof that Joses had been held prisoner in NOLA vamp HQ, they would be there pronto, probably not waiting for any parley date decided upon. Joses was already an open secret even before draining a few vamps and humans and taking off into the day. If he wasn't caught / killed truedead / whatever, that just increased the chances that the EuroVamps would declare war on the New World vamps.

When I caught up with him (when, not if), I could kill Joses outright, like he needed, or capture him, like the priestesses and Leo wanted, but capturing a rabid vamp was a lot harder than staking him and beheading him. And from where I sat, we were all screwed, no matter what I did. Rather than voice that, I sipped the *très* expensive tea.

"Our master did not drink of the blood of the son of his body. Think on this."

I had a feeling this arcane tidbit of info was important, but I didn't have time to dwell on it just then. "Yeah. Whatever. How am I supposed to track and capture one of the two Sons of Darkness, the maker of all vamps? Are you gonna show up with the Blood Cross and herd him into a silver cage?" I asked Sabina.

She still didn't meet my eyes. I wondered if that was an

admission of some kind of guilt or if she was afraid I'd read something in her gaze that she wanted kept secret. Or maybe not meeting a person's eyes was a cultural thing from her own time and people. Like not making eye contact when asking a favor or standing in a crowded elevator. Something like that. I didn't know, and there was no way to ask.

"I still cannot embrace the true Blood Cross," Sabina said. "The injury I suffered the last time I wielded it burned deep. I am not healed from the fire I suffered."

"You may never be healed enough to wield it again," Bethany said. "You should give it over to a stronger priestess. To *me*."

Oookaaay, I thought. The rift between the priestesses wasn't getting any smaller, in spite of the tea and the apparent agreement on the subject of Joses Bar-Judas.

"When it is determined that I am permanently no longer able to carry out my duties," Sabina said, starting to sound testy, "I will turn it over to another. For now, I am healing, and—"

"For now? You have been *healing* for too long!" Bethany said, anger ringing in her voice.

I had seen paintings of the last time Sabina had wielded the Blood Cross, trying to stop the Damours, a vampire-witch clan, from practicing blood magic on witch children. That had taken place hundreds of years ago, so no way was I entering what had to be an old, *old* argument. The idea of Bethany in control of that powerful icon was terrifying. The idea that Sabina might not be up to using it in a time of war was just as terrifying. I sipped and kept my eyes on my tea. Very pale, with the cream. And in a lovely china cup.

Implacable as mountain stone, Sabina continued. "I am the *Keeper*. I am able to wield the sliver of the Blood Cross and thus will remain the Keeper. I will assist Jane Yellowrock in capturing Joses Bar-Judas."

Bethany laughed. "Capture? You will die at his fangs if you try to capture him." She looked at me, her black skin seeming to absorb the lamplight. "You must call me when the time comes, if you can. There will be no way to capture our maker without me." With a soft pop of displaced air, Bethany vanished and appeared at the door, which opened and closed behind her, leaving me with Sabina.

Officially, the day sucked. If I kept a diary, that would have been the day's sole entry.

I risked a glance up at the most powerful vamp in the U.S. Well, maybe the second-most powerful now that Joses was free. She was serene, sipping her tea, the cup cradled in both pale, pale hands. "Two young Mithrans were attacked as they slept this day," she said. "Liam and Vivian were drained by a nightmare. They were brought here, to my sister priestess and to me. They may survive. Their humans were attacked as well, and are all dead. The nightmare escaped into the daylight, smoking and gibbering."

My body tightened. Humans dead. By a nightmare. Joses had needed human and vamp blood to start his transformation, and he would need human and vamp blood to continue his healing. I wondered how much blood it would take to change him from the starving bag of bones that had hung in sub-five to anything that could pass among humans. There would be more humans killed and more vamps drained if he stayed free. I nodded my understanding. I had met the two young vamps, Liam and Vivian, but for the life of me I couldn't remember what they looked like. I should have been able to remember people I was paid to protect, but there were hundreds of vamps in New Orleans.

"You will find where Joses Bar-Judas lairs and call upon me, not my sister priestess. We will bring him back to the Master of the City." It wasn't a request, which officially placed me between several rocks and several hard places. "Witches have workings that can locate and follow many different forms of sentient beings. You have entrée to the witches of this city through your Trueblood friends. Witches who, if asked, will assist in tracking the Son of Darkness."

A cold shaft of fear went through me, as I realized that Sabina was talking about Molly and Evan, who had recently been in New Orleans and who would be back soon to put together the Witch Conclave, a national meeting of the covens to try to reach reconciliation with the vamps. I was supposed to be in the middle of it all. "You're talking about me *using* my *friends*?" I said, putting emphasis on the words.

"Yes. Your *friends*." She smiled as if she had said something blissful. "You are friends with *witches*." She settled vamped-out eyes, pupils blown with scarlet sclera, on me. They hadn't looked like that a moment before. I managed not to flinch at the sight, but my breath caught and she breathed in, as if she scented my sudden apprehension. Carefully, I set the cup and saucer on the table, glad when they didn't clink with shaking hands.

"There are *witches* in this city," Sabina said. "I am a worker of magic, much like the witches. It is possible that we all may work together in this task. Ask your *friends* to give you entrée to Lachish. She will have ways to follow the trail of Joses Bar-Judas. Perhaps she and I may blend our workings together and capture him."

"Why don't you try to contact Lachish?"

Sabina tilted her head, and she made a little hummm sound, totally human and disconcerting. "With the accords under way, I had not considered . . . Perhaps I shall."

My voice toneless and carefully not accusatory, I managed to ask the most important question. "How long have you known that Joses was a prisoner here?"

Sabina didn't reply right away, but poured more tea into her cup. She didn't drink it with sugar or milk, but straight up. Finally she said, "I knew that he had been taken. I knew that he was raving. I watched as Bethany tasted his blood to determine the cause." Sabina smiled slightly, but not in pleasure. "I stood aside as Bethany lost her sanity with that one sip. And I stood aside as Amaury, master of the city before Leo came to power, brought him here and secured him in place." Her dark eyes pinned me to my chair. "I did nothing to intervene. It was my decision, when . . . events . . . led me by the nose like a horse in a twitch. I had no choice then, not with what I learned, not with what might have happened in his lair. I have no choice now."

I wasn't sure about having a choice, or what choices she was talking about. I was totally confused, but I wasn't going to argue with her. I had seen a horse in a twitch at the barn at the children's home—the horse's upper lip and lower nose twisted by a rope to hold the horse still for medical procedures. It wasn't permanently debilitating, but it looked horribly painful. It *was* horribly painful. A horse would do anything—*anything*—for the one who held the twitch.

So taking Joses Bar-Judas prisoner had been a decision forced on the vamps due to his loss of mental control? He had become a rogue vamp? Or forced on Sabina by Bethany's going insane after drinking Joses' blood? Forced on her by Amaury? And others?

"He can*not* be brought to true-death, Jane Yellowrock. He is all that we have to bargain with. He is all that we have to keep his brother, Shimon Bar-Judas, at bay. And Shimon has always been the more dangerous of the two."

I decided once again that not replying was the better part of valor and said, "Thank you for the tea, Sabina Delgado y Aguilera, outclan priestess of the Mithrans. I will" — I searched for a polite, nonbinding phrase — "carefully consider all that has been said here."

She replied to my cautious words. "You think to elude my command. The Master of the City *must* have the Son of Darkness back in his custody, alive, and soon, or many tribulations may befall. Consider carefully, before you refuse my order, the possibilities that may arise from your decision to obey or defy." Sabina settled the cup into its saucer and lifted one taloned finger, the nail more than two inches long.

I hadn't seen the talons extrude from the small flaps of skin at the ends of her fingers, just as I hadn't seen her eyes vamp out, which might mean she was pulling on her compulsive powers. I pressed my own nails into my palms, the pain keeping me alert and in my own mind, listening.

"You are attempting to construct a Witch Conclave here, in New Orleans, yes?" she asked.

I nodded, wary.

"Witches will come from all over the States and Leo will play gracious host to them and to Lachish, searching for *rapprochement*." She pronounced it in the French manner, the *T* silent, as all the vamps did.

I nodded again and Sabina smiled at me, the predator that she was peering at me through vamped eyes, her one finger still uplifted. She said, "Shimon Bar-Judas will know soon about the witches who plan to conclave here. If his brother, Joses, remains free, and they join forces, all you have sought to accomplish may be destroyed. Joses and his brother will bide in the dark, and then they will destroy every witch they can find."

She raised a second finger. "The remaining witches may then attack the Mithrans, believing that Leo set upon them." A third finger rose. "The Europeans, who watch us carefully, may choose that moment to attack the Mithrans of this city, claiming the desire to assist Joses, and if they win, they will take the hunting grounds and cattle." That meant the land and the humans. *Gotcha.*

"If we are overcome, the Europeans will kill the cattle and the witches and all that have magic and power. All these things are possible future results of *your* actions or inactions."

She lifted a final finger. "If you succeed in beheading Joses Bar-Judas and bringing him to true-death, as I know you desire, his brother will bring war upon us in vengeance. The Mithrans of Europe, Africa, South America, and Asia may well join him to ensure the death of Leo and the Pellissier clan. All that you do, every judgment you make, is weighted with outcomes in the future. The near future. All possibilities exist for you now, but every step you take to one end or another brings you and us closer to one of these finalities. The safest course of action is to save Joses and bring him to me, an act that you cannot accomplish alone. You must have help. Mithran help. Witch help. And it must be soon." She inclined her head and lowered her hand with the accusing fingers.

I remembered a moment of folded time in my shower not so long ago. Each falling droplet of water had been arrested in time and space as my Beast warped reality and bent time to her—to our—will and need. Each droplet had contained one still shot of a possible future, the outcomes to each action on my part paused and waiting. When time returned, I had staked Leo and he had nearly died. It was possible that Joses' getting free had been foretold in those droplets. It was also possible that my staking Leo had, in some way, contributed to the variety of futures that opened out before me, none of them good. Tiny fingers of fear skittered down my spine on icy hands. My fault? It could be. So much was my fault, the result of my actions or decisions.

Sabina smiled, and there was nothing remotely human left in her expression. "You understand. Good. You are dismissed," she said.

That was another thing I hated about vamps, that whole royal attitude, telling me when I could come and go. "Thanks a heap," I muttered, and forced my legs to push me up from the chair and to the door, my muscles quivering with reaction. I closed the door behind me.

In the hallway, my back to the nearest camera, I leaned against the wall to keep my knees from giving way and I gasped, catching up on the oxygen I had depleted in fear. When I could stand without the help of the wall, I texted Alex to tell me where Adrianna and Del were. I got back that the vamp was still with Leo, still in his office, so far as camera footage allowed us to tell, and Del was in her rooms.

I rubbed my arm through the T-shirt, feeling the healing energies press into my flesh, giving me ease before I texted back, *Pull up prev. research how Adrianna knew Joses. Check to see if Joses owns property for lairs. Collate with any of Adrianna's known lairs. Educated guess how Leo plans to use Adrianna re Joses.*

Adrianna was, hopefully, brain-dead, but that didn't make her valueless. If she had planned to pull Joses off the wall, then she had planned where to stash him. If they had a history, then I might be able to use that history to track him.

I stared at his instant reply of agreement. How had I ever lived without texts? How had anyone ever lived without instantaneous communication? How long before we had little chips inserted into our skin or directly into our nervous systems and brains so we could be with people all the time and never have to be alone? How long before the hive mind, integrated with AI computers, was a reality? How long before I screwed up and got everyone I loved killed?

Cell still in hand, I thought about contacting Del to see how she was, have a little girl time before I headed home, but I was too tired to do the whole "He doesn't love me" scene. Del was a big girl and I had already told one person to pull up his panties tonight. I had the feeling that Del needed something more kind. After careful consideration, I texted Amy Lynn Brown, who had known Del in Asheville. Amy was a fast-healing wonder, a vamp scion who had gone through the entire devoveo in two years, finding sanity in record time. Brown-haired, slender, and unremarkable at first glance, she had a good head on her shoulders, was calm under fire, smart, and once had been able to help a panicked fanghead at a party that went sour. Amy sent word that she was honored to pay the primo a visit.

Communication and good deeds were done, which took

some loads off my shoulders and had given my body a chance to get over the shakes—and when did I become the vamps' therapist? That left only Jodi Richoux, the vamps' liaison with NOPD, and that could wait until I had some rest. I texted Eli to meet me at the porte cochere where the SUV had been delivered from the dojo, got back a text that simply said *K*, and I headed down.

Though HQ was now quiet and inactive in reaction to the events of the daytime, I left Protocol Aardvark, Procedure B in place as I left the back of the building. Night had fallen hours past. The air was humid and hot, a storm brewing to the south, over the gulf, and heading our way. Lightning flashed from cloud to cloud, brightening the sky, illuminating the thunderheads.

In the distance, uptown from vamp HQ, blue and red lights lit up the horizon; sirens carried on the wind said it was an accident of some sort. A big one. And not my problem. Thank God.

As soon as we got home, I put the inert iron discs on my bedside table, showered, and pulled on clean sleep clothes before I climbed up onto the broken rocks in the back garden to commune with my inner Beast. Just as I got settled, the official phone rang from inside the house, the standard ringtone of Latin dance music. Looking abashed, Alex came out the side door and handed up the cell to reveal Jodi Richoux's name. Jodi was cute, with a blond bob and enough attitude to take down a vamp in a rage. And a badge to back it all up. *She's not in a good mood,* he mouthed.

I frowned but took the call. That late, it had to be business, and not the good kind. "Jodi?" I asked.

"I need you at Pauger and Burgundy in Marigny. *Now*. Park down the street and follow the lights."

"Okay." I unfolded my legs and slid across the boulders to the ground, grit scraping my thighs through the pj bottoms. *Lights on the horizon uptown. The sound of distant sirens could have been in Marigny,* I thought. *But no accident.* "What do I need to bring?" I pointed Alex to the house and he fell in behind me.

My unquestioning willingness seemed to disarm her, and Jodi said, more quietly, "I've got vamp killings, fifty-two humans, all dead where they stood."

A frisson of fear and shock raced through me like electricity, burning and sharp. I pressed a hand to my middle, thinking I'd misheard. "What?" I whispered. Jodi repeated her words even more softly, but the consonants were cutting and quick with suppressed emotion.

Oh crap. The Son of Darkness . . . Mouth as dry as paper, I asked, "Am I coming as the Enforcer or as a consultant?"

"I'm not sure." Which didn't sound like Jodi. She was always sure of my roles in things, even if I wasn't. "Maybe a little of both."

So . . . someone important was listening. And this was partly a warning. "I'll come as Enforcer and if you need me as something else, I can downgrade."

"Make it fast."

The call ended and I entered the house to see Eli standing in the foyer, waiting. "Gear up," I said, my voice hoarse. "Fifty-two humans dead by vamp."

Eli swore and took the stairs up two at a time. Maybe three. To Alex, just before I closed the door to my room, I said, "Notify HQ. Tell them to notify Leo. Tell him to stay away. Please," I added. "Tell him to *please* stay away. And if you still have a backdoor into NOPD, I want to see what they have. But only if you can do it safely."

Alex nodded, popped the top on a can of energy drink, and went to work, an all-nighter staring him in the face.

I braced my body off the toilet with both arms as I dry heaved. Fifty-two dead humans. *It had to be Joses. It had to be.* I should have found a way to stop him from leaving HQ. I should have tackled him and stabbed him and staked him and killed him. Some way. Somehow. He was the hand grenade and I should have thrown myself on it.

I had let him get away because I was hurt. Dumb, stupid excuse.

I stood upright, one hand pressed to my middle and the burning there. I should go to Jodi, right this second. I should eat. I should . . . I stopped and tried to order my thoughts. I needed to dress and get to Jodi.

And the fifty-two dead humans.

I threw off my tacky T and the ratty pj's. There was a time when I'd worn only jeans and boots and attitude, but respect for the dead suggested something more . . . formal, maybe. Like funeral clothes.

Moving on instinct, I pulled on all black—slim pants, tank, lightweight jacket, and black Lucchese boots with hand-stitched cougars on them. As an afterthought, I added the working gorget, one of several Leo had provided for me, this one sterling over titanium chain mail, and tucked my gold nugget and wired cougar tooth necklace into my jog bra, out of sight. Back before Beast and I merged so deeply, the nugget had tied me to her in some mystical way. The tooth held the DNA and RNA of the largest female mountain lion I could find. Between the two, I could find my Beast form even when I was deeply damaged. Now I didn't seem to need them, but I also couldn't let them go. Habit. A security blanket. Whatever. I almost never took them off.

As I dressed, I got a good look at my damaged arm. The scars dappled my skin like rain on the surface of a pond, if it was viewed through a spiderweb. Bands and rings of interlaced and interconnected tissue formed a network across my flesh, the white and red of scar tissue. It was pretty awful. More important, the muscles beneath looked atrophied. I stretched and the muscles didn't give. I eased into the jacket. The sleeve brushed my arm with a sensation akin to fiberglass dipped in acid. I needed to shift and see what was wrong with Beast. And shift back to complete the healing of us both.

Fifty-two humans called to me. My healing would have to wait. Ninety seconds it had taken me to dress.

I double-checked that all my papers were in my wallet. PI license, business license, concealed-carry permit, Yellow-rock Security business cards, and my new business cards Leo had provided, the ones that read:

JANE YELLOWROCK
ENFORCER to **LEO PELLISSIER**
MASTER of the **CITY** of **NEW ORLEANS** and the **GREATER**
SOUTHEAST UNITED STATES

It was dignified and offered me protection I might sorely need.

Though it might be smart to show up with every weapon I owned, I elected to go without, except stakes in my hair. Which made me feel naked and weird and caused the space between my shoulder blades to itch. Made the nausea rise in my throat, the world swimming with vertigo as I moved, ignored. I tucked the wallet into my back pocket, smeared on bloodred lipstick, and smoothed the loose hair back into the fighting queue with some gel gook.

I was using the time, the precious seconds, to steady myself. I had been in a battle. I had been wounded and was hurting. I had been socked in the face with the results of my own actions and the future results of actions not yet taken. Not so far in the past, I had let Joses Bar-Judas live, if hanging on a wall in a dungeon can be considered living, and had killed a vamp named Peregrinus instead. I should have taken Joses' head then. I had *known* he was evil, as in damned and filthy evil. I had known it on some level I hadn't understood. He should have been separated from his head the first time I saw him; I hadn't done the job. I had acted like an Enforcer rather than a rogue-vamp hunter. The fact that I had been injured and lying in my own blood back then didn't matter. I had not killed him when I had the chance and now fifty-two humans had paid the price.

Later. I'd have to deal with my life later. At the thought, something inside me, something bleeding and broken, went cold. Hard. A bloody stone in the dark of my soul home.

Beast? I asked again.

She didn't answer, but I felt her breathing and got a sense of awareness. Pain. Patience. Cat feelings that meant *leave me alone.* I no longer had time to deal with my other soul like I should, so I withdrew from her. For now.

I strode out of my room, catching sight of myself in the full-length mirror. I looked long, lean, and mean. Good. I felt mean. Though I didn't know whom I was mad at, other than myself and Leo. Not yet. The three of us met in the foyer, where Alex handed us each a tablet. There were photos on the tablets, crime scene photos. "Oh yeah," I muttered, my thumb taking me through them fast. "Death by vamp." And that thing inside me, something broken and wounded, began to wail.

When I first came to New Orleans, I had thought there were only a few parts to the town. I had learned since that there were names to every part of the place, like the French Quarter, the Warehouse District, the Garden District, and Marigny, to name just a very few.

Marigny was a slice of New Orleans–style homes, but with large swathes of it still run-down and in need of rehabbing. Lots of buildings were still vacant after Katrina, so many years ago, but there was an air of things starting to get better, lots of homes and businesses showing fresh paint, new signs, the buildings and homes a mishmash of one-story shotgun houses, double shotgun houses (houses with two front doors, one on either side of the front façade of the house, with windows centered between), Creole cottages, two-story buildings that had been subdivided into apartments, with galleries—not porches, I had learned—on both floors, with modern (and uglier) buildings interspersed.

Eli drove around the congested area, which let us get a handle on how big a space had been cordoned off. Big. Entire blocks of the city. *Fifty-two humans. Dead. Because of my decision to let Joses live.* Eli pulled in at Washington Square Park, away from the lights, noise, crowds of people, emergency vehicles, and media vans. It was still night when he parked, but I could feel dawn coming.

Sitting in the dark, he said, "The average human has five and a half quarts of blood in him. Fifty-two humans equals two hundred eighty-six quarts." He stared at me through the dark. "If they were all drained, then there is no way one vampire alone drained fifty-two humans. If it's Bar-Judas, he wasn't working alone."

I hadn't done the math, but he was right. That much blood meant multiple vamps in a feeding frenzy. I hadn't gotten the impression of multiple vamps with loss of control from the still shots the Kid had brought up. "So who did he find to follow him," I asked, "this soon after getting free? When he left his rescuers dead on the floor at HQ?"

Eli said, "The vamp in the cloak."

I rubbed my arm, but nothing came to me. I went over the vamps I'd seen in the time after the fight with the Son of Darkness. Edmund. Dominique. Grégoire, looking both pensive and worried. And sniffing the air, which was odd but not unexpected. Leo. Others. No cloak. No enemy I recognized.

The blue and red lights were out of sight, but traffic had been blocked off and the locals were out in force. The walk would give us a sense of the emotional integrity of the crowd. We got out and I closed my eyes, sniffing the air.

Weed, beer, liquor, sweat, Mexican food from a tiny taqueria that had opened after hours to satisfy the gawkers, excitement, sex pheromones, the smell of banana plants and ginger plants. Water. Urine. Stray cats. Rats. And terror, the kind of stark, sour sweat that scented of loss, of knowing loved ones were dead. On the air I heard a plaintive voice calling, "Is she in there? You gots to tell me. Is my baby in there? Tell me!" Over and over, grief like a dead body weighting down the words.

Someone else shouted, "I din' hear no shots. What kill dem peoples?"

Another one of the crowd shouted, "Tell us what goin' on!"

"Is she in there? You gots to tell me. Is my baby in there?"

"Damn cops!"

Under all the smells, beneath the worried muttering and angry catcalls, I scented a hint of aggression, not ugly, not yet, but on the edge. For now the words were mostly curiosity, not yet tuned to revenge. But it would all change. Soon. As soon as word went out that a vamp had done this.

I opened my eyes and found my partner, his back to the vehicle, searching the night. Eli had elected to wear black dress pants and a starched black shirt, no tie, shiny shoes, like a civilian. And no weapons. Without even talking about it, we were on the same page, my partner and I, in sync, which was one reason that we worked so well together, that mental consciousness of each other, like soldiers in battle, with situational awareness and comrade-in-arms mindfulness. Not that he was weaponless. Eli could kill with his bare hands. For that matter, so could I.

Eli's eyes flicked my way and back to darkness. "You gonna make it through this, Janie?"

"Yes," I said. But I heard the feeble note in my tone.

"This isn't your fault. You had no way of knowing."

I shook my head and gestured him into the street.

The sounds of our footsteps were lost beneath the crowd noise and the squeal of a siren pulling away, allowing us to move silently through the dark. As we neared the commotion, Eli's head went up, his shoulders back, and he led the way down the middle of the street, like a dance that left us striding side by side on the potholed blacktop. He looked like what he was. Dangerous. And so did I. People seemed to sense that we were trouble, or maybe that we were part of the entertainment, because the hangers-on, the curious, the partygoers rubbernecking at disaster, parted as we neared, leaving a wide gap straight down the block to the sawhorses and crime scene tape that blocked the road.

We were closer to the old woman shouting, "Is she in there? You gots to tell me. Is my baby in there? Tell me! Tell me! *Tell me!*"

My lips parted and my breath came fast and shallow.

"Is my baby in there? *Tell me!*"

A cop watched us as we neared, and sadly it was my old pal Officer Herbert—pronounced *A-bear*, in the French manner, he had told me the first time I met him. He was a career cop, mid-forties, smelling of Cajun spices and lots of aftershave, his familiar scent picked up over the crowd. He was also was a chauvinist pig, an ass, mean just for fun, and downright malicious. He hated anything that wasn't human, male, straight, and white, including me. Herbert's face twisted as we walked up, looking us over for weapons, backpacks, anything he could use to cause us trouble, the intent unmistakable on his face. I had gotten on his bad side at our first meeting, and I had never been in the mood to make nice-nice with him. I still wasn't in the mood to try. Not tonight.

"Tell me! My baby, my baby my baby mybabybabybabybaby . . ." The woman sat on the curb nearby, arms around her knees, rocking, rocking, in time with the lament. The stink of grief and fear and cheap wine was a fog around her. "My baby, baby, baby, *baaaby* . . ."

"Morning, Dickhead," I said softly, using the same name I'd called Herbert the first day I met him. In front of Jodi. This time in front of Eli, who goggled in shock. Well, his right eye twitched. A little.

"You wanna take a ride down to NOPD?" Herbert barked, his hand going to his gun.

I grinned, letting my own meanness show, a shadow of the heated turmoil boiling in me. "Not my idea of a fun first date. If I dated dickheads with badges." I wanted him to attack. I wanted him to hit me so I could hit him back. Suddenly, I wanted to hit *some*thing and I didn't care what.

Herbert's face went purple, and had he been seventy pounds lighter and twenty years younger, he would have dived over the barricade and tackled me to the ground. As

it was, Jodi appeared behind him, like a magician material-
izing out of the gloom, and placed a hand on his arm. "Jim,
why don't you take a break. You've been on sixteen hours
already. Grab something at the taqueria. On me." Jodi
placed a ten in his pudgy hand and nudged him over. Herbert shot me a look promising all sorts of horrible things,
and went.

"You like yanking his chain," she said mildly. Too mild.
She was holding herself on a tight leash.

"Yeah," I said. "He's an ass. One you used to bait me
when we first met. It was necessary at the time; I understand
that. And it never stopped me from being your friend. But
it never made me like *him*."

Jodi appeared to mull that over as she checked us out,
giving particular attention to Eli. She knew his military history and his penchant for going heavily weaponed. But
whether from exhaustion or because she recognized a familiar face in a foxhole, she didn't linger. "I won't apologize
for doing my job," she said, still mild.

"Jane Yellowrock," a female voice shouted in the distance.

Crap. The press. My stomach did a somersault. "And I
won't apologize for doing mine," I said, which, at the moment included ticking off Herbert, holding my wounded
arm steady, and trying not to throw up. "The media has now
recognized us and is starting to point parabolic and shotgun
mics at us. You want to let us in?"

Jodi let her eyes travel behind us to the media. Bright
lights began moving our way as people started running
toward us. "Those things won't pick up much past eight feet,
so you're safe. But yeah. I need you inside." She lifted the
crime scene tape just as a woman came running up, mic in
hand, shouting my name, her cameraman jogging behind her.
We three walked away, leaving her and her cronies speculat-
ing into their mics about why the vampire hunter turned
vampire lover was there. *Vampire lover.* They had been wondering online and on air for months whether Leo and I were
sleeping together. *Idiots.*

We said nothing as we followed Jodi to the corner building, the blue lights turning our skin to zombie gray. Men and
women, uniformed and plainclothes, moved grimly. They
had set up a temporary morgue under tents, the cloth sides

hiding the gurneys waiting for the legal types and the crime scene techs to release the bodies to be taken for forensic postmortems. But with multiple victims, processing started at the scene, often proceeded close by, and finished on a stainless-steel table at the morgue.

Until now, I had hoped that the number of casualties had been wrong. Five, maybe. Eight. Not fifty-two. But the portable crime scene said otherwise. It was bad. Really bad.

The two-story building Jodi led us to was large enough to support two or three businesses on the ground floor, and on the second floor, multiple apartments with a gallery, enclosed with decorative wrought iron. Holding up the gallery, matching wrought-iron poles marked the space between the sidewalk and the street, giving the lower floor protection from the sun. It was a nice-sized building, the multiple windows and doors on the first floor having jalousie windows above each, and on the second floor there were key-design windows and doors. Over it all was a fancy brickwork soldier course. I thought there might have been dormers in the roof, making a third floor a final residential area or artist's atelier, but my visual angle wasn't right to tell for certain. The building was stuccoed or plastered, hard to tell in the strobing lights. The windows and doors were all shut, and I could hear the hum of an air conditioner running.

The smell of death reached out and grabbed me.

CHAPTER 5

I Will Cut out His Heart . . .
I Will Bring It to You

Inside the main entrance, which was located on the corner, beneath an elaborate curlicued door header, Jodi handed us each a stack of paper clothing and pointed us through a narrow space along one wall. The inside of the building was hidden from our eyes, but the smells . . . they told the tale. Alcohol of every kind, old toilets, fried food—the scents of a bar and grill. And over it all rode the stink of bowels, urine, the sweet reek of blood starting to go bad.

Eli glanced at me, his eyes hard, holding both a warning and a question in his expression. I shook my head, not having an answer to whatever he needed to know. Sitting on a long bench, we pulled on the paper booties, long white paper jackets, and white hats, which looked like poofs of dough on our heads. Lastly, we snapped on nitrile gloves, the medium blue the county preferred.

Jodi stuck her head around the corner and motioned us out. She was similarly dressed, in paper and nitrile, and when we made our way around the partition into the main room, we saw everyone dressed in the paper clothing. All the living, that is.

My eyes tried to take it in as my nose went on overload with death-death-death. The dead were wearing colorful party clothes, jeans, skirts, boots, ballerina shoes, gold chains, T-shirts, button-downs, running shoes, capri pants, sandals, peasant blouses, tank tops, wifebeaters; every manner of casual dress seen at a New Orleans bar in a summer heat wave was represented. The dead were slumped at tables, lying on the dance floor, crumpled behind the bar, two prone halfway in the men's room door, one supine on the bar, as if she had been dancing the cancan and then lay down to sleep, her dress still thrown high, over her head. Some had bloody throats with signs of multiple puncture marks, the way victims look when several vamps have been at them but didn't feel the need to rip and tear. Fastidious, deadly vamps. Others were slumped so that I couldn't see their throats, and still others' heads were turned around on their spines, facing the wrong way. When the vamps were done, they had broken the humans' necks. It was much worse than the photos. It always is.

I ground my teeth and crossed my arms over my chest, gripping them with my hands. The pain that had hidden, subdued, in my flesh throbbed up my arm and hand like a bomb going off at the pressure of my fingers. Along with the pain, the pinpricks came back, tingling hot along my skin. I wanted to curse or scream. Punch something. I should have killed Joses Bar-Judas, taken his head where he hung on the wall. I had known in my gut that he was evil incarnate. I could see it in his eyes, even without proof of any wrongdoing. And I had done nothing. Worse, much worse, I had let him get by me. I had let him get free. To do this. This horror.

Hunched into myself, I turned around slowly, taking in the room. The band members were all lying with their instruments, two with guitars in hand, one guy with a trumpet, another with a sax. A girl on drums, looking as if she fell asleep across her base drum, curly dark hair with bright pink stripes painted in. Her dress was hiked up around her waist, as if—

I didn't finish that thought. But my blood heated and my heart rate sped as I forced myself away from my own shock and back to the crime scene. To that moment. To that problem. To that flood in the midst of the deluge of problems.

Eli had said that draining fifty-two humans meant 286 quarts of blood. *How many humans had been drained? How many vamps had been there? How many vamps were on the rampage?*

"Tell me," Jodi said, the words too calm.

I pushed all the questions away as the anger and guilt that accompanied them flamed high in the dark places of my soul. "You already know vamps did this. What do you want with me? Why am I in the middle of this?"

"I'll file your sympathy away for later consideration," Jodi said evenly.

I started to reply and clamped my mouth shut on the words. Closing my eyes, I said, "I'm sorry. I'm so sorry about all this." I swept my left hand out around me and regripped my injured arm. When I took a breath, it stuttered on a sob that I swallowed down.

"Okay. I wanted you to know exactly what this city is dealing with. So that you will tell me if you recognize the vampire who did this." Her tone was mild, so placid, so carefully bland, her words so precise. "Vampire," she enunciated, rage leaking into the two syllables, contained under pressure, as if she was close to explosion. "Singular."

"The math doesn't—" I stopped and looked again at the humans who showed no bloody throats and realized that the humans who appeared to have deformities had no other injuries. Their heads had been twisted around until their necks broke, but there were no fang marks, no sign of draining, and none had the pale-pale flesh of the drained. Not all fifty-two had been taken for feeding. Most of them had been killed without blood loss. Vamps didn't do that to their cattle. They might bleed their dinners dry, but they didn't kill them with their blood still inside.

I looked along the ceiling and found the security cameras, two of them, one pointed at the bar, the other at the dance floor and the cash register. One vamp, she had said. Joses Bar-Judas was old enough to have that kind of power. The words like the ashes of death in my mouth, I said, "Show me."

She led the way out of the bar and back to the place where we'd dressed. She had us remove our personal protective equipment and toss the PPEs into a bag. In a crime scene, everything would be gone over with a fine-tooth comb for trace evidence that we might have picked up and carried out by accident.

Jodi led the way outside, into the muggy heat of predawn, and into a tent set up with bright lamps, a long table, and a whiteboard. There was nothing there, not yet. But soon the table and the board would be filled with evidence and notes and comments that would later be put into computerized records. Few police departments could afford the kind of fancy computer system seen on TV cop shows, and NOPD was among the poor law enforcement departments, so the whiteboard would be front and center in the ongoing investigation. In the distance, a generator roared, a huge one, to provide power for the evidence gathering.

She left us there, and Eli pulled his cell, punched a button, and waited. I heard Alex answer, and Eli said, "Silent mode. Sync and record." He said nothing else, and a moment later Jodi returned with a laptop, an older model, that she opened and booted up.

Eli and I leaned over the table, braced on our hands, watching, as she brought up video and fast-forwarded through it. A dance bar, people having fun, a lot of hip shimmies, a little line-dance twerking, all looking silly in fast mode, some making out at the bar, a lot of drinking and eating. And then Jodi hit a button and the vid slowed down. The people moved at a normal pace now, dancing and laughing, juking and jiving, cuddling and kissing. It was silent, no audio, and the view felt odd with the lack of music and voices. People having fun are loud. Raucous.

A shadow entered the bar, moving fast, and reached the center of the room. The video stopped, and Jodi tapped some more keys, bringing the face into better focus, then tapping until we had two blurred close-ups of the man on the screen, side by side, the bar visible around him.

I had never seen him before, yet I knew who he was. I did.

His complexion was pale and scummy, with deep frown wrinkles at eyes and mouth. Tangled black hair reached his hips in tattered knots. His eyes were scarlet and black, vamped-out, glowing reddish from the lights in the room. His nose was proud, a Roman nose, half-formed but with no nostrils yet, just black holes to either side of the arching bone. He was gaunt, a scarecrow caricature of a man, an illustration from a grisly fairy tale. His beard was thin and scraggly, yet he wore clean, neat clothing, black from head to toe—dress slacks, shirt, and a black iridescent tie that caught the light. I remembered that he had killed humans and drained the young vamps, Liam and Vivian. The clothes looked like something Liam might wear. With my left hand, I pressed deep into the burning between my ribs.

"Do you know him?" Jodi asked, her voice sounding less cold, more worried. More something. "Does he have anything to do with your guys and Leo's muscle chasing a smoking human-shaped figure down the street today?"

I shook my head. "Yes. Maybe. What . . ." I stopped and swallowed down bile. "What does he look like? After."

The close-up disappeared and the video started.

The vamp raised his arms and the people all stopped. Just stopped. Skirts and big hair waved, slowing, as the people halted. Only the vamp still moved. The vamp walked to the nearest man and bent him back, over his arm. He opened his mouth, his jaw dropping, angling wide, the way older vamps' mouths did, like a snake's jaws, to allow the fangs to click down and up. These were five inches long on top and at least three on the bottom. Like a sabertooth cat. He thrust them into the man's throat. He drank. And drank. And when he was done, he dropped the man on the floor and moved on to the next person, a woman stopped in the midst of a dance move, her pelvis rocked forward. He pulled the woman to him and seemed to breathe in her scent. He took her head in his hands, and with a move so fast that the cameras couldn't capture it, he broke her neck and lay her on the floor. On and on he moved through the crowd. Drinking a few, breaking the necks of most. And as he moved, the camera began to pixel out, more and more. And he started to change.

His magic was growing as he drank. His magic was strong enough to create an EM resonance or something similar. The screen was pixelating out in broad, fluctuating blocks. But enough was left. Too much. Joses Bar-Judas—the assumption had to be correct—was healing. His olive complexion now glowed with blood-flush. Luxurious black hair reached his hips in rippling waves, and when it slid forward, it moved like silk. His eyes now looked human, light colored, maybe green, or maybe they glowed greenish from the lights in the room; I couldn't tell. His nose was proud and his beard was thick and full, with glints that might have been stray white hairs at his chin. Eyebrows like ravens' wings. He was slender and elegant and utterly gorgeous. If a fallen angel had mated with a raptor and a siren and the three had produced a son, he might be this beautiful. Even in the pixelated photos he was stunning. Magnificent. He'd stop people in their tracks wherever he went, even without vamp compulsion.

When the vamp was done with the dance floor, he stroked his luxurious beard, sliding it through his hand, thoughtfully, as he stepped up to the band. He drained and killed his way through them, one by one, until he reached the drummer; the camera caught his face as he bent over her and inhaled. He closed his eyes, liking how she smelled. I turned away. I didn't need to see more.

"Yeah," Jodi said bitterly, her gaze on me. "He's a piece of work. All that in front of the cameras. As if he doesn't care he's on camera."

Or as if he doesn't know what a camera is, I thought. "He's old. Very old. Five-inch upper fangs mean he's ancient. The way the jaw unhinged means ancient. Bottom fangs only make him older. The way he held the victims still with his mind means ancient, ancient, *ancient.* Print me a photo or send it to my cell. I'll do—" I stopped, my throat so dry I could barely swallow. "I'll get you a name."

"Leo had a problem at the Mithran Council Chambers," Jodi said, with the kind of formality she used when talking to a suspect or a person of interest. "We have reports of a human figure running through the streets, smoking and on fire, chased by a bunch of men who sound a lot like Leo's people and yours. Was it related to this situation?"

I picked through my possible responses and jutted my chin at the screen. "Probably. I could just say yes, but I never saw him in either form, not hungry and not blood-flushed and healthy."

"So what did he look like when you saw him?" Jodi asked.

I shook my head. "Doesn't matter. I want confirmation from someone who knew him. Knows him. I need to show this to Leo."

"No. No way this leaves this room."

I didn't look at Eli. He had synced his phone. We had it already. I shrugged, one shouldered.

"Leo needs to call me," Jodi said, the calm in her voice beginning to crack. "And before you say anything, yes, I know it's never convenient to drop by and visit with the cops. But if I don't get a call from him within one hour, I'll start the paperwork on getting a warrant and haul him in to NOPD. In the sunlight, in the trunk of my car, if necessary. I imagine he would find that extremely undignified. Or you can wait until PsyLED is here and they'll haul him down. You don't have many choices."

Choosing my words carefully, knowing I was walking in a verbal minefield, I said, "Is Leo a suspect? How can he be a suspect based on the footage we just saw?"

"Person of interest. Person who is supposed to know, and have control over, every vamp in his region. Who is supposed to keep the *humans* safe from *predators*," she spat, still holding in her fury, barely, but moving closer, until I could feel the anger radiating from her in heated waves. "Person who may have just lost any ability to keep the vamps out of the human legal system. Person who could end up in the *vampire version of Guantanamo Bay*," she said, her voice rising, "in a *cave* in *chains*, along with the rest of his species, if certain members of Congress have their way. And *this*"—she swept an arm to the video of the kill bar on the laptop and lowered her voice—"just made that more likely."

"Okay. I got that. Suggestion. You could go to the Council House and knock politely and ask to be let in," I said.

Jodi leaned to me, up against me, so close that her face was in mine though I stood nearly a foot taller, her calm façade cracking. She breathed, "I don't feel like being polite. I feel like taking a couple dozen guns and walking into fanghead central and shooting everything that moves. And if *I* feel that way, how do you think the rest of the city is going to feel? How do you think this city is going to react to anything supernatural after this? To the *witches*?" Her voice lowered, hissing with fierceness. "To my *people*. To *my family*."

I didn't move away. I didn't touch her. I simply pulled my wallet and removed my Enforcer cards. I tore them in half and placed them on the table, knowing what I was about to say might get me killed. By Leo. "I'm a vampire hunter. It's what I do." I held Jodi's eyes with mine, watching hers redden and fill with tears. Tears that didn't fall. "I'll start research now. I'll verify his name. I will track down and I will find this monster. I will cut out his heart and I will bring it to you. You. Personally."

"And Leo?" she whispered, her breath brushing my cheek.

I didn't know the answer to that one yet. "He may try to kill me." A ghost of a smile softened my face. "Get me a go-ahead. Call the governor and get him to give me a contract to cover liabilities. He should have one on file from the werewolf problems in Houma last winter. But I'll do it even without the contract. For you. For the witches. For these people and their families."

Jodi's blue eyes swept my face, and something there must have satisfied her. "I want you on camera with me at a press conference, live for the six a.m. news," she breathed. "I want you in full regalia. And I want you to announce that you are going after this guy. Maybe that will keep this city calm for a day. Maybe."

"Fine. Yes. I'll be there. I need to talk to Leo first, and there's not much time before six a.m."

"One more thing." Jodi pulled an envelope-shaped evidence bag from a pocket and held it out to me. "Do you know what this is?"

I took the envelope, which hadn't been sealed, hadn't been timed or dated or initialed, hadn't been listed according to crime scene number or scene sector, all of which was not according to protocol. I looked to Jodi, who refused to meet my eyes. "Okay," I said, forcing her to recognize all the problems with my seeing this. I opened the bag and looked inside. At the bottom was a tuft of something white, like a fishing fly, tied and knotted with white string, a bit of stem from a bush or tree caught in it. The leaf was still greenish, though curled and wilted. I pointed at it, the question on my face.

"You can check it out," she said. "No way can we get prints from it, and it's been handled by too many of us. DNA is impossible now."

Which meant the cops had found something somewhere and mishandled it and Jodi had absconded with a piece of whatever they had found. *Gotcha.* I lifted the hairy tuft and held it to the lamp. The white clump was composed of shorter, furry hair and longer white hairs, the tips so pure they looked almost clear. I knew what it was even without scenting it, but I sniffed anyway, drawing air into my nose, the hairs moving against my nostrils. This was werewolf hair, belonging to a particular werewolf—Brute, a werewolf stuck in wolf form. Brute and I had a long and confusing history, one that involved fights, a little blood, and an angel.

I dropped the hair back into the envelope and resealed it before handing it back. "Smells like a wet dog," I said.

Jodi stepped away slowly, pulling her control around her like a steel corset, compressing all the frayed ends, hiding all the pain inside. She shoved a strand of blond hair behind her ear and the envelope back into her pocket. "Can you still ride a bike?" she asked. "Herbert has a Harley."

I couldn't keep the snark in, though I kept my voice low, for her. "Can I sanitize the seat first?"

The laughter that broke from Jodi was as jagged as broken glass. "I might have a bottle around here somewhere."

"Then get me the bike. I'll be back as fast as I can."

"Move it. Take your partner. We need this space."

Still side by side, Eli and I left the tent.

While Herbert went for his motorcycle, I called HQ and asked for Del. "You see the breaking news?" I asked her. When she said yes, I said, "A vamp did it. Tell Leo I'm on the way in." I closed the Kevlar cell phone cover without waiting for her reply.

And dang if Jim Herbert didn't push up a customized metallic silver Harley Heritage Softail with pillion-style seat. If I thought he hated me before, the look he sent me turned regular ol' hatred into hatred times ten. "You hurt my baby and I'll make you regret it for the rest of your life," he stated.

"If I hurt that bike, I'll deserve it."

I had no idea the words came out of my mouth until Herbert glared harder. My comment made him tuck his chin, creating extra chins. It made Eli glance at me from the corner of his eye.

"Seriously," I said. Herbert might be a pig, but he had great taste in motorcycles. "I'll take care of her."

Eli and I helmeted up. I shoved my stakes into a cup

holder set discreetly in the bike's frame. My partner asked, "You're not going to make me ride the bitchseat, are you?"

"Oh yeah. And it's pillion, not bitchseat." I straddled the bike and got the feel of her balance, the weight distribution of her, the soundness of her. She was gorgeous, easy to handle even with one arm not up to my usual strength levels. "This baby's mine." I keyed her on and made a low sound of pleasure—this bike was the only good thing in this godforsaken night. I looked up and met Herbert's eyes. "What's her name?"

He frowned and hitched his pants up under his gut by his wide leather belt. "Epona. It's a Celtic goddess. It means 'great mare.'"

I smiled at him. "She's perfect."

Herbert shrugged, just a hint, but there was pleasure in his eyes. "Yeah. She is dat."

I heard a hint of Cajun in the words and I nodded to him. "Climb on, Eli."

My partner's weight settled behind me, his hands at my waist. We roared toward the crime scene tape, our identities hidden behind helmets and faceplates that smelled like Herbert and a woman. Maybe his wife.

I let Eli off at the SUV so he could swing by the house and pick up my best gear—my only set of vamp-hunting leathers now. Jodi wanted me geared up, and that's the way she'd get me—geared up to the max. Riding solo, I sped through the predawn traffic to vamp HQ.

Due to security protocols—ones I had devised—I had to unhelmet at the front gate and a guard with a slavering dog met me in the circular drive. It was Tex, a vamp with a knack for dogs and a love for .45 Old West–style handguns. "Miz Jane," he greeted me, the Texan twang throwing me off, as it always did. The dog wanted to do a sniff-and-growl greeting of his own, but Tex pulled him back. "Miz Adelaide said for you to come straight to Mr. Pellissier's office. You got any weapons on you, you got to declare 'em at the front." He smiled at me, a perfectly normal human smile, no fangs, and joked, "Our Enforcer's protocols, don'tcha know."

"She sounds like a real pain in the butt," I said, feeling my face relax for the first time in hours.

"She is that. But I'm a butt man, ma'am, so I don't mind."

With that pithy statement, he clicked to the dog and returned to his rounds.

I left the helmet on the bike, set my silver stakes in my hair, where they couldn't be missed, climbed the steps to the main floor, and was buzzed into the new steel-reinforced airlock system and metal detector, where I was met by a vamp and a human, part of Protocol Aardvark, Procedure B. The human was carrying a cross beneath his shirt, one that glowed in close proximity to the vamp beside him. They looked me over and the vamp stepped back, his nose wrinkling.

"Yes," I said, "I smell like dead humans. Deal with it. I have no weapons on me except stakes." I ignored the look that passed between them and assumed the position to allow a pat-down, which was done professionally, with minimal handsy stuff, just the way I'd taught them.

There was a time when I'd insisted that every visitor, even me, be stripped of weapons and escorted through the building, but that rule had proven kinda ridiculous when I'd needed my weapons. Now, with few exceptions, we were doing the declare-and-carry program, and so far it was working.

I knocked on Leo's door and heard him call, *"Vous pouvez entrer."*

I took a breath to steel myself and entered. The entrance was wide, with tapestries hanging on the walls, hiding from casual observers the openings to once-secret hallways, stairwells, and concealed rooms. I wasn't stupid enough to think I'd discovered all of them, but I'd done a good job of finding and mapping and putting cameras on most.

The rugs were deep beneath my boots, hand-knotted Oriental, Persian, and Chinese silk, each probably worth twenty K and with the ruined hands of child laborers to show for it. Paintings and statues were displayed all over, hung from the ceiling moldings on wire, resting on easels, posed on pedestals. There was no fire in the fireplace, either because it was already too warm in the room or because Leo was in a mood. I came to the entry to the office and stopped. On the gold chaise longue lay someone I'd never expected to see in this room again, and certainly never on Leo's feeding couch.

"Wrassler?" But the word got stuck in my throat somewhere and never emerged.

The big guy was stretched out, looking down at Leo, who knelt at the security guard's feet. Foot. Foot and high-tech prosthetic. Wrassler had lost the lower leg only a few weeks past, and without Leo's blood and Leo's contacts and Leo's money, he'd still be recuperating in a rehab center somewhere, getting physical therapy twice a day and eating crummy food. Instead he was learning how to use the new leg and being healed of the arm damage by the Master of the City himself, Leo Pellissier, who, at the moment, was inspecting Wrassler's lower arm, holding it close to his face, breathing in the scent of the skin. It could have been a lover-like moment, but instead it looked clinical, as Leo pierced the flesh with his fangs, pulled back to study the arm, and licked the new wound. He took a moment to bite his thumb pad and first pressed the bleeding thumb into the fang wounds, then placed his thumb at Wrassler's mouth. The big guy sucked the blood away the same way another human might take liquid meds from a nurse. "Thank you, sir," he said.

I stood with my feet shoulder-width apart and my hands clasped behind my back, like a soldier at rest, watching, listening to the bald-headed giant and his master. Remembering that the fanghead on his knees, healing his blood-servant, had allowed the carnage I had only just witnessed. My emotions boiled like hot tar, coating and scorching me, on the inside, where it didn't show. But I could smell my own scent, which carried the reek of stale fear and the death stench of fifty-two humans, and I knew that Leo could smell them on me also.

But he didn't turn my way. "Much better," Leo said. "Make a fist. Open. Close. Again. Yes. *Je suis satisfait.* This is improving nicely." Leo stood with the toned and lithe motions of a young, world-class athlete. "The tendon damage is much better. The surgeon did a fine job."

"Speaking of jobs, sir?"

"Waiting for you when you are well, my loyal and dutiful servant." Leo turned to include me. "If you can tolerate working *avec celle qui marche dans les peaux d'animaux*."

Wrassler nodded to me. "Janie and I understand each other, sir. And Cherokee skinwalkers don't scare me."

"Bien." Leo pulled Wrassler to his . . . feet. And supported him until the human had his balance. Leo handed the big man a cane and said, "Good day to you."

"And good rest to you, sir. Janie," Wrassler said to me as he limped past.

When the door shut behind him, Leo sat on the chaise, his knees wide, his elbows on them, hands clasped and dangling between, his eyes on me. His expression was patient, curious, concerned, purely human, his black hair loose around his face. His whole demeanor was harmless, easygoing, kind, and quietly worried, like a parent ready to hear bad tidings about his child's school grades.

I wanted to gut him where he sat.

In the place of violence, I pulled out my cell and stabbed Alex's number. "Video capture," I said, when he answered.

"Got it. Coming up now to Leo's screen," the Kid said.

I jerked my head toward the big screen that now hung above Leo's elaborate desk, where the big chifforobe full of papers, computer supplies, and the printer used to stand. It was gone now, in favor of the new device. The MOC lifted a remote and turned the TV on to the security channel. The video Alex had captured from the evidence tent at the kill bar started instantly. I stood where I was, not watching it again, but watching Leo. He was wearing thin, knit yoga pants and a fitted T-shirt, probably handmade to his measurements, sheathing him like a glove, all in a shade of blue so dark they might have been knitted from the midnight sky itself. Vampire pajamas.

There was so little movement to him—no breath, no heartbeat—that the vamp might have been a wax fake of himself. Not even his hair, hanging to his shoulders, moved. But as he watched the video of the vampire killing humans, something changed, some infinitesimal something that I had no name for. It wasn't scent, or blood-flush, or anything remotely human. Whatever it was, it was something that Beast might have understood, might have felt, while watching another predator feed. Despite Leo being a mostly sane vamp, he was still a predator, and on some level, he liked what he was seeing.

CHAPTER 6

Can Anything Survive Without a Heart?

I stood where I was as Leo viewed the footage all the way through twice, stopping, reversing, and forwarding through it, to give particular attention to details. When he had seen enough, he set the remote to the side.

He stood. Staring into space, thinking, his eyes unfocused, moving with his thoughts. I got tired of waiting.

"'I have miscalculated,'" I quoted him. "'Badly. And my people are in grave danger.' Not just your people, Leo. Humans are in grave danger from vampires. From *that* vampire. I haven't had time to pull the files or go through the basements to see if we have photos or paintings from before he turned into a bag of bones hanging on your wall, so confirm it for me. That was Joses Bar-Judas. Yes?"

"Le Créateur des morts."

"Creator of the dead? Cute. I have to kill him."

Leo's eyes moved to me, only his eyes, yet there was threat in the very immobility of his body. "If you kill the Son of Darkness, there will be war with the old ones. War as you have never imagined."

"If I don't kill him, I'm afraid that mobs of humans will

break in here and drag every vampire into the sun. I promised to give the cops his heart."

For some reason that made Leo blink, a tell that would have lost him a bundle at poker. When he didn't seem inclined to enlighten me as to his reaction, however, I went on. "Sabina and Bethany have informed me that there will be unintended consequences to killing Joses. And maybe worse consequences to keeping him alive."

"Yes," Leo said softly. "My uncle's miscalculation may prove to be costly. Mine perhaps more so."

"The miscalculation in taking and keeping Joses Bar-Judas prisoner?" I accused.

"My miscalculation about how far lost Joses' mind still was," he corrected quietly, "and what quantity of blood it might take to bring him to sanity. And my miscalculation about Adrianna's intent."

Leo looked down at the rug between his feet while I thought about Adrianna, the red-haired vamp he had carried away from sub-five dripping brains all over the carpet. Leo had miscalculated about her from day one. He had been playing her, and it seemed she had been playing him right back, one step ahead of Leo, two steps behind Joses Bar-Judas. Only now their little game had mushroomed into something much worse than Leo or she had expected: freed prisoner, brain-damaged vamp, and dead humans in a city ready to riot. "What can you tell me about the night Joses 'disappeared'?"

Leo looked up at me, a wrinkle appearing between his brows as he thought back. "There is little to tell. I spent the evening with Adrianna. She wanted something—I no longer remember what—and I refused. We argued and parted. Later, I was contacted by my uncle, who had received word about a disturbance at Acton House. He came by horse and buggy into the Quarter. It was near dawn and he was rushing; the horse was lathered. We arrived at Acton House at nearly the same time. We found the room as you will find it still, except that that night, Joses—the Son of Darkness— was on the floor, raving, insane. Bethany appeared with us as we were deciding what to do. Sabina was there as well." He shook his head, as if trying to recall events from so long ago and the timeline wasn't making sense. "There were few witnesses to the injury suffered by the Son of Darkness, no one to tell us what had happened.

"There was not time before dawn to take him to Pellissier Clan Home. Amaury decided to take Joses to the new Council House, fearing that if he was found in his current condition there would be war. If discovered at the Council Chambers, Amaury could claim he had no idea that a prisoner had been taken."

Few witnesses and *no one to tell us* didn't add up, but I didn't point out the discrepancy. Not yet. I wanted to see what else he'd volunteer.

Leo said, "Bethany lifted him and carried him to our carriage."

"So you just took him prisoner and locked him away."

"It was not my decision," he said stiffly.

"It's been your decision since the early nineteen hundreds, when Amaury died of silver poisoning and you took over."

Leo's eyes flashed scarlet and I thought for a moment he might jump me. Instead, he said, "Yes. My decision. Do you contend against it?"

"And it was your decision to drink the blood of your prisoner, thereby increasing your power and cementing your control of your territories."

"I have always done what seemed best for Clan Pellissier and the Mithrans of the Louisiana Territories." Leo bit out the words in hard syllables.

And now it comes back and bites you in the butt. But I didn't say that, settling on, "Ah." Thoughtfully, I said, "I quit my job not so long ago."

"A resignation I refused. And a renegotiation that was quite profitable to you."

A half mil profitable. "Yeah. Well, if you refuse to let me protect you *and* fulfill my word to the police, I will quit. Right now. For good." I paused and gathered myself to negotiate with the MOC. Hard to do when all I wanted was to smash that pretty face. "And I know you need me."

Leo smiled, his demeanor changing along with his peppery scent, growing more heated, like aged paper held close to a candle flame. "I do need you. All the Mithrans need you to prepare for the Europeans' visit. Your witches need you. Especially now, my Enforcer.

"Joses Bar-Judas is free. He gives evidence of being much more sane than anticipated, to have succeeded at such a feeding. That demonstration"—Leo flicked his fingers at the screen—"required intense control."

"Demonstration?" I repeated. "That was no demonstration. That was mass murder."

"Out of fifty-two humans, he drained only five, leaving behind deliberate and ample confirmation that he controlled the rest of them with his mind alone. He was leaving evidence. Proof of his power." Leo tilted his head, watching me, taking a breath of my anger and the smell of death clinging to me. "When Joses was hung on the wall, electricity had only just come to the city. There were no such things as cameras to record his prowess or his ability to control his cattle. I doubt he has had time, or will take time, to educate himself on all the technological marvels of this present era."

I had already figured that out. He'd had no idea he was being filmed. And that lack of knowledge on Joses' part might help us to find him. I pulled my cell and texted orders to Alex for the upcoming search. To look through traffic and security cameras around the kill bar until he found which way JBJ was headed. I expected the Kid was already doing that, but I needed to cover all my bases.

As I keyed in the text, Leo said, "You may give the police the heart of Joses Bar-Judas. The rest of him you will give to me, including his head, to bargain against the Europeans. Agreed?"

There was something wrong in there, though I couldn't tell what exactly. I hit SEND and met Leo's gaze, hesitating. The MOC lifted a single eyebrow, managing to appear both patient and amused. "Can he survive without his heart?" I asked.

"Can anything survive without a heart?"

It wasn't an answer, but telling me *including his head* didn't mean that Joses' head had to still be attached. Leo wouldn't have said the words unless he meant them exactly the way he phrased them. Wiggle room. He was giving me wiggle room. Or there was something else afoot. This negotiation might give me a way to dance through all the possible dangers suggested by Sabina. I'd have to think about it.

I said, "The New Orleans Police Department will see you today. Tonight or this morning. At your convenience or not, they really don't care. And frankly, neither do I. I have about ten minutes before I have to gear up and get back to that scene"—I tilted my head at the TV screen, where Joses Bar-Judas was still killing humans, over and over—"that scene that stinks of the death of Joses' *demonstration*. I have to address the media—in your name or without it, it's up to you. And I have to promise the populace of this city that I'll find the monster who killed their people and bring their sense of safety back." I'd cut off the head of Bar-Judas and offer it up to the citizens of New Orleans on a silver platter if I could figure out how to do it without starting a war, but I didn't say it.

Leo looked away, his eyes moving up and to the left, the way some humans' eyes do when they're recalling something. "His heart to the keepers of the peace. Ironic." His eyebrows pulled down into a slight scowl that might have been remembered dread. "That is how it began the last time—rioting in the streets."

I wanted to ask him what *last time* he was talking about, but I didn't have time for a history lesson.

He said, "I have lost much of the power of my house this night. To kill the maker of us all would be to lose it all, everything and everyone. Yet I understand that I have no choice but to put a price upon the heart of the Son of Darkness." Leo looked a little lost, a little uncertain; then the smile widened and the calculation snapped back in his gaze. "I accept your temporary resignation as Enforcer. I will hire Jane Yellowrock, vampire hunter, to track the . . . Did you call him a monster? Yes, the monster, who killed the humans. To track him and to take his heart.

"Tell the witch-child policewoman she is welcome here during the night or the day. I am at her command. Should she decide to await the night for her interview, I will make myself available at New Orleans Police Department, at their central headquarters' location, for the duration of the dark, to provide what answers I may to the questions by any and all law enforcement officials. My attorney will attend me.

"No matter how the police may wish to handle the law enforcement portion of this hunt, I will hold a press conference at dusk, in the front drive, provided there is no rain, and in the ballroom should inclement weather dictate."

Leo stared at me. "As to the hunt for the monster, as I

told you, his modern name was not Joses son of Judas Iscariot." He pronounced it *Yo-sace, son of Ioudas Issachar*. "The name he used to enter this country was Joseph Santana. That is the name you will tender to the police and use in discourse with me and my people, and among your team, henceforward. Any other name will mean nothing to the officials and may place us in more imminent danger."

One good thing. It was a lot easier for my American mouth to pronounce.

He punched a button on his desk and Adelaide Mooney said, "Yes, sir."

"Come to my office, Primo. We have plans to make. And send for my Enforcer, Derek Lee, to join us."

"On my way, sir," she said.

The MOC placed both hands flat on his desk, leaning forward slightly, staring at me. "The lair apartment which Joseph Santana used on his royal visit here, from which he disappeared, over a century past, is still intact. I will see that Adelaide sends you the address. Perhaps you will detect something there that I missed, so long ago."

"I'm not sure how that will help me catch him now," I said. Leo lifted a brow, ever the elegant and refined killing machine. I decided on a new tack. "'So long ago.' You mean when you took him prisoner and told the rest of the vamps that he was simply missing?"

Leo smiled, and he suddenly looked far less human and far more like the lethal predator he was. When he spoke, he sounded the soft, deadly killer that he hid from the world. "*Oui, mon petit chat.* That is one version of the old tale. There are others. Once in his apartment, you may scent out the ones now helping him from the tangled scents of the day he was taken prisoner. You may find papers that might show where he has gone to ground. And somewhere here, I may have other such papers, if they were salvaged when my clan home burned, and if they were brought here."

That was a lot of *ifs*, so I wasn't holding my breath. When the clan home burned, Leo's scions and blood-servants were busy saving the valuable art and jewels. Obscure hundred-year-old paperwork might have been ignored.

Del entered and stood at the entrance. Leo didn't look away from me to her, but kept me in the harsh light of his dark gaze. Carefully, formally, as if the words had special meaning, he said, "Adelaide, you act now as official witness. Jane Yellowrock may speak and act in my name prior to dusk. At dusk, she will be dismissed as my Enforcer. If she missteps, and does harm to the one for whom she searches, it is upon her to accept retribution, not this clan, this city, or the Mithrans sworn to me."

Great. So that was why he'd wanted me released. But . . . that meant I could do what needed to be done to stay alive and keep others alive. It was a nice little dance step around the truth. I let a small smile escape.

Leo's pupils widened, his sclera bleeding slowly scarlet as he spoke. "From that moment onward, until such time as the mass murderer known as Joseph Santana is contained and his heart given to the human authorities, the services of Jane Yellowrock, in the capacity of Enforcer, will be no longer required. Her duties will be taken over in entirety by Derek Lee."

"I have so noted," Del said, her voice soft.

"As part of her search, she is to be allowed access to any part of the Council premises, including private apartments, is to be given any and all information, papers, and access to any human or Mithran she may wish to question. All will give her complete and full truth."

"I have so noted," Del said again, and I realized that this was a form of ceremony, hopefully one that didn't require a bloodletting to seal the deal.

Leo transferred his gaze to Del and said, "You may wish to bring in my former primo to assist with any papers search. He was here when my clan home burned and oversaw storing my art and other salvage from the house."

That former primo was my significant other. Boyfriend. Whatever. Bruiser. I fought the urge to grin like a fool at the thought of working with him.

To me, Leo said, "At dusk, you will be dismissed to fulfill your chores for the New Orleans Police Department, and to fulfill a new contract with the Master of the City of New Orleans. Any choices you make contrary to that contract will be upon your head."

I let my smile widen and knew it to be an ugly, menacing smile. "I can live with that." I let my expression add, *But I don't know if you can.*

"Before dusk, you will acquire your papers and writ

of . . . tracking. Yes. Tracking the monster, the murderer of humans."

"With permission to take his heart," I added.

"With that exact authorization and that exact wording." His smile had widened to the full-toothed grin of a hungry predator. His fangs clicked down. And I remembered two things. Only hours ago, Leo had lost it—again—and savaged Gee DiMercy's throat, and silver stakes were poor weapons against the MOC. I'd tried them once and he'd been healed. Holding me with his eyes, as if he could read my thoughts through my skin, Leo said, "Prepare the contract, my primo. Contact the mayor, and then the governor, that I may speak with them. Find the papers that came here from my clan home when it burned and give them to the vampire hunter. Go, Jane Yellowrock," he said to me, "or I will drink you down."

I went, backing slowly until the door hit me between the shoulder blades. I closed it silently behind me and let go the breath I'd been holding. "Holy crap on a cracker with toe jam," I whispered. I shuddered hard and moved away from the office at speed. I was halfway to the front door when I was able to slow my breathing and my heart rate. "Ducky. Just freaking dang ducky."

All those rocks and hard places started dancing in my brain: The rock as stated by Sabina. The rock of Leo wanting me to *capture* but not kill a murderer. And settling for me taking the murderer's heart. The hard place of what I'd promised to Jodi, that I'd place the needs of the humans in front of Leo, no matter what it cost me. The safety and danger of working outside the job of Enforcer—the freedoms and the strictures both. Working for the mayor and the governor *and* Leo. Media meetings. Wondering what the European Mithrans would do to Leo in the face of these calamities. Wondering what life might be left in a Son of Darkness once I took his heart. And what the EuroVamps would do to the heart taker.

CHAPTER 7

You Wet Your Pants?

I stopped back at the house, parking the sexy Harley in the side alley leading to the small courtyard in back, and pulling the iron gate shut. The iron-on-iron clang felt like safety, like home. I leaned into the gate and closed my eyes, letting the weight of the last few hours blow out with my breath, letting it drip like water through me and down, off my fingertips and out the bottoms of my feet, the tension draining away in rivers of relief. *Home . . .*

When I opened my eyes, I saw a flash of light across the street, something white moving at speed. It was too fast for me to identify, but I could rule out lots of natural and supernatural creatures. I guessed it was Brute, the white werewolf who had bitten Joses— No. *Joseph.* From now on, it was Joseph. Joseph Santana.

I left the helmet on the bike. I missed my Harley, Bitsa, way more than I had expected to.

Eli met me on the back porch. Gallery. Whatever. He was wearing his new vamp-hunting gear. And he looked totally *awe*some. Matte black leather with sheaths, holsters, loops, military combat-style boots, and a utility belt that was built for the Hulk. He also carried a gobag big enough to hide a fully automatic something-something and a dozen fully loaded extended clips. With his brown skin and his close-cropped Army Ranger–style buzz cut, Eli Younger looked like a centerfold from a *Guns & Ammo* magazine.

My partner had once told me he would never wear leather, but the defensive benefits of the newest witch-spelled / Dyneema-threaded / Kevlar-enhanced / silver-plated–titanium–chain mail augmentations had changed his mind. I stopped on the low steps and asked, "Has Sylvia seen you in the new gear?"

The grin Eli gave me said, *Yes, she has* and *We had fun taking it off.* Sylvia Turpin, sheriff of Adams County, Mississippi, was Eli's honeybun, and what they did in the sack was of no interest to me at all. "Never mind," I said, waving away any attempt at an answer and looking longingly at the rock garden as I entered the house. It would be a long time before I got to check in on my Beast. I massaged my arm through my clothing, and the skin felt charged, as if I were standing on carpet in the winter and static electricity had coated my flesh. Prickles of pain radiated out from my fingertips. "Come on in," I said to Eli. "We need to talk while I gear up."

I waved to the Kid, who was still sipping energy drinks. He had made a pyramid tier of them up along the side of the table he used as a desk, and he looked like he was wired to the max, his entire focus on the integrated screen and the smaller screens that surrounded him. "Info when you want it," he said to me, "but you gotta boogie. Press conference in twenty-seven minutes."

"Yeah. Thanks." I crossed the house to my room but left the door cracked so they could hear me. There wasn't time for worrying about high school–variety boy-girl awkwardness, but there was the need to maintain lines of propriety. Or my prudish nature. Or both.

Eli said, "I put your clothing and leather gear on your bed and the weapons gear on the kitchen table. You're missing a blade, a fourteen-inch vamp-killer."

I flipped on the light switch and saw the gear on my bed. "Yeah, I remember. It needs replacement, blade and hilt both. They were damaged beyond repair in the fight at HQ. The spell the vamp used on me burned it to slivers." I eased the shirt off and inspected my arm in the overhead light.

The thick scar tissue was an odd, pale red tracery, as if someone had drawn lines and whorls on my golden Cherokee skin and filled the spaces between with pink marker. I hadn't noticed the redness in the heat of the shower earlier. *Weird.*

"I'll add a new vamp-killer to the list," Alex said. "You do know those things are expensive, right?"

I touched one of the red lines and felt a faint shock quiver through my skin. "I've noticed," I answered wryly. "Leo gets the bill for that one, though. Send an invoice to Raisin, and make sure you get an acknowledgment. As of dusk, I'm no longer the Enforcer and things will change."

"Say what?" Eli said.

I felt their interest practically zing through the crack in the door. They moved closer to hear better, shuffling on the wood floor while I pulled on my best leathers, debriefing them on everything Leo had told me and everything I had deduced about Joses/Joseph. I finished with, "So if Jodi comes through on a contract with the governor and/or the mayor, I'll have the unenviable job of removing the heart from Joseph Santana and taking it to Jodi Richoux."

"We'll," Eli said.

"We'll what?" I asked, hooking the reinforced leather jacket over my silk knit T. Oddly, my arm felt better with the jacket over it, the slight pressure of the thick materials giving me ease. I really needed the healing T-shirt given to me by some witch friends, but no way was I appearing on TV in a fuzzy purple T with a red dragon on the front.

"*We'll* have the unenviable job," he said.

"Musketeer crap," the Kid said.

I smiled and opened the door, my fingers busy rebraiding my hip-length hair, my injured right fingers not working properly, making my movements awkward. "All for one?"

The guys didn't answer, but I guess they didn't have to. In the kitchen, I strapped on the tactical thigh rig and adjusted its holsters for weapons at thigh and shoulder, and this time, for maximum effect, I strung the M4's harness on too. I accepted the weapons as Eli handed them to me, checking the loads on the semiautomatic handguns, making sure there were no rounds in the chambers as they went into holsters. Then I slid the blades and the stakes into the specially made sheaths in the thigh rig and in the leathers.

And the boots. And my braided hair that I had wrapped into a big bun.

"How about this one?" Eli asked. He was holding a gift from Bruiser, an antique Mughal Empire blade Bruiser had given me when he declared his intentions to take our relationship to the next level.

"A little too fancy?" I asked.

"Good PR for the media should someone notice it and ask," Eli said, which could have been unusual thinking for the shooter, except that he'd been teasing me off and on about dating Bruiser.

"The MOC's hot-chick Enforcer has a *boooy*friend," Alex said.

Eli chuckled, the sound evil. They knew I'd turned down multiple requests from the media—local and regional—for interviews about my relationship with the vamps and their humans. But this time, I might need the media to help keep the public hysteria down. I remembered the scent-feeling-taste of riot-worthy fear hanging in the air outside the kill bar.

"Fine. Give it here." I ignored their surprise as I figured out how to strap it through the stake loops, but high, near my hip and groin. The silk velvet sheath looked like rubies against my black leathers. "Okay. Eli, you're right." I held in a sigh, knowing if I let it free, I'd sound like I was whining. "We need to make an *appearance*." I made little bunny-ear quotation marks in the air. "I suggest I ride in on Herbert's Harley and you follow in the SUV."

"Helmet off," he said, "silver stakes in your hair."

Louisiana had no motorcycle helmet law, so that was feasible, but it suddenly struck me as funny that Eli was thinking about media impact. "You going into the personal image business, Eli? PR with a gun? Big bad Army Ranger in makeup and eyeliner?"

He scowled—twitch of lips, harder eyes. "Wasteful and inefficient."

"I'll take that as a no." I adjusted the silver stakes in my hair so they formed a crown out around my head. "Okay, Kid. Text Jodi. Tell her we're on the way. Make sure we can get through from the park. And remind her that she wanted regalia," I added sourly. "I don't want a video of a cop patting me down on the morning news. When we're done with the media dog and pony show we need a plan of attack. I want Joseph Santana's heart in my hands."

Most of the streets in the area were one-way streets, and despite the early hour, the crowd and the media had made them all impassable. But by the time we got close, the cops had opened a narrow corridor starting at Washington Square Park. I pulled in front of the SUV, slowing, letting the media and the crowd get an eyeful and an earful. The Harley announced us with that signature rumble, the pistons firing at uneven intervals due to the V arrangement of the cylinders, that specific Harley engine design that made me miss my bike more than ever.

Over the engine roar, I heard a lot of chatter about me, half-flattering, half-unflattering, and a lot of it salacious, but at least no one took a potshot at me. Or if they did, they missed.

The cops had commandeered an empty lot at Burgundy and Elysian Fields Avenue, and Eli and I pulled in, parked, and made our way to the makeshift stage only a few minutes before six a.m. Jodi met us there. She had freshened her makeup and combed her hair, but she looked tired, the kind of tired that came with a life of stress, bad food, scorched coffee, and impossible hours. She gave me a modified nod and indicated that I was to join her at a tent near the stage, which was a flatbed trailer with temporary stairs at the back.

Behind her, in the shadows of an evidence van, stood Sloan Rosen. He was watching me with amused eyes, knowing my outfit and general badass getup were for the press, and probably critiquing my entire ensemble. I'd known Sloan almost as long as I'd known Jodi. Like her, he worked with the woo-woo squad as part of NOPD's SCD—Special Crime Division. African American, inked with gang tats and prison tats from his time undercover, Sloan had had a hard time finding a comfortable place at cop central, a safe place, considering the price the Crips had put on his head. He was married and had kids, and so he needed the job and the benefits and the retirement package that preceded Hurricane Katrina and the city's financial woes.

He nodded to the side and lifted a finger. I gave him a half nod and turned the bike over to Herbert, who pushed it into the shadows as I met Jodi at the tent. Thunder rumbled from far away, the low, rolling resonance that was as much echo as the sound of distant lightning.

Jodi ran her eyes from the toes of my Lucchese boots to the top of my silver stakes and laughed. It wasn't a mean laugh, so I grinned back. "No one knows who our suspect is," she said. "Facial recog has turned up zip so far. Tell me something I don't know."

"Like most older vamps, he's gone through names. According to the chief fanghead, the one he entered this country under was Joseph Santana. Leo is calling the governor and the mayor to approve my appointment and contract as chief rogue-vampire hunter. At dusk I will be fired as Enforcer and given a contract by Leo to hunt Santana, which will provide him some protection against Santana's pals when I cut out his heart. How about your end?"

"Not bad," she said. "The governor's contract is being faxed to your office now, the fee to be paid by a local man whose son is inside the bar, on the floor, the result of a hungry fanghead; one of the drained ones." Her face fell, showing for a moment the despair of dealing with the grief and anger of the populace, while at the same time having to be professional, cool, calm, and able to protect and serve.

Carefully, so as not to rock the precarious emotional balance she was preserving, I said, "Just to clarify, Yellowrock Securities doesn't take orders from the donor, or any state or federal law enforcement agency. I'll be working under contract to the Mithran Council, but under the direct command of the governor." Jodi's lips tightened as if she was about to disagree and I rushed ahead. "But I will keep you, personally, in the loop. We provide each other intel and backup as needed. Agreed?"

Some of her strain eased. "You're not going to make me pinkie swear in front of the press, are you?" she asked.

"No. You're not gonna make me talk, are you?"

"Yes." She grabbed my right arm and pulled me toward the stairs. "Come on. It's time." I managed not to hiss in pain and, with my good fingers, peeled her grip free as we walked. Jodi didn't notice my discomfort. But . . . *I'm gonna have to talk?* My heart rate sped.

In a mild state of panic, I climbed the creaky stairs to stand to the side, behind Jodi and the new mayor, with Eli next to me. A suited man stood on the other side of the mayor, his demeanor practically shouting FBI or PsyLED, his expression suggesting that he was too good to rub shoulders with the locals. He didn't even glance at Eli and me, and I felt my partner evaluating him. "Civilian," Eli muttered, just loud enough for the guy to hear. The cop turned, finally deigning to look us over, taking in the weapons we carried. "Piss his pants if he met a fanghead in a dark alley," Eli finished, louder.

I managed not to laugh, but it was a near thing. The suited cop flushed darkly.

"You are evil," I whispered to Eli.

"You just figuring that out, babe?"

"Ladies and gentlemen, citizens of New Orleans," the mayor started. I listened with only half an ear, more interested in the smells and sights of the crowd, and their mob-related body language, than what the mayor was saying. Yada yada, blah blah blah, a stream of political inanities, a lot of "keeping you safe," more yada yada and blah blah.

Then the suited guy stepped up and promised that the state police and state government would be backing up the locals in any way they needed, the moment they were asked to participate. A newsy type shouted, "Why aren't you helping now?"

The cop turned, looked directly at me, and said, "The city of New Orleans has decided it would rather put their trust in armed *bounty hunters*"—which made it sound as if we were so much dog poop on the sidewalk—"than in the resources of Troop B of the Office of State Police."

"Jane Yellowrock?" a man with a camera yelled back. "What good is the lover of the Master of the City in a hunt for fangheads?" The crowd rumbled agreement and the state cop smiled at me, smoothed his lapels, and stepped aside.

Great. Just freaking ducky. I broke out in a hot sweat and, after a space of uncomfortable seconds, during which the crowd got louder and uglier, I figured out how to lift a foot and push it forward, walking slowly to the podium. Jodi shot me a glance of hidden amusement, and I realized that she had heard us baiting the cop. *My partner and his big mouth.*

I was taller than the suited cop, and I reached forward,

adjusting the main mic higher so I wouldn't have to bend over. Only as I worked with the mic did I sense that my height and the need to adjust the world to my size were playing a part in calming the crowd. Predators in the wild knew that size was no indicator of dominance or strength. I was bigger than Leo Pellissier and Joseph Santana, and they were way bigger predators than I was. But the humans quieted as I worked, waiting.

When I figured I had their attention, I cleared my throat and said, softly, into the mic, "I'm Jane Yellowrock. I came to this city to track and kill the vampire who took down an entire unit of cops where they stood. You've seen it on YouTube, uploaded by someone in the Pellissier household, the way I took that killer down. The look of his teeth—not a regular vampire at all."

"Sabertooth vampire," someone from the middle of the crowd yelled.

"That mutant, insane vampire, whatever he was, was not a Mithran. You've heard them call themselves that, right? Mithrans?" I caught some nods and felt the cameras on me. Sweat trickled beneath my leathers, tickling. My mouth went dry. "That thing I killed was something other, something unknown.

"And in Natchez, where I was sent by Leo Pellissier, I was able to bring down what the Mithrans call Naturaleza vampires, the ones that treat humans like cattle, like possessions. The vampires here in New Orleans treat humans like ..." I almost said *equals*, then almost said *friends*, and ended up with: "valued employees, with contracts, rights, and importance. It's my job to take the Naturaleza kind of vampire out. The kind that kill humans. The crazy ones. Even the very rare, powerful ones, like the ones capable of holding armed and trained cops, families, and innocents immobile and seemingly ..." Words failed me, and I floundered until I came up with: "tranquil, under the power of compulsion, the power of their minds, and drink them down at leisure. The police, especially state-level bureaucrats, don't have the training, equipment, or expertise to accomplish the kinds of hunts that Yellowrock Securities has always done so well."

"Hooah," Eli murmured softly, using the syllables left over from his army days that meant lots of different things, all of them good. I had no idea what I'd said that made him so happy, but it didn't really matter.

I stared out over the crowd, feeling the sunrise. My injured arm was aching. I wished I had some water. My mind was blank. *Oh. Crap. Where was I?*

As if sensing my budding panic and reading my empty mind, Eli opened a bottle of water and placed it in my hand. I drank and handed it back.

"Thanks. Sorry. I'm not used to public speaking. Anyway. Um. Right. Killing insane vamps, even powerful ones, is what I do. It's what Yellowrock Securities does. As of this morning I have informed the Master of the City, Leo Pellissier, that come dusk I will no longer be under his employment. At dusk, I will accept a writ from the Mithran Council . . ." I paused and made sure to frame my words to the contract that Leo was offering. ". . . to track the killer and bring him down. At that time I will also accept a similar contract from the mayor and the governor. I need a contract from each, to cover any territories I might need to enter in the course of this hunt."

"So what'll you be doing until night?" a reporter shouted.

"Why do you need three contracts?" another shouted.

"Yeah," a slurred voice agreed from the edge of the crowd. "Sittin' on your ass all day?"

"Was it a young rogue, escaped from the MOC's lair?" another reporter shouted, others on the edge of her words.

"Pellissier let one go?"

"Yeah! None of us are safe, not with fangheads in this town!"

I raised my voice and leaned into the mic. "Until dusk, my partners and I will be using the resources of the police department and the Master of the City's libraries to research the Mithran database for any intelligence we can find about the rogue vamp. For now, I *will* tell you that it was not a *young* rogue vampire. And we already have a name, courtesy of the Master of the City."

I smelled Jodi's and the state cop's shock and paid it no heed. The crowd shouted, words and questions overlapping, anger and curiosity like a toxic haze on the already scent-laden air. I softened my voice and the crowd quieted to hear, as I said, "Just prior to this news conference, I shared the name that the rogue vampire last used with NOPD. Yellowrock Securities will work directly with Jodi Richoux, under contract with the Mithrans, and under direct orders of the governor of the great state of Louisiana, to find and dispatch this rogue-Naturaleza vampire, who is a danger even to the Mithrans in this city."

"Wait! You're telling us that the killer will kill vampires too?" a woman in front shouted.

"Yeah." I remembered the sub-five basement at vamp HQ. My voice dropped even more, to a bare murmur that made them quieten and shush one another. "He already has, striking at the Council Chambers, killing Mithrans before he killed here, among the city's humans. He got away, leaving bodies behind. Leo Pellissier wants him stopped too."

"That's a bunch of bunkum," a reporter shouted into his own open mic. A gold cross caught the light on his work shirt. "All vampires are killers! They need to be staked!"

"Judge not lest you be judged," I paraphrased mildly, before his anger could spread into the crowd again, turning the gathering into a mob. " 'Vengeance is mine; I will repay, saith the Lord.' 'This is my commandment, that ye love one another, as I have loved you.' You wear a cross. Be careful which scriptures you pick and choose from to give you a reason to hate. My understanding is that the Almighty gets kinda riled at hate of any kind."

The world whirled around me and I stepped back from the mic, ignoring questions shouted from the reporters and the human observers. Taking the water bottle from Eli, I drained it. "Got another?" I asked him. He pulled a second bottle from his gobag. "Mr. Prepared."

"Always. Nice speech. You pee in your pants?"

I spluttered with laughter and the tension that had clamped down on my body eased, the world only wobbly now, not spinning. "No. Thankfully."

"Good. Let's get outta here before things turn ugly." I followed him to the SUV and climbed in, rolling up the windows. They were tinted for vamps, so no one could see in. I ripped off the weapons and the sweaty jacket and threw them into the backseat, massaging my arm. Eli concentrated on getting us out of the mob.

*   *   *

As we rode through the sunrise, a pinking of the gray clouds, Eli asked, "So. About your career in politics."

"Shut up or I'll hurt you," I said, knowing I sounded pouty, rather than like any kind of a threat.

He slanted a look my way. "You did good."

I looked out the window, surprised and embarrassed by the kindness and pride in his tone and not knowing what to say. I wasn't sure anyone had ever been proud of me before. It felt weird.

As if he knew that, Eli changed the subject. "How do we track the Son of Darkness? How do we kill the Big Bad Pure Ancient Evil that made the suckheads? Because, while I'm going to enjoy that immensely, it sounds . . . difficult," he said, the pause suggesting that he had come up with and discarded other terms, like *unmanageable*, *unachievable*, even *impossible*.

"I don't know," I said. "I don't know if killing him will make things worse, like Leo said, or better, like my gut tells me. Our contract with Leo says we can take his heart, but I don't know if that will kill him or not."

"You mean we could cut out his heart and he might not die?"

I shrugged in answer.

"That would ruin a perfectly good day."

I smiled, my fingers working the skin of my injured arm, pressing deep into the muscles.

The silence in the SUV cab grew deeper as the sky brightened and Eli processed my statements. I rubbed my arm harder, wishing for the dragon T-shirt. The world spun and halted, spun and halted, a sickening motion that made me want to toss my cookies. Or toss the water I'd just drunk.

"I got an idea," Eli said, his voice far too casual, the inflection off somehow. "What about using the blood diamond to track him? All we'd need are some witches we trust."

I flinched. The blood diamond was a black-magic, blood-magic artifact that had been empowered by the sacrifice of hundreds of witch children. And I just happened to have possession of it. My arm ached more and I pulled up my sleeve to discover that the lines traced on it were darker, or brighter. Redder anyway. I hid them beneath the silk T-shirt sleeve.

Someone I trusted once accused that I'd find a reason to use the blood diamond. That I'd justify using the blood-magic power to do good, and that using blood-magic power for any reason was a long road to hell. I said, "So, no."

"No, what?" I forced my eyes open and looked at Eli. And realized he hadn't spoken, he hadn't suggested the blood diamond. Eli's eyes were on the road, hands at two and ten. The SUV was stuck behind a cement truck, trying to navigate the narrow, one-way streets. Eli hadn't spoken at all. I had been dreaming. Hallucinating. A chill started between my shoulder blades as a single huge raindrop landed on the windshield, a splatted star reaching out from the puddled center. With no more warning, rain pelted from the cloudy sky and grayed the city around us into a misty, watery film, a return to the darkness of predawn. Eli slowed and turned on the windshield wipers, his motions efficient and smooth as always. Around us, the typical New Orleans deluge isolated the interior of the car from the rest of the world, making it familiar and cozy, despite the rising humidity brought by the storm. *Crap on crackers*. Eli hadn't spoken. "Nothing," I said.

I didn't think I should close my eyes again. Not just now. I studied my hand in the dim light of the rainstorm. It looked like I'd been beaten by two-by-fours. Bruised and broken looking.

My cell buzzed and I pulled it to see that I had a file from the Kid. I opened it and read his latest bit of research. Raising my voice to be heard above the water pounding on the vehicle, I said, "We need to talk about witches we can trust. Sabina said to get the Truebloods to introduce us to the witch coven leader here, but I'm not planning on taking that route if I can help it." Molly had problems that she needed to deal with, without helping me again. I'd been hard on our friendship—for a good cause, to save lives, but still. If I could avoid using Molly, I would.

"Good. Molly has family. Kids."

I nodded. He understood. I blinked, yawned, and forced myself to concentrate on the file open on my cell. "I took a minute, earlier tonight, to get Alex to look her up, and Lachish Dutillet is the leader of the New Orleans coven, a person of color of Creole descent." I skimmed the file. "And crap. Her daughter disappeared under the rule of the Damours, so she has no reason to talk to me or to help the fangheads."

"So we'll just hop on over there and change her mind?"

I didn't know if he was serious or not, but it didn't matter. "I have no idea how to convince her to help us," I admitted as I examined her photo. She was maybe mid-fifties, salt-and-pepper hair, Creole skin and eyes. Pretty. A bit stout. I showed the poor-quality photo that Alex had captured from somewhere online to Eli. "She has to hate vamps."

"You could tell her you killed the vamps who were killing the witches."

"Eh," I grunted. I didn't think that would help. But Jodi might, with her familial witch connections. If I hadn't run away from the press conference like a cat with her tail on fire, I could have asked her in person. I texted Jodi, *Intro to NOLA coven leader? Today?*

Instantly I got back from her, *Yes. Have made calls. Lachish willing. Things in works now.*

"Well. How about that," I said. "Jodi already contacted her." Eli grunted in acknowledgment. I flipped back through my info on the coven leader and said, "*Lachish* means 'she who walks, or exists, of herself.' It's biblical." Eli said nothing. "Names are important. They mean things. For instance, *Younger* could mean your ancestor was a younger son. *Eli* means 'uplifted' or 'ascended.' "

Eli snorted. "I do belong on a pedestal sometimes." Before I could roll my eyes he went on, "And what does *Jane Yellowrock* mean?"

" 'Gift from God, gold.' But my Cherokee name, Dalonige'i Digadoli, means 'yellow-eyes, yellow-rock.' *Yellow-eyes* because I'm a skinwalker and, hey, the eyes." I pointed at my face. "*Yellowrock* for the gold the white man found in the Appalachians that eventually caused the Trail of Tears, so the *yunega*—white man—could take our land."

"So your name is both a gift and a curse."

And that was something I had never thought of before.

CHAPTER 8

Eye of Newt

It took forever to get home, with the rush-hour traffic and the rain affecting visibility. I closed the files, too tired to concentrate, and lay my head against the headrest while I massaged my injured arm. If I'd had my bike, I would have been soaked to the skin but home a lot faster. I had forgotten how much easier/faster/better it was to navigate city streets on a bike. I missed Bitsa. I had left a voice mail for Jacob, the Harley Zen-priest master motorcycle mechanic in Charlotte, North Carolina, who was trying to put her back together again, but he hadn't returned my call. Jacob lived along the Catawba River and had originally built Bitsa from the rusted remains of two Harley panheads I had found in junkyard-graveyards. I knew Bitsa was in bad shape, but it was taking an awfully long time to get her back. And . . . he should have called. He just should have. I felt a tear trickle down my cheek, heated and burning. I missed Bitsa. Which was *not* stupid. It *wasn't*. Fortunately, Eli didn't notice in the dull lights.

We finally got to the house and Eli parked on the street, the rain still tapping down in a light shower. Oddly, I was sorry the ride was over. It had been nice. Stress-free. Vamp-free. Eli opened my door for me and stood there, in the pattering rain, waiting. I watched him. He looked kinda odd, and I asked, "What's wrong, Eli?"

"I dunno. You've been rubbing your arm for the last few hours." He leaned into the SUV. "You have tearstains on your face. You've been . . . *crying*?"

He said that like I never cried. I cried. I cried anytime I needed to. I pulled up my sleeve and extended my arm. "I think I'm hurt."

Eli paled. I made a face, swung my legs over from the floorboard to the street, and started to stand. My knees buckled. Eli caught me, sliding his arms under my legs and around my back, lifting me from the SUV. The jolt drew out a gasp, and I cradled my hurt arm across my chest. Eli kicked the door shut with a foot. "Let's get you inside and check you out. I have a feeling you need to change into your mountain lion form. Fast." I didn't reply, and Eli carried me into the house.

At his desk, Alex was rolling back and forth in his new desk chair, with the energy drink cans in a different formation at his feet. "You two get married?" he quipped.

"No. Something's wrong with Janie. She needs to shape-change, and I don't know how to get it done."

"Ummm. You think I do, bro?"

"Yeah, bro, you nosy bastard, I think you do."

"That's a bad word," I said, massaging my arm through my sleeve. I held up my hand. "Look. I'm turning colors." My hand and arm were traced with red, like vines growing under my skin, and blooms of purple bruises flowered between the vines. It was pretty.

"Never mind," Eli said. "She's worse than I thought. Get in the SUV. We're taking her to that Cherokee shaman she goes to. Move!"

I was suddenly tired. So tired. I lay my head against Eli's shoulder, and then down on the backseat of the SUV. After that I was being jostled by the movement of the seat beneath me, jerked around, pulled this way and that. At some point I began to moan as darkness spread beneath my skin. "Hurts," I murmured. "Hurts bad."

"I know. We're getting you to help. Hang on."

I felt someone remove the rest of my weapons and harnesses. My boots. And then I was being carried again. And undressed, but it was okay because Aggie One Feather was doing that, not the Youngers. And then, dressed in something white that itched on my skin, I was carried outside again and into a dark, heated, smoky-smelling place.

I heard drums, soft and slow. I smelled stuff burning, green things, dried things. Coarse and acrid and cleansing, stronger than the wood of my soul home fire. Rosemary, juniper, mugwort, something lemony, something coarse, like camphor, and wormwood. White sage. I breathed the herbed smoke in, and Molly's voice came to me from some long-ago visit in her herb garden behind her house. *"Artemisia absinthium, Artemisia ludoviciana—white sage species. Nicotiana tabacum—wild tobacco. Each has a different scent and a different medicinal usage. Some are used in shamanism . . ."*

"Aggie's a shaman," I said. But it came out all mumbled.

"Drink this, Jane Yellowrock. Drink, Dalonige'i Digadoli."

"Holy crap." I spat and struggled against the taste, pulling away from the hands that held me. "That tastes like something you killed and let rot."

"Not far from the truth," Aggie said. "Now, drink, or I'll hold your nose and force it down your throat."

I sat up and managed to open my eyes, holding her away from me with the hand that ached and thrummed with pain. A hand that felt both cold and feverish. "Last time someone tried to dose me against my will, I called her a bitch. I think I was fourteen."

"And did she hold you down and force it into you?"

"Yes. Not fair."

"Look at your hands, Jane."

I looked. The fingers of my right hand were traced with red lines and massive purple bruises. The coldness and improbable heat I had sensed in it was aching and heavy, a cold that burned. My left hand was similarly damaged, but not quite so far along—just red lines so far. I looked at my feet and saw the red lines traced there too. "All over?"

"Yes. Now, drink. I may be able to help you. If not, Eli will take you to the hospital."

"*Yunega* medicine won't help me, *lisi*. They'll put me in a cage to study."

"Yes. That is a possibility."

"This sucks."

"Yes."

Feeling wobbly, as if I'd fall over at the slightest brush of wind, I scrutinized Aggie, who sat next to me in the sweathouse, the firelight warming her coppery skin. She had a few more strands of silver in her black hair now than when I'd first met her, but her black eyes were bright and sharp and full of mischief. "Your hair's getting long," I said.

"You're dithering."

She was right. I held out my good left hand for the fired clay bowl Aggie One Feather held. She passed it to me and I cupped it to my mouth. Drank. It was like drinking something that had died last fall. Like mold and feathers and moss and clay and horrible, unnameable, vile . . . stuff.

"Drink," Aggie demanded when I tried to lift the bowl from my lips.

I gagged twice, but I got it down. Immediately the world swirled around me, drunkenly, and the light in the dim room brightened, sharp and fierce and painful to my eyes. "Holy crapoly. What's in that? Eye of newt?"

"Sleep," Aggie said, taking my injured hand in both of hers.

Pain sparked through me like a brushfire, and I pulled away. My mouth went dry and the sweathouse spun again. "Cold. Hurts," I said. Sickness spiraled up my throat in an acidic surge. "Need my Beast. Need . . ." *Beast?* I called.

Deep in my mind I heard panting, the pained gasp of my other self. *Foolish kit. We are hurt.*

"Aggie?"

"Listen," Aggie whispered. "Listen to the drums. Let them show you the way to healing."

The drums were slow, a *beat*-beat-beat-beat, *beat*-beat-beat-beat. Slower than my heartbeat. Slower than the soft dripping of water in my cave soul home. Slower than the panting of my Beast. *Beat* . . . beat . . . beat . . . beat . . .

"Oh . . . crap," I murmured again on a soft sigh. Or I thought I murmured. Blackness and the smell of smoke overtook me.

Beast's panting melded with my breathing. Her heartbeat synced with mine. And to the drum beating. The cold that had been wrapping around me eased. My fingers curled into her pelt, gripping the loose flesh beneath. Pulling it around me, rough and coarse and smooth and warm. So warm. I sighed, my breath brushing the longer hairs at my/ our jaw, tickling. *Warm.*

Beat . . . beat . . . beat . . . beat, *beat* . . . beat . . . beat . . . beat. Slower. *Beat* . . . beat . . . beat . . . beat. *Beat* . . . beat . . . beat . . . beat.

And silence.

I/we opened our eyes. Our soul home was dark, silent. Not even the plink of distant water disturbed the depth of the stillness. We were lying before a fire; coals of red cedar glowed red beneath the ashes of herbs, their harsh stink still hanging in the air. Our belly was on the cool stone floor, muzzle resting on front paws, long, thick tail wrapped around and against us for warmth. We spread our fingers/toes and stretched, extending our claws and pressing them into the stone, kneading with a press, scritch, withdraw / press, scritch, withdraw rhythm. In the distance, the single boom of a drum sounded, the vibration filling the soul home, reverberating around and around and bouncing from the stalactites and stalagmites, a tone deep and sonorous, as if the cave itself were purring. After long minutes, the sound faded. We breathed the scented smoke. We listened to the silence. *We are one, of one mind and one body, but still Beast and Jane,* we thought. The drumbeat came again, with the building pressure and deep release, the reverberation lasting long, long, long, into silence.

"Jane?" The voice came from far away, the words slow and deep. "Look up. See your soul home. See the walls and the roof of the place of your safety. See what is there."

We tilted our head, trying to place the slow, deep voice that sounded like no one we knew. Her scent told us the voice was Aggie One Feather, her words calling us to a healing ceremony. Jane/Beast had been injured. Hurt by black magic. Aggie was our healer/shaman/teacher.

Jane/Beast blinked into dim light of old, red, fire coals. Seeing above us in the dome of the roof, red lines, like blood vessels, pulsing with silver and black and red motes of power and full of sick blood. Magic that hurt us was black magic. Blood magic. Like the magic of witches turned to darkness. Like blood magic stored in a stone. The blood diamond had such magic, magic that sent out red pulses and motes of power. But Jane/Beast had the blood diamond in a safe place, kept where we could not get to it easily and use it. In a place where temptation was not.

I/we yawned, killing teeth sharp and white. We thought of the spell, the *wyrd*, that had attacked us in the hallway. The *wyrd* that Joses—*Joseph*, yes, *Joseph*—had used against us. Remembered his body when he crawled up the elevator shaft. Was many floors. Even Beast could not leap so high, could not crawl so high on metal walls.

Jane remembered.

Joseph's black eyes settled on me and his mouth opened, slowly, so slowly, to reveal a maw full of cracked and broken teeth, brown with age, and fangs like tusks in his upper and lower jaws. Even in the time bubble, Joses Bar-Judas had been able to see me, see us. Power rippled across him, sparking white and black, colder than an arctic snow, hotter than volcanic ash falling from a flaming sky. The power didn't so much dance across his skin as sizzle. So unbelievably powerful.

In the bubble that let me/us stand outside of time, we saw him alter course, shifting trajectory fractionally, heading right for us. Eli was squeezing the trigger of the subgun. From inside the bubble I could see the silver-lead rounds leaving the muzzle of the weapon, spiraling and twisting, half an inch at a time, a puff of dust and air exploding out with each round.

Joses, a Son of Darkness, ducked to miss the rounds. So fast.

Around his neck was a gold chain, like a necklace, with red things dangling from it like rubies . . . but brighter. Rectangular. Plastic? Had I seen that at the time? I couldn't remember, but I must have noticed it with some part of my mind.

I unsheathed a vamp-killer. Leaped forward, taking the time bubble with me, ducking beneath the rounds and the hot brass discharging from Eli's gun. My right arm extended in front of me, blade point forward. Pushing off with my toes, I stretched into the lunge.

Joses opened his fingers, exposing his hand. On his wrist there was a flash of . . . gold. He wore a bracelet, half-hidden by the tatters of clothing, or maybe tatters of half-mummified flesh. The bracelet was made of hammered gold in the shape of overlapping, interlocking leaves, with a bizarre setting of gold claws and horns. Vaguely familiar looking. Clasped in the setting was a mineral crystal, clear and brilliant, in the unpolished, uncut shape that nature had created. Quartz? Diamond?

The crystal spit clear motes of power, like lightning bugs on meth, darting too fast to see, even in the slowed bubble of time. Beside the clear crystal were empty horns and claws, a hole, a setting where a similar stone had been ripped away.

Oh no . . . Noooo, we thought, *pulling away from the memory.*

Lying in the darkness of the soul home, we put things, myriad disconnected things, together. And we understood. *Noooo,* the Jane part of us thought.

The Beast part of us thought, *On the wrist of great predator was magic. Predator used magic, blood magic, to escape trap and prison and cage.*

He went to the dark side, the Jane part of us thought, pulling more into herself, *like Darth Vader.* We snorted with vicious laughter. Laughter that yanked us apart with a snapping pain, to think fully as two instead of one.

Do not understand. Blood is good, Beast thought. *Blood is life. Blood is strength. Blood gives us strong mates and strong kits and fulfills hunger. Without blood, there is weakness. Do not understand that this is bad.*

Jane thought, *When the male puma concolor killed your kits, stole their blood and their life, what did we do?*

We tracked, nose to ground like pack wolf. Found male big-cat. Killed him. Beast growled lowly, the sound echoing through soul home. *Remembered taste of his blood and licked jaw. Snarled. Was good blood.*

The blood magic in the blood diamond was stolen from witch kits, Jane thought. *It is what fills the blood diamond with power. The bracelet that the vamp carried was also filled with blood magic, but . . . not of children. Of something else.*

Of vampires, Beast thought. *Tasted blood of vampires in magic that hurt us.* Stretched claws into stone of soul home floor. Scritching, sharpening killing claws.

We looked up into the roof, to strange lines that moved, thinking together and separate, thinking as Jane and Beast joined, one but two, concurrent. Lines on the roof of the soul home moved.

Pulsing lines of veins and arteries, Jane thought, *but look-*

ing clogged and bruised. Leaking? Like ... being under attack from vampire blood. But Joseph didn't bite me. And vampire blood can't survive outside of vamps. Except ... the priestess hinted that the blood of the Son of Darkness might last if it was in a relic of some sort, maybe mixed with magic.

This magic is vampire blood magic, Beast insisted. *The taste was something old, from the beginning of their kind.*

The blood of vampires powered the wyrd *that was used against us,* Jane thought, *a spell of fire and light, and ... fire and light kill vampires.*

Just as our killing teeth killed puma concolor who killed our kits.

The bracelet or necklace, Jane thought. *Or both. Oh crap. What if they were weapons of magic? Leo asked us to find what he called* "les objets de puissance, les objets de magie."

And Joseph Santana had one or maybe two when he got away, which means that Adrianna had them. She brought them to the sub-five prison to free her master or lover or whatever he was to her before he staked her through the brain. She died for her actions.

We merged closer in agreement and understanding. Together we focused Beast-vision and looked to the side of the fire that was set in the circle of stones. Saw the pile of twigs and branches, broken and dry, ends jagged and sharp. We stood to paws and stretched. Pulled muscles from toes/fingers, across paws, up legs and through shoulders. Bent and stretched, sending claws out to scrape on cave floor, forcing muscles of belly to pull and stretch. Stretch yielded and pulled into hips and spine and down lower legs. Chuffed. Cat stretch of whole body, restored after rest.

But not restored, Jane thought. *We still need healing.*

Looked at right paw. Was sick. Hairless and bruised. Licked it. Taste was of sickness, like rotten meat, crawling with maggots. This was not a thing that Beast could fix alone. Only Jane and Beast together could fix. Padded to pile of twigs and branches. Pile was much larger now. Many more branches. Grabbed branch in killing teeth, backed away, pulling, yanking, jerking, in manner of big-cats pulling fresh deer into brush to eat. Mouth flooded with saliva. Dropped branch. *Want deer. Want to hunt.*

Jane laughed. *Soon, Beast. First we have to kill the pred-*

ator that hurt Jane/Beast and killed so many humans. We have to heal from vampire blood magic.

Looked up into roof again. Drew in air over tongue and past roof of mouth, past scent sacs, with *scree* of sound. Thought, *Taste/smell of vampire blood. Vampire blood marks walls and roof of soul home, like male big-cat marks territory to find female to mate.*

Right.

Bent and put teeth to wood again. Pulled-yanked wood-plant-tasting branch to fire. Over fire, scattering coals. Lifted twigs in mouth and tossed dry, barbed things to coals, same way as tossing tiny kit to safety in back of cave. More. More. More wood. *Tasteless. Without blood. To make fire hot and high. To cleanse vampire blood from soul home.*

Flames brightened. Light and fire made *whooshing* sound. Grew high and hot and fast. Crackling fire, remembered from *time of hunger* when *yunega* cut down trees in mountains, all trees, leaving the earth bare and broken and ruined, dry limbs in piles, tossed away. Wasted. And then lightning came and fire burned everything that was left. Then rain fell and flood came and earth wept and died and washed away. Yunega *was evil,* Beast thought. *Killing earth.*

That was in the early nineteen hundreds, Jane thought. *Part of me remembers that. And yeah. They were evil. A lot of them still are.*

I/we padded, pawpawpaw, along narrow pathway between rock walls, away from fire to opening in wall, to ledge in back of cave. Leaped onto ledge. Lay in safe place, muzzle on paws, belly to cool stone. Closed eyes. Behind us, fire crackled and stank of red cedar, dry from autumn heat and winter snow and summer sun. Smoke filled soul home but did not choke or smother, like fire that burned the earth.

Yawned hard. Licked jaw. Groomed killing claws and paws. Went to sleep.

When I woke, I was lying on the ground in the sweathouse, curled in a fetal position, my head cradled on my arms. My body stank of sweat and essential oils and the residue of smoke. My mouth felt like a troop of monkeys had partied in it.

I ached all over as though I'd been beaten, but I uncurled and pushed myself up to my butt, sitting spraddle-legged as the last of the dizziness from the medicinal drink eased away. "Hey," I said.

Aggie sat across from me, her arms around her bent knees, her chin resting on them. Her eyes looked worried. I knew without looking that the ceremony hadn't taken. I didn't want to look at my body, so I kept my gaze on her.

"I tried all that I know," she said softly. "I even tried a few things my grandfather used to combat what he called white-man plague—what I think was probably smallpox." A trace of a smile crossed her mouth and was gone. "I took pictures of you and sent them to some medicine men and shamans and wisewomen I know. One of them accused me of 'ridiculous use of technology for ancient tribal healing.'" She shook her head, and I could see the dried sweat salt at her temples. "I called medicine men of the Western Chero-kee. I even sank so low as to call a medicine man of the Great Plains region, claims to be part Arapaho and part Cree and part bastard white man. He texted me back that it was a dangerous thing and for me to dig a hole in the ground, hit you over the head with a shovel, and bury you. And mark the ground with warning signs."

"Thanks for not doing that one." My voice sounded hoarse but better than I'd expected. Stronger. Aggie passed me a bottle of water and I opened it and drank it down, still without looking at my hand.

"No one knows what magic harmed you, but we all agreed, it was black magic. And we all agreed that only you could heal you. So I tried to get your animal form to come forth."

I sat up straight at that one and forced up the courage to look at my hands. They looked . . . fine. And I realized what was wrong with Aggie. She had finally seen me shift into my Beast. Or maybe my half-Beast form—which might, in re-ality, be worse. "Ummm. Okay. What did you see? And did you use your phone to take video or pictures of that?"

"I saw a dark fog flow from you and cover you, shooting with bright silver lights and blue-gray sparks. I saw your skin sprout hair and your bones twist. The sounds weren't exactly like the sound of breaking bones, but they were quite . . . disturbing. I saw you change, but into nothing that I knew, nothing that I could recognize. And *no*." The skin of her face pulled down and her chin lifted in insult. "I would *never* disrespect *utlvgi*—one who comes to me for *v-gatahv-i*—by revealing anything about their private healing ceremonies. When I took photographs of you, it was only of your arms and hands, not your face."

"I'm sorry," I said, ducking my chin and looking away. "I guess . . . I knew that." She crossed her arms, waiting. I vaguely remembered that *utlvgi* meant sick. But, "*V-ga-ta-hv-i*"—I sounded out the word—"means . . . 'knowledge,' not 'healing.'"

"When black magic is the cause," Aggie said, "only wisdom and self-knowledge can provide the healing." She indicated my hands. "You have accomplished much, as you see. But it has not been enough. The red lines are still there, barely visible beneath the skin. I do not know what knowledge is needed to complete your healing, so I cannot guide you."

"Ah." I pushed myself to my knees and to my feet. My stomach growled and my limbs felt weak, like my knees would buckle and I'd fall over if a stiff wind hit me. Heck. I'd fall over if a slight breeze hit me. "Where's Eli and Alex? I have a hazy memory of them being here."

"They are visiting with my mother. She has decided that their mother was part Coushatta. She is tracing their lineage."

I started laughing and stumbled, catching myself against the doorjamb like a weeklong drunk. "*Uni lisi* is a dangerous woman."

"Yes," Aggie agreed, sourly. She took my elbow to help me from the smokehouse and into the early afternoon sun. It didn't hurt where she gripped, not like a bruise, but I was aware of the flesh, a distant ache. *Yeah. Not totally healed. And not good. But better than dying, which I had a feeling I had been.* I blinked into the brightness, the world sharp and distinct, yet with full-spectrum color—Beast-vision still with me, tied into my own.

Behind the sweathouse, out of sight of the road and *lisi*'s house, I showered in the cool well water and dressed in the clothes the guys had brought me—jeans and the fuzzy purple dragon T-shirt, which felt wonderful against my skin. After pulling my hair, which had come loose at some point of my partial change, into a knot, I slipped my feet into flip-

flops and walked to the house. From it came wonderful
smells of grease and pork and spices, like boudin balls and
Cajun peppers and all good things to eat.

It was two p.m. by the time we finished with the appropriate and required visit (which meant the lunch that had
been picked up from a Cajun fast-food joint by Eli) and
said our good-byes. I fell asleep as soon as the SUV pulled
out of the drive. The last thing I heard was Alex saying, "Are
we gonna tell her she snores?"

CHAPTER 9

A Lot of Blood and Some Magical Mojo

The power nap did me good, and by the time we reached the French Quarter / Central Business District area, I was awake and pointing the way to the bank where all the magical goodies were kept. We were exhausted and it was probably selfish of me to make the stop, but I had to know if the half-remembered glimpse of a gold bracelet was reality or a dark dream. Grabbing an empty gobag, I entered the bank.

No one looked twice at the dragon shirt, even in the heat wave, but they did look at *me*, too tall, too lanky, and too recently on TV. *Go, me.* As I was led out of the lobby and into the long, narrow hallway where private storage was offered to the patrons, I heard whispering and muttering behind me. I gathered that the bank patrons, and probably some of the staff, identified me from the news and replays of the press conference. But nothing totally unexpected or negative happened, and no one tried to shoot me, which was always a plus, and something I thought of often lately.

Unfortunately, I did feel the instant attraction of magic as I entered the safe-deposit box room. My skin started to tingle and burn, and the red lines on my hand brightened, the closer I got to the safe-deposit box that held the most dangerous of the magical trinkets I had collected. I spread my fingers, seeing the red lines brighten, the flesh of the digits looking soft and delicate, like they were trying to swell. I tucked the hand into a jeans pocket and keyed open the three boxes I rented, before following the teller into one of the small, private viewing rooms.

As soon as she left, I held my hand over each box in turn, and even blindfolded I'd have known which box contained the blood diamond, as my injured hand practically sizzled with heat, and the red lines glowed brighter as I held it over the one box. With my left hand, I lifted the safe-deposit box lid that called to me, and the burning of my right hand increased tenfold. But now Beast pressed down on my brain, her claws extended, and pushed the pain away, kneading, just as she had done in the healing ceremony. "Thanks," I muttered aloud to her, not taking my eyes off the box.

Inside, in its black velvet jewelry bag, was the blood diamond.

With my good left hand, I opened the drawstring and eased the gem to the lip of the bag, holding the blood diamond in the velvet with the tips of my fingers, careful not to let it touch me. The stone, when not in use in a magical ceremony, usually looked like a pink diamond or a washed-out, pale ruby, the size of the end of my thumb. It was faceted all over in large, chunky planes, which I had figured out were its natural crystal shape. It was hanging on a heavy gold chain, the gem encased in a thick focal setting shaped like horns and claws—just like the setting on the gold bracelet I'd glimpsed worn by Joses Bar-Judas, aka Joseph Santana.

I stared into its depths as the gem sparkled and danced with lights, the internal lights of black-magic power. It was beautiful and ugly and probably the most powerful thing I would ever see, having been fed with the soul energy and life force of witch children sacrificed over centuries. It had belonged to the Damours, and I had no doubt that Santana would want it.

I also had no doubt that whatever Santana had done to me, I now was susceptible to the lure of the gem. My flesh wanted the diamond, wanted to cup it in my hands, to press it to my heart. My breath sped and my heart rate doubled. "Yeah. That totally sucks," I said aloud.

I forced my fingers to open, let the gem fall to the bottom of the heavy velvet bag, and I drew the drawstring shut. I had a lead-lined pouch that I sometimes stuck silver crosses in so the light from vamp-glow wouldn't advertise that I carried a weapon against them. I'd carry the gem in that, just in case the lure of it got too bad. I set the velvet bag on the table. From the box beside it, I pulled out the iron discs created from the spike of Calvary, and the pocket watches that contained more of the iron, and set them on the table. They felt different too, warm to the touch of my fingers. *Well, ducky. Black-magic stuff seems to recognize me now.* Glowering at the discs, I debated taking everything in the boxes, but if we lost the battle with the Son of Darkness and he killed us all, then Santana would own everything. As a witch and a vamp himself, one of the oldest undead on the planet, he would likely be able to use it all, just as the Damours had done. I put the biggest slab of iron discs and the black velvet bag holding the blood diamond into the empty gobag, closed up the boxes, and got the teller to help me return them to the long slots. Tired, scared, and unhappy with the direction of my thoughts, I left the bank and strode into the afternoon sun.

In the SUV, the AC running full out, I laid back my head and let my thoughts have free rein. It occurred to me that the children who had been sacrificed to power the gem in my gobag had been innocent. Only the Damours' intent had been evil. The intent of the vampire-witches had destroyed the children and then twisted the power of their innocent souls to evil. That intent was a kind of . . . *faith*. A faith in death and evil. Troubled, I opened my eyes to stare out the window as Eli drove us toward home, passing lawyers' offices, homes, apartments, dental clinics, and storefronts, all in old houses that carried the spirit of New Orleans' décor and architecture. And I saw one in particular.

"Stop!" I said. "Pull in there!"

Eli hit the brakes and whipped the wheel, slinging his passengers against the doors. Alex cussed as his tablet flew from his hands and clattered to the floor. "Sorry," I said to them both, as I popped the seat belt, opened the door, and dropped into a trot to keep up with the still-moving vehicle.

"Damn it, Jane!" Eli said, by way of reprimand.

"Sorry," I said again, deciding not to say anything about

the cursing, under the circumstances. I slammed the door and trotted on to the building. The storefront took up a wide lot with parking in front under a tree and on the street. One half of the storefront was empty. I felt a small space open up inside of me and fall through, like a sinkhole into the deeps of the earth, pulling in things after it.

The small church I had been attending had been in the storefront. It was gone now. A FOR RENT sign rested in the front window. I stepped slowly closer and pressed my forehead and my damaged hand against the glass. It was empty from wall to wall, the concrete floor swept clean. I had to wonder how long it had been since I had attended a service, how long since I had prayed. Since I had communed with nature. Since I had done *anything* spiritual. How long since I had called out for peace and help and . . . Too long. I was exhausted, broken, wounded, and still feeling the weight of the deaths in the bar. *My fault. All my fault. I should have killed Joses Bar-Judas the first time I set eyes on him.*

And how was it possible that killing another sentient being would have been better than letting him live? How was it possible that my committing murder was better than letting a prisoner go free? In hindsight, I knew I *should* have killed the Son of Darkness. But if I had killed the vamp hanging on the wall, as my instincts had wanted, just guessing that he would get free and kill humans, it would have been murder. Could I have lived with myself? Could I live with myself now? I dropped my forehead to the window glass.

I heard the SUV doors open and closed my eyes. Not wanting to see the guys whom I was putting in danger on this hunt. *My fault.*

I banged my head once on the window glass, caught in the emotional and philosophical and theological cesspool of my life. The window didn't offer any suggestions, but it did rattle nicely. I laughed, but it sounded more like a sob.

"Jane?" Alex asked. When I didn't answer, he said, "Your hand still looks weird." When I still didn't answer, he finished with, "You're acting kinda weird too. Like, almost, you know, drunk."

Without looking at him, I took a step away from the storefront, held out my hand, and pulled up my purple sleeve. The red-tattoo-looking veins were less bright under the shirt's healing energies, but they were still there. "Well, crap. Drunk makes sense. I'm blood-drunk. From a spell thrown by a vamp who was starving to death, contaminated with silver, and then suddenly got a lot of blood and some magical mojo." I pulled my sleeve down and stared into the empty building through the dirty glass. "I'm blood-drunk and still have a blood-magic spell working in me." *And I haven't yet told you about the blood diamond. That too.* "I need a cure. I dunno. I was thinking the church might have an idea how to heal my hand."

The Kid nodded, his reflection in the window glass. "That makes sense. The church didn't close down. It moved to a bigger building. I've pulled up the address."

I whirled away from the window and looked down at the Kid. Only, not so far down as before. He was taller than he had been, standing at five feet ten or so now, and the nascent muscles I had seen before had gained definition. How odd . . . I reached up and patted his head. "Thanks, Kid. You've grown. Can you take me there?"

The sentences held one non sequitur after another, but nothing threw Alex. "I know. I'm grown up now. And yes. But why do you think a *church* can help you?" His tone suggested that churches, in fact, any kind of spirituality, were hokum.

I held out my hand and took a slow breath, facing the truth of what had happened. I was hurt, and until I figured out something to fix it, I was sidelined. Just like a human. "Vampire blood magic did this. I think only something the opposite of vampire blood magic can undo it. I tried Cherokee fire and cleansing smoke and it helped but it didn't totally heal. Apparently I tried to shift but didn't make it." I thought about Beast, who was still and silent in my soul home, wounded, just like me. "And I honestly don't think I can shift on my own. So, maybe, holy ground?"

The Kid gave me a one-shoulder shrug and we climbed back into the SUV. The guys talked a bit, then we drove a while, crossing under I-10 on Governor Nicholls Street, heading nearly opposite from the house and the nice comfy bed I needed so badly.

There were parts of Governor Nicholls that looked safe, like a pleasant place to live, with blooming plants on the galleries and well-kept homes, businesses, and yards. And then there were the other parts, with busted chain-link fences, busted windows, boarded-up doorways, and walls that were covered in urban street art and gang signs. The little church was in *that* part of the hood. It had taken over a small one-story house with the traditional double-shotgun front — a door on the left and a door on the right. The house had freshly painted yellow siding and dark green window shutters that were closed against the heat of the day. A new steeple perched on top of the roof ridge, and the sign in the small yard read, THE CHURCH, which seemed information enough for me. We parked, and I got out into the heat and humidity, which instantly tried to smother me, as if Mother Nature had shoved a hot sponge over my face. I carried the gobag containing the blood diamond and the iron spike discs in my good hand, and my feet dragged me from the vehicle in exhaustion.

I opened the gate, walked to the gallery and under the porch roof, and tried the door. It was unlocked, which, in this part of the city, was just weird. I pulled the iron discs and the black velvet bag containing the blood diamond and gripped them in my damaged hand. Tossing the gobag over my shoulder into the small yard, I knocked and opened the door. I took a step inside.

The things in my hand caught fire.

Well, not really, but they started smoking, so I whipped back my hand and flung them into the day. They landed together in the sparse grass of the yard. I poked at my hand, which seemed fine, though maybe a little tender. Eli got out of the SUV and stood over the things I'd tossed, staring and thinking. Then he picked them all up and put the things back in the gobag. "You need to tell us something, Janie?"

"Yes. In a bit."

He zipped up the gobag. "We'll hold 'em."

I blinked back tears. They trusted me even when it looked like I was sick. And maybe dangerous. "Don't go to sleep," I said. "You'll wake up with the SUV on blocks, the wheels gone, the engine pilfered, and your pockets picked of the maniacal, magical, mystery toys."

Eli gave me a look that I interpreted as polite interest but was really only a slight twitch I might have imagined. "They could try. But then, I never sleep. Don't get yourself hurt again. Yell if you need us."

I nodded and went into the church, closing the door behind me. My right hand instantly started to ache, but I tried to pretend I was fine and called out, "Anyone here? Preacher? Pastor?" I couldn't remember his name, and any scent was hidden beneath the reek of fresh paint. Massaging my hand, I walked through the dark foyer into the sanctuary. The daylight in the long, narrow building was shuttered away, but the air-conditioning wasn't up to the job of the heat wave. The air in the old building was close and humid, smelling of New Orleans' pervasive mold and the overriding paint stink, outgassing from the white, sun-heated walls. The floor was new hardwood, my flip-flops slapping. The white pews were old, looking as if they had been repurposed numerous times, sporting multilayers of paint at every scratch and nick. The rostrum on the uncarpeted dais was ancient, a scarred, fancy cross carved on the front. Celtic cross? No, the upright was longer than the arms. I didn't know. Couldn't remember, the effects of being blood-drunk from a witch spell thrown by a master vampire. The back wall showed no place for a choir but did have a half wall directly behind the rostrum and a door to either side. The smell of chlorinated water came from the half-wall opening, indicating a baptismal pool.

Rubbing my thrumming arm, I continued down the central aisle, making noise, picking up the scents of children, sweat, old cigarette smoke, and aftershave beneath the paint. From the back of the building I heard a toilet flush and smiled. Preachers had to pee too.

"Preacher?" I called again. I heard one of the front doors behind me open, and Eli's scent swept through the old house turned church. So much for staying in the SUV in this heat. Nosy human.

"Yes?" From the door to the left of the rostrum a man came. Well, he was male and human, looking about twelve, no matter the scraggly mustache he sported. Yeah. Same church, same preacher. He held out his hand, walking closer. "I'm Charley—" He came to an abrupt stop about ten feet away, staring. His hand slowly fell. "You used to attend our congregation."

I nodded.

"You stopped coming."

I nodded.

"You're Jane Yellowrock. The vampire hunter."

I nodded again.

"What can I do for you, sister?"

I moved my massaging hand to my elbow, where the ache seemed to increase. "I don't know. Not exactly." I held out my damaged hand to show him the brightening red lines and felt my body listing to the side. I compensated by shuffling my flip-flops on the floor and caught my balance. "I was hit by a witch spell. One cast by a powerful vampire. I tried fire and light to drive it out, thinking, you know, vampire blood and the sun and all that. I don't know what to try next. But I thought"—I gestured to the half wall behind the rostrum—"I thought maybe holy water."

"We don't believe in holy water, sister. But I can pray for you."

"You don't believe that the water recently used for baptism is touched by God? Because I can assure you"—I laughed, more a titter than a real laugh, sounding so very drunk—"vampires are scared silly of it."

"Holy water is not the same . . . Never mind. Have you been drinking, sister?" he asked, earnest and kind—too kind—in his desire to help. Made me want to deck him. "If so, there are programs to help. I can assist you in finding them."

"Preacher," Eli said, striding toward me, his boots silent. "The lady hasn't been drinking. She's one of the few things standing between this city and another bloodbath, and she needs help. So, if you don't mind, we'll be taking advantage of the holy water in your baptismal thingy." Without slowing his pace, Eli picked me up and carried me past the preacher.

"Sorry." I waggled my fingers at the twelve-year-old human as Eli and I rounded the corner and the boy-preacher vanished from sight. "Sorry," I called out, louder. "I'm saying I'm sorry a lot today," I said to myself. Louder I added, "Sorry Eli's so bossy."

"Love you too, babe," Eli said. And he threw me into the water.

I'd been baptized in a bend of a river when I was a teenager, the water in the swimming hole deep, cold, and still. I hadn't thought about that in ages. But as I landed in the chlorinated water, eyes open and burning, seeing the blue tile and handrails beneath the water, the little rubber patches on the bottom of the pool to make it less slippery, loose strands of my black hair floating above me, I remembered. I remembered it all.

I remembered the feel of the preacher's muscled arm beneath my hands. The wet chill of his hand on my nape, his other hand over my nose, closing it off. The sensation that jarred through me as he braced his feet on the rocky bottom and lowered me down. The way the brown water closed over my head. Chill. Remembering the sight of his face through the water, rippling.

The rush of water as he levered me back up, the sound of splashing. The sound of singing. The intense smell of river water. The feel of the river bottom beneath my bare feet. The knowledge that I was supposed to be a new person, and reborn. Again. I remember thinking that. Reborn. *Again.* As if I had been reborn before. And I had been reborn, every time I shifted. But this time, being reborn from the river water, it was supposed to bring me peace.

I wasn't sure what peace really was—the English word hadn't made a lot of sense to me at the time. I hadn't known what it would mean for me, the rebel, the troublemaker at the children's home, but I knew I wanted it. Wanted to throw myself into that sensation of tranquility, that new life that the preacher and his Bible had promised I would find. And as the chill water sluiced from me, there had been . . . something. Something—

I hit bottom.

Beast screamed deep inside, a devil-cat scream of territory claiming, of rage, of might. The gray place of the change pushed into the clear water, making it roil with bubbles and heat and cold. I felt Beast's pelt pressing against my flesh, abrading underneath. My bones snapped and split and cracked as they reshaped, so fast, so much faster than not so long ago.

My skin heated, a searing, burning, scorching pain, the pain of dipping my entire body into a boiling pot, steam rising, blistering. Blood burst from the flesh of my right hand, up my right arm, into the clear water, a thin cloud of reddish mist, fading, dissipating into the pool, turning it murky. Pelt erupted from my skin. Deep inside me, Beast screamed again, the vicious sound of victory.

I crouched in the pinkish, brackish, dim water, at the bottom of the shallow pool, completely submerged. I was pelted all over, fingers, hands, legs, ankles, and lower paws stretching the stupid flip-flops. I pulled out my purple shirt and saw the pelt extended over my boobs, all the way down into my jeans. *Crap.* Buried beneath the water, I felt my face, finding the usual half-human, half-puma face with large, outthrust jaw and cat nose, human forehead and eye sockets, with pelt all over, forehead, whiskered cheeks, and chin. Instinctively, I kept my head down and nose flaps closed, so water didn't get into my puma nose. Human hair still covered my scalp, a black cloud of it floating in the water. I opened my mouth, felt of my teeth, the taste of chlorine bitter, almost soapy, and oddly salty. Though I had mostly human teeth, my canines—top and bottom—were long, like tusks. And . . . I had puma ears, rounded, movable ears that were set cat-high on my head.

This was a different shape from my previous half-cat form. I was pretty sure I didn't like it. But at least the burning, aching, of my injured hand felt better. I made a fist. Opened my tawny-haired hand with the too-big, knobby knuckles. My Beast had a beautiful golden color. Slowly I stood up in the pool, water rushing, subsiding from me in a wave, the chlorine already bleaching out the blood. I stood on the tiled bottom and met Eli's eyes.

"Well. The hair's new," he said.

I grinned, and it must have been pretty scary, because he said, carefully, "Jane?"

"Yeah. Gimme a minute." My voice was mostly mine, but lower, hoarser.

I ducked beneath the water again, feeling like a guy from the Old Testament, who had dunked himself beneath water seven times to be healed of a disease. Beneath the water, I thought about my Jane form. What I looked like when I was human shaped. For reasons I'd never understood, I couldn't move from my pure Beast form to my pure human form in the daylight, but the half form had seemed more amenable to shifting in daylight. Gray mist blended into the water a second time, boiling energies, flashes of light and shadow.

I changed again. The pain was worse, far worse than moments before. *Too soon,* I thought. *And not soon enough.* I crouched beneath the water and screamed, a gargling, cawing sound of misery, with no way to draw breath. My bones slid and crunched. Blood spiraled from my fingertips and into my mouth from my gums. I spat, the water churned by the gray energies.

The pain faded slowly, a burning, icy torture along my skin. The need for breath forced my feet underneath me, and I raised upright, sucking in air that was mostly hair and water, draining along my scalp. I coughed and took another, looking at my hands, touching my face. Human again. And only a fading tracery of red lines. "Yes!" I met Eli's relieved eyes. He nodded and pulled his cell, saying, "Lock the doors, bring the gobag inside. Return to the SUV."

From somewhere off to the side, the preacher said, "Sir, you have to leave. If you don't—"

"Father, the lady needs some prayer time. You're gonna give it to her."

"Sir. I don't want to have to call the authorities."

"Bro!" Alex shouted, the word echoing in the long room.

Eli lifted his hands, and through the opening in the half wall flew a familiar tan gobag—Beast's bag, which I carried with me when I changed shape. Eli caught it and gave me a chin jut that ordered me to get out of the water and go left. I stepped out of the pool and took the gobag, entered a room with a cutout female silhouette on the door, one from the fifties, wearing a long, wide skirt, maybc with a crinoline. It was painted Pepto pink. So was the austere little bathroom, where I rinsed my hair in the sink and dried off using coarse towels stacked on metal shelving. The clothing in the gobag was thin cotton everything, but at least was dry.

I met Eli at the door to the restroom / changing room, and he looked me over, clearly making sure I was human and covered. He pointed to a small door I hadn't seen earlier, and I ducked out into the sunlight. But on the way, I saw the baptismal water. It was no longer blue and clean. It now had an odd tinge, with a froth of brownish bubbles along the sides.

I had desecrated the baptismal pool. Something unknown, something like horror and shock and revulsion, quivered along my body. Something evil had been left in that water. Something evil that had been inside me. What if I hadn't gotten it all out? What if something was left behind, a taint, a smear of dark magic?

I made my way to the SUV, trudging through the heat in

my new flip-flops, trying to make sense of what I had seen of the water. It had looked shadowy. Not muddy or dirty or dyed with blood, as I might have expected. It had looked *shadowy*. As if something loomed over the water, cutting out the light, the corners and bottom brownish and smoked over. I got in the front passenger seat of the SUV, which was running, the AC on high, and examined my arms, ankles, shins, feet, hands, and, in the sun-visor mirror, my face. No red lines. Not anywhere.

But somehow, I didn't think I was totally cured.

Eli got in and eased into the sparse traffic, assuring me he had pulled the drain on the pool and set it to empty, making certain that the contaminated water was removed from the baptismal basin. He had also made a generous donation to the church. Then he pulled into a Popeyes fried-chicken joint and handed a bucket of extra-crispy to me.

I was generous—I gave each of the brothers a leg. I devoured the rest, ten pieces, four biscuits, and a tub of mashed potatoes that my skinwalker metabolism demanded for energy replenishment. Shifting almost always required food. Shifting and moving through time required something like penance—a sickness that nearly killed me the last time I used it, the recovery taking too long. Too dang long. Today, I wasn't sick, but the caloric needs were greater than usual. I still felt empty when I finished the bucket of chicken, but exhaustion took me under and I closed my eyes on the way home, my head against the headrest, my thoughts gloomy and uncertain. And wary. As if something watched me through the darkness of my own thoughts, its sights on the center of my back, between my shoulder blades.

CHAPTER 10

I Have the Scratches to Prove It

I woke in my own bed, when a heated body climbed in beside me and wrapped his arms around my waist, pulling me close. "Spooning," I mumbled.

"Courting and living in sin," Bruiser whispered back. "And your partners are gone to make groceries, so we have the place to ourselves."

"Yeah?" I managed, waking up more slowly than I would have liked. *Making groceries* was strictly a New Orleans term, and it sounded odd coming from Bruiser's mouth.

"Yes," he said, a low thrum of need in his voice. He pressed his lips to the back of my neck, his hands spread wide across my stomach. His scent filled the tent of the covers, his usual citrusy cologne changed to something that smelled like blue cypress and oak moss, with a small amount of frankincense and a hint of . . . *catnip. In bloom.*

I rolled over in his arms, an action that twisted me in my own hair but brought my nose into contact with his chest. "You smell good," I said.

"I'm glad you like it," Bruiser said, tilting my chin up so our mouths met. His fingers slipped beneath my T-shirt and slid it off over my head. Brushed the lower curve of my breast as he did. I sighed into his mouth, a soft moaning sound.

"I had it blended with you in mind," he whispered. And that was the last thing we said for a long, long time.

We were dressed and brewing tea and coffee when the guys got back, banging through the side door with bags of groceries. The Kid dropped three bags of veggies and one of canned, pasta-based dinners and sugary cereal on the kitchen table and took off to his tablets, muttering into his earbud cell something about encryption coding. Eli entered more slowly, placing his six bags of tofu, yogurt, green stuff, and steak on the table beside his brother's. He looked back and forth between Bruiser and me and he might have smiled.

I didn't look at his face long enough to judge, but my own flared and heated. "Shut up," I grumbled.

"Babe," he said, and grabbed a carrot and a stick of string cheese to munch as he put away the groceries. Stacking stuff on the top refrigerator shelf, he asked Bruiser, "What's the latest on the action at vamp HQ? Janie got hit pretty bad yesterday."

Bruiser smiled and went to the foyer, bringing back a leather satchel, a cross between a backpack and a briefcase, but looking expensive and well-worn. "Leo, Del, and I went over the data from the attack on Jane, and the Master of the City suggested some reading material from the library." He set the satchel on the kitchen table and removed three heavy tomes from it, along with sealed files of loose papers, the files made of acid-free materials that had been treated to preserve antique paper, papyrus, sheepskin, and anything else the ancients had used for writing. He laid the books to the side and spread out a cloth on the table before placing the files atop it. He donned white gloves, smoothing the fingers into place.

Bruiser had been given a classical education, meaning that he could read ancient and modern Greek, Latin, and several more modern languages. He had previously been translating a Latin-ish history of witches from the original hand-bound manuscript, and so far, he had discovered a lot of history that we might be able to use when the Euro-Vamps came calling, but nothing about the bag of bones formerly hanging on the wall of sub-five and currently running around the city killing people. Not a thing. Research into things historical and not yet scanned into the clouds of the Internet was more time-consuming than I'd expected. He had been at it for several weeks.

"The escape of Joseph Santana," Bruiser said, "and the deaths in the bar have necessitated a change in Leo's usual modus operandi. He is suddenly much more helpful in directing me to materials that might assist our research. Of course, having access to Reach would have been more helpful than any reading material, but I'm taking what I can get."

Reach—the world's foremost researcher on all things vampiric—had disappeared from view following a visit by some particularly nasty vamps and a human torturer. They had hurt him and I hadn't been able to discover how badly or where he was now. I hoped healing on some sunny beach somewhere, sipping umbrella drinks and working on his tan. Reach was a treacherous, double-dealing, entrepreneurial backstabber, who would have sold his mother to the highest bidder, but we had done business for a long time, and no one deserved to be tortured. No one.

"With the focus now shifted from the European Mithrans' visit to Joseph Santana," Bruiser said, "I've done some prep work in the material suggested by Leo, scanning for names used by Santana over the years, and trying to find information about his magical abilities."

Eli made a snorting sound while putting away three dozen eggs, a bunch of celery, and a big bag of sweet potatoes.

Bruiser gave him a lazy grin. "Oddly enough, the search led me to the *arcenciels*, also called *serpentes iridis*."

Eli closed the refrigerator and leaned a hip against the counter. "What do the dragons of light have to do with Santana?"

Bruiser said, "They, or the human magic users of the time, may have left behind some magical implements." I thought about the hints of gold I'd seen on Santana, at neck and at wrist. And the *wyrd* that had fried my body. What if the spell he had spoken had been augmented by an ancient artifact? What if the *wyrd* had been a spell created by the *arcenciels* or ancient magic users?

"I do have something new for you all," Bruiser said, and I got up to freshen my tea and Bruiser's coffee. "First, Leo's humans are tearing the Council House apart looking for documents pertaining to Joseph Santana—properties, habits, humans who might still be alive to offer him a lair. Second, the address of the lair from which Joseph Santana originally disappeared. The room was supposedly sealed and remains untouched to this day. It's a remote possibility that Santana, in his currently unstable mode, might return there to lair, as a place that he remembers as comfortable and safe. Or there may be papers there that will lead us to a current lair." With two fingers, he extended a folded slip of paper to Eli. "This will take you there. The caretaker has the keys."

I let myself relax against the kitchen cabinet for just a moment and sipped my tea, my eyes lingering on Bruiser, showing him with my smile my appreciation for his efforts. The look he gave me back was a little more warm and made me think about his efforts in the bedroom earlier. I dropped my head, letting my hair slide forward, over my face, to touch the oversized mug at my mouth, hiding my heated cheeks.

"Jane has told me about her injuries and the way she was healed," he said, his eyes on me and the words feeling weighted, as if they carried more import than appeared on the surface.

Not quite as gently, Eli said, "Yeah. About that. Jane? Why did you go get the blood diamond and the iron discs out of the bank?"

The house went silent, Alex in the living room, suddenly standing at the opening to the kitchen, all three men unmoving, watching me. I hadn't told Bruiser about that yet. I put down my mug and pushed my hair behind my ears and over my shoulders to hang down my back, using the opportunity to think through how I wanted to respond.

"Jane?" Bruiser asked.

"Something about Santana's attack," I said, long after I should have spoken to fill the silence, "reminded me of the blood diamond, back when the Damours used it." For the Youngers, who hadn't been with me then, I said, "Adrianna was there the night of the fight with the Damours. She was part of the blood-magic spell that they were trying to invoke. The night they tried to kill Angelina and Little Evan." *My godchildren. I had nearly gotten them killed.*

I held out my right hand, fingers spread, and studied it. It looked normal. But it still felt off. Just a little. Just a very, very little. "On sub-five, Adrianna and Mario had scratch marks at neck and wrist, as if something had been ripped off each of them during Santana's escape."

I could almost feel Bruiser's mind work, thoughts clicking into place. Softly, he said, "I remember that night, not long after you first came to work for Leo. You fought the Damours and killed them."

"All except for Adrianna, who Leo saved. Nutso, insane, psycho vamp, and he still won't let me kill her."

"In that fight," Bruiser said, "did your blood touch the blood diamond?"

Staring at my right hand, I made a fist, watching as the muscles bunched and tightened, remembering the tracery of black magic through my skin. I nodded, a jerky motion, up and down. Eli cursed. The Kid's eyes went wide.

"How did your blood come in contact with the blood diamond?" Bruiser asked. "Walk me through it, step by step."

"One of the Damours—I called him Baldy—was holding the gem in one hand. I had a cut on my cheek from a branch, from running through the woods in the dark. I know. Idiot civilians," I said before Eli could. "He was trying to kill me and I was trying to kill him. He touched the diamond to me." I touched my cheek, remembering, fear crawling up my spine like slithering snakes, sinuous and cold, swallowing my strength. "Into the cut, into my blood. And he spoke a *wyrd*, activating the spell." The feeling, the pain, had been so very similar to what had happened when the Son of Darkness attacked. I lifted my cooling tea and sipped, but it did nothing for the dryness of my mouth.

"When I was in the baptismal pool"—I opened my hand again and turned it over, seeing my palm with its three deep, smooth lines and myriad tiny ones—"I was able to remember the fight with—let's call it skinwalker clarity. Santana was wearing a bracelet when he came up from the elevator shaft. It had a setting crafted for two stones." I stopped and took a breath. "But one was missing."

Alex swore softly. Eli pursed his lips, staring at my hand.

"I went to the bank and . . . when I held my hand near the blood diamond, I could feel the magic in it. I could feel Santana's spell on me. In me. Even now."

Eli said, "If the blood diamond was once part of the bracelet worn by the Son of Darkness, and if the diamond still in the bracelet is magically connected to the blood diamond, then you might now be connected to the bracelet. Possibly even accessible to the Son of Darkness himself. He could find you through the gems' attraction to each other and to you. Through your blood."

I nodded again, more slowly, knowing what he was going to say. It wasn't prescience. It was just knowing my partner and the way his mind worked. The way my mind worked too.

"Bait," Eli said.

"No! I forbid it," Bruiser said.

Which was such an old-man thing to say that it made me smile. "You can't stop it," I said, setting down the tea mug and rubbing my right hand in remembered pain. I recalled the strange sense of being spied on earlier, that awareness between my shoulder blades. "The holy water and the shift may have mostly healed me, but I think—" I stopped abruptly, knowing how weird this would sound to anyone not in the room. "I think the bracelet knows where I am. Maybe not all the time, but—" I stopped to reconsider. "If it recognizes my blood, it could be used to track me. Meaning that I should put it back in the safe-deposit box, I know that, but if I do that, then . . ." *I can't use it. No. Not what I wanted to say.* I changed it to ". . . we can't use it ourselves to lure him to me or to track him with it, you know, in case the witches have that ability."

Bruiser set down his empty coffee cup and asked, "Can you track him? Can you feel him with or through the diamond?"

"I don't know. I think it would be stupid to try all on my own. Which is one reason why I want the intro to Lachish Dutillet. She could put up a protective circle or something witchy." I waved a hand to indicate there were a lot of things magical that could be done and that I had no idea what might be involved.

The doorbell rang, and I jumped up to answer, feeling, literally, *Saved by the bell*. It was a delivery of pizza from

Mona Lisa's, ordered by the Kid while we chatted about ways to capture a killer and my magical problems. Bruiser kissed me on the top of the head and left while I paid the delivery guy. Even in the midst of people dying and my body being eaten up by spells, I could appreciate the view from the back side, and Bruiser had a veeery nice backside. He turned as he stepped into the street and smiled at me. It was one of those special smiles that people in relationships offer each other, smiles that say so much more than the movement of lips and face. Bruiser's said he'd had fun in my bed and would be back in it soon.

While we were eating, my cell vibrated. I opened the Kevlar-backed cover and started to say hi. I never got the chance.

"Why didn't you call me?" My best friend sounded mildly annoyed with me, and whether quietly seething or furious, an angry Molly was dangerous, because her earth-witch gift had gone wonky and started killing things. I ran through what I might have done this time, but no member of her family was in danger and I wasn't bringing problems to her door. And though Molly was powerful, there was no way she could know that we had been talking about the night I nearly got her children murdered in a blood-magic ceremony. So, for once, there was no reason why she should be upset with me.

"Ummm . . . Hey, Molly," I said carefully. "Why didn't I call you about what?"

"About an introduction to Lachish Dutillet. Why didn't you call me instead of Jodi Richoux?"

"Beeecause you are far away and—" I stopped as understanding hit me over the head, and started over. "I'm an idiot. I'm sorry. I know that you're planning the Witch Conclave, and that has to involve Lachish Dutillet, doesn't it? And because I didn't call you and tell you I needed to see the coven leader, you got blindsided. And probably embarrassed. I was trying to be nice and not bother you. I'm an idiot."

The silence over the line told me nothing, and though I wanted to babble to cover the hush—a totally uncharacteristic urge—I decided that not saying anything was the smart thing to do. Keeping my big mouth shut wasn't easy for me, but I was getting smarter. Slowly.

Alex shoved a megabite of Mona Lisa Special pizza into his mouth to smother a laugh. Eli just looked amused and helped himself to another slice of the spinach pizza. Both guys were listening avidly, probably wondering if Molly would lose it and try to kill me.

"Molly?"

She blew out a breath and let go of her anger, which was a step in the right direction for the control issues my friend was having, control over her magic and emotions. In the background I heard the musical anti-spell playing, the one created by Molly's husband to dampen her death magic.

"I'm sorry," I said, "in case 'I'm an idiot' didn't say it clearly enough."

"Okay. I was just . . . surprised," she said, her tone suggesting a shrug, still anxious sounding. "There's a meeting next week between Lachish and the Master of the City's primo to discuss topics for the parley. I'm going to ask Leo's Enforcer to be on hand to present the security arrangements for the conclave." Which meant me, because she didn't know that temporarily, I wasn't Leo's Enforcer. "The meeting has been moved up because of the death of the fifty-two humans and the blood-sucker that's loose. Jodi talked to Lachish and suggested that the fanghead might have used magic as well as compulsion to hold the humans down."

Jodi had been studying the video too, probably with the help of a PsyLED agent, and had clearly drawn some interesting conclusions. A little warning from her would have been nice, but I held that in, saying, "We need to chat about that. I have info. And some problems. And—"

"The conclave is flying me in, so I have to go. I don't know the arrangements yet, but I'll see you soon."

"Wait! Are you staying with us?" I asked. "And are you bringing KitKit?" KitKit was Molly's cat and familiar—not that witches have familiars, and suggesting such a thing to a witch is as big a faux pas as suggesting that vamps sleep in coffins. But the cat helped to keep Molly's death magics in control, so technically, Molly had a familiar. Weird. But Molly Megan Everhart Trueblood was never ordinary.

Molly blew out a breath and the last of her anger with it. "Damn cat," she muttered, letting me know her kids were close by. "KitKit has categorically refused to get in a travel crate, and I have the scratches to prove it. So I've drugged her, stuffed her in, booked the fastest flight I can, with the fewest layovers, and hope to all that's holy that she's still asleep when we arrive. And yes. I'd like to stay with you, since cats aren't welcome in most hotels. The kids are staying with Evan because of, you know, crazy suckhead vampire who might be able to do magic, in your town, killing people. I'll let you know about the meeting. Gotta go." The call ended without my getting a chance to update her on the mess she was walking into in New Orleans. I thought about calling her back, but there should be time to do that when she was on the ground. And besides, if the witches had been talking to the cops, Molly might know more than I did.

I looked up at Alex. "Call Katie's housecleaning service to get in here fast."

"Good thing we kept the litter box," he said. "Texting the cleaning service in to clean and to move my stuff to Eli's bathroom." His thumbs paused over his tablet. "Kids coming?"

"No." I quoted Molly's comment about the vampires as I lifted the last slice of the Special and took a big bite. Around it I said to Eli, "You do know that even the spinach pizza has carbs and fats, don't you?"

"Shhh," Alex said. "I told him it was fat-free, organic veggies, tofu, and goat cheese."

I chuckled through the mouthful and drank down Coke. It felt wrong on some level to stop and eat and take a break and chat and laugh. Fifty-two humans were dead and it was our job to find the killer, but we had all learned over the years, separately and together, to take a break when we could, sleep when we could, and eat when we could. That if we met a killer vamp when we were hungry, sleepy, tired, and emotionally drained, we'd lose and lose bad. So we took our break, and we ate, and we recharged. We had to.

When there was nothing left in either take-out box, I shoved the last half slice into my mouth and pointed to my room. "Weapon up." Except it came out more like *'Wa'on'uu.*

"Yeah," Eli said. "Full gear. Just in case Joseph Santana was stupid enough to go back to his old lair."

"Before you leave, there are contracts to sign, messengered over from the governor's and the mayor's offices. The powers that be have signed them already, and our lawyer has approved the language. And so have I," Alex added, sounding just a bit smug. Alex was self-taught, but the boy genius could read legalese like the best attorney in town. I trusted his evaluation. We all did. But no way was I gonna tell him. His head was too big already.

Most of Esplanade Avenue in the Quarter was well preserved, well kept, and not cheap digs. The address where Joses had laired long ago, the night Leo had essentially taken him captive, and where he might even now be asleep, in a hole in the walls or floor, or under the house in a vault, was a two-storied, narrow-fronted house that was nearly four times deeper than it was wide, with two different kinds of columns holding up the short front gallery and the roof. The wrought-iron front gate and iron lattice-style gallery fencing didn't match either, but were still quintessential New Orleans. The front windows were narrow and long, with working shutters, and the house had lots of fancy woodwork, potted ferns, blooming flowers in hanging baskets, and fancy little tasseled awnings over every side window. Most important, the address sported a small, gaited parking area in back and evidence of retrofitted central air. Due to the parking and the five air-conditioning units, there was no courtyard area or garden, but I figured the owners were more concerned about protecting the Bentley Mulsanne and the brand-new Mercedes-Benz coupe parked in back than in growing their own fresh flowers and veggies.

New Orleans' pretty, aboveground vamp lairs were never what I was expecting, not with my Asheville background of mountain caves and underground nests. Here, they were usually aboveground, often delicate and sweet-looking, painted in pastels like lavender and morning-glory pink and sunshine yellow. So unvampy.

Leaving most of my visible weapons on the car seat, I went through the small gate to the front porch, rang the bell, and stepped to the side of the door, out of the way. The door was solid wood, old but well preserved, painted charcoal, with a bronze mail slot in the middle.

Eli waited at the street, the SUV idling and a nine mil loaded with silver aimed at the door, just in case the vamp we were looking for answered his own door in the daytime.

The woman who opened the door was surprising. She

stood maybe four feet six and was even skinnier than I had been before I bulked up; she probably still shopped in the children's department. Her hair was bobbed straight at the chin and dyed a stunning shade of pink, a color that enhanced her remarkable eyes—an emerald so vivid that I forgot to sniff her out. Literally. When I did take a breath of the ice-cold air that was billowing out, she smelled of lilacs, sea salt, copier toner, and blood-servant. She was wearing a severe, dark green suit and a frilly blouse in a pale shade of jade green. On her lapel she wore a brooch composed of clustered pearls and an emerald that even I knew was priceless.

She lifted her arched, pink eyebrows and asked, "May I help you?" Her voice was Minnie Mouse with a severe cold, both high-pitched and husky.

I passed her a business card—the personal one that read, JANE YELLOWROCK, and below that, HAVE STAKES WILL TRAVEL. It was sort of a joke, one appreciated by the older blood-servants and vamps who remembered the black-and-white cowboy TV series. The pink-haired woman was no exception. She tittered.

"Do I welcome a modern-day paladin onto the premises?" Before I could respond, she motioned me in with a grand gesture. "Welcome, Ms. Yellowrock. Will the elder Mr. Younger be joining us as well?"

I motioned Eli in and heard the distinctive sound of a round being ejected from the chamber as he walked up to me. He handed me my sidearm, which I rechecked and holstered. The woman didn't bat a lash. She closed the door behind us and gestured to us to sit, saying, "You may call me Pinkie. I fulfill the requirements of maître d'hôtel here at Acton House." On someone else the nickname and the hair might have been laugh-worthy, but on Pinkie it worked. She was tiny, but there was something about Pinkie that demanded respect and good manners. She had an accent I couldn't place, but it wasn't French, Spanish, or Germanic. Maybe Swedish? Or some kind of Russian-type language?

As in most houses of its kind, the front room took up the full sixteen-plus feet of house width and the rest of the house went straight back, each room opening into the next, until a stairwell offered other alternatives. The furniture was period antiques: lots of carved dark wood, curlicues, marble tops, blackened mirrors in gilt frames, old paintings of unsmiling humans and vamps in stiff poses, uncomfortable-looking furniture, old rugs, lots of doodads, and that pervasive old-house smell—camphor, dry-rotting wood, delicate cotton, and fading vegetable dyes. The couch I sat on was as hard as a board and stank of old horsehair and dust mites.

Pinkie took a seat on a tiny upholstered chair, just big enough so that her toes touched the rug beneath. She was wearing patent leather Mary Janes. She was adorable. A weird part of me wanted to hug her, but I had a bad feeling that underneath the cuteness, she was armed and dangerous.

"How can I help you?" Pinkie asked. "The new primo was not very forthcoming, except to say that I was to have the private room keys in hand."

"We need to see the lair of Joses Bar-Judas," I said.

Pinkie's forehead formed neat little rows of wrinkles in confusion.

"Joseph Santana," Eli said. "That lair. It's supposed to have been locked for decades."

"Since he vacated the premises under unusual circumstances," Pinkie said, nodding. "Yes. Room two-oh-one. Come with me, please." She stood and led the way through the next room, which was a formal dining room with a gas-log fireplace. Over her shoulder, as she moved to the right and into a short landing, she said, "I've always wanted to see the best guest suite."

"Guest suite?" I asked. "This is a what? A vampire boardinghouse?"

"Yes. Of a sort," she said, starting up the stairs. "Acton House was widely used back in the day, before the Mithrans acquired the property they now use as their Council House. Visiting Mithrans had special needs and requirements back then, don't you know. Humans to safeguard them by day, to give them alibis when necessary, protection from light, access to suitable paramours, healthy blood supply, safe and comfortable sleeping arrangements, and access to European five-star chefs. Acton House provided it all, and we still do, when called upon, though at the moment, our rooms are empty."

"You've never taken a sneak peek at the sealed room?" Eli asked.

"Of course not," Pinkie said, surprise in her voice and in her scent. "That would have been a betrayal of trust." Our footsteps were hollow in the wide stairwell, and faintly, I heard a tinkle, as of metal tapping metal. We passed a heavily curtained window that let in no light. "Though I didn't know it when I took this contract—not back then, so long ago—taking that peek, as you put it, would have contaminated the scene with my skin cells, my hair, and my scent. I do watch all the latest crime shows," she said, as if letting us in on a big secret. "An addict of them, in fact. And I'm aware that a sealed crime scene is most important." Her pink head nodded in agreement with herself, shiny pink hair rocking back and forth.

We reached the second floor and entered a very narrow hallway leading back toward the front of the house. The hall was no more than twenty-four inches wide, and as I looked both ways along it, I saw four doors to the rear, one at the stairs, and one at the front. Six rooms, maybe four of them bedrooms, assuming some of the vamps shared a bathroom.

"So you didn't seal the room yourself?" Eli asked from behind me.

"No. Certainly not. I haven't been caretaker here *that* long. My predecessor, Professor Acton himself, the scion of the owner, followed the orders of the heir of the master of the city at the time and sealed the room. It was sealed the very morning that young Master Pellissier gave the order. No one has entered since."

I put it all together. Young Master Pellissier would have been Leo. Who was having his humans tear HQ apart looking for records about Joseph. *Gotcha.*

And Pinkie wasn't kidding. Maybe a television magician could have gotten through without leaving a trace, but no normal human or vamp could have, not unless the film and fiction writers were right when they suggested that vamps could turn into smoke and slide under doors and through cracks. From the hallway, the door was padlocked, three metal strips screwed into the woodwork of the jamb and through rings set in the door; each ring had a lock, besides the one in the door itself. Over the years, the wood had swelled from the Louisiana humidity, and the house's foundations had settled, pulling the framework out of plumb and sealing the door tighter still.

Pinkie pulled a ring of keys from a pocket and held them close as she read the labels. Starting at the top, she unlocked each padlock, bending back the metal strips as she worked. The metal wasn't overly pliable, and it groaned as it was bent, but tiny little Pinkie was a lot stronger than she appeared.

When the door was unlocked, she indicated that it was ours to open. Eli slipped in front of me, knelt, and pulled a small light, checking all around the edges for . . . I had no idea, not in such an old room, but Mr. Paranoid didn't heal as well as I did, so I let him take whatever precautions he wanted. Once he was assured it was safe, he stepped back and I took the old metal knob in my hand, feeling the lines that had been etched or pressed into the metal when it was made, leaves, I thought, or a fleur-de-lis. Then I thought about a shotgun set up to fire when the door opened, and I stepped to the side. Eli and Pinkie both stepped to the other side, as if reading my mind. I twisted the knob, which made a dry, creaking sound, made much worse as I pushed on the door, swollen into place, wood against wood. I set my shoulder to it, the door groaning like a human dying, still thinking about the possible shotgun. But no gun went off.

The smells that rushed out of the dark, overheated room were mice, damp, mold, old wood, rotten linens, old blood, and . . . dead vamp.

CHAPTER 11

A Sleepover with My Bestie, Adrianna

Death, even old death, has a smell.

The vamp skeleton was lying on the floor beside the bed, her head a few feet away.

"Holy Mother of God." Pinkie crossed herself and took a step back. I took two steps in and closed my eyes to get a better scent pattern of the dead and of the room. I breathed in through mouth and nose, but making no noise. Not a true, catlike, flehmen behavior, just some good breaths of the sealed space, and I found that I could identify varying scent signatures of several people—vamps and humans—who had spent time in the room. There was no recent sign of Joseph Santana or anyone else, just old, old, *old* smells.

Once I was satisfied of that, and of the scents I had taken in, I opened my eyes and gestured Eli in. He stood to my left, the open door to his side, his body positioned to cover the hallway, the room, and me. Security was second nature to him. Together we studied the dead vamp and the scene before us.

She had met true-death wearing a long, vertically striped blue dress with a high waist, ribbons, lace, and a locket pinned to her chest. Her head had met true-death wearing long blond hair up in a bun, and a perky hat. The mice had been at it all, and her hair had been a nest for more than one family of rodents. Said nesters had eaten the soft parts of the vamp, but surprisingly, most of her bone structure and tendons were still intact, if dried out and brittle looking.

When Acton House had been retrofitted for AC, this room hadn't been included in the renovations. Room 201 had a door that would open out onto the front gallery and tall, narrow windows, all sealed shut, which accounted for the heat, all with shutters, which were latched closed from the inside.

More critter nests were between the shutters and the window glass. Yet more had taken the best location inside — within the pillows and mattresses on the four-poster rice bed. The bed was hand carved and had been made up with silk sheets and feather pillows, faded and disintegrating, but probably the height of style and comfort in the late nineteenth and early twentieth centuries. Curiously, I didn't sense any mice in the room now, but maybe the heat had driven them out. Maybe the room was their winter home. I suppressed a grin, which I knew Pinkie would consider unseemly.

The floor was wood; the walls had been papered. Moldy shreds of pink roses and darker pink stripes were falling in curls where the walls weren't blood splashed. There, it was brown and dried and had been partially eaten by mice. The rugs were gnawed and threadbare but had once matched the wallpaper in color tones. A bedside table held a hurricane lamp, a carved ivory and wood pipe, and a book, along with the ubiquitous rodent droppings.

A turn-of-the-previous-century bathroom stood open and looked as awful as the rest of the suite. The chifforobe doors were closed and warped, a key dangling from a chain on one little knob. A pair of shoes lay in a corner near a small overturned chair. A tea cart was beside the chair, its contents splattered with blood. From the spatter I could tell that the teapot had been broken prior to the beheading.

Eli pointed to a place on the wall where no blood marked the wallpaper. The killer had likely stood there and taken the blood spatter with him when he left. Great lot of good that observation did us. Any clothes and trace on the killer would have been long gone by then, and the blood silhouette wasn't over-helpful except to suggest height, which had been average.

I moved farther inside and pulled my cell phone, taking photos and sending them to myself and to Alex. The days of memorizing a crime scene and drawing it out on pads of graph paper were long gone. So were pads of graph paper, probably.

To the side of the dead vamp I saw a gleam and carefully stepped around her outstretched skeletal left hand to get a good photograph. The shiny thing was a quartz crystal, the kind found in nature, but this one had been a really spectacular specimen before it was busted. I had seen one in this condition before. They were used by master vamps and by witches as cages for *arcenciels*. The sentient, shape-shifting dragons of light were from another plane, beings who could slow or bend time the way I could, but much better. The master of such a creature could force it to bend time or could borrow its magical ability to that end if he knew how, making the master an unbeatable adversary. But if the dragon creature got free, its bite was dangerous at best and could be deadly if untreated, even to vamps.

And oddly, Bruiser had mentioned *arcenciels* as part of his research, research initiated by Leo, who had been in this room on the day that the Son of Darkness had been hidden from the world. Leo had surely seen the shattered crystal that day, but I knew for certain that he'd had no idea what it had been used for, because an *arcenciel* had bitten him not long ago, which was when we had all learned the nature of the creatures and their poisonous bites. At some point after being bitten, the Master of the City had mentally added the busted crystal in this room together with the existence of *arcenciels* and with the condition of the Son of Darkness so long ago, and sent Bruiser searching.

Right. That made sense. And Bruiser had not told me that because I was supposed to draw my own conclusions. Basic police work. Everybody observe, then everybody share. Conclusions were more likely to be correct with that formula than if one person told all the others, which would slant everything. I understood it, but it ticked me off.

"Whatever we think we know about the night Joses went missing," I said, staring at the crystal, "is wrong."

Eli agreed with a slight nod. Though his words were unspoken, I could hear him thinking about the crystal, his thoughts probably paralleling my own. He said, "No mention of a dead fanghead."

Pinkie cleared her throat warningly, but Eli didn't retract his fanghead insult with the more polite *Mithran*. He squatted onto the balls of his feet and gestured to the vamp. "Something in her fingers, hidden by her dress, and"—he bent in closer—"she's wearing a glove on this hand."

I moved to his side as he pulled a thin-bladed knife, leaned forward, and pressed the flat of the blade against the striped dress fabric. Rather than moving, the skirt of the dress crumbled with a dry *shushing* sound and fell into dust on the chewed glove beneath, exposing what she had held.

The female vamp had been holding a silver stake in her gloved right hand. The tip was corroded, as if vamp blood had been on it.

"Huh," I said.

"Who was here that night? Could you tell?" Eli asked. Meaning could I smell them.

"This much blood and this many years makes it hard to smell anything," I said, telling the truth and yet not answering the question.

Pinkie looked at me curiously. It was obvious that she hadn't heard the whole "Jane turned into a mountain lion in Leo's car" story that was still making the vamp rounds.

"Would you excuse us?" I asked her. Pinkie's pink brows went up, making her forehead do that wrinkly thing again, but she nodded and walked away. When I heard her patent leather shoes tapping on the stairs I said quietly, "I remember seeing a painting at vamp HQ on sub-four. Adrianna and a blond vamp, arms around each other. They looked chummy. I've never seen the blonde alive except in the painting, so this could be her. Maybe."

"Chummy in a culturally appropriate way for the time, or in an 'into her panties' kind of way?" Eli asked. "Because if they were lovers and she died here . . ."

That was a really good question and a better observation. "If they were lovers, then we have motive for a lot of things." More softly, I said, "And if the broken crystal means what I think it does, then we have a lot more interesting things going on than we anticipated."

"I'll take a photo shoot on sub-four," Eli said. "Been

meaning to get photos of all the paintings down there before they get moved to Leo's new place. Scents?" he reminded me.

"I should have changed into a bloodhound before we opened the door, and it's too late now. The scents are so faint that it's going to be impossible to tell which people were here before the death, during the death, or after the death. I smell Joses—Joseph—though not with the sick smell he had hanging on the wall in sub-five. Here he smelled the way he did in the kill bar; the walls here are permeated with his scent, meaning that he stayed here for a long time. I smell Adrianna and the dead vamp. I smell Leo and Bethany and Sabina and another male vamp who could be Amaury, and maybe an *arcenciel*." I frowned, not knowing how to deal with the other scent I had picked up, except that it couldn't be kept a secret. "Most importantly, I smell Immanuel."

"The thing masquerading as Leo's son?" Eli looked around the room as if the creature I had killed might be hiding in a shadow.

"The *u'tlun'ta*," I said. "Liver-eater. Spear-finger."

"The insane skinwalker," Eli said, gently, shifting his eyes up to me from where he crouched on the floor.

I couldn't make myself look at him, but I nodded. "The thing I'll turn into someday, when I'm old and go insane and start eating people."

"You don't know that. What we do *know* is that Immanuel spent decades trying to find ways to greater power and ways to control the psychosis that was eating away at *his* mind," Eli said. "Not your mind. His."

I nodded, knowing Eli was right, but not knowing how his thinking would relate to my possible future. As far as I had been able to determine, skinwalkers *all* went nutso and started eating humans.

"So," Eli went on, "if we look at this crime scene in light of that need—the need to hold on to his sanity—why was he here? What did he hope to accomplish?"

I shrugged. I had killed Immanuel, the only other skinwalker I had met in modern times. The insanity of the psychotic killing machine had been a vision into my own future unless I died first, which seemed a much better alternative than eating my friends.

"Jane!" Eli said, his voice harsh, cracking like a whip. I snapped my head to him. "Do your job."

I blinked and took a breath. Smelling the stink and the age and the puzzle before us. "Yeah." I blew out the breath. "Thanks. If we look at Immanuel's modus operandi, he took power by drinking down lots of humans, and vamps with more power than he had. So maybe he and Adrianna and our headless Barbie here busted in and tried to drink Joses down. Maybe they wanted to kill him. Maybe they let him drink from them. Only problem is that Leo said Adrianna was with him the night Joses disappeared. Did she do Leo and then come here? To barter with Joseph? More blood and sex for the favor Leo refused her?"

"No damage to the door," Eli said, his eyes scouting the room again, "so she didn't break in." He stood and stepped to the tea trolley. "Three cups, but four saucers. No, wait." He leaned into the wall and said, "Four. One on the floor, broken. Santana was expecting company. He welcomed them in, brought them upstairs where it was private, got room service or a servant to send up tea. It started out proper and polite."

"Okay," I said. "I can see that. So maybe they were going to have tea and crumpets, or a business meeting, or a group blood and sex orgy, and things got out of hand."

"Or maybe they were going to let him feed off them in return for a sip of his blood. It's powerful enough for Leo to hold him prisoner for over a century so he could drink it. It had to pack an even bigger punch when Joseph was sane and well fed with the blood of other vamps."

"Or maybe they planned to trick Santana and just steal his blood. Some kind of power play." It was the sort of thing vamps did. I'd seen Leo after one such gang blood attack when he'd been nearly drained dry. It hadn't been pretty.

Eli walked around the room, taking care where he placed his feet. He opened the armoire, pulling on the small knob and then inserting his other hand in the bowed top of the door and yanking. The wood squealed and the door popped open with a splintering crack. Inside were piles of clothes that had rotted off the hangers and more evidence of mice. A small travel bag was on the bottom and Eli opened it, shook his head, and left it open. "Empty." He continued his survey. In a bottom armoire drawer, he found a second leather satchel, much like Bruiser's in style, meant to hold papers, but constructed of soft leather. Its mouth was open, and it was full of paper scraps, an ancient mouse nest. If the papers had once been important, they were now ruined, chewed and stained with mouse droppings and body fluids. With enough time, maybe an antiques specialist could restore the papers, but time wasn't something we had. Which left Leo's search at HQ.

If I hadn't been mentally wacko the last time I saw him, I could have beaten the truth out of Leo about Adrianna and about what happened the night that Santana had been taken prisoner. I made a mental note to carry brass knuckles next time I saw the MOC.

Eli said, "They might not have planned anything other than a meet and greet. We have no evidence to go on. But we do know that something went wrong."

"Like maybe Joseph Santana tasted Immanuel," I said, "and recognized that he wasn't just a fanghead, but an *u'tlun'ta* in fanghead skin. And that was when the poop hit the prop."

Eli nodded, considering, agreeing. "Could be. Could not be too. There was a short, fast fight. Not enough to break the furniture." He turned his head toward the room door and I heard a phone ring, an actual ring on a landline, and then Pinkie's voice answering, her tone professionally pleasant.

Eli said, "Headless Barbie tried to stake someone, let's say Santana. And let's say he was wearing the *arenciel* crystal. The crystal broke, and the *arenciel* bit . . . someone."

If captured and imprisoned in quartz crystal, *arenciels* could give their master control over time, much like I had over time when I was in the Gray Between—if I was willing to suffer the illness that followed. The one who captured an *arenciel* didn't have to worry about being sick after. Just about being bitten and poisoned if the creature got free.

"Some ones, maybe. And then, after the *arenciel* got free, one of the others beheaded her."

Eli nodded. "Maybe in retaliation for breaking the crystal."

I bent over the decapitated head to get a look at the damage to her vertebrae near her skull, then at her shoulders. "Whoever took her head was no novice. It's hard to take a head, and this was done with a single strike. Long sword, most likely, not a short sword, vamp-killer, ax, or hatchet."

Eli moved to where he thought the beheader had stood and mimed a sword strike at the likely location of the Barbie's head, when it was on her shoulders and not on the floor, when she was alive—undead, whatever—and standing. "Not much room," he said. "Unless . . ." He moved to the foot of the bed and examined the bedpost. "Sword strike continued upward and embedded the blade here. Discoloration in the nick. Blood probably. The wood is slivered, indicating that it took some effort to get the weapon free." Eli turned his attention to the blood spatter on the wall, which clearly marked where the swordsman had been standing. "We're assuming the sword's master was Santana, but that's an assumption neither backed up by, nor refuted by, the evidence."

I thought about my sword lessons. "He wouldn't have had only one weapon. A short sword to back up the long sword, probably, considering the close quarters. When one blade stuck after the beheading, he'd have used another and pulled the sword free later. If he lived. If not, then someone else did. You're right. Assumptions at this point are stupid."

"We work with what we've got," Eli said, ever the pragmatist. "So the crystal holding the *arcenciel* got broken, Santana was bitten, making him have both *arcenciel* poison and . . ." Eli looked around the room, thinking, evaluating. ". . . and maybe skinwalker blood in his body at the same time, though that too is an assumption."

"*U'tlun'ta*, not just skinwalker, blood," I clarified. Because I could never forget what awaited me at some point in my future. "It makes more and more sense that Joseph was bitten by the *arcenciel*, because he was captured shortly after whatever took place in this room," I said.

"We know Leo's predecessor ordered that Joseph be taken prisoner, but it might not have been *here*," Eli countered. "Leo might have tracked Joses from here, found him elsewhere when the SoD was injured and weak from an *arcenciel* bite and from drinking liver-eater blood. In which case Leo or Amaury could have taken him from anywhere."

"Right." I toed the rotten rug, which shredded beneath my faint kick. "We know that Leo drank from Santana for decades. He also drank from someone who had been bitten by an *arcenciel* at some point because when he was bitten not so long ago, he recuperated quickly," I said, "an immune response that may have saved his life. We know it wasn't Immanuel, because if he'd tasted Immanuel's blood, he'd have recognized the taste of my blood as being the same species. So we might be able to draw the conclusion from this broken crystal that Santana was bitten by the *arcenciel*"—I held up a second finger—"and that the poison made him crazy enough to be taken captive. That still leaves us with lots of questions and not enough answers."

"What we do know is that the next morning, when this room was discovered, Joses—correction, Joseph—had been disappeared. At some point after that, the room was sealed; at some point Joseph was turned over to Amaury or Leo; at some point Bethany tasted Santana's blood; and at some point the SoD was hung on the sub-five dungeon wall at fanghead HQ. At which point he was a raving maniac."

"Yeah." It wasn't enough. I didn't know enough. As usual. "We need to ask someone what happened that night. And try to get a straight answer."

"Good luck with that. Adrianna, Joseph, and Leo are the only ones still alive to question," Eli said, amused. "One has scrambled brains, one is drinking people to death, and the other has never been overly forthcoming with the truth."

I thought about the brass knuckles and beating the truth from Leo. Reluctantly, I said, "There's Bethany."

"Ditto on the loony tunes," Eli said.

"I wonder where Leo got the painting of Adrianna and Barbie. It was with stuff that came from his clan home when it burned, but I never saw it until it was on sub-four. Bruiser said Leo was searching for things pertaining to Santana, so I have to wonder how many other things and bits of evidence there are."

"Diaries?" Eli asked. "Dear Diary, Today I intend to stake the Son of Darkness. Then a sleepover with my bestie, Adrianna."

"Okay. Ha-ha. But what about newspapers? Gossip columns were big in the day."

Eli's mouth turned down and he nodded as he considered that. "Alex can check through archived newspapers. I'll look on sub-four and search the room Adrianna used at HQ." He frowned. "It's on sub-four too."

"Nothing vamps do is coincidence. I'll talk to Leo." With or without brass knucks and the use of physical violence. "He was here. I need to know more about what he saw." I started out of the room.

Eli looked at the damaged bedpost. "Sometime soon, we need to get in some more sword practice. We may need it."

"Until further notice, we carry multiple silver crosses and silver ammo."

"I'll get some holy water from a priest I know," Eli said, "because I doubt we'll be welcomed back to The Church anytime soon."

I stuck my hands in my pockets and frowned at that thought. I had liked the small church and the earnest preacher. "Let's get out of here and get Pinkie to reseal the door. We may need back in later. Or not. But until we're done with the room, Leo needs to leave the dead vamp." I yawned, all the energy I had been expending suddenly gone. "And I need a nap."

"This one alone, so you actually get some sleep?"

"Shut up," I said, too tired to blush.

We said our good-byes to Pinkie, gave her instructions about the room, and made it to the vehicle. Eli turned on the radio to a local channel to hear that there was a crowd gathering outside of vamp HQ, demonstrating about the Fifty-two Killer. Swell. They had named him. That was never a good sign. I fell asleep on the way home, and when we arrived, Eli sent me to bed like a little girl. I was so tired I didn't argue.

CHAPTER 12

So Many Things I Couldn't Say Aloud

What felt like only minutes later and long before dark, I heard a knock on the front door. Pulling a pillow over my head, I tried to ignore it, until I heard a soft meow. In one flowing, fast move, I shoved back the covers, rolled to my feet, grabbed up the robe hanging over the bathroom door, shoved in my arms, and yanked open the bedroom door. Molly stood on the other side, the foyer lights tinting her red hair, a small cat in her arms. Her scent filled my nostrils—fresh-baked bread, herbs, soil, and cat. Heedless of the claws, I threw my arms around my best friend and her familiar.

Neither one responded instantly, but a heartbeat later, I heard a thump, felt the vibration of something heavy hitting the floor. *Suitcase,* I thought. And one of Molly's arms came around me. The gesture was hesitant, then grew more firm as she pulled me closer. The cat between us started purring.

The hesitation in my best friend had been odd. But so was the feel of her in my arms. I realized that I had never hugged Molly. Not spontaneously. Maybe not at all, ever. I wasn't a hugger. Which was really stupid. I should be able to give my best friend in the world a hug. And then I thought that maybe Molly was afraid to hug people now, what with her magic being so wonky. And so maybe this hug was good for both of us in ways I couldn't even speculate on. "I missed you," I said.

Molly said, "I missed you too."

I wasn't sure how one backed away from a friendly hug. That wasn't covered in ballroom dance class. So I patted her shoulders with both hands as a warning that I was getting ready to move, and stepped back, freeing her. The calico cat—who was still tiny but was probably nearly full grown by now—jumped out of Molly's arm and onto my shoulder. Her claws sank lightly into my flesh, which made me hiss in discomfort, and she clung close as she stuck her nose into my ear, still purring. Molly, one hand still gripping my right arm, smiled happily up at me.

"I'm glad you're here," I said. "So, so, *so* glad."

The light in Molly's eyes dimmed, and she lowered her gaze from my face to her hand on my arm. "Something happened to you." She released me and stepped back, looking me over. "Your aura is all wrong. What happened?"

"I was going to tell you earlier, but you were trying to catch your flight."

"Jane was hit with a spell from a very old vamp who started life as a witch, Molly," Eli called from the kitchen. "It messed up her skinwalker magics. Why don't you freshen up? I'll toss some steaks on the grill and put a salad together. Then we can debr—visit."

I smiled at Eli's change in vocabulary from military to civilian-friendly. And kept my eyes on Molly. She looked great.

"Your room is waiting for you, Miz Molly," Alex said. "Clean sheets, fresh towels in the bath, and the cleaning service even dusted the ceiling fan." To me he added, "They'll be back tomorrow to clean your room. They got the rest of the house while you snored." He picked up Molly's bag, which she had dropped when we hugged, and carried it upstairs.

"I don't know which statement is weirder. You getting hit with a spell and having your skinwalker energies all out of kilter or you having a housecleaning service." Molly said. "You were hit with a spell?" she prodded.

I rubbed my arm where she had gripped me and lifted my cat-weighted shoulder in what would have been an off-hand shrug if she hadn't looked so worried. "Yeah. A bad one. I guess we need to talk."

"Yes. We do." Molly turned and went up the stairs, leaving the cat purring into my ear.

Dinner was more than just steaks and raw green stuff, and from Molly's perspective it must have seemed perfect. Eli had made a broccoli casserole with cheese, baked fresh rolls, and a blackberry cobbler, which was a more family-style meal than the fat free, low-carb, raw veggies and protein, or pizza, that we usually ate. I had to push the cat away twice while I devoured my bloody rare steak. No wonder the cat clung to me. I was the only one who knew how to eat meat. Even Eli ate his steak less bloody than mine.

While we ate, the boys caught Molly up to date on the supernatural happenings in New Orleans, especially the parts that pertained to me, the vamps, Joses/Joseph, the kill bar, and the spell I'd been hit with. I listened with half an ear, using the opportunity to let the current events settle into some sort of order in my mind. And wished I had an order for the events in the vamp boardinghouse.

I sliced steak and ate, sopped bloody meat juices with rolls, chewed, swallowed, and drank iced tea, listening until they reached the part about the spell and what it did to me.

Molly watched me carefully as Eli described everything that had happened. When he was done with his monologue, Molly set down her knife and fork and said, softly, "I want to know the exact sequence of events the night you saved my children from blood-sacrifice at the hands of the Damours. Not the fighting parts, but the part where your blood came into contact with the blood diamond."

"Are you sure you can listen to this without getting upset? Your magic . . . ?" It had been a long time since we talked about the night when her children were in a witch circle about to be sacrificed.

"Yes," Molly said, irritation lacing her voice. "I'm fine."

I pushed the last bite of steak across my plate with my fork, no longer hungry. I put down the fork and rubbed my right hand with my left. *Odd. It was my right hand that night too.*

"I was with Derek and some of his men, in the woods of the park. By the time we found the vampire-witches, they had started passing the gem—the blood diamond—from person to person. Each one of them cut themselves with a glass athame, obsidian, I think, which I later found out meant it was chemically inert."

Molly nodded in agreement, her dinner forgotten. KitKit jumped into her lap and Molly absently stroked the cat.

"Anyway, they each dripped blood onto the diamond. It got brighter and redder each time, as if it took power from each of them or was activated by the power in the blood of each of them." I closed my eyes, as much to keep from seeing Molly's face as to help me remember. The scene of the black-arts ceremony opened before me, as if imprinted on the backs of my eyelids. I started sweating; my breathing sped.

Beast rose in me, padding to the forefront of my memory. *Stopped them,* she rumbled at me. *Killers of kits. All dead except the female with hair like blood.*

She was talking about Adrianna, and though cats don't see color the same way humans do, Beast had learned to use my eyes, much as I had learned to use hers. She understood the concept of red.

I nodded to her and went on. "We had to see how they set up the circle to stop the ceremony and take the diamond, but we also had to interrupt it before the circle was solidly set, or we'd be locked out of it and too late to act. After all five of the participants had sacrificed their blood to the gem, the leader, the bald-headed vamp, took up a solid-silver athame, which meant he was about to start the children's sacrifice." Remembered fear shivered through me and the words caught in my throat. My voice was tight when I went on.

"I made sure the sliver of the Blood Cross was easy to hand but still in its bag. I had been warned that it could damage me if I got pricked with it." I shook a hand as if waving away that thought. "Anyway. It was my job to get to the leader and prick him with the wood. We attacked. Derek's men opened fire with silver shot. The leader—Baldy—took some hits. They all did. But even with silver, the vamps weren't falling. We ran into the clearing. I cut my face on a branch." I touched my cheek, remembering.

"It happened really fast. Hicklin, one of Derek's men, died, his death blood hitting the circle, powering it. Derek stopped Baldy's blade with his own, saving Little Evan. The magic had already started to rise. The spell of the circle attacked us as if it was alive, as if it had a mind of its own. Motes of power burrowing under our skin."

"Like the magic that attacked Leo when he was fighting the blood duel," Eli said softly.

I nodded but didn't open my eyes. "The men were still shooting and the weaker vamps started the death keening. It was awful. We killed Rafael Torres, who was Leo's enemy and was mind joined to Adrianna. Derek and two other men staked her.

"I dove for Baldy, but he seemed to know I was coming, what I had planned. He reached out and shoved the blood diamond into my wound. And he said a *wyrd*. I had never felt pain like that, cold and searing hot all at once." The memory flooded through me, as if it had been only waiting for the right moment to attack me again.

The gem had been icy, cold and flame. Just like the spell I was only recently rid of. Colder than the dark of space, colder than a night spent in hell, as the life force was ripped out of me. "I went limp. The gem was tearing all the warmth from my body, and I could *see* it happen, could see the life force move out of me and into the gem in a single heartbeat."

My mouth was dry as memory brought it all back. The pain had seared every nerve, twisted every muscle. "I was dying. I knew that," I whispered, more a rasp than human speech. I swallowed against the pain but it gave me no real relief. "The *wyrd* was a spell," I said, explaining it to Eli and Alex, "but not like the *wyrd* that Santana said. This was a three-time spell, meaning you had to say it three times to invoke the power. The first utterance froze me, paralyzed me. I couldn't even take a breath. I fell, leaving Baldy standing over me. I was dying, but . . . I had to save the children."

The silence around the table was intense. I didn't open my eyes. I had finally told Molly and Big Evan that their daughter, my goddaughter, Angelina, had gathered raw power and thrown it at Baldy, an offensive weapon of concentrated energies, guided solely by her need and intent. But the Youngers didn't need to know that. At the same instant Angie Baby had released her power, however, the leader had spoken his spell again. So many things I couldn't say aloud to protect my godchildren.

I opened my eyes and looked at Molly, but was talking to the Youngers. "Baldy said the *wyrd* the second time, and this time the *wyrd* power went up and out to do something. I don't know what."

Baldy had been hit with Angie's power and he hadn't spoken the third *wyrd*. He hadn't bent to kill the children or spoken again. And then Angie Baby touched me and sent her energy into me, but this time with the intent to heal me. Both nascent workings had worked. Her raw, guided magic had saved my life. And Molly knew what I was leaving out and why.

"I pulled the sliver of wood from its bag. It burned some, but not much. Baldy was wearing the blood diamond, still coated with my blood, around his neck on its chain. And I launched up at him." I reached out with my right hand, fingers and thumb miming the grip from that night, as if I still held the wood from the Blood Cross. "It pierced him, in his chest, just below the gem. His blood pulsed out. Up and over the gem, mixing with my blood, and then over the wood of the cross."

"Mixing," Molly said, her voice soft.

I nodded, realizing now that something had happened that night, something unexpected and unknown. "The spell broke. Baldy caught fire at the point where the Blood Cross touched him. He almost exploded with a white heat and flame. It consumed him from the wound out. My fingers flamed. My hair caught on fire. I remember the smell. All the vamps were dead. All the humans were either dead or dying, the motes of power from the *wyrd* spell still attacking them. But he hadn't finished the spell. He never said it the third time to invoke it. But I didn't know how to save the other humans."

Angie Baby had told me to use the blood diamond to stop the magic. I'd had no idea how to do that, but I had no better ideas. My voice dropped as I recalled the last of that terrible night. "I pulled a silver vamp-killer and dug the necklace out of Baldy's burned rib cage and held it up. And nothing happened. And I started this ... this death laughter. The kind crazy people do when the world is ending," I whispered, remembering the sound, remembering that Angie Baby had saved me and that I couldn't say that aloud where others might hear. "The power of the dark spell stopped.

And it flew back into the diamond. And all the children lived. And all the humans lived except Hicklin. I liked Hicklin. He was good people."

"Oh, Jane," Molly breathed.

Baldy's spell wasn't the same spell spoken by Santana, but it had contained the same kind of concentrated, enormous power. Power that had been gathered and shaped but never released. Was that unspoken spell like a weapon, primed and aimed but never fired? Was all that power still in the gem, waiting to be used? I opened my eyes. "I used the gem myself, didn't I? When I wanted the gem to call back its power, it did. My will made it happen."

Molly looked down at her hands, holding the cat, which had fallen asleep in her lap. After long moments, she nodded, the motion jerky, as if unwilling.

"I'm tied to it, aren't I? Not just able to be tracked by it, but tied to it. *Joined.* The blood diamond and the bracelet that the Son of Darkness was wearing. And because of that, I'm tied to *him.*"

She murmured, "You are likely tied to the Blood Cross, *and* the bracelet, *and* the diamond."

"So . . . what do I do?"

Molly shook her head. "I don't know what. But I have a bad feeling that we'll find out soon. And worse, Lachish may be able to see that you are tied to a black-arts artifact. She'll know just how dangerous you are and how dangerous Joseph Santana is. And she may want to kill you for it."

"She can try," Eli said.

"The biggest failure of that night was that no one went back and beheaded the vamps," I said. "I should have. It was my job."

"You were hurt," Eli said. "You had to get the children back to their parents."

"So I didn't finish my job. Making all this my fault."

"Leo knew. It was the MOC's ultimate responsibility," Eli said. "The buck stopped with him. And he played a different game."

"Game," I said. "Vamps have always played games with human and witch lives. I doubt it's changed much now. I have to wonder if it ever will."

CHAPTER 13

Manis and Pedis and Gossiping About Boys

When Eli and I pulled away from the curb in front of my house it was after dark and we still had no idea where the murderer had laired during the day. We had no idea where he would attack that night. We hadn't killed him, hadn't even tracked him. And Molly had no idea how to keep me from being tracked by the blood diamond—which was in my gobag, to keep it away from Molly. Not that I believed she would give in to temptation and use it. Unless she thought she had a reason. Kinda like me, but way worse. I might be able to use the stored energies in the diamond to power . . . something. But Molly could use it, direct its energies like a precision tool, her death magics melding with it. And forever changing who she was. Her death magics told her that she *should* use it.

I saw Mol's witch energies flow over the house, warding it as we drove away, her once blue-tinted power now shot through with other colors, none of them pretty.

I slumped down in the seat, pressing Jodi's cell number on speed dial. There was no answer and it went to voice mail. "Calling you at the woo-woo room," I said, and pressed END before hitting her office number. When she answered, she should have sounded professional. Instead she sounded snarked out. "What the hell do you want?"

"Dang caller ID," I muttered. "Update for law enforcement. We found an old lair today. No bad guy there." A true-dead vamp lying on the floor, but there were a lot of reasons not to tell her just then: the jurisdiction was murky on dead vamps, Jodi didn't have time to work up a cold case, and she wouldn't care about dead vamps while humans and witches were in danger. "Alex is working through old property records for possible lairs for the suspect. Leo is searching for hard copies for the same and for human blood-servants who might still be alive. Eli and I are heading to vamp HQ. Did you have your little talk with Leo yet? And if so, did you play nice or did you haul him in to NOPD in the trunk of a car in broad daylight?"

"That interview has yet to take place." Jodi's voice rose into a snarl. "The governor nixed it. So you tell the MOC that the city's in lockdown thanks to his fangheads. That means no tax money from restaurants, hotels, or other sources of tourist income. Meanwhile, every cop on payroll is on duty and riding the streets, two to a car. It's costing overtime—lots of overtime. Law enforcement morale is at a post-Katrina low at the same time that the populace as a whole are getting itchy trigger fingers." Her words sped up and I held the cell out for Eli to hear better, though I doubted that he had missed anything so far.

"Every guns-and-ammo business in the city and most of the parish has sold out of silver-lead-mixed ammo and handguns, and inventory of high-powered rifles is down to single digits. Liquor sales are at an all-time high, making the populace trigger-happy and mean. And we've already pulled a dozen drunk and armed good ol' boys off the streets. They're in lockup now, making a racket I can hear in my office."

Which was in the basement. Right. I started to comment but Jodi rushed on. "The media is bitching about witches and vamps, and to make my day even better, the state senators, representatives, and the oh-so-not-helpful governor are heading down for photo ops in time for the evening news. Which I have to attend," she barked.

"Ah," I said, understanding. Jodi was an investigator first and foremost, not a pretty-faced spokesperson for the TV screen. "How about the Master of the City asks you and the government bigwigs to his headquarters for a little tête-à-tête about the ongoing investigation?"

"I have a better idea. Ask him to invite the PTBs over and do a press conference. Without me!"

I gave an uncertain huff of breath. Leo was a totally political animal, and on-screen, he practically glowed with elegant bonhomie, but informing him he needed to play kiss-up wasn't what I had planned for tonight. The MOC didn't like it when I got bossy. "Ummm . . ."

Jodi pushed. "I can get the politicians to vamp HQ in time for the ten o'clock news. Tonight."

"I can ask."

"Do that. Call me back." The call ended.

"You need a girls' day, you two, manis and pedis and gossiping about boys."

"Bite me, Eli."

My partner just chuckled.

The crowd of protestors and spectators was bigger than I had expected. Way bigger. They lined the sidewalk beneath the second-story gallery across from the Council Chambers six deep, and the smell of booze and weed was strong. So was the smell of aggression. I could hear them muttering through the body of the armored vehicle. Muttering and shouting the usual vamp hate slogans. *Vamps go home.* (Where was that?) *Humans only. Kill the vamps. Stake the vamps.* The usual. But there was an underlying energy to it this time. Aggression. Anger. Purpose. They got louder as we pulled into the circular drive in front of vamp HQ.

Cops, both on scooters and mounted—on horses— patrolled up and down the street itself, keeping the travel lanes open. There were two marked cars patrolling the side streets. When we emerged from the vehicle, the shouting got louder. They knew who I was. The entire group took up the catcall. "Vamp whore! Vamp whore! Vamp whore!"

Wasn't that sweet?

They got louder with the insults as we climbed the steps to the front entrance; the armored glass did little to mute the taunts. We were decked out in vamp-hunting gear, the new headsets, and weapons, which meant we had to go through the usual pat-down by HQ's armed security guys. These were the new guys, who had come in from Atlanta after I beheaded the master of that city, and while I had worked with them, I didn't know them as well as I did some of the older men. They weren't good ol' boys, but they were just as jumpy as the rest of the New Orleans populace, maybe more so, because the Son of Darkness had to have a grudge against anyone at his former prison, and he had mad powers. If he wanted back in here, he could make that happen, and that meant he'd likely come through them. No one would be safe. In fact, I seriously doubted that anyone would be left breathing. Or unbreathing.

At the elevator, Eli said, "I'll be on sub-four."

"I'll meet you there when I'm done."

Leo's office door was open. I had never arrived there to find it open, and seeing it wide made me feel off-kilter. The MOC looked fine, however, and was sitting in his swivel chair to the side of his desk, where I could see him, staring at the large screen mounted behind his desk. One elbow rested on the desk, his head on that hand, his legs crossed. He looked like a human city boy, a metrosexual, dressed in slacks and a loose shirt, relaxed, and gorgeous enough to make women and most men drool.

The security monitor was synced to his TV screen, giving Leo a vision of both main and back entrances in continuous view, and a rotating series of screens from other cameras. There were too many cams for one person to monitor, and before the current troubles, I had been working to arrange it so that the less-used cameras were run by simple computer programs that would collect data, collate the changes—people passing, whatever—and show only the changes, when called upon. That job wasn't finished yet. A lot of things weren't finished yet. If I died, someone else would have that responsibility.

Was I morbid or what?

I decided on a good offense being the best defense. "Evening, Leo. Two things. One, I need access to Adrianna. Two, Louisiana senators and representatives are flying in from Washington. A press conference with the Master of the City, at his Council Chambers, with the mayor and the governor would be good PR and might help to settle the humans." Leo didn't move, didn't react, and I couldn't tell by sight or smell if he was tense, terrified, or relaxed. "I'd like Jodi to arrange it."

Leo still didn't react, and I hated it when vamps did that still-as-a-block-of-marble thing. It made me want to do something annoying. So I walked over to the gold chaise longue, jumped up into the air, and landed flat on my butt and legs. It made a satisfying creak of springs and a very solid *whump*, followed by a sound that might be best described as a *sproo-OOO-ooiing*. "Oops," I said. "I think I broke your feeding couch."

Leo was watching me from the corners of heavy-lidded eyes, his mouth curled in amusement. "Yes. I do believe you did," he said. He cocked his head and his black hair slid along the curve of his jaw, as soundless and gleaming as black silk, until it rested against the edge of his hand. I knew how it felt to touch that hair and curled my fingers under at the memory. "As of dusk tonight, you are no longer my Enforcer," he said. "You cannot be bound. You are not a blood-servant, whose thoughts and loyalties are known to me. Tell me, Jane Yellowrock. Why do I keep your blood in your veins? Why do I allow your continued existence?"

"I amuse you. And I'm valuable to you, both now, to catch Santana, and when the ESs get here."

"Ee-eses?" he asked.

"European suckheads."

Leo let the small smile widen across his face. "Amusement is important to the very old among us," he agreed. "You may not have access to Adrianna." Which confirmed that she was still undead. Undead with scrambled brains, but undead.

"Adelaide has collated what information I have on the Son of Darkness, though my people are still looking for a safe, filled with deeds, that was rescued from the clan home and delivered here.

"You may inform your policewoman, who is the daughter of witches—do not think that I have forgotten that, my Jane—," he added as an aside, "that I will meet with the senators, representatives, the governor, and the mayor, here, in time for the late-night news." He pressed a button on his desk. "Adelaide, please see to it that the elected officials, state, local, and those arriving from Washington, are invited here for drinks and a private discussion, to be followed by a press announcement in the ballroom. Standard security precautions will apply to the press."

"I'll arrange it all, Mr. Pellissier," Del said. Her voice sounded dull and toneless. Competent, yes, but dull and toneless.

"Thank you," Leo said, ending the connection.

I swiveled my body so I was sitting on the edge of the chaise and facing Leo. "Adelaide Mooney is a skilled and capable lawyer. In her last position to the blood-master of Clan Shaddock, she assisted with all manner of things political, legal, and"—I rolled my hand in the air—"vital stuff. Shaddock's *assistant* did the secretarial things."

"What are you trying to say, my Jane? That I mistreat my primo?"

"No. That you should use her for the important stuff and let your secundo do the invitation-level stuff. You're wasting an asset, and that isn't like you." I propped my elbows on my knees and placed my fingertips together in front of my chin. I had a lot of subjects to cover and not much time, but this seemed important. "I'm betting that you're sleeping with her, drinking from her, and making her feel worthless all at the same time. Stop being stupid, Leo. Send her flowers, one of those handwritten notes you do so well, and start treating her like she deserves."

"She deserves for me to be in love with her," Leo said, stopping me. "Sadly, I am not." And weirdly, he did sound sad, as if his life would be much easier if he was in love with Del.

"So give her better jobs and stop sleeping with her. Let her develop a relationship with someone else, which won't happen if all the other vamps know you're poking her."

Leo murmured, "Poking her?" his words now laden with laughter. It was only now that I realized how stiff and tight his voice had been. The stress of dealing with the escape of Santana had to be wearing on him.

"Yeah. Tell me more about the night Santana went missing."

Leo went still again, but this time it was the stillness of a rabbit caught out in the open. He hadn't expected me to ask about that, or at least not then.

"Tell me about the *arcenciel* and the broken crystal

prison and the dead body at Acton House. You sent me there, so you had to know what we'd find."

Leo took a breath, filling his lungs, his eyes far away as if he gazed into the past. He said, "To tell you about the night the Son of Darkness did not rise is to tell you about only the end." Leo's tone and words slid into that mesmerizing vamp cadence, the tonal qualities like silk velvet, stroking the listener's very soul. "It would be like telling you only about the finale of a film, without telling you about the first three acts, without telling you of the conflicts that arose and were resolved, or the dialogue, or the musical score." His eyes were dark, the irises nearly as black as the pupils, his lashes long and full, Frenchy black. His jaw was firm and his olive skin smooth, if far too pale and perfect for a human. Leo Pellissier was beautiful, as most vamps were, and he wasn't above using that beauty to get what he wanted, but there was no tug of compulsion now, no sense of deceit or of spin. Instead there was bewilderment and more than a hint of worry. "But we have no time to share all that happened, to allow you to see, and understand, and know for certain the nuances that made his visitation and his disappearance so devastating."

"Disappearance," I said evenly.

Leo shrugged a languid shoulder, rolling, but it looked staged, planned, something to make me think he was relaxed when he really wasn't. "Disappearance is what we called it for so long, to protect us. It feels right to call it thus, even now, with the truth revealed. The might and weight of years."

"Okay. I get that. So just start with the twenty-four hours before the sunset when he was discovered to be . . . not himself."

"It feels strange to speak it aloud," he mused, "this secret I have kept so long and so well." He shook his head as if shaking away his bemusement and settled his body into the desk chair, the motion so human and yet so graceful. "I remember few details about the week prior. It was Mardi Gras, and there were feasting and dancing and balls aplenty. There were parties at each of the clan homes. One in particular in Mearkanis Clan Home. There were two women there that Santana liked, both human blood-slaves, sisters, twins. They were tiny and Asian, their blood a rare vintage even for him. He was besotted and wanted to add the Ming sisters to his stable."

I took note of the word *stable* (as if the women had been horses) and the location, filing both away.

"He offered their master a goodly price for them both, with a promise of immortality, but was refused. The humans became a bone of contention between Santana and Mearkanis Clan blood-master Mishael Chrysostomos. He turned the women and made them his scions to keep them out of Santana's clutches, and both later rose to great power among the Mithrans, one as blood-master to Clan Mearkanis. Had Blood-Master Ming herself not disappeared, we might not be facing such calamities now."

"Wait," I interrupted, not able to help myself, and putting two and two together with my known history of the clans. "The former Blood-Master Ming, of Clan Mearkanis, started out as a blood-slave? And . . . her name was *Ming*? Like the blood-master of Clan Glass in Knoxville?"

"Yes. It is rare that one addicted to Mithran blood will rise to such leadership positions, but both Ming sisters were strong. Though Clan Mearkanis is no more, the name Ming still rings with power. Ming is *remembered*." He said the last word as if it had meaning in a ceremonial sense. "If Ming's heir did not deface them, there are paintings of Ming and one of Joseph Santana in the rooms she once claimed as her own."

I wanted to ask all about the Mings, but I *needed* to hear the story of Santana, and it seemed like Leo was being a little more forthcoming than usual.

Leo leaned over and pressed a button on his desk, ringing for tea to be brought up. When he was done he rearranged his features into a more pedantic cast, and I knew that the storytelling was ended and the business of recalling the past, with its myriad slants and biases, had begun.

"Though I did not attend, there was *un petit bal* at Mearkanis Clan Home, full of pomp and ceremony, but according to those who attended, it was *tout à fait ennuyeux*." He translated without my asking, "It was utterly boring. It began at ten of the evening and ended two hours after midnight, which made it a dismal failure."

A faint smile crossed Leo's face and his voice began to sound more French as he took the trip into his past. "Successful parties of the time lasted through the night and often into the next day, taken into lairs and . . ." Leo waved the thought away with an indolent hand, but I got the idea. Caligula had nothing on the vamps.

"You weren't there?"

"No. *J'ai eu d'autres plans*." When I raised my eyebrows in question, he added, "I had other plans. In the early evening I was with Adrianna and one of her friends. Adrianna wanted something, I no longer remember what. When I refused her, she and her paramour left in a righteous fury."

"You drank from them and boinked them and then turned them down."

Leo shook his head, his black hair swinging until he tucked it behind his ear. "Americans have such crass names for lovemaking."

It didn't sound like lovemaking to me, but I kept my opinion to myself.

"Later in the evening, I was with Katie and one of her new girls. In the days after, I discovered that when Adrianna and her friend left my apartments, they went to the Mearkanis *bal*. Santana left the party with them, *ce qui a peut-être contribué à l'éclatement de la soirée*. Forgive me. Which may have contributed to the breakup of the evening.

"In those times of horse and carriage, travel across the city was time-consuming and often used for business or lovemaking or even sleep. We know that when the trio arrived at Acton House, their clothing was awry and the scent of blood was strong in the closed confines of the carriage. Santana ordered tea and a small repast to be prepared, and the three retired to his room. They were later joined by others, but these were not seen by the maître d'hôtel. There was clearly a scuffle, though no one heard anything out of the ordinary."

"Of course, with vamps, screams and loud noises were commonplace."

"*Oui, oui. Vous dîtes la vérité*. When the maître d'hôtel, Professor Acton, brought breakfast just after sunset—a young mulatto boy, as ordered—he discovered the room, with the body of Adrianna's paramour on the floor, and Santana, who was on the bed. The professor sent the boy to collect me in my rooms, and I sent word to Amaury, who was across the river in the clan home."

A young mulatto boy, as ordered. A boy. For breakfast. It took effort, but I kept my face clear of my thoughts, and my heartbeat even and steady. Not easy when I really wanted to smack Leo for his callous cruelty. "What shape was Santana in?" I asked, my words flat.

"Pardon?"

At Leo's polite query, I clarified. "When I saw him in your dungeon, he was a bag of leather-covered bones. What did he look like when you found him?"

"Physically, he was thin, his flesh rough and browned, as if scarred, what is called keloid scarring. He had lost the ability of coherent speech. He had lost the ability to control his bowels. He was raving and dangerous, and when my uncle arrived he established control and sent us into action. We gathered Santana up in his coach and carried him to the Council Chambers, which were much smaller and less stately than now, but which had the deep basements spelled to keep out groundwater. We removed the scions from the lowest basement and secured them in a separate scion lair. We prepared the wall for Santana. Amaury sent me back to seal the room at Acton House, and he put out the word that . . . *le Fils des Ténèbres avait disparu avec les marées.* Meaning that Santana had sailed on the tide."

"So who was the fourth person at Santana's party?"

"I do not know. No one does."

I knew. Immanuel. Not that I'd tell Leo that his son had been there. Too much angst where the dead heir was concerned. "And the young boy? The one who was supposed to be *breakfast?*"

Leo's eyes lost the glossy light of distant memories and focused on me, taking in my body language and scent. His eyes went steely. "He entered my uncle's employ, where he served, *happily*, until the end of his days."

"Yeah. I'm sure he did." And this time I couldn't keep the loathing out of my voice.

"Times were different then, *mon chat*," Leo said, his words laced with threat. "Social and political mores were different then. It was nothing to see such a boy selling himself in the streets to buy a crust of bread. Do not judge what you cannot comprehend from your easy life in this day and time."

To which I had nothing to say. Nothing at all. Not I, who

had helped my grandmother kill a man when I was five, more than a hundred fifty years ago.

"You are dismissed."

I stood and left the room, but not because he had told me to.

My head full of Leo's voice, like velvet sliding along my mind, I left the office and followed Eli to sub-four, tracking him by smell to the odd little room I had discovered once before. That time, I had entered through a hidden stairway that opened in the closet, to find everything rotted and hanging off the hangers. The room beyond had been in as bad a condition, so dusty it was a health hazard. It had been sealed off, as if a shrine to someone departed. Only later had I learned that the room had been Adrianna's. I'd had the secret stairway access closed off and sent someone in to clean out the place, but I hadn't been back to inspect it.

I came in through the hallway. The room was totally different, with new carpet, the walls painted with shiny golden tones. There were new, copper-toned linens on the modern, Swedish-style, black-painted bed, the furniture having sleek lines and contemporary chic. I sniffed, picking up Eli's scent and the slightly older but still powerful scent of Adrianna. She had spent enough time there to imprint on the room, she and two human blood-servants. No one had mentioned them, and I had a feeling that they were among the humans who had been laid out on the sub-five floor, drained and happy, and then turned. They'd be no use to me for at least ten years, when they finished the curing process and re-emerged as fangheads.

Eli was standing at the foot of the unmade bed, a new, wheeled, lightweight, carry-on piece of luggage in a floral pattern opened out on the mattress before him. He had shed his leather jacket and stood where he could see every angle of the room, wearing T-shirt, leather pants, combat boots, and headset. "Been calling you, babe," he said, mildly. "Pinged your cell, which you didn't answer. Called you on the headset. Which you didn't answer. Ten more minutes and I'd have been forced to come looking for you."

Which, in Eli's lingo, meant a search and rescue with dead vamp bodies left behind as he pulled me from the resultant carnage. I pulled out the small ear- and mouthpiece and looked it over. It showed a missed call. I tossed it to Eli. "When I'm with Leo, I try not to answer the cell," I said. "It would be like a soldier answering his cell when he's visiting in the Oval Office."

Eli nodded, not appeased but accepting, and tossed the headset back. "Remember to charge it. Batteries are low." His hands went back to feeling along the inside of the suitcase. "Adrianna and her blood-servants were planning a quick getaway," he said. "Packed, papers ready"—he tossed a packet to the bed and four passports slid out—"four first-class airline tickets to France."

"Which is where the European vamp council meets," I said. I watched him, studying the room. It was awfully neat for anything Adrianna touched. "Why four airline tickets? And whose is the fourth passport?" I asked, knowing the answer.

"Thought you'd never ask," Eli said, flipping the suitcase over, checking the zippered pouches. "Joseph Santana." He glanced up and back to the work, now searching the bed.

"They planned to take him out of here," I said, only a little surprised. "How'd they get a passport for a vamp who's been missing for decades?"

"I have Alex working on that, but I'd be surprised if the Kid gets anywhere. Joseph's papers originated in France, with an entrance stamp for last month. It's real and legitimate."

"Last month?"

"Yes. Adrianna's visit to Leo had to originate with the European vamps."

I blinked, watching Eli's hands as he continued the search into the drawers and the closet. "Yeah. That makes sense."

"Been thinking about our need to track all visitors while they're in HQ," he said. "Armbands are still our best bet, with locator chips we can ping as needed, and that send out an alarm if cut off. Maybe headsets too, but both could be removed. I've had Alex looking into feasibility and cost estimates."

"Getting European suckheads to wear tracking bracelets will be tricky."

"They'll think it's insulting," he agreed.

"Okay. Add that to the list of things to 'Figure out Before Suckheads Arrive.' FOBSA."

"No one's touched this room since we saw Adrianna last," Eli said, concentrating on the task at hand. "She packed light. A corset, silk jammies, a silk dress, and lots of lacy underthings." He held up a demi-bra that was wired, constructed to provide lots of lift, and was mostly see-through lace. It had to itch. I made a face that said *yuck*. Eli gave me his business grin, a twitch that went nowhere, and lifted a thong with one finger of the other hand. Double itch.

"Makeup case, shampoo, lotion and perfume stuff, and jewelry case."

"Jewelry case. Lemme see." I held out a hand and he tossed me a padded, cloth-covered box, which I caught and unzipped, to reveal a lot of gold. Real gold. Ancient stuff that Adrianna had hung on to for centuries. There was a gold cuff bracelet shaped like a snake climbing her upper arm, and an etched gold torque. The torque was shaped like a half-moon, to rest on her collarbones. She had been wearing the bracelet and necklace the night she and her two pet scions had tried to kill me. Kinda hard to forget something like that.

I ran my fingers over the Celtic symbols on the torque, and magic tingled on my skin. "Why not wear her good jewelry when she went to see the Son of Darkness? The dress she was wearing was fancy, so why not the gold jewelry?"

"Would it interfere with a magical working?" Eli asked, stuffing the lacy nothings back in the luggage.

"She was wearing them the night she was staked by Derek's men, and that was a mega-spell. So I don't think so. She was wearing them when the painting was done, and by the clothing, that was a long time before Santana went missing," I said.

Holding the jewelry case to my nose, I sniffed. The scent of magic on the gold was weak. If the scent had come from a spell or working placed on or in the pieces themselves, then it had been used up long ago. If the gold had simply been in the presence of magic for a long time and had picked up the trace scents, then it might have been there recently. But the scent of magic was definitely there. "I can't tell if it was ever used in a magical working or not. I'll have to ask Molly if gold is ever a part of active workings."

"Gold transmits electricity. Electricity is energy. Magic is energy. Therefore, gold *should* transmit magic."

"Yeah." I zipped up the jewelry box. "Too much of this is all about the past, and the past is written by the victor, if it was written at all." I frowned as something tickled the back of my mind. "I don't know. Something feels all wonky about this whole thing."

"Ya think?" Eli ran his hands over and under the pillows and across the linens, doing a vamp-bed pat-down. Satisfied there was nothing there, he lifted the mattresses, checking under each one before bending to one knee and peeking under the bed. I went to the closet and found three pairs of shoes, two pairs of which were five-inch stilettoes: one pair in black ostrich skin and one pair of high-glam, high-gloss ruby sparkles, like what Dorothy might have worn if she danced on a brass pole for a living. I held up the ruby pair for Eli to see, putting that pole-dancer image together with the lacy undies, and it wasn't so farfetched. I chuckled at the image and put the shoes back in the closet with the third pair—dainty sandals of gold leather. Odd that she hadn't packed them.

"What?" Eli asked.

"Nothing," I said, shaking the image away. "Ask security where Adrianna is. Leo wouldn't tell me, but they might not know that he told me no."

Eli tapped his mic and asked the question. And smiled slowly at the answer. "Copy that," he said. "Meet the Enforcer and me at the door to the secure room." He tapped off the mic.

"Tell Alex to turn off the cameras on the way there," I said. "Leo had the security program up on the screen in his office."

"I do like the way you think, Jane Yellowrock."

CHAPTER 14

She Blew Blood Bubbles

The jewelry case under my arm, I followed my partner up to sub-three floor and into one of the newly cataloged and mapped inner passageways. We went up half a floor and were met by Juwan. "Legs," he said, as he swiped his palm over the reader. I nodded and the door whisked open, a modern sound that I associated with polished steel and rubber seals; the air contained in the chamber was let out in a pressurized, icy whoosh. It smelled of Adrianna and blood. A lot of blood.

Instantly, I remembered the first time I saw Adrianna. Red hair, curly and wild, had fanned out around her, flowing to her waist. Resting on her collarbones had been the gold torque etched with Celtic symbols, and the gold snake cuff climbed one upper arm. Her dress was cerulean blue shot with gold threads, knotted toga-like on one shoulder, leaving the other bare. The bare shoulder had been splattered with my blood like a tattoo of my death. She had looked then like some ancient and feral goddess, her blue eyes not quite sane.

This time she was in a small, white, featureless room, one with a smooth, sloped floor, a drain in the center, and steel mesh cages, like small jail cells. It was a scion lair. Her cage was made of woven steel strands, making it pliable but very strong, with a stainless-steel, tray-like bottom. The edges of the tray were cupped to hold an inch of mixed blood congealing in the bottom, and Adrianna's unbreathing, lifeless body lay coated in the blood like something a chef was about to barbecue. The hole the silver stake had made in her head was still gaping. Gray matter seeped into the blood from the head wound.

"Wait here, please," I asked Juwan.

"Whatever the Enforcer wants," he said, succeeding in sounding insulting, while letting me know without saying so that he was checking out my butt. I really needed to take Juwan down a peg. Or three.

Soon, I thought, and recognized that it was Beast thinking, not me.

Hey, Beast. Missed you, I thought back at her.

She chuffed. *Good blood smell.*

The door *shushed* shut behind us, leaving Eli and me alone with the brainless fanghead.

"Rob Zombie, Eli Roth, and James Wan, move over," Eli said.

"Who?" I asked as I moved into the room, taking in the sights, smells, and the uncanny silence. This room was not on our maps, and it had been soundproofed. Which was scary all on its own. It was small for a scion lair—the place vamps kept their insane scions until they came through the devoveo, found some control over the hunger that made them little more than ravening animals, and were ready to reenter society and life with humans. What I called the curing process, but not aloud in front of vamps. This room had been constructed with six cages; all but Adrianna's were empty, which was smart. The smell of all the blood in the steel pan might have driven young vamps into a frenzy.

"Three of the best horror movie directors alive today," Eli said. "Alex is not gonna believe this. What—" He stopped and moved closer to get a better view of the body. "What is this place?"

"Modern version of a scion lair, but not a typical use of one. This is a blood burial done on the cheap. I smell three vamps' blood, Leo's, Bethany's, and Grégoire's. All powerful, two of them relatively sane, and all willing to sacrifice some blood to the cause, apparently."

"Why doesn't it stink?" Eli asked. "It should be rotting, like vamp blood always does."

I remembered the real blood burial I had seen before, when Katie, Leo's heir, had been buried in the blood of all the vamp clans. It had taken quite a while for every vamp in New Orleans to make an offering, but even after the last one donated, the blood still smelled fresh. Not rotting. And vamp blood was supposed to go to rot instantly.

Good blood smell, Beast had thought. And she was right. Which was odd.

"I don't know. But we keep this to ourselves. Let's go." I started for the door.

"Zzzzaaaaa . . ."

I turned and met the insane blue eyes of the naked vampire lying in blood. Adrianna took a breath, and when she blew it out, she blew blood bubbles. Gross. She was alive. Undead. Whatever. It creeped me out. I shoved down on my shock and walked to the cage. With one hand, I lifted and dropped the padlock. It clanged a deep echoing *bong* in the empty room. The padlock was huge; the shank that went through the cage's steel rings was bigger around than my thumb. Which was probably smart. Vamps in blood burial came back from being temporarily true-dead extra strong, and more wack-a-doodle than they had been before.

"Zzzzaaaane."

"I'm here, Adrianna. Next time I see you, I'm taking your head. Fair warning. You've survived one time too many."

"Zzzjjjaaane."

"Let's go," I said, heading for the door. "We've got a Son of Darkness to find."

"Zzzooosaaaace," she said.

I stopped at that, the door to the hallway a foot from my nose. "What?" And then it clicked and I turned around. "What about Joses?"

"Heeee . . . Heeee . . . Ccccommme."

"Groovy. Then I won't have to hunt him down, will I?" I made a fist and banged on the door. It opened on the first hit, and I nearly hit Juwan in the head with the second bang.

The look Juwan gave me and my fisted hand was insolent and insulting and a put-down to my gender, my race, and my . . . everything. Standing in the narrow hallway, I grinned at him, showing blunt human teeth. Beast rose in me, the gold glow reflected back at me from his dark eyes. His expression didn't change, but his scent did, warning me.

Juwan attacked.

I blocked the first three punches, expecting him to move in and knock/knee/lever me to the floor—a typical guy move to get the female on the ground where they think she deserves to be—so the fourth punch was unexpected and landed, hard, on my jaw, knocking my head back and making me bite my tongue. The fifth landed in my gut. I actually gave him an *oof* of grunting reward before I countered with a couple of punches of my own, moving in close.

The next moves were nearly Beast-fast, punching fists, stabbing fingers, bodies maneuvering for leverage to get the other guy down. Juwan danced back and kicked up, the kick a feint, hiding a hand-stabbing thrust to my throat. I dodged the thrust, grabbed his leg, and whipped it high. His own leverage and torqueing force turned him. But Juwan had planned on that, and his other foot came around. Powered by me as I forced up his leg.

The whirling kick landed solidly against my temple, in a move eerily like the sparring between Daniel and Eli only days prior, and I went down with him. Landing under him, limbs tangled, seeing stars. Beast growled low in my throat and swiped my brain with her claws, clearing my muscle memory, if not my eyesight. Still half-blind, deducing his body position from what I could feel, I kicked. Striking with the heel of my foot. Because I wasn't above hitting a guy where it hurt.

The kick landed. Juwan inhaled with a squeak, curled into a tight V, and started making sounds like a wounded bird, *gack, gack, gack*. And cupping his genitals. I rolled to my feet and stood over him, my eyesight coming back in patches, like digital pixels.

I normally knew better than to let Beast off her leash in a spar, but Beast didn't like Juwan any better than I did, and female big-cats don't play with males. They mate or fight, and killing isn't beyond them. Juwan's assault had been a sneak attack, and as far as I was concerned, there were no rules in sneak attacks, not even rules against kicking a man when he was down. I took a breath and blew out my adrenaline. Working my jaw, tasting blood, I palpated my temple, which was bruised. If I'd been human I might have died from that one. I would certainly have been unconscious.

I opened the lair room door and drew on Beast's strength as I bent my knees and picked up Juwan by his hair and belt, hauling him into the room none too gently. We both grunted, me with effort, Juwan in pain when his head banged into the doorframe with a hollow *thump*. I tossed his lousy butt into the cage farthest from Adrianna and locked the door, taking the key with me.

"I wouldn't have hurt you so bad if you had challenged me fairly, in the gym," I said, my voice sounding like me instead of Beast's growl.

Juwan's reply was another *gack*, and I wondered if I'd ruptured something with that last kick. Not that I cared. I took the jewelry case back from Eli, who was lounging against the wall, looking bored. As we left the room, locking the door, I jutted my chin down the hall, saying, "Too bad I had the cameras turned off. That would have been interesting on YouTube."

"Babe. He nailed you with that kick."

"Yeah. He did." And that look . . . Juwan was a woman hater. I wouldn't be surprised if he had some unreported assaults in his past. We rounded the corner and took the stairs to the main hallway as my vision came back, along with the beginnings of a headache. Softly, I said, "Tell Alex to do a deeper background on Juwan. Hire someone to talk to people in his past. I want everything back to his first-grade teachers, his first girlfriend, his first everything. I want to know if he was nutso or if he was paid to take me down. Or compelled. I'm betting on compelled, because otherwise he'd have attacked me when I was alone."

Eli nodded and tapped his mouthpiece, relaying my request to Alex.

I added, "Get him to check and see who spent time with Adrianna, now or in the past. See if you can get a master vamp to drink Juwan and read him—all the way back until he first learned to walk if that's possible. If Juwan was part of Adrianna's feeding and/or sex team in the short time she was here, heal him, get him out of security and out of HQ. And while Alex is at it, I haven't kept tabs on Adrianna's old blood-servants or scions. Back when, she had two blood-servants, Sina and Brigit, who were moved to Clan Arceneau, if I remember right. She also had two scions, Lanah and Hope, who are true-dead unless Leo found a reason to try to save them too. They need to be checked out."

Eli nodded. "Relaying that to Alex now. He'll handle it."

I nodded and touched my temple again. "I need Tylenol."

We were in the SUV and driving away through the crowd— which had settled down a lot—before I remembered that I still had the box of gold jewelry under my arm. But maybe it was smart, after all. Molly might be able to pick up something from the traces of magic on it. As if she sensed the fact that I had thought of her, my cell rang.

"Hey, Mol. What's up?"

"The coven leader of New Orleans wishes to meet with you and Sabina, the outclan priestess of the Mithrans."

The formal speech pattern of invitation, and the fact that Molly had called Lachish the coven leader, which was her title, not her first name, meant that Lachish was probably listening in. It also meant that this was likely about the vamp/witch parley scheduled for later this year. A meet-up wouldn't be a problem, as Sabina was already considering contacting Lachish about the Son of Darkness. *Go, me!* I gave a not-too-belated, "Am I supposed to ask Sabina?"

"No," Molly said, a droll note entering her tone. "That's my delight."

"I'm in with the whole parley-rapprochement-kiss-and-make-up thing, but I'm a little busy at the moment, trying to find out where the Fifty-two Killer is lairing up in the day. Any chance you can help me with that?"

"Methods to track the killer are the subject matter of the meeting in question," Mol said.

"Oh. Okay, coolio. I'll see if I can arrange that. When and where?"

I pulled a spiral notebook out of my gobag—real paper and everything—and took down the info. Still sounding formal, Molly said, "The coven leader asks that you bring something belonging to the vampire who killed the humans in the bar."

I stopped taking down the info in the little-used notebook. "Why?"

Molly sighed, the sound of her breath loud in the speaker. "I have a feeling we'll be helping you to locate him so you can stop him. It's not dangerous," she said before I could ask, "in theory."

"Yeeeeah, *right*." I vaguely remembered seeing Eli scrape the wall where the Son of Darkness had hung. "I'll see what I can do. Gotta go. Got another call." I tapped the screen and said, "Jodi."

"Not bad, Jane," she said, sounding a lot more happy than last time we talked. "Leo is playing gracious host for a press conference to coincide with the late news. I want you there too."

"I'll do my best," I said, "but I have an appointment shortly and have no way of knowing how long it'll last."

"Try to squeeze me in," she said. Which I took as a command since she used the tone cops do when issuing orders—acerbic and strident—and ended the call before I could reply.

To Eli I said, "We're popular tonight. Our dance card is filling up fast."

"One thing at a time, Janie. Witches before vamps before cops."

"Tonight, that works."

The meeting with Molly, Lachish, and Sabina was scheduled to take place at sunset in Louis Armstrong Park, a greenway with a theater and other buildings dedicated to the arts. It was a safe place and time for witches to meet. Earth witches would have access to the ground and growing things, water witches would have access to the waterway that wended through the park, air witches would have access to the currents of heated day air and the falling cool of night air, moon witches would have access to the night sky, and vamp-witches would have access to the dark. But first we were meeting Derek in the Garden District to look over a vacant clan home—the property once owned by Clan Mearkanis, where the party took place on the night Joseph Santana had disappeared. Ordinarily, searching a place that a killer had been in more than a hundred years ago would be a stupid waste of time, but Ming had been there that night, and Ming had risen to a position of power over that same clan, in that same house, and not that long ago, at least in vamp terms. There were paintings of Ming and Santana there—maybe. If they hadn't been painted over by Ming's heir. And, possibly, Ming might have left documents that might pertain to Santana. Who knew what we might find there? If we were lucky.

We tooled around the heart of the French Quarter, checking on three properties that Santana had owned, one across the street from the Royal Mojo Blues Club, the small house burned and covered with graffiti, one on Conti Street, and a block of buildings on Frenchman Street. There was no sign of or scent of the SoD at any of them.

Even with the detours, we got to the Garden District early, with sunset still ninety minutes off and the sky a hazy gray of smog and clouds. Eli parked on Chestnut Street and we got out, locking the gold stuff in the SUV, setting the alarm, and taking in the neighborhood. Eli whistled and I couldn't disagree with the notes that said the neighborhood was exclusive and pricey.

"When I first came to New Orleans," I said, "there were eight clans: Mearkanis, Pellissier, Rousseau, Laurent, Desmarais, Bouvier, St. Martin, and Arceneau." I counted them off for Eli. "Of the eight clans, four once kept official clan homes in the Garden District: Mearkanis, Arceneau, Rousseau, and Desmarais." Now, thanks to a vamp war—small by vamp historical standards, but still pretty influential—there were only four clans, Pellissier, Laurent, Bouvier, and Arceneau. "That leaves three fancy digs in the Garden District empty: former clan homes for Mearkanis, Rousseau, and Desmarais."

Eli chuckled, an evil sound. "Some might say you've been rough on the fangheads in New Orleans."

More like an opportunistic bunch of vamps had used my appearance and the death of Leo's heir at my hands to start a coup d'état, and had failed, but I didn't go there, except to acknowledge, "Some might. This"—I waved my arm like a game show host at the grand old house—"was Mearkanis Clan Home. According to what we now know, the Son of Darkness attended a party here the night he disappeared."

"And you think we may find something here about Santana?" There was something in Eli's tone that said he thought I was either dense or thinking a little too wishfully.

"I don't know what we'll find, but with vamps it's always layers of things, starting back before God made turtles."

Eli took the place in like a soldier, checking out high

locations in neighboring houses where an enemy might place a sniper, noting the lack of tall fences and razor wire, with only the ubiquitous wrought-iron fencing at the front and a stuccoed brick wall at the side street. A stepladder or an excellent high jump was all an attacker would need to gain access to the grounds. The windows weren't barred, or high off the ground, or secured except for shutters and thumb latches. There were numerous entrances and, yeah, easy access via two streets.

"Nightmare," Eli muttered.

I was pretty sure he didn't see the huge, two-storied, pink stucco home as a New Orleans architectural archetype, with its multiple galleries and arched green wrought iron, or its porte cochere, discreetly located in the back. Or its double bays or arched windows. And the grounds with the ancient live oaks and palms, flowering shrubs, and flawless lawn. For Eli, it was all secondary to security. I thought it was pretty and wondered how many years I'd work security before I lost the ability to simply enjoy a setting.

One of Leo's armored SUVs pulled up and parked behind our vehicle. I remembered when the former marine in the passenger seat drove an old panel van and I rode a way-cool Harley bike. Now I was driving an armored SUV, wearing combat boots and leathers. He was dressed in casual trousers and a button-down shirt with the sleeves rolled up and the tie loose at his throat like a businessman—and he had a driver. I couldn't say I liked the changes in either of us. It was definitely a different Derek, though still looking fit and trim and in fighting form. Drinking vamp blood will do that to a guy.

Derek got out of the passenger side, giving the place the same once-over Eli had, and he frowned. I hadn't expected Derek there and didn't like his body language or the scent he was giving off, both of them aggressive and defensive, a spiky scent full of testosterone. He pivoted on one foot, like a soldier in maneuvers, and looked us over. And frowned. "Wait here," he said to the driver and closed the door.

"You like this setup?" Eli asked him, gesturing to the house.

Derek shook his head, his eyes hard. "Hate the place. But designing the security for it was before my time."

"Historical commission would have refused any changes,"

I said, casually. "In cases like this it's monitoring and armed guards or nothing."

"People are insane," Eli said.

"Not really," I said. "The inside of the house would have been full of hungry and sleepy vamps by day, and hungry and grouchy vamps by night. It's my guess that anyone who broke in would become some vamp's dinner."

"That is one kind of security," Derek said. "But guns level that playing field." Changing the subject, he said, "Leo said you might want to check out the place for traces of Joseph Santana. While I'm here, he also wants me to start an eval on upgrade needs, to include physical structure, interior, and security, which I'll turn over to a few contractors and designers for cost analyses." Which verified my claim about the layered motives for everything Leo did.

Derek jangled some keys. "Let's check out the inside."

The best word for the house was *magnificent*. Though *bizarre* had its place in the description too. And cold, even in the heat wave, with the AC on and run up to frigid. The vibes the place gave out said it had not been a happy place, while the décor suggested that if money could have bought happiness, the vamps and humans who had lived there would have experienced unrelieved joy.

Marble foyer, lots of fancy woodwork moldings and window trim. Wide-plank flooring, leather upholstery, burled-wood antiques that I thought might be from the Art Deco period. There were old-fashioned hand-painted wallpaper and a staircase that could have come straight out of *The Sound of Music* movie. Or maybe out of *Gone with the Wind*. Whatever. The big problem with the ambiance, besides the pervasive cold and the deep silence, was the bloodstains. Like, everywhere. A battle had been fought there. Maybe more than one. And while the bodies had been removed, the mess hadn't. A major fight for clan dominance had taken place there. Or . . . or Leo had massacred every vamp in the place. The old blood still had a stink to it. So did the old fear and horror.

I glanced at Eli and he tilted his head at me. He'd seen what I had. But when I looked at Derek, he looked . . . something. Something still. Something not right. Tense and surprised and . . . something. He pulled a weapon from his spine holster, a small semiautomatic, and checked the weapon.

It made that unambiguous *schnick* as a round entered the chamber, ready to fire. Eli did the same with three weapons, but he reholstered two of them.

I could have told them that no one had been there in months, but they'd have still gone through the procedure. The place had that kind of atmosphere. We separated and the guys started quartering the downstairs.

I trailed after Eli, moving slowly, letting my mind wander again through the history of Clan Mearkanis. The clan had been led by Ming, who disappeared from her sleep lair and was presumed dead. Immanuel was believed to be her killer. Which was oddly like what had happened to the Son of Darkness. Rafael Torres, her heir, had taken over as blood-master and immediately launched a covert war against Leo. He had wanted to be master of the city.

Neither of Clan Mearkanis' leaders had reputations of happy-happy, joy-joy, and the house vibes said it had been a painful and difficult place to live for a long time, even before all the blood was spilled. And then Ming disappeared and Rafael took over. Rafael had not been a nice man and had taken an instant dislike to me. And I mean, really. What's not to like? When he was taken out in the vamp war, his clan had been disbanded and subjugated into the surviving clans.

More important, Rafael had been Adrianna's blood-master *and* mind joined to her. She had suffered horribly when he died. And when she was staked. Most vamps wouldn't have survived either, let alone both. And Rafe had been behind her original attack on me. *Crap.* So much to remember. Vampire relationships were all tangled and snarled into a bloody and politically disruptive history. Keeping track of all the enemies I had made and the ones I had gained by proxy was getting to be really difficult. I needed an outline tree of them all. Maybe I'd get the Kid to make me one.

The Mearkanis house was huge, with a living room, a dining room, a great room that opened into a kitchen with a sitting area around a gas fireplace, and another sitting area with a breakfast table in a bay window and planters on low shelves and hanging from a tarnished bar in the ceiling, all full of dead plants. There was a tea bar, coffee bar, and wet bar, and in the kitchen proper were marble countertops above fancy painted cabinets and top-of-the-line appliances and a brick oven, like you might find in a pizzeria. There was a big mudroom off the back that opened onto a laundry room. There were back stairs switchbacking up that I presumed were servants' stairs.

And everywhere I looked were bloodstains. In the foyer, on the dining room table, splattered all along the living room wall's bookcases, in the brick oven, for Pete's sake. It was worse on the stairs, as if a group had been herded there and systematically killed off. And by the smell, it wasn't only vamps who had died. Humans had died there. Adrianna had survived the massacre and the war itself. I didn't smell her blood or her presence anywhere.

I hadn't been part of the vamp war. If I had, would all these people have died? Could I have kept them alive? I crossed my arms over my chest and tucked my hands under my armpits against the pervasive cold. This sucked. I started up the stairs, pausing at the bloodstains on the landing. The stains didn't make sense. Just from the grouping, I was guessing four vamps had died there, but the scents said only two had died. It didn't make sense.

The second story was marginally better, decorated the way a whorehouse might have looked in gold-rush days with silk, antiques, and lots of bedrooms. There were only a few bloodstains, these behind doors, in closets, in bathrooms, places where vamps had hidden. In one room two humans had died protecting a vamp, part of a defensive action behind a barricade of bullet-shattered furniture. The master suite no longer had Ming's tastes, having been transformed into a man cave for the new blood-master, all heavy furniture, with hunting trophies hanging on the walls: deer, elk, and one moose head over the bed. I closed the door and opened the one next to it; this one belonged to Adrianna, her scent flooding out. And she had been there recently. But not through the hallway. Not through the house at all, or I'd have smelled her.

I walked in and stopped, taking in her room. It was long and narrow, the walls painted a deep rose shade and centered with a canopy bed laden with silk sheets and draperies and tasseled ties in half a dozen shades of pale shell pink, with a silk rug on the floor in the shape of an ammonite shell. It was pale shell pink too. Not colors I'd have associated with Adrianna. Scarlet or royal blue, maybe even gold, but not pink.

There were no bloodstains there. I bent over the bed and caught the scent of Adrianna, fresh and strong. She had slept there within the last week, and not alone. I pulled down the comforter to see several long scarlet hairs on the pillow, entangled with as many blond hairs. The feather mattress beneath was shaped into one depression wide enough for two bodies, yet no scent of human wafted from the sheets. She'd been there without her human blood-servants, which was odd behavior for a vamp unless the assignation was with another vamp and it was secret. I breathed deeply of the mingled scents. Adrianna had taken a vampire lover. The scent was familiar, but mixed with Adrianna's scent and her perfume, it was difficult to distinguish at first. It almost smelled like . . . Dominique. Dominique, who was heir to Clan Arceneau, second to Grégoire, Leo's lover. If I was right, then this horrible situation was about to get sticky in the political and vamp-bedroom sense.

Dominique had reason to detest me, for not understanding a stilted invitation once upon a time, leaving her chained in silver and starving. Old history to me. Probably like yesterday to her.

At the closet I opened the doors to see a line of hanging dresses, skirts, and blouses, all in silk. Folded on slender, stacked shelves were rows of silk knit T-shirts. Shoes were tucked in little pockets hanging on the back of the doors, the heels sticking out for easy color coordinating, and three sets of shoe pockets were empty, matching the number of pairs found in Adrianna's room at HQ.

I felt around, running the clothing through my hands, checking every seam, every pocket, every hem. I pulled out every pair of shoes, checking the toes, and in the bottoms of the hanging shoe pockets. I reached around everything on the shelves, bunching my hands on the silk for anything hidden. The upper shelf of the closet held hats, and I checked each one. Nothing.

In the narrow bureau beside the closet were drawers full of underthings, in lace and more silk. Adrianna had a serious silk fetish. The bottom drawer was empty, and I dropped to one knee so I could sniff the drawer. Until recently, paper had been stored there, along with something faintly magical, like maybe Adrianna's gold jewelry that was now, and still, in the SUV. Maybe the gold jewelry Santana had escaped with. Beside the bureau was an indented place on the rug, roughly rectangular, like the shape of the bottom of Adrianna's suitcase, found in HQ.

I went to the window, which was unlatched, opened it, and leaned out, seeing the lattice on either side of the opening. They looked like lattices for vines and flowers to climb, but they were made of sturdy metal painted dark green to match the hurricane shutters. The two vamps had climbed up and inside instead of coming through the house. Weird.

Back in the hallway, I looked into each room and counted, evaluating the mattresses. If the vamps had double bunked and pulled out sleep couches, more than twenty could have stayed on the second story. Nearly thirty had certainly died there. Leo had won the vamp war. I didn't like him very much right then.

I went through the place again, taking the time to look at the paintings, which were stacked on long, narrow shelves on the walls, made of molding turned upside down, to make deep nooks. The paintings were propped in the nooks, some two and three deep, but set in place so you could tell the subject matter. One room had portraits, and I went through them until I found a gilt-framed one that had to be Santana. He was heart-stoppingly gorgeous. And he was wearing a bracelet on one wrist, made of overlapping gold leaves. No stones showed, but it looked like the bracelet I had seen when he escaped HQ. In the crook of his arm was Adrianna. She stared at him with a look on her face that was . . . passionate, avaricious, jealous, claiming, afraid, and victorious all at once. The artist had been a master to paint all that into her expression. It was terrifying. And it explained everything.

A third story was under the low pitched roof, and Eli and Derek were there, standing in the entrance, not speaking, each seeming lost in his own thoughts, except that Derek was watching Eli from the corners of his eyes. I pushed between them and through the opening. It was hot, decorated for low-level blood-servants or blood-slaves, and had been trashed. Or the humans who had lived there were trashy. Either way. Pizza boxes, beer cans, dirty laundry, unmade beds, and personal belongings were scattered everywhere.

But at least no one had died under the eaves. No bloodstains.

Silent, we took the back stairs to the kitchen, where the guys went through the cabinets and refrigerator, which was growing something black and slimy and smelled of rancid meat and soured blue cheese. Sotto voce, Eli asked me, "Anything?"

I shook my head no and waffled my hand. "Adrianna and a vamp who smells vaguely like Dominique slept here for several nights in the last week. No papers in her room. No one died there."

Derek said, "Leo wants this place usable. Suggestions?"

I frowned at Derek, and Eli said, "From what I see, you need a forensic cleaning crew in here, new wallpaper or an artist to restore the painted wallpaper if it's worth keeping. New rugs where any old ones can't be cleaned."

"And," Derek said, sounding perfectly sincere, "a good smudging to get rid of the dead people hanging around."

My social skills were such that I didn't know if Derek was being serious or not. He looked serious, and he smelled serious, but . . . Dead people? Ghosts? I looked around the kitchen again, seeing the bloodstains. Creepy, yes. But ghosts?

"We're going," I said. "Sunset is close and we still have no idea where Santana is." I pivoted on a heel and headed back to the front, the guys following more slowly.

Behind me, Eli said, "If Leo wants it usable for vamps and not to sell, the place needs a tech update. From what I've seen, Clan Mearkanis' tech was stuck in the late nineties." He nodded to a small desk near more plants. There was an old PC on it, with a tower, a fat monitor, and a stack of discs.

"And a total security overhaul," Derek added, "with full attention to motion sensors inside and out, and alarm upgrades on windows and doors. We can sub this out or do it ourselves. How much and how long would it take?" he asked Eli.

I answered, sounding cross, "Yellowrock Securities doesn't care. We have a job: to find Santana. Nothing more."

His tone placid, Eli said, "If Leo pulls some of his own team off of the HQ updates and off his clan home, the security part could be done in a month. But other than that, what Janie said. We're busy."

A tone sounded and Derek pulled his cell. "I gotta take this." Turning for the front door at a jog and leaving us behind, he said, "Lee here. Go ahead."

The door closed behind him and the quiet of the old house closed around us, the icy air pressing against my skin. "Eerie," I said. Eli was frowning and looked puzzled, but not about the temp. I asked, "What's wrong?"

My partner gave a minuscule shrug, a closed-off gesture that didn't invite conversation, as his eyes followed the high ceilings and traversed the walls, moving from blood spatter to blood spatter, and along the floors from splatter to splatter. Though patience wasn't my strong suit, I figured Eli would get around to talking when he knew what he wanted to say, so I wandered into the foyer, waiting.

Finally Eli followed me to the entrance, his boots as silent as mine. He said, "You know, most women would have pestered me for answers to their questions." I shrugged. We had already established that I wasn't most women. "So, yeah," he said. "Something's wrong, but I can't put my finger on it. I understand why Leo wanted us to check this place out, but why send Derek too?"

"He said security evaluations, remember?"

"Derek could do that alone," he said. "Why are we all here together?"

Something did feel wrong about that, but I hadn't been able to tell what. Now the strange feeling in the room seemed to press in on me more firmly, my body shivering once from the cold. "Yeah. He could." I moved so I could see Leo's new Enforcer out the windows. He was facing the side street and he looked angry, but his position was such that I couldn't read his lips, even if I'd known how. I moved to another window to check on Derek's driver, but the SUV's tinted windows didn't let me see in. Derek looked back at the house and I stepped away from the windows, though I knew the light was such that he couldn't see in. Derek reached inside the SUV and pulled a weapon, readied it for firing. I didn't like this. I unsnapped the holsters on my nine mils, freeing them for drawing. Eli was staring out the windows, watching Derek, his face expressionless.

I turned in a circle, once again taking in the lower floor. "Did Derek seem surprised at the number of"—I rolled my hand from one blood splatter to another and then another—"deaths that took place here?"

"No. He didn't." Eli glanced from Derek to the blood-stained rooms around us and back. "Was Derek working for Leo during the vamp war?"

"Yeah." The cold closed on me with icy claws, and I checked on Derek again. He was bent over, his head inside his SUV, his weapon down beside his leg. He had said guns were equalizers in a war with vamps. Why had he drawn his gun?

"Juwan," Eli said.

I thought back to Juwan. What had someone learned when Juwan was interrogated? What if Juwan was acting under Derek's orders when he had attacked? What if someone had called Derek and warned him that I was onto him? What if I was paranoid? What if I wasn't paranoid enough?

Eli bladed his body so he could keep Derek in his peripheral vision and looked back into the house. "That one is head height. So is that one," Eli pointed to blood spatters high on the wall beside the door. "Then below them, on the floor."

I followed his finger, putting it all together. "They were shot, head shots, not staked. Not killed in sword fights or blood duels. Just shot and then beheaded," I said. *Execution-style.*

"Human soldiers did this. Not vamps." Eli and I both positioned Derek again—still at his vehicle, but I realized I hadn't seen the driver and I couldn't tell if he was there or not. We turned, quickly quartering the room, counting the wall spatters and the floor splatters. They matched. Eli said, his tone musing, "And Derek did say that guns were equalizers. Can you tell if he was here then?"

"Not unless he was injured. There's too much vamp-blood smell. It's been too long."

"He's coming back. He's got something in his hand."

"Not a gun. Paper." The gun was missing. In his spine holster?

"Still." Eli stepped into the living room, taking cover behind a small bureau, which allowed him to see the entire foyer and keep me out of the line of fire. He pulled his sidearm and readied it for shooting. "Just in case Derek just got orders from on high to take us out. Or he's changed sides and is working for the European vamps. Or some other scenario we haven't considered."

"Crap," I said. But I rolled my head on my shoulders and blew out my tension, pulling on Beast, who rose in me and sent tendrils of power through my bloodstream. "No shooting. I'm taking him down and asking questions later."

"Good by me."

I positioned myself so that I'd be behind the door when it opened. When Derek opened it, I stuck out my foot. He tripped. I rode him down and banged his head on the marble. He went still. Easiest takedown ever. I picked up the paper he had been holding, which turned out to be an envelope, one of the fancy kinds Leo used. I suddenly had a bad feeling about knocking Derek out. Concussions could be healed by a vamp, but insulting a vamp's hospitality might result in waking up dead. I flipped the envelope over and saw the word *Lachish* written on the front, in Leo's fancy penmanship. "Well, crap," I said.

"Don't move," a soft voice said. I looked up to see a guy in jeans and T-shirt, with a weapon pointed at me. Juwan was holding the gun, and he looked way too pleased to see me in his sights at a time when his boss—Derek—was unable to do anything to help or protect me. Juwan had been the driver. Or had followed Derek. Someone had let Juwan out of his cage at vamp HQ, healed him, and sent him after me. His finger began to squeeze the trigger. Rather than reply, I dove to the side, dropping the letter and drawing two nine millimeters. Juwan's weapon tracked me, and I heard the first shot.

CHAPTER 15

By the Fluids of His Undeath

The next shots were overlaid, concussing and echoing. Half-deaf, I heard a muffled shout as I hit the floor, sliding, swiveling all at once. Only to see Juwan fall. Blood on both thighs.

In a leaping crouch I crossed the floor and shoved the guns away from the fallen man, checking him for additional wounds. Except for pinpricks of closed fang wounds on the skin at his jugular, there were none, but Juwan's left leg had sustained arterial damage, and blood was spurting into the room. Eli dropped to the floor beside me and went to work, medical supplies appearing from pockets and pouches. He sliced open Juwan's pants with a small blade and tore open a sterile package—the latest medical wonder, developed for battlefield injuries, injectable, foam, pill-like blocks, contained in a modified syringe. Still deaf, I dialed for help on my cell and held the phone to Eli's head for him to handle. Fortunately, his headset had protected his hearing in one ear. Then, while he worked to stabilize Juwan, I gathered up all the unfired weapons, my gobag, the envelope addressed to Lachish, and all Eli's extra ammo, and carried everything to the back fence, dropping them over and beneath a shrub, where it would be hard to spot them from any direction. Just in case.

Minutes later an ambulance and police were out front, probably called by nervous neighbors, and the primo had called a lawyer from Leo's high-priced firm. The attorney was on the way, my partner was in handcuffs, in the back of a cop car, along with Derek's driver, and the cops would soon want me at cop central for questioning. Because, yeah, we had one unconscious guy and one shot guy lying on the foyer floor, with evidence of multiple shots fired. But, *ummm*, we also had a crime scene with multiple blood-stained sites, and no record of police being called to address a vamp problem. How did I explain that? I couldn't. I had guesses, and all of them might be wrong. After all, it looked like I'd been wrong about Derek and his driver being out to get me.

I caught Eli's eyes through the unit's side window, and he gave a single quick nod, off to the side, away from the ruckus. It was a tacit order for me to make our next appointment without him. It also meant that he had likely overheard someone saying I should be arrested too.

I frowned but nodded. I had given a preliminary statement to the cops, little good that it did, and if I stuck around, I'd be in cop central for hours while Joses/Joseph was still on the loose, with backup from some traitorous vamp at HQ. Pulling on Beast's stealth abilities, I slid into the early shadows and along the house to the back. I leaped the low fence and picked up all the gear.

Crossing yards, courtyards, and streets, jumping fences, and weaving through the falling dark, I hoofed it out of the district, calling for a cab on the way. I hadn't contacted Rinaldo in ages, but he was working the dinner shift and said he'd pick me up in ten. I emerged on Jackson Avenue and spotted the cabbie in the rush-hour traffic. Which was even more heavy than usual. I was going to be very late to the appointment with Lachish, Molly, and Sabina. On the way, I texted Alex with the deets of the ambush and told him to start reviewing all video showing the entrance to the scion lair where we had trapped Juwan. Fat lotta good it did us.

I entered the park off of North Rampart Street, rushing up to the iron fence and leaping, grabbing the cross piece at the top, below the stylized, blunt spikes that pointed to the sky. Using my momentum, I levered my body up and over, landing silently on the grass in a crouch. The place smelled like water, grass, flowering plants, pesticides, and other poisons, but not crowds of people. There hadn't been an event there that day, and if one had been one scheduled for that night, it had been canceled due to the vamp affair and citizen safety. The only sounds were the traffic, the splashing of the fountains, and the movement of the breeze.

I pulled on Beast's sight and let her night vision, which was so much better than mine, take over. The world turned into greens and silvers, shading off into gray and blue. No reds, not much in the way of yellow, but everything sharper and cleaner and clearer. There was also something I was learning to recognize might be hints of ultraviolet or fluorescent colors—letting big-cats see body fluids the way a crime scene tech would under a black light. Though I had to work to see them, they were occasionally present in night vision, even in human form.

On the breeze, I smelled witch magic.

Keeping to the shadows and downwind of the scents, I followed the magic smell, moving across the grounds and the narrow walkways, across bridges over pools of water that had been sculpted to look natural, until I reached the redbrick main building. One side had shutters closed over the windows, a space between the building and a wide pool, and an open lawn with few trees and no privacy, except the shimmering of the magic that hid the gathering. It wasn't an invisibility charm—there was no such thing—but the obfuscation charm made it hard to focus on the women in the circle. I was supposed to be in the park at sunset to be enclosed in the circle with them. Yeah. I was late. I wondered how much butt kissing I'd have to do to make up for being so rude.

Poured on the grass with what smelled like powdered chalk was a circle; I stood outside it, watching, waiting. Inside the circle, which, in my Beast-sight, flowed up from the ground looking like a wall of pale white wind, were five witches, sitting equidistant from one another. There was no chalk pentagram or pentacle, but I could picture an imaginary star from their positions. I didn't understand witch workings, though I had learned that there was nothing inherently evil about the star shapes. Pentagrams and pentacles were simple geometry through which energy could flow without stopping, just as it could within a circle, but with points at which the energy could be drawn off and used in a working. A star was a way to control power, like a resistor or regulator.

Molly had once told me that magic users could have used squares, equilateral triangles, or a golden rectangle (a Greek mathematical concept), but the five points of a star—the shape taken from the shape of the human body, just as Leonardo da Vinci had shown with the Vitruvian Man—had proven to provide the best geometric and mathematical stability for a working, and was best when five magic users came together to work energy to a purpose, what laymen called a spell.

The woman I identified as Lachish, an air witch, was sitting at the east and was directing the energies of the working. Molly, an earth witch, was sitting to her left, with Sabina at the fire point, and two others at the moon and stone points. I recognized the last two as Butterfly Lily and her mother, Feather Storm, not their real names, but the only names I'd ever gotten, the two wearing similar flowing skirts and feathers in their hair. The two witches had only weak power and were used by other local witches as routing stations, or bodies through which the workings of energy could flow.

It would be rude, and possibly dangerous, to interrupt a working, and since I was late, I dropped to the grass, crossed my legs guru-style, and pulled patience to me like a cloak. My crosses had started to glow in the presence of the vamp, and I tucked them beneath my shirt to both preserve my night vision and avoid offending Sabina. I could be patient. *I could.* If they'd hurry up. Within ten minutes of my arrival, Lachish dropped her hands to the ground, bringing down the wall of energy. A slow breeze escaped and tugged at my braid before dissipating, and the tingle of faint magic danced across my exposed skin.

Lachish held up her hands when Molly would have stood to greet me, and my friend settled back to the ground, her expression guarded. "You are Jane Yellowrock," Lachish said.

"I am. I . . . uh . . . I come in peace."

Molly rolled her eyes and even Lachish looked amused. She looked a lot like the photo I had seen, though her face was more lined and sun damaged than the picture had indicated. She looked like a farmer, with short, stubby fingers and blotchy, grooved skin. She smelled of horses and chickens and green hay and strong magics.

"No. Seriously," I said. "I'm not currently working as the MOC's Enforcer. I come as a partner in Yellowrock Securities, and, yes, we have a contract to do upgrades on the MOC's properties, but I owe the vamps only the loyalty to keep Leo and his properties safe, not to take on other duties like causing trouble for witches. Oh. And I have a letter for you." I reached to my side and pulled the envelope from the gobag. It looked rather the worse for wear, the paper creased and scuffed, but the blob of wax that held it intact was still doing its job.

Lachish motioned me in and broke the circle by dusting away the chalk. I stood and stopped, glancing to Molly. "Weapons?"

"Silver and steel must be left outside the circle," Lachish said for her.

I grunted in dismay and started stripping off the weapons and crosses, my belt buckle, harnesses, and anything else that might interfere with the magic they were working. I kept the ash-wood stakes, but against a master vamp, they were likely worthless. I was about twenty-five pounds lighter, and considerably less secure feeling, when I was done. Leaving my weapons outside the chalk, I stepped through the opening, approaching Lachish across the grass. She snapped her fingers and I felt residual energy spin from the circle, and a tiny flame of witch-light appeared at Lachish's side. It took serious control to create a witch-light from damping energies, and even more to keep it going and stable. Lachish was showing off and letting me know that she was not someone to be trifled with. And she kept seated, another show of being in control while I came to her.

I lowered the envelope and the leader of the New Orleans coven took it, broke the seal, and removed the letter within. She read while I waited, sneaking a look at Molly's face, which was asking me what the letter was for. I shrugged back, also with my face, pulling all the muscles down to indicate that I had no idea. Leo could have given the letter to me earlier, assuming it was written then, or could have given it to Sabina to bring, but he hadn't, so this was an addendum, or . . . whatever. I was a glorified messenger girl. Sabina—vamp face like a white plaster statue—looked neither surprised nor expectant, so that was no help.

I took a look at the two weaker witches, mother and daughter. They looked and dressed alike, wearing filmy skirts and peasant blouses, pastel feathers and shimmery crystals in their earrings. They had been injured last time I saw them, but they looked okay now.

"This—" Lachish stopped. She looked at Sabina, sitting cross-legged to her left, the old vampire looking more peaceful than I had ever seen her. Sabina's white, *white* skin and her white wimple gleamed in the darkness, her humongous vampire teeth were retracted on their hinges, and her eyes were almost human looking. "Did you know about this?"

"It is no secret that the Master of the City of New Orleans intends to parley with the Witch Coven of New Orleans and the Witch Coven Council of North America," Sabina said. "As I have spoken, Leo Pellissier knows that the Mithrans are guilty of much evil against witches and have great reason for contrition. There is ample sin for which to pay penance. And though the evil against witches began long before he had the power to end it, he accepts responsibility for foul deeds. This is the beginning of . . . not payment for the lives lost, for that is never possible, but an offering to show that he intends peace and protection for *qui operatur magicae*, the *opus virtutis*, in his hunting grounds."

Lachish looked to me and I shook my head before she could ask. "I'm thinking Latin," I said.

Lachish's teeth flashed white in her witch-light. "I know what the words mean, Jane. I was about to ask if you knew what this was." She indicated the envelope.

"I have no idea. All I can tell you is that looks like Leo's handwriting on the outside, and his seal was intact until now."

"He chose an interesting messenger boy for his offer," she said, and I was pretty sure the "messenger boy" comment was meant to be both demeaning and full of curiosity. Fortunately I'm hard to insult.

To Molly, Lachish said, "The Master of the City has deeded a piece of property to the coven to be used for the conclave and for future coven needs."

"Wait," I said, feeling suddenly sick. "Is it the property on First and Chestnut streets?" Lachish nodded and I settled to my seat in the grass, our eyes now level. I said, "There may be a problem. It may be a while before the house is released by the police."

Lachish's eyebrows went up in affront, as if I meant that Leo had deliberately deeded a problem property to the witches.

"Leo didn't know when he wrote the letter," I said quickly. *Or maybe he had. He had to know about the blood inside.* "A man was shot there today, and also crimes took place in the recent past. It's a crime scene at the moment. But it won't involve the witches. I don't think." Well, that certainly made her feel all better. *Not.* "There'll be quite a few bullet holes to repair, but Leo is handling that. Or I will. And the place needs a good smudging, according to Leo's head of security and new Enforcer."

Lachish's eyebrows were still up. I realized I was running on at the mouth, and also that what I had said made Leo sound like a tightwad or a guy who would deliberately give a bad gift.

"Look," I said. "The mess with the shooting today was all my fault. I kicked a guy in the nuts earlier after he jumped me in a hallway. Then my partner shot him in the legs."

"Both of them?" Lachish asked politely.

It took a sec, but I realized she was smiling at me. Well, laughing at me with well-bred restraint, of course. "Yeah. Both nuts, both legs. Eli's a good shot. I'm thinking a traitor vamp set him on me."

Lachish said, "We can discuss this offer and its ramifications later. For now, we're wasting time. The moon won't be up long tonight, and we have a monster to find."

Crap. I breathed in a slow, relieved breath and the witchlight fluttered. It looked like I was going to have help after all.

Molly said softly, "Jane, we're aware that you're tied in some way to Joseph Santana. The sun's down and he'll need to feed. Soon. He may already be hunting humans to drain and kill. Are you willing to be bait for us to track him and possibly lure him here and capture him?"

I knew why Molly was saying it all aloud. Stating the obvious and getting permission were part of the ceremony, making certain that it was clear to all assembled that I was a willing . . . *sacrifice* was the wrong word, but it was close. Closer was her word choice and Eli's. *Bait.* But there was something in her eyes, some warning, that told me Molly hadn't yet informed Lachish about the blood diamond, which happened to be in my gobag. I wasn't sure how to deal with that, but I had trusted Molly all my adult life, so I nodded to let her know it was okay to tell if and when it was necessary. "You're going to try to make him come to us, here," I said, tapping the gobag so she would know I had the gem with me. "Yes, I'm willing."

Molly hesitated, then nodded. We were good to go.

Less than two minutes later, I found myself in the middle of an inner circle, sitting like the witches, cross-legged, Eli's and my gobags between my knees, our weapons and metal equipment—knives, stakes, guns—still in a pile outside the biggest circle. Not having them near me made me more than uncomfortable, but Lachish assured me I would be safe in the warded circle. *Yeah. Right.*

Sabina, the old outclan priestess, was watching me through the dark, her gaze piercing and steady, as cold as a block of ice. At her right knee was the black velvet bag holding the sliver of the Blood Cross, the greatest weapon the vamps owned. It struck me as odd that she had it, as there was no silver cage to herd Joseph Santana into, and Leo wanted him alive-ish. Heart removed, of course, however dead-ish that left an old vamp. I formulated that question aloud to her, but more along the lines of, "I was hired by Leo to take his heart. Do you plan to kill Santana true-dead?"

Lachish answered for her. "Sabina has informed us that our prey is a truly powerful vampire. It's possible that no steel or silver cage will hold a vampire that strong; therefore, we've devised a cage of energy. We'll place you within, call him here through your tie to him, and pull him to the boundary of the outer circle. The moment his flesh touches those energies, we can cage him in the inner circle, within the *snare of thorns*, the ward devised by the Everhart sisters and granted as a gift to us."

"Wait a minute," I said. "I'm *inside* the cage meant for Santana?"

"Yes," Sabina said, her tone placid, "at first. And if he cannot be held in this cage, and if I cannot best him one on one and keep him there in a test of our joined power, then I will use the Blood Cross sliver and send him to the light." Which was vamp for killing him true-dead, which went against Leo's proscriptions, and her own, and Bethany's, for that matter. "As you would say, I have planned for all eventualities, even the most dire."

Worst-case scenario, I thought.

"It's okay, Jane," Molly said. "The circle you're sitting in isn't activated. The moment that Santana touches the outer circle, you'll feel it. We all will. Then you just have to roll over the inner circle, on the side away from him. You rolling over the circle wall will activate the *snare of thorns*, and the energies will then pull Santana inside."

Yeah? No. "I don't like being inside a cage, even if the door's wide open."

Sabina said to me, "You have agreed to be our lure. You brought the stains of his life force, the fluids that were hung upon the wall with him?"

I hesitated. This sounded too simple. And too dangerous. Though not as dangerous as what the fifty-two humans had experienced. What choice did I have? "Yes," I said, after the pause had gone on too long. "I brought it." I opened Eli's gobag and dug around for the gauze. I reopened the packet and set it on the grass between my knees, making sure it wasn't touching me, or the chalk of the inner circle, and that there was plenty of space for me to roll or somersault over it if needed. I didn't like this. Not one bit. I didn't like that witches I didn't know were in charge. I didn't like that Sabina was involved—a fanghead so powerful she could probably do what Santana had done and immobilize us all—and who was a witch herself. I didn't like that Sabina and Lachish seemed so chummy. I didn't like that two very weak witches were finishing out the circle, instead of five strong witches. New Orleans had plenty. Why two weak witches? Was I missing something? Yes, of course, I was flying by the seat of . . . of someone else's pants, which was stupid and dangerous. Mostly, I didn't like that Molly was there. I wanted her safe at my house. Dang it all.

I hung the gobags around my neck and made sure I had ash-wood stakes within easy reach in my bun. If it came to a physical fight, wood wouldn't kill an old vamp, but it might immobilize him long enough for me to break the circle and get my weapons. If the cage I was sitting in didn't hold him. I looked at Molly, my misgivings clear even by witch-light. She gave me back a look that said she was worried too. *Great. Just great.* I mouthed, *Does she know about your magics?*

Molly shook her head, the motion tiny, to keep others from noticing. *Crap.* She hadn't told Lachish that her magics had gone to the dark side, from strong earth magics with a hint of moon magic, to death magics. "Molly—"

"I'll be fine," she interrupted.

I compressed my lips together, holding in the words I wanted to say.

Lachish looked back and forth between us, but when neither of us spoke up, she indicated that all the witches should sit and take up their implements for a working. As an air witch, Lachish took out a necklace of feathers: hawk, owl, and one long, golden eagle flight feather. The two weak witches already had theirs on the ground—the moon witch using a fist-sized moonstone, polished and bright in the night; the stone witch using a dark green stone the size of her own bony knee, smoothed by water. Molly laid a gnarled stick of wood in front of her knees. A whole, small tree, based on the way it twisted off at both ends. I sniffed and recognized the scent of the plant. Rosemary. The last time I'd seen Mol cast in a group working, she had used a live rosemary plant, and she had killed it with her death magics. Now she used the root, trunk, and branch of a rosemary plant, and I had to wonder if the aromatic dead plant was the one she'd killed that day.

"What do I do? Just sit here?" It felt like time-out at the principal's office when I was growing up. Except the scenery was nicer than the principal's tiled floor and army green walls, and the outside air was better smelling, even in the middle of the city at night.

Good food smells, Beast thought. *Want to hunt.*

"Pretty much," Molly said.

I just smiled, stretched my neck, rolled my head, and rotated my shoulders, getting ready for ... anything. But mostly to move fast. I was sitting so that I was facing the two weaker witches, and so that Molly was at my back. She'd had my back at workings before and I trusted her to smack me with her magical root if I needed to do something, a thought that made a titter tickle in the back of my throat. *Nerves.*

"Breathe in," Lachish told the witches, "and breathe out." Her witch-light fluttered and went out. "Again. Slowly. And"—she lifted her hands into the air—"we are together and we are separate, as the circle of power that binds us rises, making of us like-minded family."

There were several kinds of workings witches could do, from manipulated energies that changed human perceptions—like glamours and obfuscation spells—to *wyrd* spells, where the energy for a working was prerecorded into a single word or phrase. *Hedge of thorns* was a protective shield spell that Molly and her sisters had created, and which combined a warding and a modified *wyrd* spell. Santana had used offensive battle *wyrd* spells against me, and he'd nearly killed me. There were also summoning spells that called a specific person, and communication spells that allowed witches to talk over long distances, though with the advent of cell phones they were little used these days. There were also the off-the-hip workings that accomplished something new, but they came with inherent dangers and outcomes that were often difficult to predict. This spell started pretty simply, with the witches matching one another's breath patterns, even Sabina, who didn't need to breathe.

The outer circle began to glow again, that pale moonlight color, silvery gray, opalescent and feathery, a soft sheen of energy. Beast pushed into the forefront of my mind and the circle changed color, glowing brighter, but now with dark green shadows that moved, as if the wind pushed forest leaves against the surface, as if vines crawled up from the ground to meet at the center overhead, a dome of protective power. In the distance of the park grounds, I caught a glimpse of white, flowing like a mist, or perhaps a ghost, across the lawn. Then the magics brightened and I lost sight of it.

"Begin," Lachish said.

Molly said, "We are protected here. We ward our space with the power of the air, the moon, the earth, the stone, and the power of fire. All power gifted by the Creator, spirit gifted by the Great Spirit, who moved over the dark waters . . ."

I jerked in surprise as fire flickered up, golden among the moonlight gray and the green of the leaves. There was something pagan and elemental about Molly's wording, unlike

the workings that she usually performed, and I had to wonder how acceptable it was for me, a Christian and a Cherokee and a skinwalker, to be sitting in the center of the
witches' working. It occurred to me that since I was part of
the working, my spirituality might cause glitches in the func-
tionality of their joined magic. Maybe I should have thought
about that beforehand. And I had stopped listening as my
thoughts took me into potential, unexplored problems.

Lachish said, "I call Joseph Santana. By the fluids of his
undeath, by the bodily soil of his captivity, I call him. I sum-
mon Joseph Santana. Come, Joseph. Come." Nothing happened.

Sabina took up the working and said, "Joseph Santana,
you seek the power of the Lost Diamond."

The gem in the gobag grew hot against my skin. I
whipped my head to Sabina, eyes wide. And then to Molly,
who stared at me in horror.

Sabina said, "She who holds the Lost Diamond is here,
among us."

I had agreed to being used as bait, but Sabina somehow
knew that I had the blood diamond. She was *using* it to
power the spell, bringing Santana there. *To us.* And from
her expression, Molly hadn't known any of this was going to
happen.

Sabina said, "You are called, Joseph San—"

In a single instant everything went wrong. The air split
open with a burst of wind and a flash of light. Thunder
cracked. Power sizzled through the ground, stinging me
where I sat. The grass along the outer chalk circle flared with
flame. The fire whooshed, creating a wind, and roared up
along the dome of the witch circle, stealing my breath and
making my ears pop. I roped the gobags close to me, the one
with the blood diamond painfully hot, but at least not yet on
fire. The fissure in the air was like a gaping wound spilling
ropes of light, tongues of fire, and gusting wind instead of
blood and viscera. I could hear Sabina still calling, though
her words were lost beneath the clamor.

I placed my hands to either side of the gauze, flat on the
ground. Lifted my weight up and forward, toes beneath me,
ready to somersault away.

The air thundered again. Something dark and opaque
appeared in the cleft of light. It grew in size as if it ap-

proached at great speed. Thunder crescendoed. I narrowed my eyes against the brightness. Joseph Santana emerged through the rift of light, on the far side of the outer circle. Hanging in the air. Dangling. He screamed and dropped something. I felt the thump through the ground.

The outer circle split as though cut by an athame. The night wind and the stench of burning grass blew in. So did Joseph Santana. I had an instant of warning and Beast slammed through me, pushing me up and over the chalk line, like a gymnast over the vault horse, hands on the ground, body rolling high. Beneath me, the grass caught fire, scorching my hands. I tucked and rolled, over and through the grass fire. Heat blasted my thighs and hands. I tumbled, hit the earth jaw first with an *oofing* grunt, and rolled, grabbing at the ground to stop my momentum before I damaged the outer circle.

Predator! Beast screamed, her power shooting through me.

The space where I had sat was now much more than a small chalk circle drawn on the ground. Walls were rising from the soil, energy growing up like vines, becoming solid, energy that glowed and tremored with power.

This looked dangerous for the nonmagical nonwitch. Sweat adhered my clothes to my body like some kind of slimy glue. Heat radiated from the gobag like I'd stuck a burning piece of charcoal in it. My heart raced like a broken drum. My breath felt scorched on the heated air. Yeah. This officially sucked.

CHAPTER 16

Silver Motes of Power Slo-Mo-ing

The inner circle blazed fire like a flamethrower. An inverted *hedge of thorns*, built to work like a trap of power, turning a witch circle into a prison and a cage. *Snare of thorns* was an apt name. Heat broiled out, reaching for the vampire hanging in the air. The clap of thunder was so strong it shook the earth, and I squatted, my weight distributed on toes and fingertips. The gobag smelled like burning cotton and plastic, but the heat against my side began to dissipate. The inner circle glowed the color of crystalized blood, from the burning grass up to the top of the dome of the outer circle, like a noose tightening on the inverted ward. Inside was Joseph Santana.

He was crouched as well, our eyes on a level, one knee up near his chin, one hand on the burning ground. The hand wearing the bracelet was held in the air, fingers fisted. Flames licked at his skin and clothes. The bracelet was fully exposed on his wrist. The crystal in the setting spit a mixture of shadowy and clear motes of power, darting in a complicated spiral. Beside the clear crystal, the empty horns and claws looked dark, a hole waiting for the twin of the stone. In the same instant, I felt an answering heat in the gobag.

The stench of burning fabric again increased. Santana's eyes fell on the bag at my side. *Oh crap . . .*

Joseph shouted, *"Glaciem!"* Power like lightning shivered through the air. Abruptly the flames on the grass inside the snare went out. There was no smoke, only charred grass, the stink of old fire, blackened pants legs, and singed shirt cuffs to indicate the flames had been there at all. And now a ruff of frost lined the ground and coated the singed grass inside, the ice crystals taking on the color of the trap and cage. The ground looked like frozen blood, sparkling.

Santana was partially vamped-out, his eyes blacker than the darkest hells, the sclera looking like gelled and clotted blood. But his face was purely human, his fangs not visible. His long black hair fell in waves to the ice and covered his hand, his spread fingers already healed of any burns. He was dressed in a tuxedo, one so impeccably fitted that, even as he crouched, it conformed to his body perfectly. Yeah. He had helpers out there, and not just Juwan.

Joseph Santana himself, however, gave no appearance of having ever been human; rather, he looked like something carved by a master sculptor. His skin was the white of a marble gravestone, as slick and smooth and glowing as polished moonstone, and he gave off an aura of power that seemed to crackle through the air we breathed. Through the veil of the *snare of thorns*, his eyes settled on Lachish. He looked way too calm for a guy trapped in a cage. And my weapons were outside the circle.

Something's wrong, I thought to Beast.

Predator . . . Beast gathered my body in tightly, flooding me with adrenaline. My eyesight sharpened again, the world growing brighter. *Danger . . .* My heartbeat and breathing sped, scents taking on a sharper intensity.

The fingers of Joseph's upraised hand snapped, a sharp popping sound. Softly, he said, *"Strangulo."* The power of the *wyrd* spell pulsed through the ground. Lachish grabbed her throat and fell to the side, her mouth open and eyes wide in terror. Over the magics and the burned earth I could smell her fear, like the stink of castor oil and burning fennel.

"Sabina," I whispered, a warning in my tone. "Molly?"

"Working on it," Molly said, breathless. "Lachish, ward yourself! We can hold the cage."

Joseph pointed at the two weaker witches and said, *"Dor-*

mio." Again I felt the spell as it rippled beneath the earth, and instantly they both fell asleep, toppling to the side. As they fell, Lachish managed to raise a pale blue ward around herself, the energies flickering and unsteady, but they were enough. She gasped in a breath, crying and shaking, hyper-ventilating. I realized that the magics Joseph Santana was using were strong enough to pass through the ground beneath his fingers, under and through a warded circle, and still be deadly. I wondered how the ice he'd placed on the ground might be helping that, but it was an isolated thought in the midst of thinking, *My weapons are* outside *the circle!*

Sabina raised one hand toward Molly, who reached back; energy crackled between their hands, blue and red electricity arcing between them in the air. Sabina held her other hand toward the trap and said, *"Solidus. Profundus."* The bloody energy of the inner circle's *snare* went brighter, richer, as their combined strength supported the existing working. The walls now looked like plasticized safety glass running with blood. *"Stabilire,"* she said, a heartbeat later. Her spell somehow put out the last of the flames in the large circle, and a wind blustered through, blowing away the stench before it died.

Even as the priestess said the words, Joseph turned the bracelet toward Molly and said, *"Demorior."* And nothing happened.

Molly whispered a curse. "Son of a witch on a switch. That was close." She was sweating, the vivid scent notes of terror on the air.

Without looking, the prisoner lowered his hand and picked up the gauze that had helped to bait the trap; it was burned to a crisp. He sniffed it, his nostrils moving delicately, before dropping it back to the ground. He stood, moving like a trained dancer, loose and balanced, but with something off, something not quite right, not quite human, in his posture and the movement of his joints. He raised both hands like a mime on a street corner, but far more mesmerizing. Pressing his palms against the trap the witches had set for him, he ran his hands up and down, along the walls of power, as if testing their strength.

My weapons are outside the circle. And the blood diamond was getting way too hot. How many of them were drawing on the power stored there?

His head rotating on his neck in that creepy, typically vamp, reptilian manner, Joseph looked back and forth between us all, taking our measure, as if seeing more than normal beings could. His eyes settled on Molly, and he lifted the wrist wearing the bracelet, angling it at her. Then he crouched and pressed the bracelet against the icy dirt beneath him. *"Sanguinem ad mortem,"* he said. Molly made a small sound, like a child in sleep, and blood gushed from her nose. Beast snarled deep inside me, her pelt rubbing against the underside of my skin, itching, tingling, her claws making my fingertips ache. Molly bent forward, her eyes wide, circled in white, murmuring, *"Hedge of thorns."*

I jumped back as another small ward appeared inside the outer circle, this one the red-tinged energies of Molly's strongest working, the warding created by the Everhart witch sisters. This one completely encircled her, a sphere of power around her, deep into the earth. Her bleeding slowed and Molly coughed, spitting blood, and wiped her nose on the back of her wrist. She was quivering; her other arm encircled her waist as she bent forward in pain. "I'm sorry, Sabina," she whispered. "I can't. I'm hurt."

Beast-energies and mine flowed together like streams merging, her soul and mine joining. *Mother of kits,* she thought at me. *Predator harms mother of kits.* I showed Santana my blunt human teeth in a snarl, but he ignored me, angling his bracelet toward the priestess. The gobag at my side was flaring hot, and smoke curled up around me.

Sabina vamped out, her eyes going black and bloody, her jaw changing shape to allow three-inch fangs to click down from her upper jawbone. They looked enormous, hanging down below her chin. "It is not of my choosing," she said, the words spoken with the precision of a verdict. She stood, her body also moving oddly, as if her joints worked backward. Her right hand rose over her head, her fingers bent and twisted like broken bird feet, her talons black and knifelike. Inside the outer protective circle, power gathered in dark motes, like a swarm of black, metallic bees, potent enough for me to feel on the air like the buzz of a power saw. Sabina held the black velvet bag in her other hand, the sliver of ancient wood exposed.

Joseph ignored her energies collecting, as if her power was unimportant, his eyes alighting instead on the sliver of the Blood Cross. He opened his mouth, a ghastly sight as his jaw unhinged and his mandibles separated, the lower dropping down. His fangs, the uppers five inches long, were massive, clicking into place, dwarfing hers. He looked like the spawn of a lizard and a fighting insect, joints taut and sharp, his frame altering shape, his shoulders rising, neck stretching. His talons extended, and even through the cage of energies I could see the cutting edges, like razors. He hunched, incongruous in the tux, no longer remotely human. "Sssabina," he said, the word soft and sibilant. "It has been long. I see you still possess that which is mine to give."

Sabina took a step toward the inner circle, her white skirts blacked at the hem by the grass fire. Another step brought her halfway across the small space. Smoke rose from the velvet bag holding the vamp's greatest weapon as she neared the *snare of thorns.* "Too long, *Le Créateur des morts.* And never long enough." She rotated her hand and said, *"Contego."* A sheath of energies spread out from her right hand, a shield of protection curling around her, created from air and moonlight and the shadows cast by a bright moon.

Joseph stared at the shield and he chuckled, though the sound was nothing like a human might make, broken and raspy and cawing. "You have drunk of my blood. You joined those who used me while I hung in the darkness. A prisoner."

"No," Sabina said, her brow creased in concentration. "My sister priestess lost much from your blood. Seeing dark memories." As she spoke, her magics strengthened, coalescing around her. Sabina was buying time as she gathered herself. The gobag at my side flamed, and I dropped it at my feet, gripping an ash-wood stake with my good hand.

"I watched as she fell deeper into the madness of your mind, a loss of self. Instability followed, for long years after.

"I did not drink of you, only of others. But after a time, the poisons that tainted you were there, in the collective blood, shared among us all, though weakened, so that we did not all succumb. But I tasted of the venom, and I perceived how to remove the poisons that had infected you, that came from you, and how to absorb only the strength of your holy blood. Then"—she smiled, a grisly expression, and her power swept around her, dark and intense—"then I gained much. I gained all that you were and more."

She extended her left hand toward the inner circle/trap/
cage. *"Foramen clavis,"* she said, and she touched the sliver
of wood to the cage. The energies parted as the point of the
wood passed through. The ground beneath my feet shuddered and tilted. I bent my knees to catch my balance, my
hands out to the sides. The ground moved again and I saw
the tips of Sabina's fingers touch the scarlet energies. Flames
shot out. *Oh crap.*

The fire whipped across her shield and shot beyond it, to
cover the walls that held Joseph Santana prisoner. From his
hand ice emerged and coated the cage. The two went immobile as the flame and a coating of ice met and smoky-toned
energies sparked out. I lifted a shoulder to protect myself
from the heat and flames, watching the contest of wills and
powers. It didn't look as though it was going anywhere fast.
Still crouched, I crab-crawled the inches toward Molly, who
was staring at the confrontation, slack jawed, drying blood
on her face. Behind me, the gobag was in flames.

As I neared her, Molly's head tilted toward me, and her
skin paled. Her eyes widened. Slowly, she focused, but she
wasn't looking at *me*. She was looking at the flaming gobag.
Molly held out her hand, palm up. "I can make this stop,"
she said, her voice toneless. "I can make him go to sleep so
you can take his heart. I can pull the life out of him. I can
take his power and make it mine. And save us all. Give."

"Molly? What—"

"Give me the amulet."

I stopped moving. The gobag flared, golden flames licking upward as the stench of cotton and plastic rose on the
air. The *hedge of thorns* protecting Molly glowed brighter;
she was drawing on the diamond. *Crap.* Her death magics
were extracting power from the diamond, even though she
wasn't physically touching it. And the energies were changing Molly into something that wasn't the Molly I knew.

Beneath my skin Beast screamed, *Predator!*

She meant Molly. *"Give,"* Molly said. The dark power
was changing her right before my eyes. Reaching down, she
started to swipe away the *hedge of thorns* she was hiding
behind.

The gray place of the change, the Gray Between, erupted
from inside me, gray and silver clouds of energy, dancing
with blue and silver motes of pure power. Beast shoved

through, her claws piercing the skin at the tips of my fingers. Pelt sprouted along my arms and the backs of my hands. Pain scraped across me like a knife flaying flesh from my bones. My spine bowed with the pain, then arched back. I threw back my head and screamed with my Beast. My paws burst through my boots, my claws shredding the leather. My body bent back and slammed forward, somehow ending up with me on all fours, close to the outer circle ward, but facing both Molly and the inner circle. I snarled at what I saw.

Molly dropped the *hedge of thorns*, keeping the circle open, ready to reactivate the instant she got the diamond. She laughed and crawled forward, toward the gobag. *Predator,* Beast screamed. *Strike now.*

I fisted a huge knuckled hand and drew back. I hit her jaw, full on, at about a third of my usual strength. Molly's head whipped back and her body fell, unconscious. Physical strength and sneak attack against magical energies? *No contest.*

To my side, the outclan priestess was leaning against the fiery wall of the *snare of thorns*, the sliver of the Blood Cross pressing the inverted ward inward, the energies bending and giving. Inside, Santana was growling, a hulking nightmare creature, any pretense of humanity ripped away.

Softly, Sabina said again, *"Foramen clavis."* The energies of the *snare* gave way and her arm disappeared inside the trap. In the same millisecond, Sabina caught on fire.

The creature inside the trap, the *thing* that used to be human, so long ago, the thing that—by his own volition and his foolish and selfish actions—had created all the fangheads, reached around the sliver. He grabbed Sabina's flaming wrist with his clawed fist. He jerked her toward him.

I knew, between one heartbeat and the next, that this was the end. The Son of Darkness was breaking free. There was no way I could control him. And if he bested me, he would have the blood diamond. Around me, my energies—Beast's energies—took over.

Time altered, decelerating as if someone had put on the brakes, as if they had gelled every movement, every thought but my own. All I had time to think was, *This is gonna be bad.* Beast didn't disagree.

The Gray Between was my greatest weapon, when it gave me the ability to shift shapes—and my greatest danger, when I used it to bubble or fold time. Something about using the gift, about folding time, caused me to bleed internally. And when I shifted back, I didn't heal like I should. But it was too late to halt the process now.

Around me the world had almost stopped, the dance of my own silver motes of power slo-mo-ing, seeming to vibrate in place. At my feet—my paws and ruined boots, rather—Molly lay on the ground, her *hedge of thorns* gone. She had fallen across the remains of her protective circle, and she was vulnerable to anything inside the circle with us.

Within the inner *snare of thorns*, Sabina was being yanked into a physical battle with the big-bad-ugly. Her clothes were burning, her skin was burning, her lips were snarled back, her left hand leaning forward, aiming at her prey. Her other hand was behind her at her belted robe, reaching for a silver stake partially visible there. If she had time, if silver hurt a vamp as old as Santana, Sabina might have a chance. But her best weapon, the sliver of the very wood that had made Santana's father, was being twisted back against her. Santana versus Sabina was going to be a no contest in the wrestling arena. And what would silver do to the energies massed between them? Would we all go bang?

According to all the legends, if the sliver of wood touched a vamp, the fanghead would explode in flames. I had seen it happen, though never to a vamp as old and powerful as Sabina or Joseph Santana. This was why Beast had taken over and forced the time-shift onto us. In about five seconds real time, Molly would be dead. So would I. I had resisted Sabina once and lost. Santana was stronger than she was. We were all dead . . .

My gut started the now-familiar gripping, a twisting, tearing, grinding agony. I ignored it. If my body worked this time as it had the last time I/we had folded time, I had a few more real-time moments before I was incapacitated. I walked to the outer circle. I could reach just outside the circle and grab my weapons. I could. It would destroy the wavering protective ward instantly, but that was a real-time instantly. I could take up a blade and be ready when the *snare of thorns* fell, and try to cut out the Son of Darkness' heart. *Decisions, decisions* . . . I reached through a gap in the wavering energies and drew out a vamp-killer, lifting it through the energy gap and across the circle. Instantly I felt a snap of pain and knew I'd destroyed the ward.

Trying to breathe through the gathering pain, I stepped to the priestess' side and eyed the terrain, the stability of the inner and outer circles. They were both dropping. The *snare of thorns* wall was falling, spaces opened between the flames, as if the energies were burning away. There was no place to hide. I reached one arm inside the cage, angling my arm through the flames, careful to not touch the stressed energies, hoping to ease the vamp-killer through another opening and cut out the heart of the Son of Darkness. But when my jacket brushed the edges of the energies, fire leaped through my arm and along my nerves. It felt like my flesh had ripped from my arm in one long, exquisite pain. Hissing, I lifted myself away from the contact and smelled burned flesh. *Crap.* I'd cauterized a wound, like a brand. Gasping, I stepped back and reconsidered.

Okay. Plan B. There was always a Plan B, right?

Delicately, I eased one arm back through an opening and took the tip of the wooden weapon, the sliver of the Blood Cross, in my fingers. I pulled the splinter of wood away from Sabina. The velvet bag around it was soot and ashes, and a flake was falling in real time, hanging an inch away. I eased my arm back through the trap wall and snagged the wood through my collar to hold it in place. The back of my upper arm twinged and pulled and I felt wetness gathering inside my leather sleeve. *Best not to let my blood touch the energies of the snare again,* I thought.

The abdominal pain hit like a colossal fist, doubling me over. I gagged, the retching deep and ripping. My guts snarled and twisted. My breath stopped. I retched again and I tasted blood on the back of my tongue, salty and vile, mixed with burning stomach acids. "Not yet," I whispered. *Not yet.* I measured the distance from the falling outer circle to Sabina with my eyes as I walked back to her and snagged the silver stake from the back of her robes. With no other planning, I forced myself upright, reached in, and, one by one, I broke Santana's fingers to force him to release her. The bones broke with deep, cracking sounds, like a bass drum hit four times. It took muscle to accomplish anything when time was folded, but I managed to separate Santana's hand from Sabina's wrist.

I grabbed her nonburning arm and threw my body into a judo move, heaving the priestess up and over. For an instant Sabina's energies merged with mine and I could sense her disconcertment, a nearly spiritual vertigo, but she left my grasp so fast that it didn't last, and I turned away, leaving her hanging in the air, angling toward the pond nearby, robes flapping out like wings. Oddly, the fire that coated her didn't feel hot. It was one good moment in an agony of bad ones, and I retched again, this time spitting blood. *Not good.*

I went to Molly and hefted her up and over my shoulder, coughing on my own blood. I carried her through the dying energies of the witch circle and away, into the dark. I lay her down in the shadows of the brick building, in the opposite direction from Sabina. Molly didn't wake. As I stood, something inside me tore and I fell against the side of the building, unable to breathe. I wouldn't be able to lift the other witches still inside the circle, not now. But I couldn't stop. I still had to deal with the big-bad-ugly in the trap, a trap that was clearly falling apart, leaving him able to kill us all, because I wasn't going to be able to stop him. Not like that. I pressed a fist into my middle hard enough to touch my spine, if the knotted muscles hadn't stopped me.

The pain only increased, choking me, doubling me over. I hadn't prayed in a long, long time, and there wasn't time now to make things right between God and me. I said, "Need a little help here. Just let me get back to the Son of Darkness long enough to stab him."

God didn't answer. I didn't really expect him to, not with a prayer like that. And the pain wasn't going to ease up. I pushed myself upright and stumbled back toward the circle, walking like I was on a three-day drunk, and lurched through the crashing energies. Halfway to the inner circle, my guts rippled and twisted. I hit the ground with both knees and gagged, blood in my throat. "No," I whispered as tears of agony gathered and fell, dripping off the tip of my nose and collecting around my mouth. "Not yet." The tears tasted salty, and I licked my dry lips as I pushed up with both hands. I got one back paw beneath me before my abdomen wrenched and I threw up. Like the last time I had spent too much time outside of real time, it was pure blood. "Not good," I whispered as the world reeled around me. I supported myself on splayed toes and fingers to keep from falling.

My right hand looked reddish in the witch-light and night

shadows. Pain started in my fingertips and spread up, joint by joint. Bad, really bad, but not something I could deal with right then.

From that position I saw something dark on the ground. I remembered the thump I had heard when Santana first appeared in the rift of space. Over the stink of my own sweat and sickness, I smelled a human. Santana's dinner. I needed to get him or her an ambulance. *Right,* I thought. *First thing. As soon as I finish dying myself.*

From the corner of my eye I saw a mist in the darkness beyond the outer circle. The mist was moving toward me. No. It was racing toward me. Moving *inside* the folded space of time. Coming fast.

It was Brute, the werewolf stuck in wolf form. Brute, who had chased Santana out of vamp HQ. Brute had probably been keeping tabs on me . . . or Santana. I remembered the reports of him racing through New Orleans. The white werewolf stuck in wolf form had bitten Joseph Santana. He could, therefore, probably track the Son of Darkness.

And Brute had been in the presence of the angel Hayyel . . . along with Beast. And could clearly fold time. *Holy crap.*

CHAPTER 17

Broiled Vamp-Flesh, Still Rare

The werewolf leaped high and stretched out, passing over and through the breaking energies of the outer circle. He landed with an expelled grunt and gathered himself, his tongue hanging out one side of his mouth. His teeth were enormous, bigger than Beast's in her big-cat form, though not as large as my/our fangs in half-cat form. Brute turned crystalline eyes to me. In the glowing energies of the various walls of power, his eyes looked bright and clear and blue. He trotted up to me and stopped in front of the bloody vomit on the ground. He bent his nose to it and sniffed. Growled and hacked. He sat, front paws neatly together, and met my eyes, as if waiting for a treat.

"Sorry, dog," I managed. "I don't have a bag of rawhide for you."

Brute chuffed, sounding a lot like Beast when she laughs. He turned his head to the disintegrating trap and back to me.

I ignored him, one hand holding my stomach, kneading the knot there, and headed back to the *snare of thorns*. "I ask God for help and he sends me a freaking werewolf?" The wolf yipped and looked again at the trap. Visibly, it was failing, the energies separating. Time wouldn't wait forever. "Proof that God really does have a sense of humor."

The creature that was Santana, caught inside the *snare*, had shifted position while I tossed my cookies and rearranged my friends and talked to a werewolf. Santana's balance was now on his back foot, his head up, looking at the top of the failing trap, ready to jump. He was going to vault up and over the falling walls. I looked at Sabina, who was tumbling in the air, her clothing in flames. Her hand was blackened bone.

Lastly I looked at Lachish, who was staring through her weak ward at whatever was happening in her time. She looked terrified. She had to know that when the monster was free, he was gonna kill her and her witch friends, who were still sleeping on the singed grass.

I pinched the tip of the sliver of the Blood Cross that was hooked through my clothes. I couldn't cut out his heart. If I grabbed him, he might time-sync with me, like Sabina had, and kill me on the spot. The sliver should kill him. Or at least hurt him bad enough to give me time to save the others. I laughed, the sound similar to Santana's laughter—not nearly human. "Pop his bubble," I muttered.

The wolf came to my side and braced his four feet.

I glanced down, surprised. "I have a service, werewolf," I whispered. Brute chuffed again. I placed a hand on his back, over his shoulders, and pushed upright. Well, bent over, dizzy and retching, but at least now I had help. Moving slowly, keeping step with me, Brute helped me inch to the deteriorating cage. Once there, I used my free hand—pelted, knobby knuckled, part paw—and I gripped the wood tightly. It felt hot in my hand, as if it were about to burst into flame at the very touch of my fingers. I had a feeling that the sliver and whatever power it held didn't like my skinwalker magics or the blood diamond magics being utilized in the protective circle, and would just as soon see me dead.

Brute stopped at the boundary of the inner circle / *snare*, and I pushed up against him, levering my weight higher. I eased my hand through a gap in the trap energies. My hand was shaking, but I managed to align the splinter of wood with a patch of bare skin just above Joseph's tuxedo coat collar. The SoD didn't teleport away or get beamed up to Scotty or fold time to fight me, the *wyrd* spell he was trapped in perhaps not letting him utilize that much of his own power.

I shoved the sliver of the Blood Cross into him.

His flesh was tough inside of folded time, like the rind of a watermelon. I put my back into it and shoved. For my efforts, I got another burn across the back of my arm, but higher up, near my shoulder. I hissed with pain but kept pushing. The wood point pierced him and I saw a blot of blood just as the first flame licked out. I jerked my hand away and fell, rolling back, vomiting. Pure scarlet blood. I tucked into the fetal position. Brute stepped over me, defending me. *Dang dog.*

Now, Beast, I thought.

Around me, time unfolded with a snap that I felt through the ground, more so than heard. Brute vanished, still caught in sometime else. The outer circle fell. The trap walls fragmented and collapsed. The Son of Darkness screamed, the sound a composite: the wails of a thousand humans wounded in battle, the high-pitched screech of tearing metal, and the deep, broken reverberation of rock rolling from a high place. The vamp death scream squared.

A huge splash sounded from nearby. Sabina hitting the pond. A whoosh of flame and heat scorched close to me. I looked between my elbows to see Santana engulfed in flames.

He reached up with a clawed, taloned hand. And he ripped out a gobbet of flesh. Dropped it on the ground, burning and bitter smelling, hotter than molten steel. He was still on fire, deep inside, his flesh burning even away from the air. He screamed and I covered my ears at the painful pitch. With a pop, he was gone, flames flashing, marking a path, *fast*, away from the park.

I lay where I fell and vomited. And vomited. And felt my body try to reshape with a burning-slicing torture of fast-mutating skin and muscle. A moment later, I felt a cool hand on my forehead. Healing energies flooded through me. To my side I spotted the bluish illumination of a witch-light. I smelled Lachish. And burned grass. And broiled vamp-flesh, still rare, along with vamp-flesh, well-done, cooked to a crisp. The stench did nothing for my nausea.

On the ground, only inches from my nose but out of the visual range of Lachish, was a charred hunk of something rank and foul. I reached out and pulled the sliver of the Blood Cross free from the hank of skin and hooked it back into my collar. So much for it being a weapon of vamp destruction. Santana had enough strength to get stuck with it and still run away to fight another day. I closed my eyes and let Lachish take away the pain. It wasn't a complete healing, but her ministrations helped, a lot.

Only when Lachish had pushed the sickness far enough away that I could get to my feet did I tell her about Molly, still unconscious behind the building. Lachish wasn't happy about what she took to be a poor decision on my part, but I didn't really care. *I* wasn't happy about Molly and didn't really want to be anywhere near her when she woke. As the coven leader of New Orleans tended to her witches, I gathered up a handful of smoking flesh and the blood diamond, tucked them into the other gobag, gathered up my weapons as best I could, and walked away from the burned remains of the fiasco, into the dark.

The grass felt strange on my bare feet, something half-remembered from the early years in the Christian children's home, my soles tender and without the calluses that built up in humans. The lights of the park grounds didn't reach the pond water, but even with Beast resting within me, silent and still, I could make out the blackened wimple and robes the priestess favored. She was sitting chest deep in the pond. I moved toward her in my bare, human-shaped feet until I heard a ripple of water, the sound an alligator makes when it slithers across the surface of a shallow bayou.

"Sabina?" I said softly.

"Stay away, skinwalker, or I may drink you down. I am hurt. And I am not entirely in control when so badly damaged."

I thought about that, and about the blackened bones of her burned arm, for half a second before I pulled the gobag to me and removed my cell. I punched the number for Del at vamp HQ.

"Jane," Del said, her tone cool.

"Sabina's injured," I said baldly.

Del made a *shushing* sound of shock. It was hard to hurt an old vamp.

"We need healthy blood-meals for her at Louis Armstrong Park. Tell them to enter through the North Rampart

Street entrance, cross the footbridge, and move toward the water. She's in a lot of pain."

"Go away, skinwalker," Sabina said, her words sibilant with warning.

"How much pain?" Del's voice held a note of concern, maybe even worry.

"Third-degree burns to one arm to start out with. Burns elsewhere. I don't know how bad."

"In that state, she'll kill any human she tries to drink from," Del said. Which made sense but made me pause. "I'll send Leo. Sabina can drink from him first, and then, when her pain is eased, she can drink from the humans."

"*Ssssskinwalker . . . I thirsssst . . .*"

I took that as evidence that I needed to get moving, and headed toward the street. "That'll work. But we have a bigger problem. Santana is hurt too, maybe as bad as Sabina. He's going to need blood to heal. And then he's gonna be ticked off."

"Dear God, Jane. What have you done?"

I could almost see Del rubbing her temples and popping Tylenol for the headache I was giving her. "I'm trying to fix a problem that's been in the making for over a hundred years. Not everything is going according to plan. I'm not surprised about that and neither are you." She didn't answer that one.

"Even with humans to help him, life in the twenty-first century is going to be abnormal to such an old vamp. Santana's going to take a while to get up to speed, unless he has some willing vamp help or takes a vamp prisoner," I said, thinking about Dominique and making speed away from the water where Sabina lurked. "You need to put all the city's vamps in lockdown. *Now.*"

"Is that all?" Del asked, her snippy tone back.

"One more thing," I said, getting ticked off myself. "I'm trying to fix Leo's screwups, so make it snappy." I closed the bullet-resistant Kevlar cover of the cell as I passed the burned grass marking the site of the magical debacle. A witch-light brightened the ground and the witches who were gathered there. All four were conscious, but Molly wasn't quite ready to take on anything magical, thank goodness. The NOLA coven leader was bent over her, pale healing energies moving across Molly's face and head. My pal's eyes were closed. I didn't want to disturb her, and I hoped she wouldn't remember the attempt to take the diamond. Or the fist that stopped her. "Lachish," I said, my voice soft and measured, "you got enough mojo to put up a ward? Sabina is injured and it's gonna take a while to get blood-meals together."

"I can. And you can give her this." She tossed something to me in the dark.

It landed at my toes, and when I picked it up, I felt the warm tingle of healing energies built into a feather tied to a bit of wood. The wood smelled like baby birds and bird poop, and I realized it was a stick from a bird nest, tied to a feather. Interesting choice for an air witch's amulet. "Good," I said. "I'll get this to her. The sooner the better on the ward. Sabina's hungry and not in very good control. I'll see you later. I have a master vamp to track."

No one replied. Knowing that vamp ears were good enough to have heard the conversation, I tossed the stick-and-feather healing charm toward Sabina, before picking up my gear and moving away to North Rampart Street. When I hit the footbridge I saw a ward rise from the ashes of the original witch circle, and I felt safe enough to knead my aching stomach. The witch healing hadn't been thorough, and the pain still lurked there, knotted and tender. Worse, the hand injured by Joseph's *wyrd* spell was marked with faint red tracery again and had started tingling.

Eli hadn't called, meaning he was still in custody, so I dialed for a taxi as I walked, putting distance between me and the injured vamp. Rinaldo, the cabbie I used most often, wasn't working now, but he offered to send a pal to pick me up and take me where I needed to go. I turned left out of the North Rampart entrance on foot and looked around for possible danger. The sidewalk was empty and still. Perfect place for an ambush. I stepped into a shadow to hide and watch, following the scents on the air currents. Upwind, no one hid. Downwind was a lot more iffy.

While I waited, I dialed Jodi Richoux on her cell. She answered, which meant that she was still at the crime scene, not in her cavernous office in the bowels of NOPD central. The woo-woo room had no cell reception and never would if the big muckety-mucks at NOPD had anything to do with it.

"I don't have time for this," she grated out in lieu of greeting.

"Yeah, you do. I just injured Joseph Santana."

"What?" Her tone sounded remarkably less irritated all of a sudden. "How? How bad?"

"I stabbed him with a weapon that works on vamps. One I borrowed from a ..." I wasn't sure how much Jodi knew about vamp hierarchy, but I decided on truth. "... from the priestess Sabina. He was on fire when he got away from me. You need to send out an alert to all your cops that Santana is burned and might be looking for water sources to lair up in, as well as blood-meals to heal with, and better if he can find both together."

"Do you know how many water sources there are in this city? *Hundreds!*" Jodi said, her annoyance increasing again.

"That's the best I can do right now. I need you to let Eli go. I need him to help me track Santana."

"I need a raise and a better-fitting pair of shoes."

I chuckled softly. "I'll take you shopping if you'll set Eli loose."

"Bribing me, Yellowrock?" she asked, but her tone finally settled into grudging friendship instead of cop–to–possible suspect. "There's laws against that. Do I need to haul you in too?"

Which meant that Eli was at NOPD, possibly under arrest, and that I'd been wrong. Jodi was no longer at the scene of the shooting. "Bribing is more along the lines of what Leo might do, not me. I don't have bottomless pockets."

"Which doesn't say whether this is a bribe."

"It's not a bribe," I said, getting grouchy in reaction to her tone. "You need shoes. I need a girls' day out. You need rest. I need Eli to help me track Santana. When Santana is dead, we'll do the spa thing and shop, which you know I *hate*. We'll ask Adelaide Mooney to come with us. All this is a statement of fact. I'm *not* offering to buy you a pair of shoes."

"Too bad. There's this sexy pair of lipstick red heels at Macy's in Metairie that I've been lusting after."

I beat my forehead with a fist. Women were so confusing. "I'll buy the dang shoes if you'll wear them on a date with Wrassler. That can be a bribe. The rest of this is business."

There was a hesitation before Jodi said, "That the guy who lost a leg in the fight at vamp central?"

"Yeah. And he's down and depressed because of the injury and he always had the hots for you. He could use a night on the town."

"Really?" From Jodi's tone I had a feeling the shoes were superfluous to any agreement to a date with the big guy. She said, much softer, "You got his number?"

"I do. We got a deal? I need Eli."

"Sure. Text me his number. You can pick up Eli at NOPD at the Eighth on Royal Street in ten." The call ended, and by the ease of me getting what I wanted, I guessed that Eli hadn't been under arrest after all. Cops were sneaky. Not that I minded anything I had just agreed to. I texted Wrassler's number to Jodi and hopped in the cab that pulled up. "Take me to the Eighth District NOPD. Wait for me there and there'll be another destination and a nice tip."

"How nice you gonna be, my sister?" he said.

I looked at the cabbie in the rearview, seeing dark skin and pretty eyes. The left one had a teardrop tattooed at the outer corner. A prison tat. Great. "Twenty. And I'm not in the mood to dicker."

"Done." We pulled away from the curb and into the night's traffic. "You know you're barefoot, right?"

I snorted. "I noticed. You know you're an ex-con heading toward NOPD, right?"

"I noticed. But I got nothing to worry about. I found the Lord when I got outta the joint and made my life right. I go to the Baptist church roun' the block from the Eighth. I know the cops there. You should join us come Sunday. Nothing so good as bein' right with Jesus, my sister."

I was being evangelized by an ex-con. How weird was that? Then I remembered the dirty water in the baptismal pool at The Church and I sighed silently. "I might be looking for a new church. I'll keep it in mind."

We pulled up in front of the Eighth District Police Department and I got out, unhappy at the sight of broken glass on the sidewalk. "Here," the cabbie said, handing me a pair of neon green flops. "Client left them in here last week. She paid cash so I couldn't find her. I washed them shoes good. Was going to give them to the clothes closet at church, but you look like you could use them."

I might hate the idea of putting on someone else's shoes, but it was way better than being barefoot on broken glass. I pulled on the flops and checked the cabbie's name on the license. "Thanks, Zareb."

"Welcome, my sister. *Zareb* is African for 'protector.' I'm your protector tonight."

For reasons I couldn't name, that simple statement brought tears to my eyes. "Thanks," I said through a tight throat.

"I'll be waitin' for you right here unless the cops send me off. Then I'll be parked beside the church round the block. I won't leave you. And if you need a doctor for that belly pain, I got one who work at the free clinic. She'll see you."

I dropped my hand from where it had been pressed against my stomach and closed the cab door, thinking about the old saying of people being helped by angels in disguise, and I figured I had just met one, even if only in a small way. Feeling better for reasons that had little to do with logic, I thanked Zareb with a lifted hand and entered the main doors of the Eighth.

The exterior of the French Quarter precinct looked like a fancy hotel, two-storied, pale pinkish stone landscaped with palms and old, flowering magnolia trees. Inside were, arguably, the most friendly cops on the face of the planet. The woman behind the desk greeted me as "Honey," and told me my boyfriend would be out in a minute. When I said he wasn't my boyfriend, she offered to take him off my hands and laughed. And directed me to the vending machines with NOPD T-shirts. Seriously. Police T-shirts, hats, and police kitsch. In a vending machine. Even as tired as I was, I loved this town. But I bought a Coke instead and sucked it down for the calories. I had partially shifted and hadn't eaten. Not smart. The cramping in my belly eased with the Coke, and I bought another, drinking it just as fast.

Twenty minutes later I had Eli in the cab and we were heading back to the house, silent, not wanting to talk in front of the cabbie. Back home, I paid my bill plus tip, accepted an evangelical tract from Zareb, and Eli and I entered the house. We had a lot of catching up to do and not a lot of time left in the night.

There were a lot of things we needed. An update on any sightings of Santana or unexplained deaths that might be related to him. New wheels—the SUV had been impounded as part of a crime scene. Better garb. New boots. A bottle of antacids, which Eli had and which helped the pain in my gut considerably. A plan to catch Santana, which we didn't have. A nap that none of us were going to get. And I had to update the Youngers on Molly and the witches, which should take the shortest amount of time. Witches weren't out to kill or maim us or the community, so that was just info, or so I thought.

The Kid had a listing of places where dead humans had been found since sundown—three homeless people drained and dead not far from Louis Armstrong Park. And more recently, places where strange lights had been seen and horrible smells of smoke had been detected—four locations that were near water. The Kid had hacked the NOPD network, which no one mentioned because we needed the intel he had discovered. He pinpointed the sites on a map and sent them to our cells. Each location was farther from the park, as if the stink of burned flesh and odd, unexplained fires had been leapfrogging, moving uptown and beyond, toward the Garden District, which made something in the back of my mind feel all squirrelly, as if that direction made some kind of sense that I didn't want to think about.

The Kid stayed busy uploading all the intel to our cells as we debriefed and reweaponed up and found new boots. Blades clicked and slid into sheaths, the *schnick* of chambers sliding and magazines snapping closed punctuated the commentary as Eli gave us the short version of his time in the pokey. It was succinct. "I was taken in." *Schnick*, *snap*, *slide*, *tap-tap*, *clack*, *schnick*. "Made my one call to HQ." Repeat of same sounds but faster. "Leo made a couple calls to the mayor and the governor." Soft slide of blades being checked and repositioned, leather against steel. "I was let out."

I couldn't be as succinct, but I told the guys about the failure of the *snare of thorns* trap, about Molly trying to get to the blood diamond, about Sabina being burned, and about Brute chasing Santana. I ended with, "I can't trust my best friend and I don't know what to do about it. Or about anything else either."

The Kid said, "The first time Molly misused her gift was when?"

"In Evangelina's garden, fighting her sister off. She stole

the life force of every living thing in the garden to keep her sister from killing us all."

"And the blood diamond was present?" Eli asked.

"Pretty sure Evangelina was using it at the time," I said, sitting on the couch to pull on my last pair of combat boots. All I had left after this were my Western Luccheses, and no way was I going to ruin the pretty boots on a hunt for a big-bad-ugly. Boot shopping was in my near future. "She had already called the demon in her basement, so, yeah, she had to be drawing on it."

"Molly's magic was tainted in the garden, before she came into contact with the angel Hayyel," Eli said, testing the movement of a gun into and out of a holster. That statement seemed important too, but nothing was becoming a cohesive whole in the front of my brain. "And since then, she's been wavering close to out of control."

I nodded. "The angel Hayyel did good stuff and bad stuff to us all. It seems kinda weird that he did nothing to Molly."

"That we know of," Alex said. "Anything might have happened then."

"And KitKit?" Eli asked. "Was the cat there tonight?"

I had forgotten about the cat. "No." I sat back on the couch and closed my eyes, feeling a little weird, doing this in front of the boys, as I breathed in, sniffing for the cat. I placed the highest concentration of cat scent at the stink of the litter box in the back, in the utility/laundry room, and the whiff of cat food from upstairs. The next strongest concentration of cat pong came from behind me. I got up and followed my nose through the kitchen into the butler's pantry. The cat was curled, asleep, on the top open shelf, among some dusty teapots I hadn't had a chance to investigate, her small tail hanging down.

Back in the living room, I said, "Molly doesn't want the other witches to know she has a familiar."

"Peer pressure," Alex said, seriously, nodding. "She's afraid they'll make fun of her." Which wasn't what I was thinking, though it fit.

Eli said, "She needs to take the cat with her all the time because now her affinity for the diamond grows every time she's anywhere near it. It's black magic just like her death magics, and they feed off each other."

I looked at my partner in surprise. For a former active-duty Army Ranger who, until recently, knew nothing about magic, the guy had come a long way. "Makes sense," I agreed. "The cat has a den on the top shelf of the butler's pantry. Alex, can you handle Molly if she comes back while we're gone?"

Alex lifted a shoulder. "When I hear her coming, I'll throw the cat at her. If that doesn't work, look for a warty frog hopping on the keyboards when you get back. Find me a princess to kiss me. I want tongue."

"Gross," I said.

"Fried frog legs," Eli said with a slight twitch of his lips.

Alex flipped his brother off and we left the house on that loving family moment.

CHAPTER 18

The Stench of Barbecued Vamp

Eli's SUV had been released by the police to Leo, and a lower-level blood-servant picked us up out front and drove us to vamp HQ. Eli and I dropped the driver off around the block from the Council Chambers when he said he could get back through the mob safely, and I figured he knew about the secret entrance in the outer wall. We headed into the night, following up on police reports, answering calls from Jodi, and talking to the vamp who had interrogated Juwan—meaning drinking from him until he was blood-drunk, making him take a sip or two of vamp blood, and then reading his mind, which essentially made Juwan a plaything. It was the way vamps fed, and when it was with the human's agreement, it was legal, if morally questionable. When the human was not in agreement, it was ... despicable. Making me despicable for ordering it. But if it helped me stop the Son of Darkness, I could live with despicable. The conversation was pithy and not very informative.

"Yo. Edmund. You're on speakerphone. You get anything outta Juwan?"

"Jane. Such a pleasure to talk with you. Are you certain I can't do anything to share that pleasure with you?"

Eli laughed. More a snicker, really. And it was too dark

for him to see my scowl. I wanted to swat both of them, but Edmund Hartley was inside vamp HQ and I had a feeling that swatting Eli could get a bigger hit back.

"Eddie. Focus. This is business," I said.

"Eddie?" Eli said, incredulity lacing the word.

"You wound me, my darling Jane. When my only desire is to ravish you with sensual delights and bring you to intense heights of carnal satisfaction."

Eli's eyebrows went up. It was stupid and, with us in the middle of chasing down a murdering vamp on fire, not the right time, but I laughed, which was what Edmund intended. If I could like a vamp, I liked Edmund, and I still wanted to discover his story, but another time, another place. "Yada yada yada," I said.

"True. But are you more relaxed?" he asked.

"Yeah. Thanks. Now, about Juwan."

"For a human, he is inordinately difficult to read."

That stumped me, because Edmund, though technically a bond slave, was tremendously powerful, a master vamp under any other circumstances. "So you got nothing?"

"I saw Adrianna in a variety of lascivious positions, none of them likely to have been a result of reality, but he was definitely smitten. Other than our brain-dripping prisoner, I saw only one other Mithran, and it was a bare glimpse."

"And," I said, letting my impatience show.

"It may have been nothing. Or everything."

"Okay. I got it. I can't skewer her on sight."

Slowly, he said, "Dominique."

There were a lot of vamps. Hundreds in the New Orleans territory alone. But there was only one Dominique, and that was the heir to Clan Arceneau. Arceneau's blood-master was Grégoire. Grégoire was Leo's second-in-command. And Leo's lover. I had been hoping I had been wrong about Adrianna's partner in crime, but it seemed the scents in Adrianna's bed were not misleading. "Well, crap," I breathed.

"Yes. My sentiments exactly."

"Edmund, when the prisoner in sub-five got away, he left a pile of nearly dead humans on the floor, humans who had to be fed and turned, and a bunch of you showed up just in time. Dominique was there. So were you." Edmund didn't respond, so I asked, "Who was there first? How did you all know to come down there?"

Cautiously, Edmund said, "Dominique was standing at the top of the stairway on sub-three. She called us down, to turn the humans."

Just as carefully, I asked, "Why was Dominique at Council Chambers? Was she invited? A party? Something?"

"No. She is seldom here. I admit to surprise at seeing her, though at the time it didn't register as odd."

I remembered seeing Grégoire sniffing around sub-five after the Son of Darkness got away. Had he been smelling Dominique? I asked, "Was there any indication that she had, possibly, just maybe, been in sub-five?"

"There was blood on her dress. A fine mist of it up the front of the skirt in a slender V shape, as from an arterial spray. Human blood, fresh, by the smell. But that could have come from anywhere."

"In a V shape," I said. "As if she had been wearing a cloak and took it off after she had been sprayed with blood?"

Edmund said, "Anything is possible."

"Thank you, Edmund. I'll not divulge where I learned of this." I ended the call. I had no idea how to handle this. None at all.

Eli and I talked for a bit as he drove, trying to think like an old vamp and trying to decide what to do about Dominique and checking out every site that might lead us to the Son of Darkness, without having to bring her or Grégoire into the picture. Because going after his heir based on only a glimpse from a traitor's blood-drunk brain could get us both killed, fast.

I texted Alex to have security at HQ look for footage of Dominique before, during, and after Santana got away. I texted the security team at HQ to search for a scarlet cloak. Nifty electronics and digital toys could get us only so far; then the human eye had to take over and search. I got back a text telling me that Derek had shown up at the house, ticked off at being ambushed in the empty clan home. In the next second, I received one from Derek himself that said, *You and me gotta have this out. No more bullshit.*

I texted back, *Watch your language. Thought you mighta switched teams, hanging out with Juwan.*

No. I. Gave. My. Word.

"Ouch," I said aloud. The punctuation suggested that Derek was severely ticked off. And yeah, with reason. I had a feeling I was gonna have to make nice-nice with Derek for a long time over this. I texted back.

I am sorry. When SoD is caught we'll talk. Though I had a feeling it might be more fists and feet and less talking. I really needed to work on my social skills.

Eli and I stopped first at an alleyway near Louis Armstrong Park, not far from where Santana got pricked by the sliver of the Blood Cross. The homeless men had been living in cardboard boxes behind a Dumpster, and according to the scent on the dead men's throats, they had been drained by a burned and bleeding Joseph Santana. After that, things were less certain. The total draining of three humans had been enough blood to get Santana away from the park, but not enough to heal him completely. Not enough to put out the fire burning him from the inside out. For that he needed vamp blood, priestess blood in particular. Fortunately for us, there wasn't a priestess handy and unprotected.

Unfortunately, there *were* old vamps around and less protected than I would like. I remembered the consensus about the SoD being out of touch with modern times. There had been four clan homes in the Garden District, back then, when Santana came to New Orleans as visiting royalty. He had been feted and entertained and wined and dined—or wined and blooded—at all of them. Currently, three of the Garden District's clan homes are vacant—Mearkanis, Rousseau, and Desmarais—empty of everything but ghosts, as the visit to the old Mearkanis home had demonstrated. But one was still inhabited. Arceneau Clan Home, Grégoire's home, and Grégoire had been drinking from Santana. The Son of Darkness might want revenge. And a traitor had seen Dominique, the Arceneau heir, who was currently controlling the clan home in the Garden District while the clan blood-master waited on Leo. We went there first.

Brandon and Brian, Onorio twins and Grégoire's primos and security specialists (despite the fact that Onorios can't be bound to a vamp), met us at the front drive. The wrought-iron gate was locked, the house was dark, the shutters closed, and the twins were decked out in low-light and infrared headgear, top-of-the-line coms gear, a multitude of blades and arms, including shotguns in spine holsters, and full Enforcer regalia. I had never seen them wearing the leathers of Enforcers. And all I could think was *Oh. My. Gosh. Holy. Crap.* My reaction must have showed on my face when I exited the SUV.

"She likes the way we look," Brandon said, identified by his scent, and sounding satisfied.

"Too little too late. She turned us down in favor of George," Brian said, automatically repositioning so that his brother and he could both shoot and take us down with ease but not catch each other or the house in the cross fire.

"The way I heard it," Eli said, beeping the SUV locked and stepping behind it so he was protected but in an excellent firing position, "you boys never offered her anything. George got her by default."

"Never offered?" Brian said. "She clearly never told you about the nights in Asheville."

"She stayed in our rooms. *With us.*"

"I had my own room," I said crossly, sniffing the night and searching the shadows for signs of anything out of place. For the smell of Santana. For the smell of Dominique. Someone had been cooking spicy fried food, the smell/taste of peppers, shrimp, and hot oil on the air. No smell of scorched vamp or Dominique. "No fighting in the ranks, boys. We need to know that Grégoire is safe. Joseph Santana got burned and he'll be looking for strong vampire blood to feed him."

"And what burned him?" Brandon asked, his voice a little too silky for my tastes. And for Eli's too, seemingly, since he showed the nine mil he had drawn, aiming it between the brothers. I took two steps to the side so I was out of the line of fire. "It's okay, Eli," I said. "Sabina's sliver of the Blood Cross burned him. She's burned too, but Del is sending Leo to her." And if my answer let them believe that Sabina was burned when the priestess wielded the sliver of the ancient weapon against Joseph Santana, well, I was learning to lie by omission way better than I wanted. It made the skin between my shoulder blades twitch, as if God was watching and wasn't happy with my methods.

"Is the priestess okay?" Brian asked.

"Arm burned to blackened bones. Not in very good control."

The brothers looked at each other and flipped their

night-vision goggles out of the way. "We've heard tales about the months after she used the Blood Cross to stop the Damours back in the late seventeen hundreds. It was bad."

Brian rested his left elbow on the hilt of a sword. "Amaury cleaned out his scion lair and locked her in. It took the better part of a decade for her to heal enough to regain control around humans. Or so they say."

Or so they say was a common phrase humans used around vamps, because vamps explained nothing and offered even less fresh intel. Vamps were born and bred on secrets. Or rather, raised from the dead and nursed on bloody secrets.

"Some say she didn't come back to herself until Amaury put her on a boat and sent her to the Europeans. They fed her on the oldest Mithrans. The Sons of Darkness even offered blood," Brandon said. "Or so they say."

"Old tales," Brian said, and changed the subject. "Grégoire is safe, here. He rose with us at dusk, fed, and is currently on conference calls with his businessman in the Philippines."

"Here?" I asked.

"Yes. Why?" Brian asked.

"Who's watching him?" Eli asked.

"As per the orders of the *Enforcer*," Brian said, his tone going glacial at a perceived questioning of his decision-making process, "we're integrating the teams. With our master are three of the new people from Atlanta and four of the Tequila boys." Team Tequila had been with Derek since the beginning.

"No offense, Grandpa," Eli said, his expression and tone proving his words a lie.

"None taken, Sonny."

"I can't take you anywhere," I said to Eli. And then I asked the Onorio twins the really important question. "And Dominique?"

"Away. With her scions."

"I'll need that address," I said slowly.

The twins altered position in the dark, the difference subtle but certain. They were ready to draw weapons. "Why?" Brandon asked.

I shifted my own position, just as delicately, to keep any stray shots from neighboring houses. It was like a dance. The boys might like me, but if they thought I was the slightest threat to their master, they'd hurt me bad. "Because there is some indication that she was involved with Adrianna." Behind me, Eli's weapons ratcheted as he readied two, seemingly at the same time, which took dexterity. My partner wasn't subtle at all.

The twins glanced at each other, and some indefinable communication occurred, a twin thing where layers of exchanges were taking place, even as they glanced back to us. Brian said, "You understand that this request places us in a difficult position. You understand that as head of clan security, we know the most personal and confidential details of our clan Mithrans' lives and are charged with their protection, well-being, and their privacy."

"I do. I know how to protect those who give me the information I need," I said. "And I know that we have a killer on the loose who threatens the delicate balance of safety between the Mithran world and the human one."

Silence settled between us as the two thought and impatience crawled under my skin. No way to bash the info out of them, but I wanted to. Thoughtfully, Brandon said, "Dominique is in love with Grégoire."

I considered that for a bit, before saying, "And Grégoire is in love with Leo."

"Yes," Brandon said, his tone weighty. There was a lot of meaning in that simple word.

"Our clan heir has a new lair in the Garden District, but we don't know where," Brian said, the words formal and guarded. "Dominique has been staying there often, for the last few weeks. When she comes home she smells of blood. Mithran blood."

"Does she smell of sex?" I asked.

The brothers glanced at each other again for half a second. Brandon said, "Not sex with a man."

"I see. Let's go, Eli. Call us if you need us," I said to the twins. "If Dominique shows up here, I suggest that Grégoire protect himself. No telling who she might bring with her. And if Grégoire wants to stay at HQ, for any reason, including being attacked by someone close to him, let us know. He may need a convoy and diversions."

"We've seen what the vampire you're hunting can do," Brandon said, gravely. "We'll be careful."

"Yeah. Do that."

Back in the SUV, I said, "Idiot."

Eli said, "I was just having a little fun. And so were they."

"Maybe." I leaned my head back on the headrest and closed my eyes as we motored down the street. "But you're still a pain in the ass."

Eli choked at my use of language and I smiled into the darkness, letting my shoulders droop into sleep. Eli woke me when we reached the first body of water, a family pool. I didn't even have to step out of the SUV. I could smell the stench of burned vamp from the open window, along with the smell of pesticides and dog poop. And Brute. But no dead people. I marked it on my map on the cell and closed my eyes until we reached the next site, a fountain in a park I didn't recognize. It was empty and stinky and tainted with were-taint also. As were three of the other sites. At none of them did I smell Adrianna.

We drove through the Warehouse District and I told Eli about the Damours, pointing out the warehouse where they had lived, a building where they kept the long chained secured to metal beds in a big room with a dead human they had fed to their progeny. I pointed out the building vamps used for parties, and an old church now owned by a vamp and kept as a daytime lair, which was weird.

At two of the sites I smelled dead humans and left the SUV, making my way close to the bodies to ascertain that no one was left alive. In New Orleans, it's warm most of the year and homeless people can live outdoors in relative ease all year round, needing only tarps for rain protection, and lots of bug spray. At the first site I scented two dead middle-aged men smelling of booze, and the cops were already on-site, carrying the cop version of AK-47s and wearing their kill faces. We drove on by.

At the second site I held up a hand, indicating that Eli should wait in the vehicle. I drew my M4 shotgun and moved across the weeds of a vacant lot. I found a dying campfire and an entire family, including a teenager, all curled in sleeping bags. Drained.

I stopped as the scent of this death burned my nostrils, my lungs, scorching through my bloodstream. I moved into the campsite and bent over the boy, drawing on Beast's senses. He looked too young to even shave. Worse, he was smiling.

I had a hard time drawing a breath. *He was smiling.*

Something like horror slithered under my skin, and I closed my eyes, turning away, hunching. The thing that had hung on Leo's wall had done this. I had let him get away. I had let him live when I knew the first time I set eyes on the thing, it needed to die. Leo and I shared responsibility for this death. For all the deaths caused by the monster.

Kit. Killer of kits must die, Beast thought.

"Yeah," I murmured.

I loosened my grip on the M4 to keep from accidently firing or damaging the weapon with my anger and breathed shallowly until I found a measure of control.

Sniffing the site again, I detected another scent. Brute. The werewolf's growing anger was pungent on the night wind at the campsite, and I figured that if the werewolf caught up with Santana, there would be a miniwar on the spot. Maybe I'd get lucky and be there to help. I backed away from the camp to the SUV.

Eli pulled from the curb. "Details," he said quietly, reading my body language.

I shook my head and dialed Jodi. Eli listened as I made my report, and Jodi was quiet, an awful, broken fury flowing across the cell to me, like a wave of emotion. When news of this hit the airwaves, there would be a reaction in the city, one that would put every supernatural at risk, or pit one species against another until full human-on-supernat civil war was possible. But at the moment I didn't care if every vamp in New Orleans died in their lairs.

With dawn only hours away, my skinwalker metabolism had healed my body enough to allow me ease of movement and breath enough to feel like I'd survive. I still hadn't seen to Beast, but I would get to her soon, I promised us both. *Soon.*

Alex had sent us a new address, one that had been called in to 911, about a bad smell and odd lights. The address matched the vacant Rousseau Clan Home in the Garden District, and though we had two other locations to check, we were close enough to Rousseau to take it first. Eli drove around the entire block, getting a feel for the house and grounds, entrance and egress, the layout and footprint of the property. It was going to be hard to approach safely and covertly, but we needed to take a good look. The burned-flesh stench came from around back. "He's been here," I told Eli. "Recently. Real recently. As in, could still be here."

The Rousseau Clan Home was close to the street, and the grounds in front of the home were small but lush, with palms and what might have been a banana tree and night-flowering jasmine. The lot was slim but deep, and the two-story house was weirdly U shaped, narrow across the front, long and deep, with a very narrow hallway and gallery down the right side of the back of the house to the rear of the lot, where the house spread out again. From what we could make out in the security lights of neighboring houses, the back section of the house looked like it might be the same size and footprint as the front half. The pool was in the courtyard, surrounded on three sides by the house and by a tall brick fence on the fourth, giving it privacy. The chlorine smell was strong enough to override a lot of smells, but not the stench of barbecued vamp. And the seclusion wasn't enough to mute the sounds of splashing.

"Call in fangheads or Derek to assist?" Eli asked.

"I say no, but it's your call," I said. "I want access to take down whatever needs taking down, with finality, and without vamps sticking in their noses. But I'll also heal better than you will."

"Keep HQ on speed dial and get me help if needed, but I say we go in alone. Stay close," Eli murmured. "It's too deep to divide up." I nodded and we triple-checked our weapons, pulled on the new headsets, leaving the SUV parked on the street, unlocked, windows open, in case we needed to make a faster-than-normal getaway. At the left corner of the lot, partially hidden behind the banana leaves, I boosted Eli up and over the ten-foot brick fence. It was his turn to take point. He tapped his mouthpiece, telling me it was good, and I pulled on Beast's strength to jump and grab the top, swinging myself over.

"Show-off," he muttered good-naturedly into his mouth-piece, as we moved along the open left side of the house to the courtyard. The central garden area had been kept up and was lined in more plants, both the flowering and the vegetable variety, and the center was tiled in peachy orang-ish terra-cotta, the pool perfectly in the middle of the tiled space. We hid in the shrubs, checking the place over.

The courtyard was overlooked by the wraparound second-floor gallery and the patio beneath it on the first floor. The house was dark and the gallery was streaked with the long shadows of predawn. Up there, anyone could be hidden anywhere. In unison, we eased our right earpieces away from our ears, keeping one ear tied into coms and protected against explosive deafness, but allowing us to hear anything closer.

There were low ambiance lights on in the shrubbery, giving just enough illumination to tell us that there was no one in the open, yet the pool tiles were running with water, draining away from the pool. And the runoff looked darker than normal, probably mixed with blood. I was holding a vamp-killer and the M4 loaded with silver, but the stink of blood and vamps and scorched flesh told me it might not be enough. Maybe if Eli was carrying a man-fired missile, an SA-24, I might feel secure. *Might.* I stood silent, sniffing, letting the shadows and the scents tell me what I needed to know.

Santana was no longer alone. By the scent patterns I counted five humans, all smelling of stress and fear, probably barely alive from blood loss, and maybe two other vamps, but the scents were hard to read beneath the chlorine and the stink of Santana burning. His being on fire might make him easier to kill, but it wouldn't make him easier to get along with. I breathed steadily and discerned the vamps' location on the warm, humid night air. Indicating their scent positions as best I was able, I held two fingers curled down near my mouth, like vamp teeth, then held up four fingers, before pointing in two different directions.

Eli made a cutting motion across his own throat, asking me if they were kill targets. I thought about it, hating to be stuck in this position—the position of deciding who lived and who died. Or, rather, who remained undead and who found true-death. I held out a hand, palm up, as if serving him a plate of hors d'oeuvres. The gesture said, *Your choice.* I hoped it indicated that if the vamps were prisoners, no. If they were willing participants, yes.

I patted the left side of my chest to indicate a heartbeat and pointed where I smelled humans. Eli nodded and flipped down his ocular. I eased out of the foliage to give him better room and visual access. He flipped back and forth between the low-light and the infrared oculars and used his entire hand to point out where the humans were. All five in one location.

Pulling harder on Beast's night vision, I spotted something close to the far end of the pool, silvery and ... The vision resolved into humans, all together, lying in a pile, unmoving but still alive. Barely. Inside me, Beast growled low, the vibration juddering my chest. They had been drained and might be so close to death they couldn't be saved. This was going to be messy.

For half a second, I debated calling in SWAT and medic, but I decided that the vamps might just finish off the humans if they heard sirens or smelled cops. And I reconsidered calling vamp HQ for backup. It was a risk to do neither, but ... Undecided, I held up my vamp fang-teeth gesture and then pointed, asking if the vamps were stationary. After feeding, they might show on infrared, but they always showed on low-light. Eli pointed to lounge-type garden furniture beneath the gallery. An unmoving form reclined on each one, which I could see now that he pointed them out. The vamps were the full length of the courtyard apart. I nodded. Then he pointed up and inside the part of the house farthest from the street and made a waffling motion. There was something hot up there, showing in infrared on his PIR device.

Like maybe a vamp on fire. Yeah.

Two on the lower floor near the pool, one or two upstairs. Why couldn't they all be in one place, easy to herd up and dispatch? I pointed to the vamps on the lounges and mouthed, *Go.*

We separated and raced in, Eli to the right, me to the left. Eli's vamp was lying facedown. It raised up and Eli took it—him or her—from behind, his left arm around the vamp's throat, his right stabbing up into the vamp's rib cage. In a human it would have been a kidney strike, a killing stroke that would sever the main artery feeding the kidney and the main nerve keeping it healthy. It was said to be so painful that a human taken down couldn't even draw breath to scream but would bleed out and die on the spot. Silently.

Didn't happen quite that way with the vamp. The death wail was an instant ululation that echoed off the house walls and into the night. The other vamp leaped high, toward Eli from twenty feet away. If the vamp had used his vamp speed, I never would have had a chance—there would have been a pop of displaced air and Eli dead on the ground. But the vamp was in predator mode and leaped, like a wolf onto prey. Still drawing on Beast, I leaped too, judging the vamp's speed and direction even as I shoved off with my back foot. We hit in midair, about two feet from Eli and the vamp he was now fighting.

The next moments were blurred images of vamped-out predators, both female, ripping and tearing at us with talons and fangs. The sound of blows landing. And the overwhelming, night-blasting explosion of an automatic subgun as Eli emptied the extended magazine into the vamp he'd stabbed.

Over that, I heard nothing, not even the screaming of both vamps in mortal danger.

Eli's vamp was falling, mostly in two parts, but still alive, somehow, her face in a rictus of fury. Mine was on the ground, a silver stake in her heart but still clawing at the lawn, trying to reach me. I kicked her over and rammed in a second stake. And then six more for good measure. The stink of nitrocellulose, corroding silver, and vamp blood filled the air. Finally the staked vamp lay still, weirdly not yet true-dead, but close. She looked like she had been in intimate contact with a porcupine. I chuffed out snarling laughter that I couldn't hear.

The face of the vamp at my feet resolved into someone I knew. I checked out Eli's opponent, who was unmoving also. I knew them. Lorraine and Cieran, formally of Clan Desmarais, or maybe of Mearkanis. I didn't remember and it really didn't matter, because both clans had lost in the vamp war last year and the vamps who had survived had been seconded to Clan Pellissier. In Pellissier they were the lowest of the low, as all vamps from defeated clans were. But more important, they had once served as scions to Adrianna. She had turned them; they were her children. It was no accident that they were here with Santana. It had to have been planned from the beginning, though whether Santana had found them or they had found him and brought him here to recuperate I might never know. Not now. Because no way was I leaving them alive.

Eli was already moving for the nearest door, ramming a new mag home in his small, automatic subgun. I fell into place at his left. The door to the long, narrow hallway that separated the front half of the house from the back was unlocked, and we entered, Eli taking point, which my Beast didn't like at all. But I knew Eli could survive a frontal attack by using the minigun, and I stood a better chance than he did of surviving an attack from behind.

But the place was empty, cool, the air-conditioning running with a soft hum. It smelled a lot like the Rousseau Clan Home, of old vamp blood and mold, but there was also an overlay of Clorox. In the last few hours, someone had been there to clean. Beneath the smell of cleansers were the fresher smell of human blood and the stink of scorched vamp. Joseph Santana, aka Joses Bar-Judas, aka the Son of Darkness, was there. And so was a female vamp. Dominique. There was no longer any doubt. Inside, I cursed.

My hearing was returning and sirens sounded in the distance, still muffled. Eli muttered, "Dang nosy neighbors, upset over a little weapons fire in the middle of the night."

I laughed, but it sounded odd, too deep, my Beast close to the surface. From overhead, in the second-floor hallway, I heard a thump and crash. Eli's gun followed the sound, held close beneath his arm. But nothing came through the floor.

Since the AC was still on, that meant that the power was on, and with one hand, I found a light-switch panel containing eight switches and one of those round dimmer switches. "Lights," I said, warning him. He flicked his goggles out of the way. I flipped all the switches and stabbed the dimmer. Lights came on everywhere. My eyes watered. Outside, I heard a pop of vamp movement and whirled. A flash of something pale showed in the now-illuminated courtyard, and I smelled the receding stink of burning vamp. Santana was taking off. Over the fence at speed.

The cops were pulling up out front. I wasn't gonna get a chance to chase Santana down. But I did mark the direction of his exit by the smell and by a glimmer of light in the night. He was still burning, like the way human flesh burned when pure potassium got embedded in it. I was guessing that when he tore the sliver of the Blood Cross out of his neck, he didn't get all the fire and now was being consumed by the flames of the Blood Cross. I couldn't think of a better way for him to go, even if it meant war with the EVs.

From the other end of the house, I heard something

crash. "Window," Eli said. Outside there was a muted thump. The other vamp getting away; Dominique making a hasty exit.

I holstered the weapons and dialed Alex. Succinctly, I said, "Call the cops and Leo. We're at Rousseau Clan Home. Cops are here. Santana got away. Dead vamps and drained humans. We need to be able to track Santana. We need medic for drained humans and vamps to heal any that might survive."

"Copy. Eli?"

"We're both good."

The connection ended and moments later, cops rammed the Rousseau front door and the first wave poured into the house. We were standing with our weapons on the floor and with our hands high when the cops raced through the front of the house and into the long hallway. They scooped the weapons into the corner, put us in handcuffs, and shoved us to the floor, where we stayed. I got a good look at the front half of the L-shaped house; the back entrance to the hallway opened into a huge yellow kitchen with modern, fancy cabinetry, yellow- and brown-veined granite cabinet tops with lots of quartz and mica flakes inside that made them gleam in the lights. Beyond, I caught a glimpse of a living area with brown leather furniture, a luscious leather that screamed *expensive*. I could see a yellow silk rug beneath the furniture that probably went for forty thou, and crystal chandeliers overhead that were probably worth even more. The window treatments were full of tassels and drapes and swags and looked tacky to me, but I probably wasn't cultured enough to appreciate them. The kitchen was spotless and the smell of Clorox flooded out, suggesting that Leo had—literally—cleaned house to remove any signs of the vamp war. And then Santana had shown up.

With a frisson of worry, I had to wonder if the nearly dead humans had been his cleanup crew.

We sat on the floor, silent and still, not answering questions, until a familiar figure appeared, wearing a fancy suit with prison tats below his sleeves, an incongruous mixture among the uniforms. The detective walked up, stopped, and stared down at us, his face expressionless but still oozing menace. I figured that was a skill he'd learned undercover in prison among gangs. There was still a price on his head

set by the gangs, and the powers that be at NOPD didn't
know what to do with the hero cop, so they had dropped
him into the basement with Jodi Richoux. "Sloan Rosen, as
I live and breathe," I said. "You do that whole 'badass in a
suit' look well."

Eli slanted me a glance. He didn't know Sloan well, because the detective worked opposite shifts with Jodi in the
woo-woo department. Eli's glance said he'd sit silent unless
called upon for more. I inclined my head a fraction, saying
I got the message.

"You the ones who called in the medic?" Sloan asked,
watching the byplay, his dark skin gleaming under the too-
bright lights.

"Yeah," I said. "Vamps drained some humans. We got
two of the fangheads. Two got away."

Sloan stepped to the vamp who had been chewed in two
by the barrage of bullets. Then he looked over at the façade
of the back half of the house, which was peppered with a lot
of bullet holes. He toed the vamp. "Bit of overkill, don'tcha
think?" Out in the courtyard, medical personnel were attending to the humans, separating them from a limp pile
into individuals.

"No. She had been drinking on"—there was a microhesi-
tation before I finished—"Joseph Santana, the vamp who
killed the fifty-two humans. He's the most powerful vamp
I've ever encountered, and his blood gave her extra healing
abilities. She didn't go down and stay down. My partner had
to *put* her down."

Sloan stared at me, his eyes narrow. My hesitation had
not gone unnoticed. Nor had the unnecessary info I'd offered to cover it up. "He one of the two who got away?"

"Yeah."

"And you didn't chase them?"

"Coulda tried. But we kinda had cops heading our way,
aiming guns at us," I said. "I didn't want my partner to get
shot. Is it okay to take off the cuffs? My fingers are falling
asleep."

Sloan thought about that for a while, chewing a tooth-
pick, which I thought was a totally noir finishing touch,
what with the suit and the tats. After making us wait long
enough to bother normal humans, Sloan gestured to one of
the three cops standing guard. The cops uncuffed us and

stepped back, weapons still at the ready. Sloan gave us a "get up" gesture and we stood, shaking out our muscles. I said, "I called Mr. Pellissier to send over a vamp to feed the humans. Maybe we can save them."

"They better not turn 'em," one of the cops said. "'Cause the only good suckhead is a staked suckhead."

The other cop laughed. "Yeah. Like these two. Good shooting, man," he said to Eli. "Too bad you can't take 'em all out."

Sloan frowned. Vamp racism was rampant in large parts of the city, but the cops were usually better at keeping it hidden. The death of fifty-two humans by one vamp had brought a lot of the latent hatred and fear out in the open. I decided not to respond to the comments, and Eli followed my lead. Sloan gestured to the two cops, stepping out into the courtyard. The last cop looked no less friendly about vamps, but he also looked like the angry, silent type, a guy who had a hard-on for anything and everything that wasn't like him—white, middle-aged, out of shape, and unhappy.

Eli and I exchanged glances that were full of meaning, mostly about needing to get on the road and after Santana, but I had a feeling that if we tried to leave, the angry, silent cop would happily shoot us in the backs.

Sloan returned in minutes, looking grim. "Two human victims have expired, and a third is receiving CPR. A fang—A vampire is here," he corrected himself, "named Edmund Hartley. You know him?"

"Yeah. He's good people. He has a gift for healing. 'Bout this tall"—I held out a hand—"slender, nondescript, mild-mannered looking. Like a librarian." I leaned around Sloan and spotted Edmund in the courtyard. "Yeah. Him."

Sloan frowned. "Okay. I'll let him feed them. But we'll keep weapons on him."

I figured Edmund would be insulted, but he wouldn't do or say anything against the weapons. He was too low in the vamp hierarchy to do that. I pointed to the end of the hallway. "Mind if we check out the back of the house? That's where we think Santana and the other vamp were before they heard gunfire and took off. In which case we'll need our weapons."

"Knock yourselves out," Sloan said. "I'm calling the ME's office and Homicide."

I took the statement as a hint that if we wanted out of there, instead of getting caught up in the investigation, we needed to slide away without asking permission. We reweaponed and hoofed it to the back half of the house. It was actually set up as a totally independent second home, the décor similar but contrasting to the front half, and more expensive. Lots more expensive. There was leather everywhere—the soft stuff that would make good gloves—and gilt everything, and the crystal chandeliers were even bigger than in the front of the house, the rugs even fancier, and the drapes even swaggier. If that was a word.

My guess about the drained humans had been right. The crew hadn't finished cleaning, and there were fresh and old bloodstains here and there. It was getting uglier by the moment. We moved through the house, from the entry beneath the gallery, through the pale yellow and cream kitchen, the breakfast nook, the coffee bar, and the wine bar, taking in the damage. In the wine bar, someone had decided to try a little of everything, and there were empty and partially empty bottles, broken bottles, and spilled wine everywhere. Along with signs that more had taken place there than just a lot of drinking. My chest went tight as I studied the place with eyes and nose.

There was blood—fresh, not old and brown—here and there, in sprays along the walls, in small puddles—and other bodily fluids. Some of it was human. Some was from the vamps we had killed. Santana had partied there and drank his fill. My ribs hurt as I put it all together. Santana had raped his way through the hostages.

If we had started the night's search there, we could have taken him down and saved the humans.

Eli swore as he recognized what the evidence suggested.

"Yeah," I said, the fury so heated beneath my breastbone that it felt like a hot, liquid pool, like molten stone. "I know." I rubbed my sternum with a fist, trying to ease the pain. We moved on through the house, finding the royal-style bathroom where Santana had bathed in a magnificent marble tub, trying to put out the flame that persisted, burning inside him. There were knives strewn about the place, showing traces of blood. I bent and sniffed one, catching the reek of scorched vamp and the scent of saliva. I had a feeling that Santana had tried to cut the fire out and that Dominique had indeed been there, helping, and had licked the blade clean. *This dude needs to die.*

I didn't realize I had spoken it aloud until Eli said, "Let's get to it."

Under cover of night, we slipped out of the house and into our SUV.

CHAPTER 19

Too Much 'Tude and Not Enough Manners

We followed the stink of the Son of Darkness for miles as the sky lightened with the coming dawn. Santana dipped into pools and bayous and even puddles along the way. Eventually I lost the scent and thought about returning to the house for my bloodhound fetish necklace to keep chasing him, but if we caught up to him, that would have left Eli to take out the Son of Darkness alone, a vamp who was smelling more and more of the stink of madness. Pain can do that to anyone, and a previously poisoned and insane vamp might stand a greater chance of insanity than even a regular vamp.

Not that I told Eli that my reason for staying in human form was to keep him from having to fight Santana alone. I wasn't stupid. But before Mr. Macho and I could go home and get cleaned up, we had to check out the locations of the final 911 calls. Thankfully, we could do that on the way back to the house, backtracking through the city.

The first location was near a small park I wasn't familiar with—Samuel Square. The address was on Loyola Avenue, a new town house. We rode around the block, scoping out the place, before we pulled over and got out. Dawn was minutes away when I took a deep breath, over my tongue and past the roof of my mouth.

The smell of blood met my nose instantly. "Oh crap," I whispered.

Eli was holding weapons before I could finish the words.

"Dead humans. And Brute's hurt," I said.

Eli frowned, a real frown, harsh lines bracketing his mouth. There was nothing we could do for the dead except call Sloan. But a bleeding werewolf was a lethal werewolf. The cures for the werewolf bite, from were-taint contagion, were only sometimes successful and required spending a lot of time in bed with Gee DiMercy and . . . Eli would probably rather shoot himself than go through the cure. I stood a better chance of surviving unchanged than Eli did.

But the presence of an injured werewolf meant I needed advice and probably help. I pulled my cell and ran my fingers through my contact list. I didn't have a lot of friends, and the list of the ones who could help with a werewolf were few and far between. Like, two.

"Call him," Eli said.

I knew he meant for me to call Ricky Bo LaFleur, my ex, but I still hesitated, my fingertip hovering over the name.

"Soul is the other choice, and she'll follow PsyLED rules and regs. Rick is a cop but he'll put you, and Brute, and this city, before protocol."

I blew a raspberry and punched Rick's name on the screen. I heard the line open, the near-silent sounds of linens and a mattress moving and groaning. The soft sound of a woman murmuring—Paka, the liquid syllables of her native African tongue, questioning. "It's okay," Rick said. "Just work."

Just work . . . I pressed my lips together to hold in the retort. Calling him an ass wouldn't help me.

The ambient sound changed, then changed again as a door closed. "Jane?" Rick said a moment later. The single word was filled with all sorts of meaning. *Is it really you? Why are calling? Are you nearby?*

"Brute's been injured," I said, without intro. "I smell his blood. It was probably done by a powerful vamp I'm chasing."

"The Fifty-two Killer."

"Yeah, but cute names the press have given him don't begin to tell about this guy."

"I've been reading into the situation in case I need to come down there."

That made sense. Rick knew the city better than any other PsyLED special agent. "I need to know how to capture Brute without getting bit, and how to help heal him. When a were can't shift—" I stopped midthought.

Rick laughed, but the low sound was grim, not humorous. "They're deadly. I have firsthand experience. And I'm betting you can't sneak up on Brute and knock him out, like you did me."

"Yeah. Kinda used that one on him already."

"You did always hit first and ask questions later." He sounded like he was taking a trip down memory lane and it was all rose petals and kisses.

"How do I stop him?" I bit out the words.

Rick hesitated, then said, "I left a few things in a public storage unit on Tchoupitoulas Street." He gave me the unit number. "Do you still have my house key? It fits the lock."

An uncomfortable warmth filled me, not sexual, but heated all the same, as if someone had just injected hot-pepper sauce into my veins. "I have it." Dang it. I had it on my key chain in my pocket. Why hadn't I tossed it? Was I still— I stopped the thought before it was born. No. I wasn't. "What do I do?"

He told me how to get in and what to do and how to deal with Brute. When he started talking about a special rifle, I passed the cell to Eli, who took the particulars. When he was done, Eli listened a moment longer and then said, "Yeah, man. Sorry. But thanks." He closed the phone and handed it back to me.

"Let's go," I said. Eli nodded and we drove away from the scent of bleeding werewolf. "What did he ask you?"

"Is she okay? Is she waiting on me?"

The peppery feeling reared up in me. It was anger, not something softer and sweeter. "*Hu-whaaaa-at?* Am I *waiting* on him? Like some lovesick fifteen-year-old with too many hormones and not enough brains? Am I *waiting on him*? You got to be freaking *kidding me*!"

Eli slanted a glance at me, his dark eyes catching the passing park lights. He was amused.

"Well? Am I?" I asked, and I couldn't avoid the street-snark head roll.

"No, babe. I'd say you moved on and up. Way on and way up."

"Okay, then." I sat back in the seat and realized I had just acted like a fifteen-year-old with too much 'tude and not enough manners. I scowled at the street and then felt my mouth curl up into an unwilling smile. "Am I waiting on him. As *if*."

Eli chuckled softly. I relaxed into the seat, my fifteen-year-old-teenager fit passing. I had moved on a long time ago, but something about Ricky Bo still pushed my buttons. Not the hot, jump-in-the-sack buttons, but the hot, want-to-belt-him buttons. They were located in close proximity in my brain. I think they were located close in humans' brains too, which was why people fell out of love and into fury so easily. *Design flaw,* I thought, and laughed along with Eli. As he drove, Eli contacted his brother and told Alex to get inside the security system at the storage unit and shut off the cameras. I was tired or I'd have thought of that. Eli was right. I needed a nap.

Even in the Big Easy, traffic thinned just before dawn, letting us get to the storage unit in record time, where I covered us in the hallway while Eli went inside. The trip would have been a lot faster on Bitsa, but when I saw what Eli left the unit carrying, I shut that thought up. No way could I get away with carting *that* on a Harley. It was a long, charcoal gray case. A gun case. A honking *big* gun case.

Back in the SUV, Eli opened the case and placed the weapon in my lap before driving away. It looked like a ... I had no idea how to describe the weapon except that it was long barreled, matte black, and looked really high-tech. It was a gun, but a gun like I'd never seen before. "Uncle Sam's R and D department at DOD would be very unhappy to learn that our friendly PsyLED cop has that pretty baby," Eli said, sounding satisfied and wearing his smallest smile, the one he saved for military hardware and tactical ops.

While I inspected the gun, he called Alex again and told his brother to restart the security system. There would be no record of our visit.

The gun was heavy and had a scope, but no place for a

standard magazine or clip. "Okay," I said. "I'll bite. What is it and why do we have it?"

Eli voice took on that pedantic but affectionate tone used by all gun lovers when they talk about a weapon. "It's the military's new, fully automatic version of a Dan-Inject dart gun. The man in the field calls it a Bongo, after an African elephant that needed sedation and transplantation to an area with fewer humans."

"Fully automatic?" I quoted, turning the weapon in my hands, careful to keep my fingers away from the trigger.

"In this case, the term doesn't refer to the method of firing rounds, but to the darts themselves. There are five or six different meds included in each dart, so they can be calibrated in the field to the species and weight for dosing, so one weapon can be used for various different-sized animals. And retrieved and reused."

A frisson of fear shot through me. "And they have a sedative that will work on a three-hundred-pound werewolf?" *What about skinwalkers?* But I didn't say it. Not yet. If Eli knew the answer to that question, it put our entire relationship on a completely different standing.

"Seems so," he said, smelling stress-free and sounding relaxed. "It's nearly instant sedation—*true* instant sedation being a thing of novels and the movies. Using civilian and veterinary sedatives, sedation takes ten minutes to half an hour on most species. The military version is faster, taking about half that time because it's a two- or three-part med. The first part is a fast-acting paralyzing agent. It takes the target down, makes them relaxed, makes their limbs feel heavy. The second part puts them to sleep. For werewolves, there's a third part, a very slow-acting sedative to keep them under longer, so they can't start to wake up, panic, shift, and/or bite."

Drawing my courage up around me, I said, very softly, "And for me? What does our dear, kind ol' Uncle Sam have for skinwalkers?"

Eli's scent changed, and the look he shot me this time was thoughtful as he processed my question, what it might entail in practice, and what it might lead to in our future. "So far as I know, and so far as my nosy, snooper brother can find out, the U.S. military is unaware of what you are, beyond some kind of magical creature. Alex was able to find one report that suggests you're a witch of some kind, one previously unknown."

"They asked you to watch and report on me."

Eli's eyes went hard and cold and he whipped the vehicle over to the curb, braked hard enough to rock the armored SUV on its reinforced undercarriage, and slammed it into park. "You got something to ask me?"

"Yeah," I said softly. "The guy who asked you to spy on me? When you decked him, did he bleed much?"

Eli snorted softly, the sound way more refined than my own snort. He closed his eyes and scrubbed his face, the action showing just how tired he really was. My partner needed sleep, much more than the power naps he'd taken since the death of the fifty-two, since the growing death toll among New Orleans' marginalized and least protected citizens. Softly, musingly, he said, "You really are a cat, baiting and pouncing on the unwary. And no." He dropped his hands and met my gaze across the darkened interior. "I didn't deck him. He was in one piece when I walked away. But any chance of ever serving with the military went down the drain with that decision."

There was something in his tone that said the story hadn't stopped there. "So who's watching me?"

"Alex."

I didn't react externally, where a human could detect it, but my heart rate leaped and sped.

"They approached him when I turned them down. They offered him to end his term of probation. We decided to take their offer, and so he's been feeding them info for the last few months. He's a free man now. And whoever it was who wanted info has been firmly convinced that you're a witch of limited power who came into Leo's employ by stealth and deceit."

Holding myself still, I considered what Eli had said. From one perspective it was a stunning betrayal, and my heart hurt, far deeper than I had expected. They should have told me. But from the perspective of a military man, one grounded in strategy and tactics and need-to-know, it probably seemed like the smart thing to do. With Alex collecting data, Eli knew who all the players on the field were: who was watching me, who was collecting information, who was spinning it, what it looked like when it was reported, and who it was being reported to. Except for the last part, it was all in the family.

My tone just as mild as his, I said, "You didn't think about telling me all this?"

"I did. But." He turned his eyes back to the road and pulled into the sparse traffic. Passing headlights created planes of illumination and zones of shadow on his brown-skinned face. He was thinking, trying to find words to tell me something important, something he found difficult to say. "You were making money. You were seeing George. You were happy for the first time in a long time," Eli said. "I didn't see a reason to tell you something unnecessary and bring you down, not for a situation that would never affect you. Did I screw up?"

"I think so."

"You're not sure?" Eli snorted again and slanted his eyes at me. "That is such a girl remark."

"Yeah. It is. Doesn't change how I feel about you and the Kid conniving behind my back. How would you feel if I did something to try to keep *you* safe or happy or something?" And I knew it was a mistake the moment the words left my mouth. Because Eli grinned, showing teeth, the way Beast shows teeth—to make a point, and not a nice point either.

"You mean like you not shifting into an animal with a tracking nose because you're afraid to leave me to fight Santana alone?"

I let the question hang in the air between us for a while because, well, he was right. Which I hated. I frowned at his self-satisfied grin and finally said, "Is this what family does? All this conniving and arguing and keeping secrets? 'Cause I don't like it."

Eli's face fell into what might have been his normal, regular, ordinary smile, had the Rangers and service to his country not beat all the softness out of him. "It's okay, babe. You'll get used to it."

Which made me feel all warm and fuzzy, because that meant that he and Alex weren't planning to take off any-time soon. They were sticking around. Being partners didn't mean they'd stay. Being family meant they'd stay. "I'm sorry I didn't shift."

"I'm not. That sucker woulda eaten me alive and spit out the bone splinters."

I laughed softly. "Yeah. He would. And thank you for telling the U.S. government lies about me."

"Anytime, babe. Anytime at all."

We got back to Samuel Square Park and tootled down Loyola Avenue as the sky grayed and the shadows changed depth, shrinking, drawing into themselves, as if the sun injured them. The new town house smelled of fresh paint, adhesives, wood, and floor finisher—lacquer or whatever they used to make wood shiny. We got out and I lifted my head into the wind currents, drew my lips into a snarl, drawing the night air into my mouth and over my tongue with a soft *scree* of sound. Flehmen behavior. Beast behavior.

Over all the outgassing building materials, I smelled fresh plantings, turned soil, and flowering plants, primarily jasmine, a floral that seemed designed by God himself to ruin my nose. Along with the floral bouquet, I scented chlorine and burned vamp flesh and fresh and old werewolf blood. My lips fell back into neutral and I shrugged at Eli, who had a tiny smile on his face. My cat-like responses didn't bother him at all, which made me even happier on some level I didn't look at too closely. The Youngers were becoming family, which meant that they had power over me, over my emotions. I'd cry like a child if they left me. "All the scents, including the biggest concentration of dead human and werewolf blood, come from the backyard. There's a pool."

Eli clicked the dart to the highest dose, shouldered the oversized trank gun, tossed a massive gobag over one shoulder, and moved away from the street. I followed. "What's the plan?" I asked.

"Well, we could go in slow and easy and hunt him down, step by step. Or I could get a good vantage, and you could race naked through the backyard and draw him out. And then I could shoot him."

"Naked."

Eli's grin widened. "Works for me."

I almost said something snarky and then I realized he was pulling my leg. "How 'bout I keep my clothes on."

"That'll work too, but the video won't be nearly so much fun to watch later."

I shook my head in resignation, then rolled my head and

neck on my shoulders, working out tension. "Okay. Gate." I checked the wind, pointing to the downwind side of the yard, to a gate that was padlocked. "That entrance."

Using a huge pair of metal cutters he removed from the oversized gobag, Eli had me in the fenced yard in minutes, backing away and closing the gate silently behind him. Then he did a little more covert B and E, traipsed through the house, and took a position on the second-floor balcony, looking out over the pool; I knew he was in place by his scent, flowing down with the humid breeze. The backyard was decorated like a courtyard, with palms, and heavy land-scaping along the three fenced walls, with the wall at the house covered with blooming jasmine, the scent so strong it nearly made Beast sick. She sent me a mental image of her claws raking the wall of jasmine down and tossing it into the pool.

Eli said, softly, "Go."

CHAPTER 20

His Most High Toothy-ness

I readied my M4, but even with the shotgun and its silver-fléchette rounds, it would take a lot of ammo to kill a were. A *lot* of ammo. The M4 was nearly idiotproof, requiring little or no maintenance, and operated in all weather conditions, even New Orleans' storms. The smoothbore, semiauto shotgun could fire 2.75- and 3-inch shells of differing power levels, in any combination, with no operator adjustments. It could also use standard ammunition or well-made, hand-packed rounds without replacing any major parts. It utilized the autoregulating gas-operated—ARGO—firing system, with dual gas cylinders, gas pistons, and action rods for increased reliability. It could fire, be adjusted, or be field-stripped, totally without tools. It was perfect for close-in fighting in low-light operations like the night might turn into if we were partially but not totally successful in our aims.

I racked the slides on two nine mils, which took some good ambidextrous moves, rounds in both chambers, both loaded with silver. I called out, "Hey, Brute. Where are you?" Nothing happened, so I called him again, adding, "We're here to help you." Which was sorta true, but the call was to no avail. The wind shifted, swirling slowly as the dawn air currents followed the Mississippi River, bringing the scent of dead bodies and water, and the smell of werewolf blood, old and sour, fresh and weak. But there was no sound or movement. No visible sign of the wolf, not even when I drew on Beast's night vision, which turned the garden area into silvers and grays and greens.

I spotted the bodies. These didn't look or smell like homeless people. These smelled like shampoo and perfume and fear. Lots of fear. He had taken his time, a leisurely blood-meal with the terrified human females. It was hard to tell much else from the blood-scent and the feces. He had torn them apart and left them piled near the diving board, like so much human leftovers.

But I didn't smell the sickly sweet scent of were-death, just blood—werewolf and vamp. I gathered that the werewolf had gotten there after Santana finished dinner. Maybe both had been injured in the fight that took place there. That was a cheerful thought. I wondered what effect were-taint might have on the old vamp. If we were lucky, that was the second time the wolf had bitten him.

The wolf still hadn't appeared, and I *so* did not want to go looking under the banana leaves and the elephant-ear plants and the other big leafy plants that could hide a three-hundred-plus-pound werewolf. It was the perfect way to get ambushed. I'd rather bring him to me, which would give me at least a little warning. So I whistled, softly. And said, "Here, Brute! Heeeere, boy! I got a treat for you." Doggy talk. Werewolf trash talk. Talk sure to anger the were enough to bring him to me, even if he was gravely injured. "Here, doggy-doggy-doggy."

Deep inside me, Beast snorted with laughter and I had a mental image of her slashing the wolf's nose with her front claws. "Here, doggy-doggy-doggy," I called.

Eli didn't react, but I smelled his amusement, a happy scent, like bacon-flavored ice cream. Leaves rustled at the back of the garden. At my side, I saw Eli in my night vision, two fingers pointing. He had the were in his night-vision headgear.

"Here, doggy-doggy." I heard a low growl and called again, "Heeeeeere, doggy! Come on, boy!"

The growling stopped but Brute didn't come charging. The harsh scent of fresh blood swirled by on the wind. I walked along the side of the pool. "Brute. We're here to help." *Yeah. With the sound of two guns readying to fire.* I was stupid sometimes. "Seriously. I don't plan to shoot you. Unless you try to bite me. Then I'll fill your sorry butt with silver. Come on out. *Please.*" The leaves—banana leaves—rustled again, and I blew out a frustrated breath. I was gonna hafta go looking. And maybe get bit. Again. I hated this.

Placing my feet with careful precision, I approached the banana plant, the stink of blood and injured dog wrinkling my nose. "Brute?"

With the business end of the gun in my left hand, I pushed back the leaves. And found Brute.

The white werewolf was lying in a pool of his own blood and looked wrong. Just wrong. His back legs bent the wrong way, his throat had been ripped open and still leaked fresh blood. He had been beaten, mauled by vamp fangs, and maybe whirled by a vamp, twisting his back legs until they broke and splintered. He was barely breathing.

Dying, Beast thought at me. *Will go to angel Hayyel.*

"No. Not in my plans," I said to her, setting the safeties and holstering all the weapons. I had rounds in each nine-mil chamber, which was a stupid way to holster them, but I might need the weapons. Fast. So I left them there, stupid or not. Louder, I called, "Eli! Injured werewolf. Near death. Rick said we should get a vamp to feed him if he was injured. Suggestions?"

I heard him land in the garden after leaping off the second-story gallery, a deliberate choice on his part, as I knew he could have landed in total silence. Thoughtfully, he said, "Not really. Leo and his people hate werewolves."

"Yeah. Well, if he dies, we'll lose any and all info he gained from fighting the SoD. So give me vamp names in order of likelihood."

Eli pulled a minipenlight and inspected the wolf, the light flashing over the bloody body so fast, I couldn't tell what more I was seeing. "He's barely breathing," Eli said. "Blood loss, shock. Leo owes you a boon. The so-called big honking boon. You could call him."

That was true. I hesitated, my fingers poised over my cell phone in my pocket. A boon that big was worth a lot more than a werewolf's life. Which was a horrible, foul, selfish thought; my old pal guilt gripped me in her cruel hands and

twisted. But that boon could save my own life someday. Or
Molly's. Or those of my godchildren. How much was Brute
worth? I hadn't realized I had pulled my cell until after I'd
dialed Bruiser.

"Jane," he answered, warmth in his voice. With just one
word, I could tell he was tired, sleepless, like me. Pulling a
second all-nighter, except for the short nap in my bed.

I blushed. I could feel it creeping up my neck. "Santana
and Brute fought. Brute's hurt. I need him alive to tell us
what he knows about Santana. Joses. Whoever. And I have
to call Jodi, to report the three women Santana killed, so I
need Brute handled *stat*."

Bruiser rephrased carefully, as if he wasn't sure what I
had said. "Santana fought Brute and the werewolf is still
alive?"

I looked around the garden, only now seeing what my
nose had told me. Blood was spattered everywhere. There
were broken pots and overturned lawn chairs. "Yeah." I
bent low to hear the soft, wheezing escape of air from damaged lungs. "Barely."

"I'll be there in ten." The call ended.

I stared at the cell. Bruiser hadn't asked where I was. He
didn't have to. Bruiser *knew* where I was. All the time. I
cocked my head, holding the cell that was a leash and a
prison and a spy, thinking. Wondering if I had exhausted the
ways that I could turn the cell to my advantage.

Beside me, Eli put away the penlight and turned on a
larger flashlight, the beam so bright my eyes teared up. It
was the brilliance, not the vision of the battered dog, that
brought my tears. *Wolf,* I reminded myself. *Werewolf.* Not
dog. It wasn't a dog covered in blood, seeping from dozens
of wounds. Not a dog with glazed eyes. A wolf. A werewolf.

One who was dying. One who had saved my life once
upon a time. Who had gone into battle with me against
common enemies.

"Well, *crap*," I said, kneeling in the bloody grass. Getting
anywhere near an injured werewolf who couldn't shift to
heal himself was stupid. Helping said werewolf was suicidal.
"Medical pack." I held back my hand and Eli placed the
mesh bag into my palm as if he'd had it ready and waiting.
"I am not predictable," I said as I unsnapped the pack and
pulled on nitrile gloves. They were Pepto pink. Cute.

"Sure you are, babe. I'd treat the throat wound first. And try to not get bit."

"Thanks," I said making sure the sarcasm was properly expressed.

I eased my hands under Brute's jaw and applied pressure to the werewolf's throat, to either side of his esophagus, so he could still breathe. He was unconscious or too close to death to snap at me. His breath rate was fast, his heartbeat was faster, stuttery, uncertain. His body smelled sour and sick, the smell of death clinging to him.

I felt something hard beneath my fingers, like bone or . . . metal. Holding pressure with the heels of my palms, I let my fingers follow the shape. It revealed itself to be a chain, like a dog collar, but it was too thin, too delicate. The heft and shape were more like a fashion necklace, and there were things hanging from loops on it. I slipped it from the folds of the wound and discovered that it was wrapped around Brute's bloody jaw. Keeping my flesh away from the wickedly sharp teeth, I eased it free and handed it to Eli. "What is it?"

A long moment later Eli said, "If Alex can recover any data from a bunch of jump drives hanging on a gold chain and covered with were-blood, it might be something. If the blood can't be cleaned away, then you'll have a nice necklace."

"Jump drives?" I asked. "Thumb drives, flash drives? Same thing?" Eli nodded and I said, "Reach said that Satan's Three took his data. They could have used jump drives."

"Or sent it to themselves. Or to the cloud. Or just copied the hard drives."

"Adrianna had marks on her throat near where she was bitten by the Son of Darkness." Marks that could have come from the gold chain I'd been holding as it was ripped off her. The gold chain that was dangling in Eli's fingers, the links the same size as the marks on her neck. Reach's data? One chance in a . . . couple hundred. Maybe.

Santana was a child of the Roman Empire and had been kept prisoner for the last hundred years. He'd had only a few days to learn about the modern world and would have concentrated on the things he needed to survive: food—human cattle—shelter from the sun, a safe place to lair up. Electronic hardware had to be way down on the survival list. If he took the necklace from Adrianna, it was because he thought it had significance, like magical powers. And for us, maybe it did.

"Get back to the house. Now. Before anyone gets here. Get the Kid working on it. Tell him I'll buy him a whole computer store if he can save the data."

Eli chuckled and disappeared into the night, taking his flashlight with him, leaving me in the dark with a dying werewolf, Brute's blood on my hands. "Come on, boy," I said gently. "If you die now, you'll never have a chance to get revenge for my Beast slicing your nose open." Brute didn't react, but he didn't stop breathing either, which was good enough for the moment.

In less time than he had promised, Bruiser walked into the walled garden, three shorter forms behind him. By their smell, I knew they were vamps. And by the smell alone, I could tell they were agitated, vamped-out. Such concentrated blood smell could make the young ones vamp-out and go on a feeding frenzy. "Bruiser? You sure about this?"

"Not in the least, but he assures me he can control them and that they need a challenge to remember that they are Mithrans, not simply meals to the more powerful among them."

"He?"

Magic rose; icy prickles danced along my skin, sharp and burning cold. I knew that magical signature. A fourth form walked into the garden, a man of middle height, lithe, and so powerful it hurt where his magic touched me. Edmund Hartley's power seemed to hurt the three young vamps as well, because the small group came to an abrupt stop. And danged if two of the three young vamps in the bloody garden weren't vamps who had been drained by Joseph Santana the day he escaped. Vamps who had been prey to Santana.

"Vivian, you will restrain the wolf. Liam," Edmund said, "you will open your wrists and hold them over the wolf's mouth. Rebecca, you will stand aside and wait your turn."

I rose, straightened my shoulders, and backed away, moving at glacial speed. I didn't want to incite their hunting instincts by any movement or gesture that looked like running away or as if I was afraid. I let Beast enter the forefront of my brain and glow through my eyes.

I am Beast. Beast is not prey.
You tell 'em, baby.
Am not kit.
I meant— Never mind.

When I was standing near Bruiser, arm to arm, the warmth of his body heating me through my clothes, I spoke softly. "You cannot tell me that Edmund lost his clan to Bettina. That vamp is crazy strong, and crazy controlled."

"Not everything is about physical and metaphysical power, my love. And not every battle is won through Blood Challenge. Some are won hours or days before that, in other battles, or in parley, in exchange for favors rendered or promised."

I thought about that as the scent of vamp blood grew in the closed garden. "Punishment. Being forced to fight while drained or grieving. Trickery. A big honking boon." But I'd heard nothing about a clan blood-master being punished, and though the vamp war was in full swing when Edmund Hartley lost his status and his clan, I'd heard nothing about him injured or suffering the loss of someone close to him. Bettina wasn't tricky enough to defeat this guy. I wasn't sure that even Leo was tricky enough to beat him. And then I understood. "Politics. He gave up his position to gain something else."

"We had an agreement, Onorio," Edmund said, his voice barely a whisper but laced with threat. "Do not renege."

"I abide by my word," Bruiser said.

Silence fell on the garden. I'd lost my chance to learn the secret of Edmund's change in status. The sky warmed to a golden hue, rosy at the horizon. Sirens sounded in the distance. The beginning of early morning traffic. The clank of a garbage truck in the next block. From beneath the banana plant I heard Brute's breath ease; the faint wheeze disappeared. His heart rate steadied.

"Liam, you may desist and heal," Edmund said, "while I get us out of the sun." Edmund lifted Brute and carried him inside, out of the sun's rays, and laid the wolf on the carpet, heedless of the bloodstains in the new construction. The vamps, Bruiser, and I crowded in after him and I pulled the fancy new blinds. "Liam, assist Vivian to hold the wolf. He will be stronger now. Rebecca, you will open your veins and feed the wolf."

"And if it bites me?"

"You are being well recompensed in blood-meals."

"Yeah. We are, aren't we?" The female vamp knelt in the bloody carpet, her back to me. I smelled her blood when she opened her wrist.

"Edmund," I said. "Thank you for this. I know vamps don't generally like weres."

"I detest them. I'd see them all in hell if I could. But. As I said, I am being well recompensed."

"Yeah?"

"Yesss," he said, drawing out the word. "I am no longer the lowest scion in servitude to the Master of the City. I have gained in status and my twenty-year bondage is now only nineteen. A small price to pay for a room without a view."

I grinned in the dark, remembering Edmund's lair, the room on an outside wall. And though the window was well covered by day, it couldn't be a happy thought to know that the sun was only a foot away. "Leo gave you that?"

"Yes," he said, his voice sly. "My master is generous to you."

"Oh." My grin fell away. "Yeah, Leo wants in my pants. That ain't happening."

Edmund chuckled lightly, the tone sly. "My master is patient."

I ignored that, but I could tell by a faint shift in posture that Bruiser didn't ignore it. "Is Brute stable?" I asked.

"He will be awake soon. Then I will set his limbs. It will be painful and we will have to restrain him. It might be better if you are not here then."

"Try not to hurt him. I may need him." I thought back over the local vamps' past relationship with the weres and added, "And he'll tell me how you treated him."

Edmund chuckled again, the devious tone morphing into something darker. "Werewolves do not talk. They growl and yip and whine, but they do not talk. They scream with pain and howl for help, but they do not talk."

I walked closer to Edmund. "That sounds like experience talking. It's no secret that Leo had someone *interrogate* werewolves in his possession once. And that they didn't survive the Q and A. So just to be clear, this werewolf talks. He talks to *me*. I may need him to track the Fifty-two Killer.

So make sure Brute can still talk when he gets to me, make sure he's out of pain and healed up nicely and not afraid. Or the second I take back the job, the Enforcer will put you back into an outer room." I leaned in. "This time without draperies." I turned my attention to Bruiser, standing impassively, his hands at his sides, his feet spread, his weight balanced, his eyes watching Edmund. Ready for a fight. Ready to protect me from Edmund. Which was just so cute.

I pivoted on one heel and left the house, giving Edmund my back, letting both men see that I had no fear of the vamp behind me. Dawn had officially arrived. I was exhausted. I needed sleep. But sleep was not on the menu for my day. I had to make it to vamp HQ for a little chat with Leo, a chat of an unpleasant nature, which would be even less pleasant with him up after dawn. He got bitchy then. And I had to contact the witches. And I had to deal with Molly and the problem with the blood diamond. So much to do, none of it fun. But first, I needed a shower and a change of clothes. And I didn't have a car. Dang it.

I took a taxi home. Rinaldo, the friendly taxi driver who made me a priority, picked me up on the street and took me back to my house, where I intended to change from the bloody clothes, have a quick debrief with my team, and decide what to do next. Because I had no idea what to do with all my problems.

The Molly problem met me at the front door with a sleeping, purring cat draped around her neck and Eli at her back. Mol was fully dressed in ironed jeans, a severe, button-down white shirt, and blue loafers, and I instantly could see the fine quiver running through her, strongest in her hands, her fingers tremulous. She looked exhausted, dark circles beneath her eyes; her pale skin had a yellowish pallor; her hair was pulled back in a scalp-wrenching bun. I would have almost rather had her meet me with her hair hanging wild and free. The tight, binding bun said too much about her state of mind.

"Molly, ma'am," Eli said, his voice at her left shoulder, his familiar scent grounding me. "You gonna be okay, ma'am? I'd hate to have to knock you flat like Jane did. But I will, if you get magically violent."

Molly's eyes went wide and she stepped back, past Eli, fast. Her cat familiar stopped purring.

At least he had only offered to deck her, not fill her with lead. I sighed, the breath sounding weary and irritated in the uncomfortable silence of my front door.

"Great, ol' buddy, ol' pal," I said. "You just threatened a powerful witch with bodily harm. That is the definition of stupid, just in case you were interested."

Molly touched her jaw. "Is that why I'm sore?"

"Yeah," I said flatly. "You don't remember?" Molly shook her head and I said, "I socked you. Lachish healed you. Mostly. But you look like crap."

A slight smile settled on Molly's face. "You never have babied me. Thank you for that."

"You're welcome? I think?"

I eased inside, past Molly, and shut the door. Eli backed up to the bottom of the stairs. The cat had started purring again, which had to be a good sign. "Why did you have to knock me out?"

"Because you went for the blood diamond."

Molly closed her eyes. With an effort, she kept her breathing steady. "And you have it with you still. I feel it. Okay. I think I'll put on my music." Molly left us to listen to the music her husband had recorded—music that was spelled to help her resist the urge to use her death magics. Her trembling increased as she climbed the stairs to the room she was using, the one directly over mine. In hindsight, it might have been smart to move the workout gear to that room and put Molly in the room at the back of the house. If she became the least bit avaricious again, I'd do that. Or send her to a hotel. Yeah. Better. With that course of action laid out, I went to my room and stripped out of my vamp-fighting gear.

The leathers had more blood on them than I'd expected, and it took a while to get them clean, especially the knees of the pants and the sleeve that had been burned on the *snare of thorns*. I had left my leathers dirty before and I had learned my lesson. The stink of vamp and human blood didn't always come clean later. Living with Eli had made me more attentive to the details of my equipment. I used to just rinse them with water and clean them with saddle soap or leather-conditioning paste, or maybe vinegar or olive oil, depending on the type of filth. But I was short on vamp-hunting clothing, and cleaning these leathers the right way was a three-step process starting with baby wipes, followed by careful drying with a nonscratch cloth, and last by use of a proprietary bloodstain-removal spray that had come with the leathers. The spray was a nonstinky, non-water-based leather cleaner designed especially to remove blood but not harm the finish, and it dried odor-free. I rubbed the spray in with a soft, clean cloth. No stinting on the process this time. I didn't want Santana to smell me coming, splattered with the blood of his dead ladyloves and the werewolf and me. By the time my leathers were clean, I was feeling a little less cantankerous, and I showered off the sweat of a New Orleans night, dressing in sturdy undies, slim pants, and a tank top, all in black. And my newest boots, the ones Leo had given me. My doubled gold chain and gold nugget necklace, with the mountain lion fetish wired on, made a bright counterpoint on the dark colors and made my yellowish eyes look more amber, darker and shadowed. My only makeup was bloodred lipstick.

I studied myself in the long mirror in my bedroom, thinking about my hair, whether to yank it back in a bun like Molly's, plait it into a long tail, or put it up into a fighting queue. Giving up on knowing what looked best, I parted it in a zigzag and let it hang, which I seldom did. Long hair made a perfect handle for a bad guy or evil vamp to grab to try to control me. But today it might be another kind of tool.

Bait, my Beast thought, *to bring Leo closer. To make him foolish.*

I smiled grimly and weaponed up, taking only a single nine mil and wood stakes. I was running low with all my silver stakes in a dead vamp. Remembering that made me dial Sloan Rosen. When he answered, I said, "You do know to behead the vamps, yes?"

"Your boy Edmund Hartley did that. Without permission, and against the ME's wishes. He also removed your stakes, wrapped them in a cloth, and took 'em when he left. That was a serious breach of crime scene methods and I'm sure there will be repercussions."

"Good," I said, and closed the Kevlar cover of the cell.

"One less thing to worry about." Then I had an idea and dialed Edmund's cell number.

"Jane Yellowrock," he said into the phone, the tone sounding seductive.

Beast perked up and I thought at her, *No. No way. Don't even think about it.*

"Edmund Hartley," I replied. "Do you have my silver stakes?"

"Eight of them, which will be delivered to your residence once Housekeeping has cleaned off the blood and polished the silver to a nice, bright, deadly shine."

"Ducky. Do you get a fee for beheading Leo's enemies?"

"Though my position in Clan Pellissier is markedly higher after feeding a werewolf than it was prior to that, no Mithran in my lowly position may receive remuneration for servicing his master."

Which just sounded icky, the way he said that. I said, "If you're low on liquid funds, feel free to post the beheadings under my name and orders. I'll forward my fee to you."

Edmund hesitated. "That would place me under the commands of, and under the authority of, the vampire hunter, who is currently under contract to the Master of the City. Not under the authority of the Enforcer, where I have been hitherto."

"Is that a problem?" I asked.

"Not to me, no. But it lessens the power that the Pellissier Clan blood-master may wield over me and makes me more bound to the vampire hunter."

"Is that likely to make Leo mad?"

"At you? Yes. At me? No. I have no authority and therefore no responsibility."

I chuckled, and the sound was wicked. "Make it so," I said, "and be sure to tell him all that, uh"—I paused and tried to think of a term an old vamp might appreciate—"posthaste. Yeah. Tell him all that posthaste."

"You are too kind," Edmund murmured. "For this charity, I am at your service, and I owe you a boon."

"Yeah. Whatever. I just like ticking off his Most High Toothy-ness."

I thought I might have heard Edmund choking with laughter as I ended the call.

CHAPTER 21

You Are Going to Prick My Temper

It was well after dawn when I left my room and swung out the front door, hoping to leave Eli to get a nap. No such luck. He tapped on the SUV window as I inserted the key. I set a finger to the window button and it rolled silently down. "Busted," I said.

"So busted. You can barely keep your eyes open. Move over. I'm driving."

"You've had less sleep than I have."

"Yeah. I know. Uncle Sam trains his Rangers to not need sleep like normal humans."

I levered myself over the console into the passenger seat as Eli took my place and belted in. "I'm not a normal human."

"I know that too," he said, the engine turning over. "You're part cat. Mountain lions sleep something like twenty hours a day, which means you're overdue for a long nap." Eli didn't look my way, but his mouth took on that almost-smile thing he does. "Big-cats spend the other four hours hunting, eating, and mating. And you haven't been with Bruiser much lately, except the short time . . . was it yesterday? When Alex and I went for groceries?"

That shut me up. I was pretty sure I blushed. "Drive."

"Yes, ma'am."

"And when we get there, be advised that I intend to bait Leo. A lot."

"Because we're pissed off with the MOC. I got that."

I smiled. Yeah. My partner got that. And . . . *we're* pissed off. Not *you're* pissed off. But *we're* . . . A feeling I had never experienced before rose from the deeps of me and began to spread out. It was a weird feeling—light and airy, and it made my eyes water. It was kinda . . . I didn't know how to describe it. Maybe *fluffy*. Which I'd never say to Eli. *Not. Ever.* I looked out the window to hide the tears gathered in my eyes and I was glad he couldn't smell my reaction. I stared out into the bright dawn so he couldn't see my face. "Ticked off," I said automatically. "You know I love you, right?"

"Yeah. I know. Ditto, babe."

I blinked my eyes hard to dispel the tears as we rolled through the Quarter, silent now, getting ready to bait a master vampire in his lair. Go, us.

Eli and I made it onto HQ grounds from the side street without incident. The picketing citizens were fewer there and resorted to shouting at us as we turned inside. He parked under the porte cochere and we entered through the back. The repairs were coming along nicely, the store of building supplies that we kept on hand in the garden shed out back making a big difference in the speed of repairs. The back entry was repainted, the blood cleaned away, the walls looking brand-new. The elevator doors were perfect except for a couple of bullet holes in the metal. And what're a few bullet holes between friends?

The sun was rising as we entered Leo's office. He wasn't alone, but his dinner was sleeping, possibly naked, on the chaise longue beneath a velvet throw. It wasn't the first time I'd been there when a human was asleep after servicing his or her master. But it was the first time the sleeping human had looked all of fifteen. I threw Leo a murderous glance, and he lifted a single eyebrow in reply, amused.

I bent over the human and shook him awake. He was beautiful, with black hair worn long, blue eyes, and that perfect pale skin of the Black Irish. "Evening, ma'am." Something in those two words drew rein on my budding anger. He *sounded* Irish too, and more composed than any fifteen-year-old blood-meal had any right to.

I stepped back and studied him more closely. Slender, with graceful bone structure, the shoulders of a dancer and the face of an angel. Michelangelo would have fallen in love with him and tossed the model for the statue of the young David out the window in favor of this guy. "How old are you?"

" 'Tis closing in on forty, I am."

My anger drained away like water down a drain. "Okay. Why have I never seen you before?"

He gathered the throw around him and swung his feet to the Turkish rug, sitting up. "I was rescued by Grégoire"—his voice didn't get harsh, but it did go toneless—"from a breeding pen outside of Atlanta, it was."

"Oh." I took another step back, my thoughts skittering around in my brain like rats in a cage. I put two and two together and came up with the child-man having been raised on one of the slave farms run by the former MOC of Atlanta and Greater Georgia, Lucas Vazquez de Allyon. I had killed the MOC. It was a death I didn't regret. Not one bit. I'd never get used to the way most vamps think that they own humans. The EuroVamps would only be worse. Probably much worse. If they came to America and won a war, we'd have a lot more people like this, but they'd be a lot less happy.

Running on instinct, I put the blood-meal on Leo's couch together with the human's old master, the former Master of the City of Atlanta, de Allyon, and tried to fit the puzzle pieces of the European vamps and the Son of Darkness into the picture. And the Damours. They didn't fit; none of the pieces connected. Until I added in Adrianna. She was there, on the outside of everything, her fingers in all the pies. But I could have sworn that Adrianna wasn't smart enough or powerful enough to accomplish long-running treachery, one that would have spanned decades. It didn't add up to a massive conspiracy, a long-term strategy to take over the Americas, but with vamps there were always more layers to the puzzles. And I was absolutely certain that I didn't have all the pieces. And if I was wrong, then the mystery was a huge, overwhelming plot with more angles than I'd ever be able to figure out. There was no way I'd ever learn enough history to name all the pieces on the chessboard of vamp politics.

The pretty child-man offered me a smile that was wholesome and cheerful. "My new master, Grégoire, thought I might gain some much-needed education 'n' training here at Mithran headquarters. My opportunity to acquire such knowledge was sorely lacking under my previous master."

I moved out of the way, nodding to the door, letting my body language tell him he could go. When the door shut behind him, I looked at Leo. He was doing that block-of-gravestone-marble expression vamps did. No breathing, no tightness around the eyes, no tells at all. He could smell my exhaustion and irritation, but he had few clues why I was upset. Eli moved into the room, crossing to my left for a better shooting position, an action that was second nature to my partner. Though Leo didn't turn his head, his eyes marked the movement and returned to me. Keeping my voice neutral, I said, "Education and training for Grégoire's new servants is to include . . ."

Leo leaned back in his desk chair. He was wearing what I had come to identify as probably sleeping clothes, stretchy yoga-type pants and shirt. His feet were encased in soft slippers, a match to the ones that were always in my locker downstairs. "You are aware that I need not provide you with information," Leo said, his tone equally without inflection, "and that their satiation has no bearing on your current hunt, Jane Yellowrock who is no longer my Enforcer."

I nodded, a slow incline of my head. "They will be tutored in reading, writing, and arithmetic. Computer skills. Daily living skills, such as banking, how to drive an automobile, and how to order food at a restaurant. How to get on with the populace around them. Applications are ongoing for birth certificates and social security cards for those born and raised in slavery. We are searching out relatives for those kidnapped and brought to the Americas, as is the case with the young man who just left. Compassionate therapy and counseling are being provided for those abused. Assistance in finding a new life and a stipend for those who wish to leave our service. Lessons in how to assimilate into a proper Mithran clan are available for those who wish to stay in our service."

Leo's eyes narrowed and his nostrils fluttered as he scented my surprise. "Lest you think I am too lenient, far less compassionate therapy, and a great deal more physical rehabilitation, is being provided for those humans who assisted the Naturaleza of Atlanta in the abuse of their fellow humans. Those involved in the cruelty of the slave pens, and judged irredeemable, will not be allowed to leave our employ, though they will not be harmed. What would you have me do differently, Jane Yellowrock? I would not abandon the victims of my enemy."

Dang. Every time I wanted to hate Leo, he did something that made me like him. My exhaustion seemed to compress my chest, robbing me of air, but I wasn't about to sit on the gold velvet chaise. Reading me, Eli pushed over a low, rolling stool with his boot. I sat, and my hair swished forward, the tips settling on the floor. Leo's eyes followed its movement, and I knew he wanted to touch my hair. His fingers curled under, a strangely human gesture of resistance to an internal desire.

I propped an elbow on the desk and my chin on my fist. "I need to update you. And I need to ask some questions that are gonna tick you off. So before I do that, I need your info."

Leo smiled, the utterly beautiful, totally human smile that had been his as a human, before he had been turned. "You are going to prick my temper."

"Yup," I said, smiling back.

"No one else in all my long life has provided me such perpetual and unrelieved entertainment."

"I try."

Leo laughed, his black eyes sparkling, his black hair moving with the laughter and curling around his chin, down onto his shoulders. He hadn't trimmed it in a while. I liked the extra length. "Proceed with your update."

I told him about the debacle with the witches and the Son of Darkness, leaving out the part about Molly and the blood diamond. I told him about the scene and the altercation between Derek and Juwan and Eli and me at the Mearkanis Clan Home, and about the fight and the human deaths at Rousseau Clan Home. It was clear he had heard it all before, but not from my perspective, with my insights. I told him about Brute, the werewolf, at the pool. And lastly, I told him about the deaths of the city's homeless. When I mentioned the young teenager, Leo's face went stone-still. If it was possible for a vamp to grow even more lifeless without being true-dead, Leo did that. Then he took a short breath, just enough to speak. "This . . . is unacceptable. I will contact the mayor and order the leasing of a building for the homeless. They can be rounded up and sent there for the duration of this crisis."

Leo punched a button and gave a series of precise orders to Del. They included transportation, food, portable showers and toilets, cots, furniture, and security for as many people as the city could find. It was things like this that made it hard to hate Leo for the evil, blood-drinking bastard he was, and I had to remind myself that he was the root cause of this problem, and the buck did indeed stop with him.

While he was talking, a servant entered and brought in a tea tray, with a porcelain pot and tea cozy, and three cups. Eli made a minuscule face but accepted a cup, no sugar, no cream. Leo's preference was likewise. I added extra sugar and double cream and drained my first cup before the servant finished serving us, and started on my second.

When he was finished with his orders, Leo lifted his cup to me in a gesture that said I should continue. I said, "I have reason to believe that Dominique is working with the Son of Darkness."

Leo's eyes bored into mine, his pupils widening, the sclera going slowly scarlet. "This is not possible."

I felt more than saw Eli put down his cup and place both hands on vamp-killers at his thighs. I said, "Dominique hasn't been at Arceneau Clan Home since this started. I caught her scent at the old Mearkanis Clan Home, in the same bed as Adrianna. And in the old Rousseau Clan Home. In the same room as Santana."

Leo put down his cup. The china *tink* of cup to plate was sharp and loud in the suddenly tense room. "This is . . . Grégoire will . . . *Il sera dévasté.*"

I caught the devastated part.

"But . . . this explains much that happened the morning the Son of Darkness escaped," Leo said, staring at his hands curled around the cup. "At the request of your young business partner, Derek has been watching all of the security footage. Dominique was here, on premises, and we have not been able to discover a reason for her presence."

My mouth started to form words and then stopped. I didn't know what to say.

"One of my men found a cloak in the ballroom. It was spattered with the blood of the Son of Darkness and of humans. It smelled of Dominique. I had feared she had been taken prisoner, but"—his mouth pulled down, forming harsh lines from his nose to his chin, making him look far older than he usually did, and far more human—"but with your information, it seems not. I shall inform Grégoire that his heir is excommunicated. Expelled from clan and blood. She will be killed on sight as traitor to us." He looked up from his hands, his eyes bleak. "I will place a bounty upon the heir of Grégoire's clan."

"I'm . . . sorry. I really am."

At my words, Leo blinked and his vamped-out eyes returned to human. "Thank you," he said, solemnly. "I have news as well." Watching my face with care, Leo said, "The European vampires have cut off negotiations for their visit." I couldn't help my quick intake of breath, and Leo gave me one of his kingly nods. "I fear that Shimon Bar-Judas, the other Son of Darkness, is likely to come to help his brother, now that Joses—Joseph Santana—is free."

"Without ongoing negotiations," I said, "there's no warning when they might arrive."

"Correct."

"Unless your mole is still active?" Leo had a spy in Europe, a high-placed one, who sent him information as often as possible. As often as was safe.

"I have received no word. I may assume a variety of things about the silence: our association is at an end because of Santana; my associate is unable to get word due to heightened security; my associate has been caught and is now dead. I have heard from other sources that several of my friends from centuries ago are prisoned or deceased, simply due to an ancient acquaintance; in one case it was a relationship that ended long ago, in enmity. I am operating in a vacuum. We need Santana caught and shackled quickly. No games, Jane. He cannot be killed. I need him alive as a bargaining chip."

I glanced at Eli, my reaction evident in my expression. "Politics. They always suck," my partner said.

It wasn't what I wanted, and I figured this could be the

nail in the coffin of my desire to behead the Son of Darkness. But I was still taking his heart. "Fine. But I can't defeat Santana without help." Before Leo could reply I asked, "What have you learned about Santana while searching HQ? The Council Chambers," I amended.

"There are records and a small *objet de magie* in a safe, though where the safe was placed after the fire that destroyed my home is not yet known. There are sub-basements here and storage units off premises. I have people looking. You will be contacted when it is discovered. It was my uncle's private safe and its contents might prove helpful in your search. Meanwhile, another safe of similar design, purchased at the same time, has been located on sub-four. It contains deeds that might assist you in searching for sleeping lairs." Leo opened a desk drawer and handed me a ring of keys and a scrap of paper with numbers on it. "This will open the safe."

"We'll head there now." I started to stand and Leo lifted a hand.

"Jane." I stopped. "The Son of Darkness is strong. Far stronger than any Mithran or Naturaleza you have yet encountered. I offer you my blood to give you and your second strength and faster healing." He extended his left hand, the wrist exposed.

I had no idea what to say. No way was I drinking Leo's blood unless I was dying and couldn't shift. My eyes went to Eli, who said, "We decline for the moment. But if we are in danger or injured, we will remember the generosity offered by the Master of the City of New Orleans."

I nearly fell off the low stool in shock at Eli's words. Diplomatic. My "shoot first and figure out who was guilty second" partner had just been diplomatic. Leo took it as his due. "You may proceed with your search," Leo said, with that gracious tone that the old royals used. "You are dismissed."

Eli smiled, a genuine smile, the kind he reserves for his honeybunch. "Thanks, boss," he said. I stood and we left the room.

"Boss?" I asked as we moved through vamp central.

"Yeah. Why not?" Eli said. "You get away with unruly behavior all the time. This is his battle. I'm just the hired hand. And *my master* will never come out of my mouth."

As we entered the elevator, Eli asked, "Where are we going?"

"Right now for coffee. Then to sub-four to check the safe Leo mentioned. Also, since this conspiracy to free Santana keeps widening, I want to take a look again at Adrianna's room here, and again at her room at Mearkanis Clan Home. Maybe we missed something."

"You're going to drink coffee?"

"Odd how you picked that out of the really good stuff that I just said."

"I heard it all. The only weird part was you drinking coffee."

"Yeah, well, my bones are tired." I stretched, feeling the stiffness of muscles and joints. My spine popped when I twisted, and I blew out a deep breath, exhaling some of the tension that had accumulated in my flesh. "My *skin* is tired. Even my *hair* is tired." I dropped my arms. "I need to mainline caffeine if I'm going to make another couple hours. Coffee is faster than tea. Espresso is faster than regular coffee, and I got the chef to set up a Keurig for the green room. But sometime soon, we both need some sleep."

"Copy that."

We stopped off in the green room just off the main entry in vamp HQ. After the last time I crashed in there, I had updated the room. It now had a Keurig with a full selection of everything caffeinated, a full-sized refrigerator kept stocked with fresh food in see-through plastic containers, colas, water, and various bottled green teas. There was a large microwave, and cabinets filled with canned and dried foodstuffs. The room also had a nice table and chairs and comfy, upholstered furniture. And a three-paneled screen in front of the wall that showed a sealed-over entry to the no-longer-secret elevator close to Leo's office. I might need it someday and I didn't want it to be easily identifiable.

I made a cup of espresso, passed it to Eli, and made another for myself. As I worked I said, "Did you ever get photos of sub-four?"

"I got part of it. Alex has the pics."

"And did you find the safe Leo mentioned? Is it already open?"

Eli's lips twitched. "Yes. And not yet. I thought about blowing it up, but it might make a mess of the room."

I chuckled and felt odd as the laughter moved through my body, as if I should be grieving or furious instead, and the laughter was a betrayal of the dead and dying in that city. Nodding, I took my own cup, setting the Keurig to start a third cup, this one of chai. I opened the freezer and dropped three ice cubes into the espresso, swirled the ice in the cup and tossed it back. The whole cup of espresso hit my stomach like I'd swallowed a bowling ball. I struggled to not throw it back up. "Holy crap," I managed. "How do you drink this swill?"

"Slowly. Sipping it. Like a gentleman."

I rubbed my stomach while adding cream and sugar to the chai. "That sounds yuckers."

Eli chuckled. "Sipping espresso or being a gentleman?"

"Sylvia has ruined you," I griped, referring to his girl-friend.

"I'll be sure to tell her so," he said mildly.

The coffee's caffeine hit my nervous system and I took a deep breath. "Holy cow. That feels better."

"For now," Eli agreed, while at the same time disagree-ing.

I frowned at him, took my tea, and led the way back to the elevator. I was getting tired of Eli following, protecting, and taking care of me. I wanted to do something to shake things up, shake him up. Okay, I was grouchy. Maybe it was the caffeine or the lack of sleep, but whatever. I sipped the tea, trying to remember why I was grouchy. I really did need sleep.

The main elevator opened on the huge storage room, which took up most of sub-four's floor space. Eli and I stepped off and the elevator doors closed, the cage going back up.

The room was dry, thanks to the witch spells that kept groundwater from seeping in, and was well lit, well ventilated, and packed full of vamp stuff. There were paintings stacked in front of paintings, in every corner and along the bookcases, which themselves were filled with thousands of books and manuscripts, trunks, wooden boxes, heavy cardboard boxes, hat boxes, wig boxes, and various stuff collected by the vamps who had come through HQ for centuries. There were steamer trunks on the floor, lamps, birdcages, jewel boxes, suitcases, and photograph albums. It was disorganized enough to look like a bad episode of *Hoarders*, and took up most of the sub-basement. There were tons of . . . junk. And history. And . . . *stuff*.

I wandered to the right, sipping, through trails between piles of very expensive and valuable junk, now following Eli toward the paintings that were stacked in front of the safe. "So did you ever figure out if there's a system to the junk stored here? Maybe a caretaker?" I asked.

"Bethany," Eli said, humor in his tone.

"Bethany. Crazy-as-a-bedbug Bethany. Bethany, who was somehow involved with the Son of Darkness before, during, or after he was injured? That Bethany?"

"One and the same. Seems that once upon a time, she was sane. Ish."

I sighed, stopped in front of the paintings, and stared at them, stretching my shoulders. I drained the teacup and set it on top of a flat-topped trunk, immediately forgetting it. The lack of sleep had caught up with me. My brain had shut down. But the paintings drew me.

I knew a lot of people in them. Satan's Three, dressed in the height of fashion back in the days of poufy drawers and tights, now dead. The Three and their maker, Le Bâtard, a vamp I hoped to kill someday. And Adrianna, now gibbering on the floor of Leo's special scion room. Her I'd killed more than once, yet she just kept coming back, over and over again. Next time I'd take her head before Leo could stop me. The promise was growing old.

Eli began moving paintings. I stood and watched as paintings of Leo and Katie emerged. In one, they were wearing what might have been the height of style for the late seventeen hundreds, the couple shown standing on a steamboat, black smoke belching into the night sky. Leo was looking at Katie with lust in his eyes. Katie was laughing. She had been in love with Leo for a long time. I wondered if he really understood that.

There was a painting from the last century, of Grégoire and Dominique. The two blonds stood in front of scarlet draperies, Dominique in risqué stockings and garter belt, corset, and little else, Grégoire wearing a black tuxedo and big fluffy tie. Cravat. Whatever. And a top hat. His arm was around Dominique and she was bent back, chest outthrust, one knee raised to curl around his legs, staring at him, in love with him, just as Katie was in love with Leo. Leo and Grégoire had no idea. *Men* . . .

Eli slid the painting across the floor, exposing the safe. "It's a Victor Safe and Lock, the company out of Cincinnati, Ohio. This one was patented in 1904, which we knew. The two front doors are composed of layers of steel, six inches thick, sealed with a combination lock. Inside, if it's built according to the usual style, it has five inner doors of drawers, two on top, three smaller ones on bottom, each with its own combination lock and its own combination." He held out a hand and I placed the keys and numbers in his palm. Eli went to work.

"I need more caffeine," I said, toneless and wan, as Eli managed to get the outer doors open to reveal the inner doors and drawers. My fingertips were tingling from exhaustion.

"This will wake you up. Remember that necklace on Brute?" Eli asked.

I slid my eyes from the dark metal of the safe to Eli. "I'm sleepy, not brain-dead."

Eli grinned, looking as fresh as a daisy. Dang him. "The data on the jump drives was mostly recoverable. Alex started cleaning them up and did a cursory search of a couple of them."

That woke me up. "And?"

"They were Reach's data files. Or some of them at least. Best idea on how the Son of Darkness got them is that he took them off one of his rescuers. No idea how *they* got them. Alex is downloading, collating, and upgrading our information system. Soon we'll have at least some of Reach's information at his fingertips. Then it's just a matter of reading everything so we know what we have. Which will take time, but it has Alex's total attention."

"I love your brother," I said.

"Cougar."

"Am so."

CHAPTER 22

Cast into the Day

According to Alex, who was read into the current action on Eli's headset, the safe was a standard design for this model, with thick outer doors and five inner compartments. Leo's combination numbers worked on only three of the inner doors, however. Someone had changed two of them; the right upper and center lower drawers were unavailable to us. The left upper contained velvet and leather bags that looked perfect for holding magical toys, but they held only gems and gold coins, none of which felt or smelled of magic. My life was totally off any kind of solid foundation when a fortune in gems and gold was uninteresting.

I counted the bags. Seven dark blue velvet bags contained rough, uncut gems, three red velvet bags contained faceted gems, mostly diamonds and bright red rubies, which vamps adored, and two padded silk bags contained pearls as big as my thumbnail, which Eli proclaimed were South Sea pearls and worth a fortune. I didn't ask how he knew that. Courtesy of Uncle Sam, he had traveled the world and he knew lots of things I never would. The leather bags held the gold, some of which had been minted into uneven coins stamped with Spanish words and old-fashioned heads that

Eli said were likely from the time of the Spanish invasion of the Americas. One bag held old earrings and bracelets etched and pressed with symbols that might have been Aztec or Mayan. Not counting the archeological value, I guessed the weight of the gold to be around ten pounds; Leo had his own bank. We put everything back where we found it and closed that compartment.

The two compartments on the bottom were actually drawers, and one contained a heavy, expandable paper file holding passports, the land deeds Leo had promised, with properties all over, from Barataria to Baton Rouge, bearer bonds, stock certificates, and various paper money stuff. I set the deeds aside for study later. The other drawer contained a single gold bracelet. It looked Celtic in design, heavy, simple, elegant, a snake meant to be worn on an upper arm, so that it appeared to crawl up or down. It was a match to the gold arm bracelet I already had, the one Adrianna had once worn all the time and that tingled of old magic, somnolent or fatigued, the spell held within the gold in need of recharging. This bracelet, however, was strongly charged and full of power. I had no idea what it did, but it reminded me of the blood diamond—potent and dangerous. I thought about taking it, but it wasn't mine, and while I wasn't above taking a dangerous artifact from the vamps, I also wasn't going to do that unless there was evidence of misuse. I hoped the moral imperative of "thou shalt not steal," didn't come back and bite me in the butt.

We closed up the safe and spent a few minutes poking around before the last of the caffeine wore off, and then we gathered up the deeds and went home to catch some shuteye.

I got four hours of uninterrupted sleep, which was enough to make do, but not enough to be fully mentally functional. I woke spooned in Bruiser's arms, his bristles scrubbing the skin off my shoulder. It was my favorite way to wake up, and I rolled over slowly, to keep from waking him. He was traditionally handsome in a lot ways, brown hair and eyes, with a firm jaw and sculpted nose, long and sort of bony, a little Roman arch in it. I had a thing about noses, and Bruiser's was perfect. He had a long, tall physique, muscles in all the right places. When I met him, I had assumed he was a weight lifter, though not to bulging excess, but I'd never seen him with weights in his hands. He was toned and fit. Pretty much perfect. He opened his eyes and smiled, a slow and easy smile, full of promise.

"I like waking up with you," I said. "You look amazing in my bed, wearing nothing at all."

He asked, "Finished looking?"

"Not yet, but I can take a breather."

"Good." He slid me closer and up under him and his mouth landed on mine. Heat shot out from deep inside me and I tightened my arms on him, wrapped my legs around his. The next few minutes were hard and fast and totally satisfying. And I promptly fell back asleep.

This time, it wasn't someone else who woke me, but my own overactive brain, which was sharing a confusing caffeine-enhanced dream of the Son of Darkness trying to drink down a human while his mouth was on fire. Totally unsuccessful in a horror-style comic-book manner.

Bruiser was gone, his side of the bed cold. If not for the scents of man and sex that wafted from the sheets, I might have thought I'd imagined him being there—well, that and the present he had left on the pillow. A single scentless lily in a deep scarlet color with hints of purple in it. There was a little green thingy with water in it, on the cut stem to keep it fresh. He brought me flowers almost every time he came over.

Smiling, I crawled out of bed, pulled on raggedy gray sweats, and stumbled into the living room, where the Kid was surfing, transferring, downloading, and organizing data from the jump drives. He looked as if he'd been mainlining meth, red eyed, dark curly hair rising in wild ringlets, his body twitchy, and emitting an odor of stress pheromones and scents I'd come to associate with caffeine, ginseng, taurine, and vitamins from canned energy. There was a huge pyramid of empties at his feet—four name brands of energy drink empties. He usually overdosed like this when he was playing marathon *World of Warcraft*, but this seemed worse than his usual binge drinking.

"What," he growled without taking his eyes from the screens.

He was starting to sound like Eli, and maybe a little like me, when he was irritated. Tone mild, I said, "Are we out of energy drinks?"

"Yes. And I know I'll crash in a bit, but I need to stay on this until I understand it. So again. What. Do. You. Want?"

I cut off an inch of the stem and put the lily in a tall vase with water. "Have there been any reports of humans being drained since Santana left the pool where he fought Brute?"

"No."

"Hmmm," I muttered. "I think Santana is still on fire and burning from the inside. I nicked him with the sliver of the Blood Cross, and fire usually moves upward. Like into his throat and head. He needs enormous amounts of human and vamp blood to heal, but if his throat's on fire, then he can't drink, and if he can't drink . . ." My words trailed off.

The Kid chortled. "He can't heal. Making the city marginally safer than before. All we need to do is find him. If we can."

I pulled my cell and dialed Edmund Hartley. He sounded groggy when he answered. "I will not offer my blood to a werewolf ever again. Do not suggest it. Go away."

"Good morning to you too. Is the dog still alive?"

"He is. Sleeping at my feet, bandaged, and healing at a prodigious rate. He stinks like wet mutt. He produces a miasma of gas. He runs in his sleep. He moans. I am not getting any rest, which little has now been interrupted by you."

"You sound a little like Leo when you're ticked off. I'll need to talk to Brute soon. I need to know if the SoD was on fire when they fought."

"Your needs are always most strange. But I will ask him." The call ended. I went back to my bed and to sleep.

When I woke next, my mind was running in circles and I knew I wasn't getting more sleep, so I threw off the sheets and dressed in jeans and a T, checking a nine mil and sliding it into a spine holster beneath my T-shirt. The Kid's desk had been abandoned, and I could smell him upstairs. Eli was sleeping upstairs too, the sound of two humans breathing filling the otherwise silent house. I didn't hear Molly and assumed she had awakened and was away on witchy business, mostly because KitKit was stretched out on the back of the couch staring at me. I rummaged around in the Kid's papers and found a city map, taking it and the land deeds to the kitchen table and starting a pot of tea, a good Asian black with lots of vanilla and star anise.

While it brewed, I paged through the land deeds, scanning the ancient and not-so-ancient legalese, and setting the ones owned by Joses Santana and his aliases in a neat pile. Once I had them separated, I marked the locations on the map as best as I was able, though over the past hundred years, some streets had changed names and others had disappeared altogether, making some of it guesswork. And then I found two that rang odd bells, one in Barataria, where I had once tracked Leo's son, Immanuel, before I killed him, and another down in the Warehouse District.

I had been to both locations before. At the Warehouse address, I had found the scent of my godchildren, in a closet, where they had been kept, kidnapped, until the Damours needed them for a black-magic, blood-magic sacrifice to power the blood diamond. I had always assumed that the Damours owned the property, and perhaps they had at the time I was there last, but way back when . . . Yeah. Way back when, the Son of Darkness had owned the property. He had owned land in Barataria too, under the name of Jesreal St. Anna. St. Anna/Santana. With vamps, there was no such thing as coincidence. Heedless of damaging them, I folded the deeds and left the house, closing the door quietly behind me.

Outside, it was midday and hotter than one of Dante's circles of hell. It was a wet heat and my clothes stuck to me instantly as I slid my shades over my eyes. The whole world smelled of urine, sweat, and river water. I hated Louisiana in summer. I hated the summer smells, the summer mosquitoes, and the summer everything. I hated lack of sleep. It was hard to be charming when I was sleepy. But charming was overrated.

I beeped open the SUV and slid it into traffic. This time Eli slept through my escape. Go, me.

Due to the larger-than-normal group of picketing humans in front of and along the side of HQ, it took longer to make it the few blocks to the Council House than it did to find the deed I was so ticked off about. Dang Louisiana cars. I slowed in front of the gate and put on my blinker. I half felt, half heard the gunshot. And the odd splat/squeak at my side.

I flinched and dropped low in the seat.

Beast reared up in me. *Predator! Gun,* she screamed inside me.

Almost as one unit, the crowd crouched and started to run. I could hear their screams. The second shot hit the SUV window. It left a dark, rounded mark in the glass, spider-webbing out. A third shot followed, but the window held. I yanked the wheel and roared into the Council House drive, slamming to a stop in front of the iron gate as I dialed HQ security, the back of my car hanging out in the street. Behind me there was shouting, and I got a glimpse of a horse, one of the mounted police units that patrolled the Quarter. Sirens sounded close by.

"... —n I assist you?" a man's voice came from my cell, barely heard over the screaming.

"It's Jane! I'm out front! Security code Alpha Attack! Someone in the crowd took a shot at me. Let me in. Now!" I heard more shots, more sirens in the background. I didn't want to be responsible for a cop, a horse, or a pedestrian getting shot. "Now! Now! Now!"

The massive iron gate rolled back and I was admitted by whoever was on security console detail, and I parked just on the inside of the iron gate as it rolled shut, offering me protection I didn't have otherwise. "Thanks," I said, gasping, heart pounding. I had been shot at. "What do you see?" I asked security.

Beast thought at me, *Stay in den. Safe here.*

Yeah, I thought back. *Okay.*

Through my cell, security said, "Right now, there are three cop cars in the street and one pissed-off mountie. Sorry, Janie. *Unhappy* mountie. They got three people in custody, but I don't see any weapons on the suspects. The second-story window is open, drapery blowing in the breeze."

Another voice said, "Hang on, Legs. Let me check the feed on the other cameras. I'll let you know when it's clear to exit the vehicle."

The second voice belonged to Vodka ChiChi, a guy I had worked with for some time. A guy I trusted. The first guy was one of the newbies, and I didn't remember his name, let alone trust him yet.

I breathed deeply, waiting for an all clear to exit the vehicle. Three minutes passed. As my heart rate slowed to something closer to normal, I sat up in the seat and my eyes tracked all the security updates, noting where a camera hadn't yet been installed. I would've bet money that the missing camera would have been the one that best covered my getting shot at.

Since Leo's security people were handling the installation of the outside cameras, I'd have to have a word with someone, and I was now so far beyond grouchy that I figured I'd make a really good point. More minutes passed. My former sleepiness was buried under adrenaline, leaving me twitchy and testy and ill-tempered. I stopped my fingers where they were tapping out a rhythm on the wheel, and gripped the leather instead. It was mostly nerves, but nerves were not what I wanted to display when I entered vamp HQ. I concentrated on breathing deeply and slowly. But I wanted to tear off someone's face with my claws.

"Janie, Sloan Rosen just called. He wants the vehicle," ChiChi said over my cell connection.

"Fine. He can clean my pee off the seat," I said, only halfway joking.

ChiChi laughed. "The shot definitely came from the second-story window. Cops have the place sealed off, but it looks as if the shooter got away. The other people in custody appear to be bystanders who mouthed off a little too much."

I took my life in my hands as I opened the door. Wet, heated weather blew in and I realized I was drenched in sweat. An attack from nowhere was harder than actual battle. At least in battle, I usually knew whom I was fighting. An ambush was scary, and my body was still reacting. Beast's body was still reacting. Dang.

I stepped out of the SUV and crouched at the door, inspecting the damage. The first slug had flattened into and against the driver door, at my left upper arm. The window shots were likewise embedded. If the rounds had been larger caliber, if any of them had penetrated, I'd have taken a heart shot or a head shot. My sniper was a good shot at short distances, with what looked like rifle rounds—not handgun rounds, and not frangible varmint bullets or ones that entered, expanded, and ripped holes as they exited. This looked like a bullet designed for complete penetration, in and out, the intent being to punch a knitting needle–sized hole, plunge through the victim (deer or, in this case, me) and out the other side into whatever was on the other side. My passenger door. Because of the short range and the minimal damage to the armored SUV, I was betting the cops would recover traditional "deer-getter" .30-06 rounds from the premises. A hunting round fired by every good ol' Southern boy who hunted—a blue million of them around there. Unless they found prints or got lucky, my shooter was in the wind and would never be found.

"Whoever had drawn a bead on you, they were a really good shot," a woman said from behind. My hands clenched, resisting the urge to jerk, yelp, or pull the nine mil and shoot.

Moving as if I didn't feel like I had a target painted on my back, I turned to her and saw three other armed security personnel in the drive area. Silent, I left the vehicle and strode up the stairs, the guards racing to fall in behind me, weapons pointed at the street. They had come outside at the sound of gunfire. Stupid, from a security standpoint, but . . . nice. Really nice. Over my cell, and from the guard's headsets, I heard ChiChi say, "All clear. All clear. All clear."

Inside HQ, one of the guys worked a bottle opener like a bartender and passed out Cokes to the small crowd; we clicked bottles and drank. I drained mine, the caffeine and sugar hitting my system and mitigating the adrenaline breakdown, which could make anyone feel nauseous. I accepted a second bottle. Then I thanked them for their fast response and told them to never do it again. "Seriously, y'all. I appreciate the sentiment. But you do not abandon your post without specific orders or danger to the target. I was in a Clan Pellissier armored SUV, safe from anything but a rocket launcher, and even then, I'd have *some* protection. Never race to a gunfight without intel. For all you know, someone had a gun to my head forcing me to ask for help. Or the shooter might have been waiting to draw you out the door and take you all down."

"Yes, ma'am," one of them said, sounding snarky, half laughing. "Next time we'll leave you hunkered down by enemy fire."

I recognized him as one of Grégoire's new people from Atlanta, but I couldn't recall his name. "You do that. And when I get my title back, I'll make sure of that upon order of the Enforcer," I said, this time letting steel and some of the leftover adrenaline into my voice. His eyes slid to the side. "I was in an *armored vehicle*. Afterward, I had an armored vehicle between me and the shooter's position. You aren't even wearing vests." I poked his chest hard enough to leave a bruise, so he'd think about what a bullet might have felt like. "He could have mowed you all down. Dead heroes are useless to me, people. I need people who *think*."

I set my Coke down with a hard thump, holding my arms out to the side. "Inspect my weapons and add them to the list of documented blades, stakes, and guns currently on the premises," I instructed, bringing the small group back from battle to proper protocol.

Protocol Aardvark, Procedure B was still in effect, and I had weapons, which always made me feel better, even when I couldn't use them, such as in the SUV, being fired upon. Shoving the nine back into my spine holster, I said, "Take my personal belongings out of the vehicle and make sure that Detective Sloan Rosen gets the SUV. See that a new vehicle is made ready for my use and placed out back."

A female said, "Yes, ma'am. I'll take care of it." She was blond, and I remembered her from . . . sometime. Sometime when I wasn't being shot at. I forgave myself for not remembering.

I looked at the snarky man and said, "There's an empty camera mount on the outer wall at the corner. Find out why the camera isn't installed, and see that it gets up by nightfall."

The hard-muscled man jerked upright, his shoulders going back in the way that only time in the military can produce. "Yes, ma'am. On it."

I let out an Eli-worthy smile. "And, people. Despite the tongue-lashing, thank you." With no further words, I picked up the Coke and a headset that would allow me to interact with security and made my way to the elevator, the doors closing behind me, leaving me in stale, frigid air that chilled my sweat-damp body. It wasn't really cold. I knew that. But my body didn't, not yet. I shivered hard and finished off the Coke, leaving the empty in the elevator. Housekeeping would put it in the recyclables.

I stared into the elevator door's reflective, polished surface. I didn't normally stare at myself in an elevator, or anywhere for that matter, but this time I got a good look. I hadn't rebraided my hair and it was sticking out everywhere. I had dark circles under my eyes, and frown lines pulled down on my face. I looked as peevish as I felt. *Peevish* was a good word, combining exhausted and sleepy and running on fumes, with a side order of irritation, anger, and annoyance. I smoothed my wild hair, my only concession to neatness.

My cell dinged with a text that said, *The SoD was on fire when Brute and he fought.* The text was from Edmund and it answered my question, though the data did nothing for me. Most info in an investigation actually provided nothing and ended up as loose threads of information that never went anywhere.

I stepped out on the main floor and dialed Del, Leo's primo. She was on vamp time and I surely woke her up, though she sounded perfectly alert and composed when she answered. I interrupted her pleasantries with, "I was just shot at in front of HQ. I need Leo. Get his butt out of bed and into his office, now." Face growing tight, jaw knotted, I ended the call and took the stairs to Leo's office, not wondering why people were moving out of my way. I could smell my own anger.

Leo's office was locked, a problem I remedied with a shoulder to the door, knocking the dead-latch plunger and the latch bolt free from the strike plate. Stupid finger latch. I'd been putting off changing out the cheap lock for one of the new models that scanned handprints, knowing that Leo would gripe about not being able to get into his office easily. Maybe the broken lock would change his mind.

I stood in front of Leo's desk and slammed the pertinent papers down on top, bending forward, supporting myself on one fist as I spread them for view. A tapestry moved and Leo entered his office. He was wearing the yoga pants and knit top ensemble and he looked cool, untouchable, and every inch a king. An angry king.

He moved with that inhuman grace and took his chair, deliberately placing himself below me in a gesture that clearly said he didn't need bogus gestures of height to be more important than me. And that he wasn't the least bit afraid of me.

My finger stabbed the deed. "Why didn't you tell me Joses Bar-Judas, aka Joseph Santana, aka Jesreal St. Anna, once owned *this* property?"

"I didn't know, Jane Yellowrock, who is no longer my

Enforcer," Leo said softly. "Had I known, I would have so informed you."

Which took all the furious wind out of my sails and left me tired and deflated.

"My uncle and Bethany brought the dying Son of Darkness here. They knew that the European Mithrans would hold us all responsible if they found out what had happened and that we had their leader prisoner. They would cast us into the day for the actions that resulted in his injury and imprisonment." Leo looked down to his hands and back to me, his face so very human and pensive. It was either a very real and human moment or he was playing me. I couldn't tell which. "But back then," he said, holding my eyes, "so long ago, and yet only yesterday, there were ways to hide many things that are much harder to hide today with the electronic media and digital cameras and all the changes."

I decided to change tactics. "Where did you get the bracelet that matches the one Adrianna wore?"

"My uncle had it in his possession when he died. I have seen no reason to return an object that sings with power to a blood-sworn scion who is untrue and seeks my death. And who I might yet use to my own ends."

Smart move, I thought. "Why are you answering my questions?"

Leo let a small smile slip free. "Because, while you are technically and contractually released from my service, you remain my Enforcer. I know this. You know this. Though you are currently free of the obligations attendant to that office, and though I have charged you with an unrelated task, you are loyal, Jane Yellowrock, to my people, and to me."

I frowned. *I was?*

"Any information that I have is yours to know, insofar as it pertains to the task at hand."

I scowled at him, using my ankle to hook the stool on rollers that was half beneath the desk, pulled it out, and sat, putting us on a level. "So why didn't you tell me that?"

"You did not ask. I did not think to offer. There is much that happened so long ago, and that I have forgotten, and that comes back to me often in small flashes and rarely in great shocks of memory."

Leo was being nice. Honest. Charming. Dang it. "Sometimes you really get under my skin, like a chigger or an embedded tick—which is an appropriate analogy."

"You insult when you desire a favor. Odd behavior."

"I thought I was entertaining."

Leo smiled. "I am tired. I have been informed that you were shot at while attempting to gain entry here. Are you well? I do not smell blood."

My anger abruptly evaporated. I hated it when Leo was the calm, rational one. "I'm okay," I said on a sigh and closed my eyes, scrubbing my face with both hands. "I was driving one of your armored vehicles. Now I'm turning it over to NOPD and I've requested another be made ready. Yes. I was shot at. I'm fine."

"Yes. You are," he said, a soft, almost compassionate note in his voice.

With my eyes still closed, I smiled. *Only Leo could be so totally disarming.* But I didn't say it aloud, shaking my head, instead.

Leo said, "The local police did not capture your assailant, but they did find fingerprints at the windowsill from which the shots were fired. If they are on record, there will be an arrest."

"Which will just tick off the populace even more."

"Indeed. What do you want, my Enforcer who is not?" he asked.

"I need access to the properties owned by the SoD, especially this one." I opened my eyes and tapped the paperwork. "Every room, every nook and cranny. And I need any magical item in your possession that will put out the fire of the Blood Cross. I hooked Santana and I think he's still burning."

Leo's smile widened. "I may die for your foolishness, but I will die truly entertained."

"You happiness is what I live for, Your Great and Mighty Fangy-ness."

"I could only wish that were true."

I decided not to reply to that. "Magical weapons? Something that will put out the fire of the Blood Cross?"

"I have nothing that will douse the fire of the Mithrans' creation. But what I have you may have." Leo stood and walked to the tapestry that had shifted when he entered his office. I wasn't invited, but I followed him anyway, through the previously hidden passageway into the next room, the one with the formerly secret elevator. A lot of Leo's secrets had come to light since he met me, and now I learned another. He stood in front of a bookcase, wearing his skintight yoga clothes—which showed way more of him than I needed to see, though the vision of a perpetually young, perpetually toned and fit man was no eyesore—and started removing books and putting them back. It reminded me of the trope movie scene where someone removes a book and the bookcase swings open, but was much more complicated.

After a series of moves that might have nothing to do with opening the case, and might have been nothing more than sleight of hand, he pressed a panel in the back of the bookcase and I heard a *click*. Leo replaced all the books before he pulled on the case, which took some leverage and upper-body strength. The muscles of his shoulders, back, and buttocks stood out against the stretchy fabric. I had never looked at Leo's backside in skintight knit pants before and the view was mighty nice. Again—something I would never tell him, and would only even think when I was sleep deprived and under stress.

Rusty hinges and warped wood screeched as the case opened. Inside was another safe, a twin of the one on sub-four. Leo opened it with little spins and clicks, and the thick door swung open to reveal five compartments. From the upper-left compartment he removed three pocket watches and held them out to me. "You have several at your disposal," he said. "It takes twelve to activate a witch circle, and until recently—when Adrianna used many to activate the spell to free Santana—we had enough between us."

I took the watches, letting the chains drape over my fist. Carefully, I didn't let my expression change because there was no way that Leo should know how many watches I had in my possession. And I was not gonna let him have the pleasure of knowing that he'd just thrown me. Fortunately, the MOC wasn't looking at me but at the watches in my hand.

"Since the ones that once hung on Joses were destroyed by my enemies, we are several short. This is all the priestesses had left of the iron spike."

The iron spike of the hill of Golgotha, the spike that

would allow the bearer to control all vamps. Right. The fabled weapon of mass destruction, the weapon that was said to have come to the Americas in the care of vamps fleeing the Inquisition. The one thing that would allow vamps to be controlled. Or so they said. Who really knew what it did? So far as I had been able to determine, it had never been used against vamps. All we really knew was that when twelve of the pocket watches were placed in a witch circle, one that forced witches into a full-coven working, it did as intended. Of course, it killed the witches it used, but vamps would never worry about the deaths of nonvamps.

"Question. Why didn't you give these to me the morning Santana got away?"

Leo turned back to the safe and began to close it up. He said, "I did not have them the morning that the Son of Darkness was set free. I requested them from the priestesses and they were delivered after dawn today via human courier.

"Sabina has been studying. According to what she has discovered, you must take out the discs that were smelted from the spike," he said, a safe door shutting with finality. "Shape them into any device with an edge or point. She believes that cutting or pricking one of us with the iron will place a Mithran into some form of suspended animation. Perhaps even Joses Bar-Judas. Or perhaps it will kill him. Or perhaps it will do nothing. It is only a theory. It has never been tested."

I remembered Sabina and Bethany in the library, drinking tea. Researching? "Why are you giving me this?"

"I give it to you because you once told me that the citizens of New Orleans would attack this Council House and drag us into the light of day. My Enfor— My Jane was shot at upon entering the heart of my domain. I believe you now." His back still to me, Leo finished closing up the safe. His head was bowed as he spoke, one knee on the floor, his hair falling over his face. There was something regal about his position, and something broken as well. "I was advised to not give it to you, because no matter your loyalty to me, I know that one day you may try to bring me to the sun. Giving you weapons that would help you in that task may be foolish, even with the Son of Darkness insane and drinking down the populace of my city." Leo breathed a soft sound of laughter. "Again, you being shot at changes many things."

He twisted his body and looked at me over his shoulder, his eyes fathomless black, like a moonless night over a restless sea. "The horde at my gates changes many things. It is as though I live through the revolution all over again, and I fear for my head upon my shoulders. I fear for my people.

"I do not know if the weapon you will devise will work, my Jane. I do not know what it will do at all. But according to Sabina, the outclan priestess, without the full iron spike of the Place of the Skull, it is our last chance to stop the Son of Darkness, yet keep him alive for our use. Or at least in some semblance of undeath, a hostage that might avert a war. And no. She did not tell me of this possible use until after the Sun of Darkness escaped or I would have tried it on him myself."

I figured the SoD in suspended animation would have been way easier to control than the SoD just crucified and hanging on a wall. Wisely, I didn't say it aloud. Instead I said softly, "Thank you."

Leo rewarded that with a regal tilt of his head.

I was halfway down the stairs from Leo's office when I heard my name called. I turned and stopped, mostly in surprise. It was Raisin, though I called her that only under my breath, and never where she might hear. Her real name was Ernestine, the human blood-servant CPA who handled the Mithrans' corporate finances, wrote all the checks, and upon occasion reamed me a new one for costing the fangheads money. And I had never, not once, seen her outside her nook of an office with its huge black safe.

I wondered if she knew about the deeds, financial certificates, gold, and gems in Leo's safes and decided instantly that she couldn't possibly know, because if she did, they'd be in her safe, where she could keep an eye on the fortune. "Can I help you?" I asked.

"Yes, Miss Yellowrock, you may," she said, tottering toward me, using a cane to support her right leg. Raisin had gotten her secret name because she looked like dried fruit, wrinkled, shriveled, and ancient, but well preserved—made that way on vamp blood for who knew how many decades. "I wonder if you would do me the honor of a favor?"

"Yes, ma'am." I fidgeted as she caught up with me. I had things to do, vamps to track.

"Would you please be so kind as to look in on Acton House for me? I received the most bizarre telephone call from Pinkie this morning, and now she doesn't answer. And she never goes out. Agoraphobia, don't you know."

I didn't know, but I didn't like the sound of Pinkie not answering. "What did she say?"

"She said, 'It is lovely to have the old ways back.' Just that. And then she disconnected."

A frisson of premonition raced through me. "Yes, ma'am. I'll check on her."

The crowd out front had been sent packing, but I still took the back way out of vamp HQ, bringing with me the deeds to land in all the names that Santana had used to buy property, not that I thought we were going to find Santana at any of the houses, but who knew? They might come in handy.

On my way over to Acton House, I called Bruiser and then dialed the house. Eli answered on the first ring. "You left without notifying us. Someone shot at you." His voice was toneless, totally without inflection, the way he sounded when he was mad.

"Yeah. I suck. Get weapons and meet me at the boardinghouse. Bring whatever's left of the holy water. We might have found Santana."

"And are we going to bring him in to Leo?"

"Or kill his ass. Whichever works."

"Hooah." The connection ended.

CHAPTER 23

Ashes and Shattered Bones

We reached Acton House, the old vamp boardinghouse, at about the same time, Bruiser, Eli, and I, Eli driving his old SUV. I got out, scanning the place, opening the two passenger doors for partial protection.

Bruiser emerged from the icy interior of the armored car, decked out in military-style pants, body armor, weapons, and a face harder than stone. His expression said, *I will kick your butt. Come on. Make my day,* without the need for words of any kind. Dirty Harry, times two.

Eli slammed his SUV door and tossed me a body-armor vest. To Bruiser he said, "Your driver is taking my vehicle back to HQ. No one drives an unarmored car until this is settled."

"Not even then," Bruiser said. "Change in protocol per Leo."

Eli nodded to the house and spoke to us both. "You think he's inside?"

"It would be too easy," I said. "Find him asleep, stake him, and cut out his heart? All because he went back to lair at his old haunting grounds? Nah. Too easy."

We gathered in the semiprotection of my open doors, the

house only feet away, the breeze wet and swirling, as if rain was on the way. I shrugged into the vest and slapped the Velcro closed, pulled the nine mil, checked the weapon, holstered it in the shoulder rig, and let Eli help me into it. I opened my mouth to speak and caught the scent of death. The words died in my mouth and I inhaled in a soft *scree* of sound. Eli pulled weapons, offering me cover. "Something dead. Some*one*," I said.

Bruiser whipped his head to the house. "From inside," he said.

I didn't ask how he could smell as well as I could. He was Onorio. There was a mountain of stuff I didn't know about him yet.

Bruiser took point and Eli fell in behind me, keeping me in the middle. Keeping me safe. I might have objected to the positioning, but it wasn't sexism. At the moment, they had way better toys than I did. My nine mil in a two-handed grip, I scanned the area, the house, the high places where a shooter might hide.

The solid-wood front door was closed but unlocked, the knob turning easily in Bruiser's fist. He took the left side of the door, Eli the right. I stood out of the way, feeling useless with my single nine mil and no backup mags. The smell of death was coming through the edges of the mail slot on the artificial, air-conditioned breeze. Bruiser and Eli met gazes and Bruiser shoved the door open. The two men rushed inside, split up, and stopped. Eli motioned me in.

Pinkie was sprawled on the horsehair sofa, her suit jacket folded neatly beside her. It was burgundy today, her blouse a pale pink, like her name. The pearl buttons of her shirt had been unbuttoned, the silk pushed aside, now lying curved around her rib cage, which rose high and rounded, with small, tight breasts lying far to the sides, easily visible beneath the paler pink, child-sized camisole. The exhaustion that had been dogging me welled up inside like magma in a volcano. The breath I took was jagged and harsh.

Her lipstick wasn't smudged. She was smiling. Pinkie looked almost peaceful. Or as peaceful as a human can look without a throat. One shoulder and the side of her face had been burned to the bone. Her dyed pink hair had been singed and the stink still tainted the air along with the stink of bowels released in death, the slightly sweet smell of blood going bad, and the overriding reek of burning vamp. And still Pinkie's expression was relaxed. Almost happy. A lot like most of the faces of the fifty-two people in the kill bar.

Bruiser bent over her body and inspected her throat, though I had no idea what he could possibly be looking for. He pulled two silver stakes and took them in one hand, like chopsticks, which made a totally inappropriate and half-hysterical giggle well up into my throat. I swallowed it down, but the exhaustion was so strong that I knew it wouldn't be long before I did something thoroughly crass. Or fell asleep on my feet. Carefully, Bruiser lowered the stakes into Pinkie's throat and pulled out two long black threads.

I realized he was both collecting trace evidence and testing for vamp blood. If vampire blood was present, it would burn and stink in the presence of the sterling. The familiar smell sizzled into the room. I had no idea how vamp blood got on Pinkie. I couldn't imagine a scenario—

"Hair," Bruiser murmured. "He couldn't drink so he ripped out her throat and buried his neck in the flow. He left behind his own blood and hair." Bruiser pulled out a roll of small paper bags from a pocket, removed one, and put the roll back. He inserted the hairs into the bag and sealed it. I just stared at the body. Why had Santana come here? What had he hoped to gain?

Pinkie hadn't been dead long. Maybe only as long as since dawn. If I had known about the property in the name of Jesreal St. Anna, Royal Santana, and others, and if I had been smart enough to put two and two together with Joseph Santana as a possible way that a long-lived vamp might cling to property between generations, back in the day when they were still in the vamp closet, I might have been there when he came calling. Pinkie might still be alive. I might have saved her life. Or maybe he'd have killed me dead instead of Pinkie. Might. Maybe. But at dawn, I was too busy bandying words back and forth with the chief suckhead to think, to use my brain, to keep people alive.

I shoved my shame deep inside along with all the other guilt and anger and fears and misery I didn't want to look at. So deep I'd never have to look at any of it again.

Bruiser said, sotto voce, "By the smell, I'd say that he's no longer on premises, but I could be wrong. And others might be here."

"Understood," Eli said, just as softly.

They were talking about Dominique. And more humans. We moved through the lower level, little of which I had seen, making sure we were the only ones there. Every closet, every cabinet, every place a vamp on fire might have gone to lair by day. There were plenty of null spaces, wide gaps between walls, their presence hidden by the old-fashioned architecture: behind the kitchen wall, access was through the pantry. In the floor of Pinkie's bedroom closet, we found access into a coffin-sized hidey-hole. A long, narrow room on the back wall of the house could have hidden ten standing vamps in a pinch, with access from upstairs via a brass fire pole of all things, and access to outside through a trapdoor in the floor.

Upstairs was more of the same, though all the bedrooms were as neat as pins and currently unoccupied. Except for Santana's old room. The door was hanging open at an angle, the upper hinges ripped clean away, screws showing pulverized wood. The straps had been replaced and were now twisted and stretched, torn in two. The place had been trashed, the bed torn apart, the armoire tossed across the room, and the dead vamp on the floor stamped into ashes and shattered bones, boot prints clearly seen in the rotten cloth. The Son of Darkness had been in a rage. And though the stench wasn't as bad as it had been before he ripped into Pinkie, he was still on fire. Smoldering, maybe.

I held up a hand and stepped inside the open door, breathing shallowly, then deeper, trying to separate the smells of the day from the weaker, dryer scents of a hundred years ago. I really should have shifted into a bloodhound before we came there the first time. Any chance of ever determining a scent pattern was gone now, buried beneath the stink of burning vamp and pheromones comprised of toxins from both anger and severe pain. I shook my head and waved the guys in. They made sure the SoD wasn't hiding under the bed or in the bathroom, and then holstered their weapons as they studied the room.

"He tore the satchel with the old papers in it to pieces," Eli said.

"Soooo. He came back for it, not knowing that the contents were ruined. And when he found that it had been destroyed, he had a temper tantrum."

"He took the stake with his blood on it," Eli said.

I bent over the pile of vamp dust and toed a bone fragment away. "The remains of the crystal that contained his *arcenciel* is crushed," I said. "He came back looking for something." I dialed vamp HQ and was put through to a sleepy Leo. When he answered, his voice was nearly purring, thick and rough with sleep.

"My Jane. You miss me, *oui*?"

"No." Quickly I informed him about the state of Acton House and its curator. "Is there anything you haven't told me about the night Santana disappeared?"

"This is a story like unto the five blind men who feel of an elephant. One touches a leg and says he feels a tree. One touches the trunk and says he holds a snake. One takes his tail—"

"I know the story. What does it have to do with this situation?"

"Eyewitnesses all see something different. Ask Bethany what she saw. Ask Sabina. Ask Adrianna when she regains her mind. Ask anyone and everyone what happened that night. Perhaps they all saw something different. Something useful to your search." Without a word I closed the Kevlar cover of the cell phone and tucked it away.

"Everything that has happened to vamps in the last hundred-plus years is related directly to this night. And everything that will happen in the next . . . year or more"—I made a waffling hand to indicate who knew how long it might last—"will be related to how we handle the Son of Darkness. I don't know that we even need to know the sequence of events from that night. I don't think it matters. But we do need to know where all the players are now, and whose side they're on. Bethany claims Leo is hers, but if she doesn't get her way with him," *or with Bruiser*, I added mentally, "she might flip and side with Dominique and Santana, against Leo. Because she is seriously nutso."

Eli muttered, "At which point we might be screwed." Bruiser slanted a look at me before he turned away and moved back toward the stairs. The look said lots of things: that Bethany was crazy, that Bethany might not know the difference between truth and her own blood-poisoned imaginings, that Bethany might just as soon kill us all as talk to us, that he and Bethany had unfinished business that might make her decide I was her number one enemy, that she wanted her Bruiser back as love toy and dinner, that she was hungry and we might *all* look like dinner. Lots of things.

We left the house at different times, staggering our departures. Bruiser left last, and he was on the phone calling in a cleanup team for the house. Pinkie would disappear, her death never reported. I knew that. And it made me sick.

We stopped at three other properties owned by Joseph Santana or similar names. They turned out to be rental properties run by a management agency for a shell-company landlord. Santana hadn't been to any of them. And though we had had naps, we were dead on our feet. Three days of stress and bloodshed and death had taken a toll. We had to stop or our bodies would stop us.

Back at the house, Eli parked and followed me in, pausing just behind me in the foyer. I pulled off the holster and the vest, tossed the vest across the room to the couch, and hung the shoulder rig over the stair post. I leaned into it, dropped my head, and closed my eyes, both hands on the rail's monkey tail, gripping it hard enough to hurt, hoping to hide my feelings. There were things that needed addressing. "I won't leave the house again without telling you, even if I have to wake you up and you need sleep," I said.

"Thank you," Eli said his voice quiet. "If it makes you feel any better, she didn't know she was dying."

"No." I shook my head, rubbing my forehead against my arms. My eyes were hard and dry and burning. "It doesn't make me feel any better. Pinkie's dead. And I could have stopped it. Get some sleep. We finish this tonight."

I went to my room, stripped on the way to the shower, and stood under the spray, leaning against the tiled wall, my back to the door, my head cradled again in my arms, as if the water might wash away my misery and my guilt. Tears leaked down my face, mixing with the first mist of rising steam, salty on my lips. The hot water beat into my back.

People were dead because I was . . . not enough. Never enough. Not enough to stop it. Not enough to figure out where Santana was. Not enough to kill him or capture him or . . . anything. Just not enough. And yes, I'd been told that not being enough was a normal feeling, and that wanting to

be enough for everything and everyone was me trying to fill
the gap where God was supposed to go. That didn't help;
not at all. I was trying to do my job, but I wasn't sure where
God was in all the chaos. I wasn't sure he was there at all.

The shower stall door opened behind me. I didn't turn.

Some part of me had known he was there, had perhaps
detected a faint tremor through the floor, of him walking, or
maybe smelled him, as he pulled off his weapons and
clothes. Bruiser shut the door, trapping the steam and the
heat, and stepped close, not speaking, not touching. Waiting.
I took a breath and felt my ribs quaver on a sob as I exhaled. My fists clenched.

As if that was a signal, he moved closer, closing the gap
between us. His body touched mine, paused, as if expecting
me to shove him away. When I didn't, he stepped closer still,
and leaned against me, his body long and hard on mine.
Skin as hot as the water. His hands went high, bracing his
body on the tiled wall, careful not to put too much weight
on me. As if I were fragile, breakable.

I shuddered out a second sob.

With his chin, he pushed aside my wet hair and dropped
his jaw to my shoulder. His lips found that place, right at the
base of my ear. He'd found it less than a week ago and we
had discovered that when his mouth touched it . . . like
that . . . I started to shiver.

A long, slow tremor went down my body, and my tears
flowed faster. I shook my head, not in negation, but in uncertainty. He seemed to understand that. My voice rough
with tears, I murmured into the crook of my arms, "You
think hot, wild monkey sex is gonna fix any of this?"

"No. Nothing will fix the mess we're in. Nothing will
bring back Pinkie, or the fifty-two, or the homeless, or the
three women at the pool." His jaw rubbed along my shoulder and up my neck, the beginning stubble of his five-
o'clock shadow scraping. "But an hour together, here, while
the water warms our muscles and slicks our skin"—his teeth
grazed the curve of my ear—"will clear our heads and our
hearts and help us to sleep."

I almost said my hot-water heater didn't hold that much
water, but I kept the words in. I knew what he meant. *I
knew.*

Bruiser's hands dropped slowly down the wall with a

slight screech of skin on tile, until he touched the backs of my fingers. Moving as if he were composed of heated caramel, his fingers slid along my hands and wrists, my lower arms, circling the bend of my elbows. His touch warmed some cold place inside of me, and I sighed again, this time in relief that morphed slowly, languidly, into pleasure. Something warmer than my cold misery curled in my core and settled, heavy, low in my belly.

His hands traced my upper arms, biceps, triceps, and deltoids, his fingertips giving no more pressure than the water trickling down me. The pressure increased slightly as he outlined my shoulder blades, the points and wide planes of scapulae. He massaged my shoulders, digging gently with his thumbs into the pressure points between blade and spine. When my shoulders finally relaxed, he feathered his fingers beneath my armpits and, even more slowly, languidly, down my sides, almost ticklish, almost. Not quite. Just on the edge of . . . something . . . but not quite anything. Not yet. But heated fingers, slick and slippery.

He eased his weight away, our bodies still connected at our hips, and paused, hands spread wide just at the curve of my lower back. My bones went liquid. Beast purred deep inside me. *Ours, ours, ours. Mate.*

Bruiser whispered, "I hear your cat when you breathe," as he massaged up the long muscles of my spine. I moaned, the pitch deep and low, a vibrato of need.

My eyes slitted open, to see the steam that was rebuilding in the shower stall, swirling around our feet, Bruiser's and mine. His need pressed up against me. Insistent, in contrast to his patient, languorous, stroking hands.

I smiled as his palms slid down my spine and between our bodies, to cup my buttocks. The heat of the water and of the Onorio radiated into me. His hands glided around and caught my hips, his long fingers splayed over my abdomen.

My arms skated down from cradling my head, my fingers covering his hands and interlacing. My right hand was traced with reddish streaks, still not healed from the *wyrd* spell damage. I leaned back into him, and his head came down again, close to my cheek.

We stood like that, for a long time, body to body. Silent. Content. I felt his lips curl into a smile before he spoke.

"The last time I was in your shower, I had been nearly drained by Leo and beaten into a bloody pulp by his other Enforcer. And I was alone. Totally alone."

"That sounds so sad," I whispered, my smile widening, my face relaxing.

With mate. Not alone now. With mate, Beast purred.

"It was *very* sad," Bruiser said. "Positively wretched. And to make it worse, there was this body wash that smelled like a greenhouse in bloom. No bar soap. No unscented anything. Just . . . floral bouquet soap. When I returned to the Council House, several days later, unwashed since that time, unshaven, and unkempt, Leo said I smelled as if I had spent an uncommon amount of time at Katie's Ladies."

A giggle slipped out. I do not giggle. But one slipped out. Bruiser laughed with me, his breath hot at my ear. I said, "I didn't know you showered then. The soap was a Christmas present from one of Katie's girls. If it makes you feel better," I said, "I dropped that bottle of body wash some time ago. It accidently drained out and away before I had a chance to pick it up."

"Accidently."

"Absolutely accidently."

He bit my shoulder, catching my trapezius, holding me still, like a big-cat would grab his mate. Heat blossomed in me, breasts tightening. Beast hissed and the sound came from my lips.

Bruiser's hands slipped free of mine and down along my hips, one finger caressing the mound at the center of me. And lower, across the cleft. Clever, skillful caress. I wanted to step to either side, widening my legs, giving him access, but his feet trapped mine. His body pressed against me, a tender prison. My eyes followed the movement of his fingers, such talented fingers. One slid gently between the lips and over the heart of me.

I sucked in a breath, arched my spine and threw back my head, resting it on his shoulder, my hands now spread on the wall, supporting us as he pressed harder, forcing me against the cool tile. My breath came fast as his fingers danced, curling and circling and driving me to a peak. The sound I made was nothing a human throat can mimic. A low, muted growling that vibrated my bones and hissed at the end, "Yesssss. Yesssss."

The orgasm caught me unprepared, banging my face on the tile as it gripped my body. Shook me like prey. Shot through me like lightning through river sand, burning every nerve end as if crystalizing them all at once. "Yesssss." It began to fade, singeing me here and there.

Bruiser whipped me around and lifted me, catching me under my buttocks and settling me onto him. He caught my breast in his mouth and bit. And I came again, long before he even started to move inside me.

A quarter hour later we were lying exhausted in my bed, the covers shoved off to the floor. When I could speak, I mumbled, "Are you sure that wasn't hot, wild monkey sex?"

Bruiser laughed. "No, love. Hot, wild monkey sex is what you give me when you see the *wyrds* I discovered in the manuscripts you found and gave me. *Wyrds* of power. Molly says they are *wyrds* that she and Sabina can use to ensnare Joses Bar-Judas."

I managed to roll my head on my neck. "You'll have to wait a while on any activity that requires more energy than turning my head." Bruiser gave me that grin, the one a man used when he knew he had satisfied his partner—part conceit, part lasciviousness, part wicked pride. I ignored it. "You got *wyrds*? Seriously?"

"I did. I already gave them to Molly." A smile creased his face and I rubbed my temple against his scratchy beard.

"Fine," I said, as if measuring his offer. "Next time, monkey sex."

"Hot and wild," Bruiser specified, as if this was a bargain we were striking. "But for now, we sleep. We need sleep. Even a skinwalker and an Onorio can't fight well on no sleep."

I rolled over and pressed my backside into his lap, scrunching into him until we were skin to skin from top to toe. "Okay. Wake me when it's time to kick SoD heinie." I closed my eyes and slept.

I woke when Bruiser rolled to his feet and stretched, our mingled scents coating the air, wafting from his heated body. "Don't forget your promise," he murmured to my ear.

"Yeah. Whatever," I said, and closed my eyes. Moments later I heard Bruiser leave the house. I flipped back the covers and showered off our fun-time smells. Playtime was over. Now might be a good time to wake up a vamp from her daytime nap. Never a fun thing to do. And made doubly unfun when said vamp was as crazy as a mattress-full of bedbugs. I braided my wet hair and twisted it up into a tight fighting bun, in case I didn't have time to do so later. While I pulled on my jeans, I dialed Eli, and when he answered I said, "Get up and armed. We've got about three hours before dusk to figure out all the causative factors of this mess, devise a plan that will make the witches happy, avert a vamp war, and have time to prepare to capture Santana sometime tonight." Eli groaned and I could hear the sheets move as he rolled over in his bed. "You said to call," I added, trying not to taunt. "I can do this alone. But if you're coming, we need to conference in the kitchen."

He swore softly and didn't apologize. "I'll be down in five." He ended the call and I heard movement upstairs.

I pulled a short-sleeved T over my head and latched on my silver-plated titanium gorget, stuck my silver stakes into my bun, and holstered two .380s in a double shoulder holster I rarely used because it rubbed the skin under my arms, but the weapons didn't show to the casual observer once I slid on a lightweight jacket. I'd sweat unless the heat wave had broken, but I could live with a little stink. I stuck a vamp-killer into each Lucchese boot shaft. Basic, minimum arms for a rogue-vamp killer. Then I hung two sterling crosses around my neck and emptied out an old gobag, filling it with stuff I might need at HQ.

Eli was standing in the kitchen drinking a fresh cup of espresso when I left my room, and over the scent of coffee, I could smell chai steeping. Alex was there as well, his head on the table, his eyes closed. He looked just the way a kid coming down off an energy-drink-induced high should look. Wasted. I poured the tea into a twenty-ounce travel mug and lifted it in a toast to Eli. With my knee I nudged Alex. He raised his head and cracked open his lids, glaring at me between his long, curly lashes, lashes that most women would kill for. I grinned at him, unrepentant. My power nap with Bruiser had revived me more than I'd have thought possible. Alex closed his eyes again and dropped his head with a groan.

"Since we're all here," I said, "I need to clarify something and correct a mistake." Both brothers turned their total attention to me. "In the Cherokee tradition, family was not necessarily related by blood, but by marriage or adoption."

A sudden tightness appeared at the corners of Eli's eyes. Alex actually focused on me. Both Youngers stared at me, silent, unmoving.

"Since you bought into the company, since you moved in here, you've become more than just business partners to me." I stopped. My throat didn't want to go on, threatening to close up and suffocate me. I cleared my voice and the tissues sounded suspiciously thick and wet. "I haven't researched the proper ceremony, and The People have ceremonies for everything, but they usually are amended and altered within clan and family." I shrugged and set the travel mug on the table. My hands were sweating. "So I thought—" My voice stopped again and I cleared it, but when I went on, my voice was rough. "I thought that, if you wanted, we could become family and make up our own ceremony."

Eli smiled, a real smile, showing teeth. Alex goggled, but his eyes appeared wet, and he blinked them quickly. Eli said, "Are you asking us to marry you, Janie?"

"No! The roles for men and women are different in *Tsalagi* society—" And then I realized he was teasing. I whooshed out a breath and wiped my palms on my jeans. "I'm asking you to become my brothers. My blood brothers, specifically. If you want to."

For the next six years, subjective time, and what was more likely less than five seconds' objective time, the brothers stared at me. Then they looked at each other. There was that wordless, instant, deep communication that took place among family. Alex shrugged. Eli shrugged.

"Why not," Alex said.

"We are honored that a War Woman of The People would adopt us into her clan," Eli said. Both Alex and I raised our eyebrows. He gave that open, warm grin again. "I've been talking to *uni lisi*. She wants to adopt us too. All of us." *Uni lisi* was the mother of Aggie One Feather, who was an Elder of The People and my spiritual counselor. "But I'd rather be adopted by you," he said.

"Yeah," Alex said. "That old woman scares me."

"Me too," I said.

The brothers laughed, and I wasn't sure why, but I

laughed with them. Then I said, "*Edoda*, my father, was of *ani gilogi*, Panther Clan. My mother was *ani sahoni*, Blue Holly Clan. Technically, because the men left their clans and entered the wife's clan when they married, I'd have been born into Blue Holly Clan, but because my eyes are yellow, I think the Panther Clan had claimed me, through my grandmother who was Panther. Also, after my father died, my grandmother claimed me and took me to her clan. I think. It was a long time ago. But that's what I think happened." I took a breath and it was shaky sounding. "So I want to invite you to be adopted into *ani gilogi*. To be my *danitaga*" — I stumbled over the word — "my blood brothers. To be my family." I dredged up the words from my distant, fractured memory. "To be my *tsidanalu*. Or maybe it was my *sidanelvhi*. My family."

"Why now?" Eli asked.

"Because before the EuroVamps get here, I'm going to write my will. It's easier to transfer money to you if you're family." *And because it's what I want. I want a family.* Didn't say it. Figured they knew it.

Alex said, "Is this where we cut wrists and share blood? 'Cause that's totally unhygienic, dude."

I hiccupped with laughter. "No. That's not in the *Tsalagi* tradition at all." Eli gave a minuscule grin at my laughter. "And we'll have to finalize this at the Propitiation of Cementation Ceremony, what we call the Friendship Ceremony. It's celebrated ten days after the Great New Moon Ceremony, so once a year, in October, to be formal and legal according to tribal law. Traditionally two men publicly exchange clothes, one piece at a time, to make them brothers for life."

Eli's eyes widened. "I am not wearing your lacy undies."

"I don't have lacy undies," I said crossly. Eli's grin widened. "Brat," I added. Just as I might have to a real brother. Eli's grin went wider. Alex's eyes were as large as saucers.

"Purification rites would follow the Cementation Ceremony, to remove any unforeseen barriers that stand between us and the Creator. And then we're family. If you want to."

"But for now?" Alex asked. "What do we do in the meantime?"

"I think we just say yes," I said.

"Yes," Alex said, instantly.

Eli's smile slowly fell away. He set his own coffee mug on the table and stood straight, at attention, the military man's regal bearing. He said, "Yes. My brother and I are honored to be accepted into the *ani gilogi* clan. Honored to be the . . ." He paused. "Sorry. I don't remember the pronunciation."

"Danitaga?" I supplied, as tears gathered in my eyes.

"Right. We're honored to be the *danitaga* to War Woman, Jane Yellowrock. Dalonige'i Digadoli."

"You said my name right."

"Yeah," Eli said, his face serious and intent. "I've been practicing. Now let's go solve the world's problems."

We walked into vamp central, keeping it light, keeping it relaxed, went through the pat-down and the listing of weapons. Eli and I put on headsets that allowed us to talk to the person manning the security console and walked to the elevator before turning the units off. On his cell, Eli asked his brother, "You have her location?"

"Yeah. I had to backtrack through hours of footage — thanks for all the time, by the way — but I located her on the security cameras. Go to the third floor and I'll give you directions to her lair."

"Which should be loads of fun," Eli muttered.

Minutes later, I knocked on the inner door of the supposed lair of Bethany, outclan priestess of the Mithrans. A human opened the door and stared out at me. He was holding a cannon, pointed dead center at my chest.

CHAPTER 24

Doing the Big Nasty

"Janie?" he said, startled.

"Wrassler?" I said at the same instant, just as surprised.

"We weren't expecting company."

"Uhhh . . ." *We as in we, a couple? Wrassler and Bethany? When I'd given his number to Jodi? Oh crap.*

But before I could say something totally inappropriate, he said, "Some of Leo's most experienced people keep watch on her when she sleeps at HQ. Do you want me? Or . . ." He looked back over his shoulder while holstering his Taurus Judge .45/.410, a gun easily mistaken for a cannon. I swallowed my heart back down into my chest cavity, where it danced a jig as it tried to settle to a normal rate and not the fight or flight of a gun in my face. ". . . or Bethany? She's awake, but she's feeding."

Which sounded just icky. "Feeding while . . . ?" I made a circular motion with my hand, trying to find a socially appropriate term.

"Getting it on," Eli supplied. "Doing the big nasty. Making the two-backed—"

"Stop."

"Yes, ma'am." But he didn't sound the least remorseful.

Wrassler just gave us a small smile. "I wouldn't have opened the door had that been an issue."

"Oh," I said. "Well, of course you wouldn't." And he wouldn't. Wrassler was big enough to be a member of WWE—World Wrestling Entertainment—but he had brains and sensitivity and long years with the NOLA Mithrans, which required a healthy awareness of all things vampy-protocol-ishy to survive and prosper. Which he'd done really well until I'd shown up, after which he'd lost a leg and use of an arm. Go, me. With an effort I kept my feelings off my face. Wrassler wouldn't appreciate either guilt or sympathy. "May we speak to her?" I said instead.

Wrassler lifted a huge shoulder in a shrug that would have moved a mountain range. "She's better after feeding. Come on in." He stepped aside, limping as he put weight on his prosthetic leg. From the corner of my eye, I saw Eli with a weapon. He'd drawn down on Wrassler, not that it would have saved my life. If Wrassler had intended my hurt, his round would have passed clean through me, Eli, the wall behind us, the wall on the other side, and probably out into the French Quarter. Or, depending on what the versatile minicannon was loaded with, it might have just filled me with shotgun pellets, taken out every organ in my chest cavity, and killed me before I could shift, like the *yunega* did my father.

I had a sudden flash of ancient, faded memory. My father dead on the floor of our home, his hands in beast-claw form. Partially changed, as he tried to draw on a beast-form to save his life. The memory of my small hand in his cooling blood. Painting my face in promise, a promise to kill the white men who had been his murderers. Which I had done.

I shook myself free of old memories when Eli put his hand to the small of my back and gently pushed me into the room. I stopped just inside the entry and stared.

The apartment was small by modern standards, a tiny sitting room on the right, a bedroom directly ahead, a bath to one side, closet to the other. But it was far, far different from other vamp rooms I'd seen. It wasn't gilded or inches deep in Middle Eastern rugs or full of paintings. The floor area was bare. Spartan. And lovely. The cypress floor was so smooth it felt like glass beneath my boots. In contrast to the empty floor space, there were shelves built around the walls, filled with orchids beneath grow lights, bleached bones, and African artifacts that should probably have been in museums. There were African tribal masks, animal skulls, tapestries, iron arrow points, twisted iron necklaces, rotting breechcloths, spears decorated with feathers, amazing carvings, bright pigments, and . . . blood. Yeah. Blood, old and grayed by time, used as coloration or to anoint some artifact in sacrifice, the ancient mixed with the smell of fresh blood on the air—sharp from the recent feedings.

The lighting was bizarre, landing on the artifacts from odd angles and unexpected positions, throwing shadows that held teeth and claws and movement as the air-conditioning came on and a false breeze stirred the feathers and cloth. Clothing and jewelry hung on pegs on the walls—wildly patterned skirts in silk and cotton, billowy blouses, ballerina shoes, silky underthings in reds and pinks and amazing blues that didn't fit into any modern-day version of undies. There were necklaces made of horn, bone, blackstone, onyx, polished marble, pearls in fabulous colors, and dozens of shades of jasper and agate. Earrings and bracelets hummed with magic. Geodes lined the shelves, cut to reveal amethyst, some kind of pink stones, darker than quartz, and some kind of blue stones, the color of the sky at dusk.

Bethany's room was pagan and harsh, uncivilized by European/American standards, tempestuous . . . and utterly magnificent. There were African phallic symbols, idols of the earth goddess, death masks like those at Madame Tussauds, all things I recognized because one of my housemothers had loved history.

Brenda. She had been the best. I'd learned how to be civilized because of her. Not civilized like the *yunega*, the white man, but civilized in the sense of humanity, long-lived and long-suffering. For some unclear reason, the suite reminded me of Brenda. Brenda who had been nothing like a suckhead.

Bethany, suckhead in question, was lying on a bed that might have come from fifteenth-century Europe, carved in Christian art of the time and magical symbols, though none with crosses. She wasn't that nutso. The bed was strung with tight hemp ropes to keep the mattress resting flat. The bedclothes were white silk. And Bethany was dressed in . . . a sheet. Nothing else. Her blue-black skin was so oiled and rich looking it seemed to throw back the candlelight. Her hair—always long, braided, locked, and strung with beads— was up in a high wrap, like a turban made of her own hair. The beads in the locks gleamed in the lamplight, as did the myriad earrings hanging from her ears.

"Oh, maaaan," I murmured. How was I supposed to talk with . . . this?

But Bethany broke the ice, sounding relatively coherent. "Skinwalker," she said. "Welcome."

I threw back my shoulders and I asked, not the questions of the hour, but the question her welcome inspired. "When did you first know I was a skinwalker?"

Bethany shrugged and the silk sheet slipped to her waist. *Oh goody.* "I knew when you shifted into the screamer cat." Her full lips stretched to reveal her blunt human teeth, the smile of a succubus, had they ever existed, wicked, entreating, passionate, demanding. "My Leo was most distressed about his upholstery but was most delighted to have found one such as you."

"Yeah. I'll bet he was," I said, my tone uncaring.

"But before that, when I healed you of the injury you suffered at the hands of my friend, I tasted your blood. Blood that I knew from before and yet could not name."

That was a lot of info from a vamp. They usually held their cards closer to their chests, but maybe the blood-feeding had made her mellow. I wasn't sure where to go with the information. The event Bethany was talking about had happened soon after I came to New Orleans. I'd been injured at a vamp party and Leo had ordered Bethany to heal me. It had been a . . . harrowing experience. But if Bethany had tasted one like me before, that could only mean she had drunk from Leo's son, Immanuel, whom I had killed. The only other skinwalker I'd met in the modern world. Of course, he'd become a liver-eater by then and was killing humans and vamps like they were his own personal buffet bar, so I hadn't really had a choice.

"When did you drink from Immanuel?" I asked, knowing it had nothing to do with Santana but unable to help myself.

Bethany shrugged again and pulled the silk sheet over her, turning on one side, so I could see only part of her face, one black eye glittering and cold and nutso insane, no matter how lucid she might sound from time to time. "We were lovers," she said, "Immanuel and I, before he went up the river to explore. We were lovers when he returned, but his blood was different then. When I spoke of it, he refused to allow me to drink again. There was no more sharing. You tasted as he did. Will you allow me to drink from you? A true sharing, not a healing?" Bethany pulled the covers away from her body in welcome.

Ick. Blood and sex. Not gonna happen. But I said it more nicely. "I'm honored. But I'm otherwise involved." Eli slanted a look at me and I wanted to elbow him. I refrained. "Did you drink from Joseph Santana the night he was taken? Did you bring him to Leo? And most importantly, did Santana drink of Immanuel before the rest of you got to him? And then did the *arcenciel* bite Santana? It's vitally important that I know what happened that night."

"You ask too many questions and offer nothing in return. No blood, no sharing, no love. What do you barter?"

I had expected this and I opened the gobag. Carefully, I removed the magically empty gold arm bracelet shaped like a snake, the one I had taken from Adrianna. "This is worth much more than answers to questions. This is—"

"The little whore's armband." Bethany thrust up her hand, rising to her knees so fast I missed the motion, the sheets forgotten. "Give." Eli tensed, his pheromones going from merely alert to something like interested. Bethany's eyes flicked from me to him and back to the gold.

"We're bartering. I want honest and complete answers to all my questions, today, now. And your assistance at some future date, such assistance to be determined."

Bethany snapped her fingers at Wrassler. "Witness."

"So witnessed," Wrassler said.

"Give."

"You understand that it has no magic at this time."

"It can be used for many things, none of them your concern. Our bargain has been struck. Give!"

I tossed the armband to Bethany. Faster than a snake striking, she leaped up from her kneeling position, stretched, and caught the gold band out of the air. Landed on her mattress with a creak of the hemp ropes. It was a slithery motion, more reptile than human, and it made my skin crawl. If the scent change was any indication, the snaky act also decreased Eli's interest considerably. Bethany slid the gold band onto her arm with such glee and covetousness that I felt like I was watching a scene from *The Ring* or *The Hobbit*, or one of those movies that Alex was always playing on the TV as background to his work space. A sick sort of desire. It made me acutely aware that I might have made a mistake giving her the band, but it was a little late at this point.

Bethany, naked as the day she was born, sat back on the sheets, caressing the bracelet. Without looking up, she said, "Ask your questions."

"Tell me about the night Joseph Santana disappeared."

She tilted her head and gave me a look so sly it could have come right out of the Garden of Eden. "No. I will not."

I started to argue and then realized what I'd said. I'd already violated the agreement. *Crap.* "Did you drink from Joseph Santana the night he was taken?"

"Yes."

"Did Santana drink of Immanuel, and Immanuel drink of Santana, before the rest of you got there that night?"

Bethany tilted her head in a way that no human could do, short of a broken neck. "I do not know. It is possible."

When she didn't elaborate, I tried to figure out a way to learn more. "Ummm. Were you there when the fight broke out?"

"Yesss," she drew out the sibilants like the snake she looked, her locks fallen in her leap and now flared out like a hood, like a cobra. The candle flames flickered and her head seemed to swell and return to normal. A trick of the light. Her eyes, focused on me, seemed to have a dark glow.

I felt the rising of her vamp power in the air, tasted it on my tongue when I took a breath to speak. "Who was there when the fight broke out that night?"

"Joseph. Adrianna and her scion. I have long ago forgotten her name. She was always unimportant. Immanuel. Me."

But there were only four teacups. Interesting. I asked, "Who got there first?"

"I do not know."

"Speculate," I spat.

Impassively, Wrassler said, "That violates the bargain."

I let a bit of Beast into my eyes. "Who was there when you arrived?"

"All of them."

"Who did you expect to be there?"

Her sly smile widened. "Now you begin to ask the important questions. I expected only Immanuel, Joseph, and me."

"Why only the three of you?" And then I got it. "Oh." To Eli, I said, "Immanuel's modus operandi. He took power by drinking down vamps with more power than he had. He had gone away tasting like one thing and he came back tasting like something else. Like a skinwalker. I bet once he realized that he could be identified as a fraud by his blood, he quit letting people who had drunk from him in the past drink from him again."

Bethany said nothing, her fingers stroking the bracelet like it was a cat. Like it was alive.

"Was there a coup d'état in the works against Leo's uncle, the Master of the City at the time?"

"My little skinwalker is gaining in insight and wisdom and treachery," Bethany said, which I took as a yes.

"Did Leo know of it?" Had he been involved in this? Did he have more knowledge than he had let on?

"No. My Leo was always loyal, if foolish and naive."

"Was Immanuel, Leo's son, behind the planning of the coup d'état?"

Bethany swiveled, leaned forward, and lay across the bed on her stomach, her bare butt arched up and bare feet in the air, her ankles crossed, her eyes avid on me. "The skinwalker is truly treacherous, like a cat with a mouse, its small screams piercing." She licked her lips in what looked like anticipation as she answered more than I had asked. "Leo would never hear evil of his beloved son, his murderous and traitorous son, who tried to kill his uncle."

Something cold and certain moved deep within me, and I asked, "You and Immanuel went to Joseph Santana to try to get him on your side?" Bethany nodded. I asked, "Maybe you offered to swear allegiance to Joseph if he'd help Immanuel?"

Bethany's lips parted and she breathed out a soft sigh. "Old betrayals. Ancient strategies that came to naught. We had an agreement. We had bought property together. But that night when we went to share blood and join together, Adrianna was there with her little paramour." Bethany's face pulled down. "They ruined everything."

I put it together in a rush. "Joseph had agreed to work against Amaury, but turned on you to work with them. They beat you to it. Did the Son of Darkness agree to work with Adrianna and the Barbie?"

"I do not know what barbie is." She looked confused. "Santana refused us."

"And while you were there, with Immanuel and Adrianna and her scion, a fight broke out."

"Question," Wrassler said, and I rephrased the sentence. "Yesss."

"And the necklace worn by Joseph Santana broke and the dragon went free? Biting the Son of Darkness on its way out? Biting Immanuel? And . . . Ohhh." Understanding rose within me. "Biting you."

"Yesss . . . ," she hissed softly, a look of near joy on her face. "Though there was little poison left in the creature."

I didn't add, *And everyone it bit went insane*, but it was a near thing. Because it was true. Santana became a gibbering bag of bones hanging on a wall. Immanuel became *u'tlun'ta*. Liver-eater. Spear-finger. Bethany got less poison from the bite, but she later drank from Santana, getting more poison, enough to go insane, and she was still crazy. And Adrianna had probably been weirder than usual ever since too. *Holy crap*. It had to have been a long time after the SoD was hung on the walls of HQ before Leo and his pals drank from him, long enough to have muted the poison in his blood. But that poison, shared through blood from vamp to vamp . . .

I didn't know what it might mean, but it couldn't be good.

I said, "Who killed Barb—the scion of Adrianna?"

"Immanuel."

"Why?"

"She staked him." Bethany shrugged again. "He was defending himself."

"Did you bring him to Leo as well as Joseph Santana when they were injured?"

"Yes. And Leo protected his son, while Amaury took the other prisoner. I thought to heal the Son of Darkness. I drank of him, though he was raving, and gave him of my blood. I do not remember aught else of that time." She lifted her index finger. "I am done. There will be no more

questions. No more answers. I am hungry and sleepy and"—
she looked at Wrassler—"and I desire a partner. Find a human to spend time with me."

"Yes, ma'am."

"And send these away." Bethany curled into a fetal position, her face turned to the wall, one hand still stroking the
gold bracelet.

We left her bizarre quarters and returned to the main
entrance, not speaking, Eli letting me absorb the information that Bethany had provided. She had given me facts, but
I understood a lot more than she had suggested. I understood what Immanuel was and why he had become a liver-
eater. I understood what Santana had wanted, and how he,
and his blood, combined with the bite of the *arcenciel*, and
the taste of Immanuel's blood, had poisoned all of the Mithrans of New Orleans so long ago. Probably making them
less sane and more emotional and more reactive, more passionate and less rational as the blood of the bitten Son of
Darkness and the bitten *u'tlun'ta* passed through them, one
by one.

Santana had planned to take over as chief fanghead of
the United States, starting with Amaury Pellissier. I was betting he still wanted that, and with his insanity decreasing
with the ingestion of so much fresh, healthy blood, and so
many years gone by to leech out the poisons, he was probably going to go for it again.

Layers upon layers, plot atop scheme atop conspiracy.
The vamp way. My way of life now, until I settled things
there, served out my contract, and left. And I would never,
ever know enough to predict anything. I'd always be flying
by the seat of my pants, because vamps' hidden histories
held all the informational treasure. That and Reach's files. I
pulled up the business number and punched CALL.

"Wise Ass," Alex said. Yellowrock Securities. *YS* pronounced as only a teenaged boy would, but only when he
saw our number on his screen. That had been made plain.

"Did Reach know anything about the night that Joseph
Santana was taken? I ask because it goes back to what Sa-
tan's Three knew and what they might have passed along to
Adrianna. And Dominique. And combined with the info
Leo gave us, it might tell us where Santana is now." I
thought for half a second and added, "I remember from the

land deeds there was property in Barataria. That was where Immanuel had property before I killed him."

"That was pretty obvious, Janie," he said, sounding sullen and cranky and more than a little snarky. "I'm working on it. But were-blood isn't easy to clean away from drives, and so far, I haven't found which drive that history's on. I'm still looking for the index file so I can figure out what's what. You'll get it when *I* get it." He ended the call.

"That's my bro," Eli said, amused.

"That's sleeplessness," I said.

"Yeah. It is."

Being sleep deprived was a problem for us all. Mistakes happened when people were sleep deprived. Tempers flared. We needed either downtime to regroup, or to end things and then take off a week to snooze and recover. Just trying to keep all the vamp relationships in place was enough to drain me mentally.

"So," Eli said as we started down the last flight of stairs to the main floor. "What did you learn in there?"

"I learned that the bite of an *arcenciel* makes vamps insane, maybe forever, or maybe just for a century or so. I learned that drinking from a vamp bitten by an *arcenciel* makes them unstable, if not insane. I learned that a vamp who had been drinking from a skinwalker and then was bitten ends up like the Son of Darkness, raving and chained to a wall."

I stopped and put a hand out to stop my partner so I could finish while still out of earshot of anyone else. We were still several feet above the main floor, looking down on everyone there. I tilted my head so no one could later read my lips on security camera footage.

"All this, all this mess, is because a skinwalker, someone like me, took DNA from a vamp's body and blood, probably planned to kill him and eat him, so he could live longer, forever, in one immortal form, at the top of the vamp food chain. All this death and problems and vamp insanity is because a skinwalker—Immanuel—practiced black magic, blood magic, and then was bitten by an *arcenciel*. And those who had shared his blood at some point, and/or who were bitten by the *arcenciel*, they were affected too. So that means that . . ." I went silent.

It meant so much—it meant everything, or it meant

nothing. Hope welled up in me. "There were no *u'tlun'ta* until the white man came. So that means that maybe ..." I stopped again, unable to voice that rare unexpected hope.

Eli did it for me. "That means that becoming a flesh-eating monster is a communicable disease, the result of a bite from an *arcenciel* that then can be passed to others. And that disease condition affects different species in different ways. Vamps one way. Maybe witches another. Maybe skinwalkers another. So becoming *u'tlun'ta* isn't a final, unavoidable, horrible way to die."

I nodded. *I might not become* u'tlun'ta. *I might be free.*

"Fine. How's that gonna help us locate Joseph Santana before he gets hungry again?"

That was the big question. And I had no idea.

CHAPTER 25

We Could Play . . . Strip Poker

As it turned out, I learned nothing from either address. Santana wasn't there, hadn't been there. No stink of burned vamp, no dead humans, no Dominique. I was fresh out of ideas until Bruiser called and Eli and I went to meet him.

"Remind me to never let you set the venue for a meeting again. There is zero shelter in the event of a firefight and zero security," Eli said at his first glimpse of the vamp graveyard.

"The location wasn't my choice. This is where she said to come," Bruiser said. "One does not say no to the outclan priestess Sabina. Besides, we're much more likely to be decimated by Molly's death magics than by a hail of weapons fire."

I wasn't sure, but Eli might have shivered. Just a little. Bruiser parked the SUV and we got out, stretching our legs. I adjusted my weapons, my hand finding the hilt of Bruiser's gift, the curved knife he had given me. The blade itself wasn't as functional or as sharp or as strong as one of my modern vamp-killers, but it carried a prophecy of sorts that might save my life if it came to that. I was taking no chances and was carrying everything that might give me an edge, no matter how bizarre.

It was just after dusk, and we were the first to arrive at the vamp cemetery. The moon was not yet up and the sky was a vibrant red in the west, fading to purple overhead, and to twilight black in the east. The sun's last rays glinted on storm clouds moving in. Far-off lightning flickered through the clouds. The mausoleums glowed white in the dim light, throwing black shadows, making broken patterns where they intersected the white shell pathways. The vampires carved to look like angels on top of the mausoleums looked almost real, as if they would lift wings and fly, swords raised in battle.

As per instructions, we moved to the center of the cemetery, where there was a small grassy area about thirty feet wide and vaguely oval shaped. Eli caught my attention and twirled his index finger. He melted into the shadows to check our perimeter. In the distance a night bird called. Nothing answered. Silence settled on the cemetery, the resting place for dead vamps. And we waited.

Lachish and Molly were late, traveling together, still going over the possible pronunciations of the *wyrds* of power, which was harder than it sounded. They had to sound out each part of the *wyrds* separately, giving each syllable its own space and not overlapping the vocal reverberations, which might activate the spell. *Wyrd* spells could be dangerous.

In the papers I had given him, Bruiser had found half a dozen of the ancient spells, all in Latin, none with proper directions, and all with dire consequences if not performed properly. The witches had narrowed the useful possibilities to three, one a summoning and two that created traps, like jails made of power. *Snare of thorns* was like Molly's *hedge of thorns*, a spell that had saved my life on more than one occasion. Since the *snare* had failed to hold the SoD last time, the one the witches were using tonight was different. And probably a lot more dangerous. It was certainly more powerful.

But we three nonwitchy types weren't depending on magic. We were decked out in our best leather vamp-fighting gear and were loaded to the nines with weapons. I even had my Benelli M4 Super 90 tactical shotgun.

The M4 was loaded for vamp with hand-packed silver-fléchette rounds made by a pal in the mountains. Fléchettes were like miniature knives, which, when fired, spread out in a widening, circular pattern, entering the target with slicing, lethal force. The fact that the fléchettes were composed of sterling silver decreased their penetrating power but made them poisonous to vamps, even without a direct hit. There was no way a vamp could cut all of them out of his body before he bled out or the silver spread through his system. And there had been nothing in my bargain with Leo about silver. Loopholes sometimes made me happy.

I opened the cock, inspected each round with eye and nose, and tested the weight distribution. I hadn't taken the weapon into battle conditions since Eli had given me the shotgun-shell holder, which was mounted on the left side of the receiver, giving me quick access to an additional six shells, but changing how the weapon rested in my hands and how it drew from the recently modified spine rig. I slid the weapon into the sheath, feeling the slight catch on the shell holder. I always had to be careful how I drew it, but more ammo in a battle was always better than less.

I also had two nine-millimeter semiautomatic handguns, six extra mags, ten vamp-killers of various lengths and weights, three throwing knives—what Beast called her killing claws and her flying claws—and my sterling stakes, which had been returned via Edmund Hartley and a blood-servant. The blades and stakes were held in sheaths, loops, specially designed pockets, and the shafts of my boots. The modern, mundane gear was heavy. Not so much the arcane gear.

On a thong around my neck, underneath the silver-plated titanium gorget, I had the sliver of the Blood Cross in a velvet drawstring bag. The blood diamond, this time wrapped in a lead pouch, the kind I kept my crosses in when I wanted to not insult a vamp, was tucked beneath the edge of my vest, over my heart. Lead worked to damp vamp energy, so maybe it would work on witch energies and keep Molly from recognizing it. I could hope.

A second vehicle pulled into the cemetery lot and parked beside our SUV. It was a soccer mom's sports van with seating for six—eight in a pinch, and it was packed with people right now. Molly and Lachish stepped out of the front doors. The back doors opened, and without consciously knowing why I pulled it, I was suddenly holding the M4. Eli appeared behind the van and said softly, "Halt. Raise your arms. And do. *Not*. Move."

Eight women halted, but they didn't raise their arms. My heart rate went into overdrive. There was too much cohesion here. Too much precision of action. They turned to face Lachish, and their witch power rose, a humming, raw beat of power that thrummed into the night. Eli was about to be a witch-fried Younger. Or the witches were about to become hamburger. "Molly!" I barked. "Are you in your right mind? And can you speak for the absence of compulsion on the witches with you?"

"Son of a witch on a switch," she cursed, realizing what was happening. She stepped to the side and lifted her arms. Independent action. "Yes. We're good. No vampire has been close to us."

I swallowed my heart back out of my throat and said, "More."

Molly hesitated a beat, tucking a strand of red hair behind her ear, and then chuckled. "Last time I was in this city, you made me prune a tree with my magic."

What I had done was make her kill a sapling, but saying that would have let the witches know just how bad Molly's little problem with her magic was. "They're good, Eli," I called out. My partner vanished again into the shadows and the hum of power emanating from the witches died away.

"What just happened?" Lachish demanded.

"You stepped out of the van like a dance troupe, organized and of one mind," I said. "Like you might if you were all under compulsion of a vamp mind."

"We've been practicing a working," Lachish said, her tone severe and laced with sarcasm. "Of course we were attuned to one another." Which made sense, and would have been nice to know ahead of time.

Before I could reply, I felt a tiny pop of displaced air and found Sabina standing at my elbow, her eyes black and flat and empty. I caught myself before I reacted, fighting to keep my adrenaline from spiking in surprise, a reaction that might be interpreted as fear—not a good reaction in the presence of an apex predator. "Sabina," I said carefully.

"This is witch magic. Go away, skinwalker. Go away, Onorio. And take your foolish human with you."

I had no intention of leaving, but I did back away to our SUV, where I handed out bottles of water to the guys before taking one and draining it myself. I kept my eyes on the witches, especially Sabina, who wore fresh, starched, habit-like whites, all the way to the wimple covering her hair. She had been burned at our last meeting, dangerously so, and now she wore white gloves of soft leather on both hands, hiding her wounds. Her fingers seemed to move more stiffly than usual, and I had to wonder how much pain she was in and how well she would handle confrontation with Joses Bar-Judas if he came to them.

As the witches walked into the central open space, I felt the tingle of magic through the ground as a circle was raised, but . . . nothing happened in the grassy area. "Did you feel that?" I asked Bruiser.

"Feel what?"

Whatever I had felt had happened elsewhere, not just there, in front of me. The sensation had been like ants running across my feet, little feathery touches, there and then gone. The sensation hadn't come from a regular witch circle, but from something else, something more finessed and subtle, more practiced.

I tossed my empty into the back of the SUV and drew on my Beast. She peered out of my eyes, lending me her night vision and pulling up a hint of the Gray Between, which turned the world into sharp focus, grays and silvers and deep sylvan greens. I turned in a circle, questing with my/our senses, and spotted something different just beyond the tree line. A soft greenish glow of power ran through the trees on the far side of the chapel, crossed the drive, just short of the road, and circled back into the trees, enclosing the mausoleums. It wasn't a ward, exactly; it was more of an early-warning system, like a magical burglar alarm, and a very sophisticated one too.

Sabina's territory had once been used by the Damours in a black-magic, blood-magic ceremony trying to raise vampires into the undead without the devoveo—without the insanity that vamps go through when they're changed. Everything in this gig came back to the vamps I'd killed my first few months in New Orleans. I'd missed the chance to gather intel back then—too busy killing things. Too sure that my way was the best and only one. Too dependent on Reach for intel, and not careful enough to gather my own. I'd learned that lesson the hard way.

Since then, Sabina had instituted modifications to her territory that I hadn't noticed the last time I was there, probably because I was in danger of losing my head last time and had other things on my mind. I explained Sabina's spell and added, "We don't have to worry about Joses/Joseph walking up to us unannounced. I have a feeling that if he tried it, we'd see fireworks."

Eli rolled his head on his shoulders and I heard a faint pop as his spine relaxed into place. "Good. I'm taking a shooter position up there." He pointed with his weapon to the top of the Rousseau mausoleum. It had a small, flat roof ridge, not quite wide enough for a normal human to lie down on, but enough for a former active-duty Ranger to get comfy and get his weapon ready. And the sword held by the vampire angel was canted at a nice angle to tie off a rappel line for a quick dismount. I shooed him with my fingers and he trotted off; I turned my attention to the witches and asked Bruiser, "What'd I miss?"

"They're drawing a double circle. No, make that a triple circle."

I snorted in disgust. "This is looking like a whole lotta hurry up and wait."

Bruiser lifted a single eyebrow in that Leo-like gesture and said, "We could play blackjack. Or strip poker. I'm very, very good at poker, so it would prove interesting."

From out of the dark I heard Eli snort, this time sounding much like my own. I just shook my head and levered myself up onto the SUV hood to lean against the windshield for a little catnap. But I found myself watching the witches, Molly in particular, as they discussed the working they were going to try and shared the carefully spoken syllables of the easiest *wyrd* spell.

"*Vo. Co. . . . E. X. Cie. O.*" They spoke the syllables with no inflection and with irregular pauses between to avoid releasing the spell. Testing a new spell was dangerous. Testing someone else's spell was triply dangerous. I hoped they had done their investigation properly, that the mathematics were correct and the *wyrd* wouldn't blow them all to tiny, bloody, messy pieces.

The witches used string and a stick to mark three circles, then went to work with small shovels, digging the circles out. It should have been backbreaking work, but I realized that they weren't creating new circles, but simply cleaning out preexisting furrows, removing the loam and grass to reveal channels made with concrete mixed with white shells. From the condition of the grass, they hadn't been used in decades, but clearly Sabina had left her territory ready to take up her witchery at any point. The string had been used to measure out and find the circles, not to create circles.

Four witches stepped back against the mausoleum walls, Molly among them, as five witches stepped inside the middle circle. The five sat in the traditional pentagram positions—which was one of the best circles for a combined working. Sabina was sitting at the position for north and clapped her hands once, to call them to . . . I didn't know what. Attention maybe. Or to announce it was time to get started. A circle opened around them, and the middle, white, concrete furrow glowed with a reddish light, flickered, and stabilized.

Sabina said a version of what I'd heard Molly say before. "We ward our space with the power of the wind and rain, the moon, the earth and all that lives upon it, the stone of the heart of the mountains, and the energy of fire. All power is gifted by the Creator, and to her we offer homage . . ."

Her? Interesting. But I didn't dispute the gender of the Creator God. He—she—whatever—had no gender, so any pronoun would do as well as any other. And calling God *it* seemed disrespectful.

The middle circle flared, merging with the energies of the far warning circle. The powers paled from reddish to pink and then to a deep purple before the circle evened out again, looking as smooth and unbreakable as plasticized glass. As they murmured, getting the rhythm right, they initiated the first steps of an inverted *hedge of thorns* in the center circle, turning a proactive shield spell into a trap spell, but this spell felt different from the ones I'd seen before, smelled sharper on the air. Yeah. This was a different trap from the one they'd used before.

The *hedge* spell smelled the way the world did in the

middle of a major thunderstorm—stronger, creating a tingle of static electricity in the air—as opposed to the way the Everhart sisters' spell felt, which was more like the air when a storm is brewing but still far off. This *hedge* also felt different from the same spell that had been opened on the grounds of the Louis Armstrong Park. They had used five witches then too, but only three had been strong practitioners; two had been weakly gifted. That night, I didn't see Butterfly Lily and her mother, Feather Storm. There were five strong witches in the working, a well-balanced blend of talents. The power signature was stronger.

So far, it was pretty much what I was used to, but with enough differences to make me wary. The witches were chanting something too softly to hear, the words not in English or Gaelic or Latin, not in any Romance tongue I recognized, all of which were languages I had heard witches and shamans use before. But it was something different, maybe tribal American. Not Cherokee—the consonants were too hard and sharp for that. But maybe something else tribal, a language that I didn't know.

Molly's mouth turned down in a frown. She didn't know the language either, but the local witches did, even Sabina. *Interesting-er and interesting-er.* How would Sabina know a local witch language unless she had been working with them? In secret or something. Yeah. *That.* More vamp games. I wondered how long that had been going on. It couldn't have started until after I'd gotten to NOLA, so probably less than a year. Maybe. Or maybe not.

They stopped speaking and the circles fell. Or they went inactive; I could see over and around the circles, but there was still a faint glow. Sabina stepped to the center of the inner circle and gestured for all the women to join her. They all came close, even Molly, who was looking more and more like a fish out of water. Sabina talked to them, her voice soothing and peaceful, but with the nine witches it was still a lot like a huddle of football players discussing the next play.

I could have listened if I'd strained, but the days of lack of rest caught up with me. I fell sound asleep. I dreamed about my soul home, but it was a confusing dream, and a different place, the walls blackened as if by fire, the smell of sour smoke hanging on the damp air. It smelled unused. It sounded silent. It felt cold and empty.

I woke when Bruiser's scent changed, my eyes opening wide. A heartbeat later, his hand landed on my ankle and I sat upright.

"No," he said. "I won't allow that."

Sabina said, "We dare not utilize the same sequence of spells and incantations and *wyrds* that we used last. We are stronger now, with time to prepare and with five full practitioners on the *regnum* circle and four on the outer *protego* circle. We have more options, but we must be prepared for the unforeseen and the unexpected. In return, we must attempt that which is untried and unanticipated."

"And what is that?" I asked, knowing I wasn't going to like it.

"We will once again place you in the center of the *hedge* with the item that will attract Santana. You will hold the sliver of the Blood Cross and the blood diamond in one hand, so that they touch. And you will drop your blood upon them."

"Which could get me and everyone in the circle with me killed if it explodes and sends wild magic everywhere."

"No. That will not happen. You have used the sliver before. Your blood has been upon it before. The diamond has touched your blood before. There will be no change except you will be able to call Santana to you with the power of your blood."

I knew instantly that they had been talking to Molly about me and that she had shared the story of the first time I wielded the sliver of the Blood Cross. She had told them one of my greatest secrets. Until now, the number of people who knew exactly what had happened the night I killed a coven of blood-magic practitioners to save her children had been extremely limited. I turned wounded eyes to my best friend, and she lifted her chin, a gesture that looked defiant. I didn't know what was happening to Molly. She was changing, and I couldn't see where the changes would take her except someplace dark and empty and alone.

"It's untried magic," Bruiser growled, sounding a lot like he had the first time I ever saw him, in the doorway of Katie's Ladies, defending Leo. Now he was defending me. Life was so weird. "That makes it dangerous."

"Worst-case scenario?" I asked.

"You burn to death," Molly said.

"That's what I always liked about you, Mol. Honest to a fault. Except when you aren't."

She flinched, a minuscule recoil at my words. Yeah. Molly wasn't so honest anymore. That hurt. And it made me mad. And it made me sad.

"Hey, Molly," I said, feeling mean. "Where's KitKit?"

"In the van in her travel carrier, from where I picked her up at the vet's," Molly said, lying through her teeth. "She'll be fine. The windows are cracked and I left her water." Her bright eyes stared at me across the darkness, defying me to share her secret, even though she had shared mine.

It was a dare. A challenge. Like a line in the sand, one that Molly wondered whether I'd cross. Would I really tell the witches of New Orleans that my best friend in the whole world had gone to the dark side? That she was drawn to the practice of death magic? My breath caught as I realized that—yes. I'd give away my best friend in my entire life, turning her over to her own people, if it meant saving her life and the lives of my godchildren. "I'll get the cage out," I said, my words slow and stiff, telling her I accepted her challenge. "A little night air will do her good."

Molly narrowed her eyes. Her hair blew out in a wind that wasn't there, a wind that instantly died. Staring at me, walking slowly backward, placing her feet with care, she stepped to the outermost of the three circles. I turned my back on her, a Beast-move that said she wasn't a threat, wasn't worth remaining watchful over. It was a dominance ploy and an insult that Molly surely recognized.

I opened the van's hatch and saw the cat cage, the tiny cat staring at me through the mesh, much like Molly stared at me across the cemetery grounds. I lifted the carrier by its handle to carry the cage to the edge of the grassy area where the witches had activated their circles.

Sabina was watching me, her expression shrewd and knowing. I had to wonder how many times in her own long life she had been tempted to take the easy way out, to try blood magic, to kill something, or someone, for an end that appeared worth the murder and the smut on her soul—assuming she had a soul. Most Christians said no vamps had souls, but as with most things religious, there was no proof. And then I wondered, what if Molly had already been there, done that, and was getting ready to betray us all? *Crap.* Too much could go wrong, including the people I needed to be able to trust.

I set the carrier down on the grass and looked up at Clan Rousseau's mausoleum, seeing the slightly darker outline of Eli Younger, stretched across the roof's ridge. Instantly I felt better. I had stopped next to Bruiser, KitKit's cage at his feet, his warm eyes on me, telling me that he knew something about Molly and the other witches was off-kilter but that he trusted me to handle it. Yeah. I blew out a tight breath, chest muscles relaxing. *Two people here that I can trust with my life, Eli and Bruiser. I can work with that.*

Deep night had fallen when the witches were finally ready, dark night, with a whipping wind and clouds building overhead, anvil shaped, moving in from the southwest. But, low to the ground, it was still and heated, the wet hanging on the air and slicking our skin, the humidity so high that our own sweat wouldn't evaporate. Lightning flickered uncertainly between the clouds, making a low, rumbling thunder, not striking down to earth, not yet, but dancing from cloud to cloud with lambent light that brightened the mausoleums and the marble vampires who stood atop each, statues of the clan founders depicted as angels going to battle. Campy just on their own. A little eerie, considering the origination story of the vamps.

The witches had planned and arranged and rearranged the alignment of the circles, setting up the two outer rings for eight practitioners instead of nine, four in each circle, with candles on the outer ring at the cardinal points of the compass, and candles on the middle ring at the intermediate points of the compass. At the north compass point on the inner circle was the new trap, stronger than *snare of thorns*, where Santana would be captured if all went as planned. Molly found her place on the innermost circle and sat—the circle called the *inretio* circle, which was Latin for *trap*. And she smiled, shifting candlelight reflected in her eyes.

"Eli," I said, loudly. "If Molly starts doing something dangerous and Bruiser doesn't stop her, shoot her."

"What is the problem?" Sabina asked.

"Chick fight," I said, "one with lethal consequences. Not something that concerns you or the others. As long as Molly is a good little girl."

"Angle of shot is acceptable," Eli said from the roofline. "Placement of shot preference?"

"Not someplace lethal," I said ruminatively, as if I was thinking about my options. "Maybe a lower-leg wound. She might limp for the rest of her life, but I'd be alive to see her all gimpy."

"Roger that. Leg wound it is."

Bruiser looked from Eli to me to Molly and lifted one eyebrow, just the one, and smiled. "Capital idea. And what is my job?"

More softly I said, "Throw the cat at her."

"I'll try that right away," he said, his tone wry, "the moment I see a demon or something, hoping to avoid a shooting. Less mess, all that blood getting all over the grass and inciting vampire hunger."

"Yeah. Okay. Whatever," I said, taking in the circles and the location and the weird storms on the horizon. No. It wasn't okay; it was scary and dangerous and probably stupid. It looked all wrong. Lightning flashed between thunderheads, brightening the sky. I did not like it at all.

"You in a Latin triple circle with witches and a priestess of the Mithrans, objects of black magic, the creation wood of all the vampires, and a death witch at the trap to the door? What could go wrong?" Bruiser asked softly, reading my mind.

"I know. Right? Easy-peasy."

"I have a bad feeling about this, Jane. Make them find another away."

I glanced at him, his body tense, leaning against the SUV, the grill at his back. He was dressed in Enforcer garb and loaded with weapons, his strong, slightly Roman nose proud and beautiful, his jaw almost square, upper-class British lips thin with disquiet. "Questions, Onorio. One: Does this look like it might work?"

His mouth turned down with an unwilling, "Yes. Perhaps. If it doesn't blow up everyone in the rings."

"Two: What kind of honor would I have if I ran away?"

He shook his head, refusing to answer.

"Three: I know you can enter the Gray Between and fight beside me. What would happen if you crossed over an active witch circle or three in the middle of a working?"

Bruiser tilted his head down and smiled at me from beneath his brows. His tone speculative and intrigued, he said, "I have no idea."

"Well, if it looks like it's going to hell in a handbasket, and throwing Molly's familiar at her doesn't work, and Eli shooting her doesn't work, pull a couple blades and try it."

He leaned over to me and pressed his lips to my forehead, his mouth fevered and dry and smooth, like a blessing more than a kiss. I closed my eyes, holding him close with one hand on the back of his head. "Be safe," he murmured against my face. I felt small tingles of magic flutter over my skin, cool and sparkling, like the tingles of sparklers from a Fourth of July celebration. "Please."

"I'll do my best."

I removed the sliver of the Blood Cross and gripped it in one hand. I tucked the iron discs in a Velcro pocket at my right hip. Overhead, the rumble of thunder sounded. Wind whipped through the cemetery, smelling of ozone and rain. Shorter strands of my hair were yanked loose from the bun, stinging my face, tangling in my eyelashes. While watching Molly, I tumbled the blood diamond from its lead-lined pouch into my palm. Her eyes found me instantly, and the stone went from icy cold where it touched me, to a pleasant warmth in my hand, to fiery, as if it had been heated by a flame. It felt as if it wanted my attention, even as I watched Molly. It was just a stone, but it felt like more. It felt . . . interested.

Curious.

Alive.

So very wrong.

CHAPTER 26

Dressed Like a Man of My People

Sitting in a witch circle—again—felt like a really bad idea. We had tried something similar once and it had ended badly. Unfortunately, I had no better ideas. And humans were dying. The fifty-two were dead. Pinkie was dead. Homeless people were disappearing. Humans were close to rioting in the streets. My choices were limited. So I stood close to the inner ring with the others, and across from Molly.

Four witches sitting inside the largest circle spoke softly, the words in unison. *"Surgent in terra,"* in Latin instead of the Gaelic I was accustomed to hearing from Molly's kin. The large outer circle rose with a brownish light and a thrum of power that I felt through the earth. They blessed it with a second spell, *"Benedictionibus lucem,"* and the color of the ward lightened into a rosy hue, like flower petals.

The witches of the middle circle sat and spoke their spell, *"Arma, mediante circulus."* The pale green energies of the middle circle rose as I figured out the meaning of the wyrds as *arm the middle circle*, enclosing them, an answering pulse that I felt in the air as an updraft rising toward the clouds.

The sky grumbled overhead. A crack of lightning hit the ground deep in the tree line, close enough to brighten the scene in flickering uncertainty. Instantly the boom of thunder sounded. *"Benedictionibus lucem,"* the witch sitting at true north, in the outer circle, said.

Dangerous wyrds, my Beast whispered at me.

Blessed light? I thought back.

Dangerous spell. Cannot tell what will happen with witches and storm. Overhead, thunder rumbled, far off and rolling closer. *Storm is drawn to power.*

Yeah. I swallowed, my throat dry and painful. *I got that too.*

Sabina rose to her feet inside the middle circle she had just helped to raise, removed a small box from her sleeve, opened it, and took out something that crinkled, a plastic Baggie, saying, *"Ad esca in captionem."* Something about a trap. Baiting a trap? Even before I saw her open the Baggie I smelled it. Raw and scorched at the same time. But not exactly rotting. Sabina had found the gobbet of flesh Santana tore out of his body at our last attempt. Yeah. Or I could use the hairs in Bruiser's pocket. I had forgotten he carried them. A little late now. I looked to him and patted my pocket. Even across the distance I saw his eyes widen.

Sabina placed the stinking flesh on the ground inside the center circle, which was all of four feet across. She pointed at me to step into the circle. I looked at Bruiser and lifted one corner of my mouth. He was holding KitKit and the small envelope containing three scorched hairs from the head of the Son of Darkness. And he was smiling at Molly. It was a really nasty smile.

I stepped into the inner circle but I didn't sit. No way. I stood, bent kneed, relaxed, balanced, with the gobbet of flesh between my boot heels. And this time I was armed to the teeth. If the weapons made the spell go wonky, they'd have to think of something else. Sabina didn't remark on the metal I carried, her eyes flickering over me in what looked like approval, before she returned to her position and sat. Wind gusted through the cemetery, the wards being air permeable. The candle flames, protected in glass globes, wavered and stuttered.

Molly looked up at me from where she sat and shivered, her eyes on my hands holding the power her death magics

red. She was sitting in guru position, her legs in full lo-
, back straight, arms relaxed. She took a slow breath, her
mile widening. All by herself, like a solo portion of a con-
cert, she said, *"In carceribus incarcero. In carcerem condidit
ignis."* Something about fire and jails and—

Scarlet fire shot up from the inner concrete trough in the
earth, so hot it blazed against my skin before it settled into
simply uncomfortable. I started to sweat. Usually wards
weren't hot, but this was a different kind of spell. Stronger
than any I had seen before and reaching up to the heavens
and the storms that brewed there.

Danger, Beast murmured to me again.

Yeah. I noticed. From every corner.

Are no corners. Circles.

I didn't laugh, though she hacked at her own humor. My
big-cat had a point.

Overhead, lightning flashed and broke apart into splinters of power. It quaked across the sky in fractals of energy,
throwing the cemetery into stark white and night black.

Several things happened in a single instant. The vamp-
angels atop the mausoleums seemed to move and shift in
the lightning light, feathered wings lifting. Illusion—eerie,
but illusion. The air smelled of ozone and force, as if gathering to be used.

The blood diamond I was holding in my left fist took on
the color of the circle, glowing the shade of blood. This was
the moment I expected Molly to try for the diamond, but
instead, she blinked and fell back, catching herself on her
hands, palms flat to the earth and arms locked. She looked
surprised, but I didn't know why.

Power from the diamond expanded and shivered through
me, unexpected, shocking, prickling like a thousand needles
into my flesh. I gasped as the pain went deeper, and my
right hand and arm began to quiver, the hand that had been
burned and scarred by the *wyrd* of Joseph Santana. The
lightning faded as I switched hands and shook the diamond
in my left palm like dice, to keep the gem from burning me.

Over her shoulder, Molly said to Sabina, "I'm ready."

Beyond the outer circle it started to rain, the drops splat-
ting and drumming and sliding down the outer ward where
it closed overhead. Not that it mattered, but I had never

figured out how magical energies were constructed to allow air for the witches to breathe and light for them to see by—which was energy and would seem to be an interference—but not allow anything else through. The witches had created the concept of semipermeable in their wards long before science had discovered it. Outside the wards, Bruiser was getting soaked. And so was the cat in her cage.

Sabina nodded to me. I juggled the sliver of the Blood Cross into my right palm, held the diamond in my fingertips, and pulled out a small throwing blade, one so pointed-sharp it would pierce flesh before I knew it had touched. "I hate this part," I muttered as I rearranged the diamond again, careful to keep a firm grip on it. I didn't want to see what might happen if I dropped it and it hit a witch circle. I stabbed the tip of my thumb. In the same instant, lightning slammed down. Hit close by, a white flash of light as pain shot through me, an electric shock that skittered along my skin, up my neck and across my scalp, down my spine to my toes. I flinched at the dual sensations. Blood welled. I wiped the knife off on my leathers and sheathed it, taking the diamond in my right hand, holding it out of the blood.

My blood slid down the pad of my thumb, stretching into the creases of the inside of the knuckle, where it pooled, welled up, and slid down my proximal phalanx, toward my palm and the sliver of the Blood Cross. My blood spread through the creases of my palm to puddle in a growing pool. When I had about a quarter-sized pool, I nudged the sliver of ancient wood into it.

Nothing happened. Five seconds went by. Then ten. Twenty. At half a minute I said, "Nothing happened." Since it was supposed to harm or kill vamps, were-creatures, and even my species, I had expected the sliver of the Blood Cross to react to my blood. I looked up from the bloody pool to Molly, who shook her head in confusion. I transferred my gaze to Lachish. "Suggestions?"

"None. Sabina?"

"None," the priestess said. "Clean the weapon and secure it safely."

Meaning keep it handy to use in case the SoD showed up, but not so close that I dropped it. Making sure I didn't get my blood on anything important, I threaded the sliver

ugh my gorget, hooking it in the links. I'd worn it that
y once before and it worked fine.

Wind swirled through the circles, sending the candle flames
jumping and dancing, like captured djinns. The wind smelled
wet, clean, rainy, and strongly of the ozone of lightning.

From my right pocket, I pulled the iron discs and carefully set them into the congealing, cooling blood of my left
palm. A jolt of energy passed through me, too fast to ana-
lyze, a sizzle of icy heat, like mainlining pure menthol, potent and prickly. And just as quickly as it passed over me,
the sensation died.

Lightning blasted into the earth close to the Rousseau
mausoleum, and I closed my eyes against the glare for a
moment. Glanced up to see the outline of Eli still in place,
being pounded by the rain. He lifted a hand to show he was
fine. Bruiser stood just beyond the outer circle, soaking wet,
in his leathers. He was holding KitKit in both hands, as
close to Molly as he could get without breaking a circle.

I took two slow breaths to settle myself and lifted the
iron discs out of my blood. Heedless of smearing my own
blood on my fighting leathers, I stuffed the discs into a
pocket. Keeping my head up and half an eye on Molly, so I
could see every threat possible, I took the blood diamond
in my right hand and dropped it into my palm, into the
blood pooled there. Time changed. Slowed. Stretched. The
raindrops hitting the ward seemed to move like warm
honey instead of water. And I wasn't causing the time shift
this time. The diamond was. I felt a distinct tug back across
the Mississippi River, in the heart of New Orleans, a pull
so strong I could have followed it like a dog with a scent.
Santana. A moment later, time sped up again and Sabina
nodded.

Yeah. It had been suggested that I could sense Santana,
that we were connected by way of the diamond in my hand
and the crystal on his bracelet. Well, it seemed that was true,
though whether I could *call* him to me was another matter. I
was bait or I was useless. And if I was bait, I might be dead.
I blew out gathering tension and tried to relax.

Together the witches called out in unison, *"Voco, Yosace
Bar-Ioudas! Joseph Santana, excieo!"*

Directly overhead, lightning struck.

I saw it crackle down, reaching for the ground right in

front of my toes. A bolt wider than my waist, shivering with power, blinding white-blue-black. Searing my eyes. A smaller bolt reached up from the ground, a thin trickle stretching high. As if guiding the greater energies down. They connected. The bolt from the heavens rammed down on the smaller thread. Hit, slamming against the earth. I heard the explosion begin, a roar that beat against my eardrums. Felt the power lift me. Saw my boots leave the ground. Saw them cross over the edge of the *wyrd* spell. Above me, I saw the impression of wings, one pair black and sooty, shadowed by the lightning, one pair white, reflecting it.

Multiple energies encased me, shocked through me. Witch magics. Lightning. Not pain exactly, not yet, but sensation—heat and cold all at once. Smaller, but distinct, I felt a sear of pain burning in my closed fist. In my palm. Where the blood diamond was resting in my blood. Maybe that hadn't been such a good idea.

I didn't hit the ground. I think I was still in the air. Flying. Stuck in time and space. The world went black. Silent. The way it might if I was dead. Or dying. Or if I did hit the ground, maybe I was dead before I landed.

A second pain followed, suggesting that I was still alive. This pain was in my chest. Over the place where the sliver of wood from the Blood Cross was snagged in my gorget, pure heat as it tagged the titanium. Oh yeah. Three bad ideas together—witch magics, lightning, and magical artifacts. The pain pulsed through me, increasing but still muted, as if stuck in balls of cotton. As if, when they released, I was going to suffer, and badly. If I survived at all.

Beast? I thought. She didn't answer.

Time had stopped for me. It had done that before. Each time I nearly died from my body's reaction. Maybe if I was dying, time would stop automatically, time and my body's perception of it, my consciousness slipping into the Gray Between. As if the two were related in causality—death and time.

I reached outside of me, and inside of me, searching for the Gray Between, the space/no-space of matter/energy where my power rested. Nothing happened. Not for a long beat of no-time. And then I felt it answer me. Sluggish. Cold. A silver mist that lifted and swirled slowly, shimmering, touched with black and silver and blue motes of power

rembled and quivered and tried to move like the danc-
motes of energy they were in real time. But there they
ouldn't quite seem to twirl and pirouette like they normally did.

I was stuck outside of time, hanging in the air in the middle of a lightning strike. Probably dying.

Light flashed at me. Sound thudded at me. Pain lanced
through me from my hand and my chest. Pain like fire and
blades and glacial ice all mixed together. An ache in my
heart and lungs and every nerve ending in my flesh, like
poison spreading.

As fast as it hit me, the sensation was gone again. A moment of real time in the real world. Separate from the world
I was inhabiting right now. Bad. I was hurt bad. If I'd had
access to my own lungs, I would have gasped and screamed
and groaned.

Jane?

Beast! Where were you?

Jane is hurt. Jane is dying.

Kinda guessed that. Getting used to it.

Come.

Instantly I was in my soul home, the cavern deep beneath the Appalachian Mountains, and I gasped in air. Cold
and damp and fresh air. I was crouched, arms wrapped
around my knees, breathing hard in this nonreality, as if I'd
been running and needed to catch up on oxygen, though I
probably wasn't breathing in my physical body, back there,
in linear time.

There, in that cavern, I was safe. It was the place where I
first was led into my *wesa* form, my bobcat form as a child
of five, and watched *edoda*, my father, shift into his *tlvdatsi*
form, his panther, one so unlike my Beast. *Edoda*'s panther
had been a black panther, the rare melanistic coat color of
the species. My first shift had taken place in the cavern that
was the physical manifestation of my soul home. I had
memory of the cave in the natural world, though I had
never been back to it. It was a real place, perhaps lost to
humankind again, since the *nunahi-duna-dlo-hilu-i*, the
Trail of Tears. It may have fallen into disuse with so many
of The People gone. It might be forgotten entirely. But there
in the Gray Between, the cavern was a real place again.
Real to me.

A faint light came from my right fist. I was holding the blood diamond, but there, it was glowing a pure white light, as bright as the sun. I tucked my hand beneath my thigh to protect my eyes from the brightness, but the glow escaped from between my fingers, shining through my flesh, illuminating my bones. I could feel no blood on the gem. There I was unwounded, hadn't pricked myself with the knife.

Keeping my fist hidden, I rose to my feet in the cave, in the dark, smelling something burning, unidentified, but inorganic, the scent acrid and dry, like hot metal and acid. There was only the light escaping from my fist, but I knew the cave as well as I knew my human form. I moved through the dark and knelt at the fire pit, one knee on the cold stone floor. Found the matches that had never been there before—matches being a white man's invention, the easy way to make fire, even with one hand unusable. But they were there then, when I needed them. I struck one, looking away from the flame to protect my night vision. Beside the circle of stones there was a pile of wood shavings and sawdust. Small, dried-out branches. Larger logs, split by an ax. I lit the tinder, starting a fire. Coaxed it to grow and spread. Added little strips of wood, and then the larger branches, until it was crackling and putting out heat.

To the side, in the widening glow of the flames, I saw Beast, curled in a tight ball, her tail wrapped around and covering her front paws. Her eyes were glowing, reflecting the flames, staring at me.

"Hey," I said to her, aloud.

Jane is dying. Must decide.

"Decide what?"

Decide.

"Not very helpful," I admonished. Beast huffed, watching me. "Dying is getting old," I added.

I looked down at myself. I was wearing moccasins, plain and unadorned, tied at my ankles with thongs. I was dressed in a cotton shirt that hung over my leggings, a fringed cloth around my waist as a belt. A medicine bag hung on a leather thong around my neck to dangle over my heart, the leather dyed green on one side and black on the other. An empty knife sheath was belted at my hip. I was dressed like a man of my people, a hunter. A warrior. A War Woman? Had we dressed as men when we went to war? Was I at war right

My hair was braided to either side of my head and hair swayed with my motion.

In that reality, the sliver of the Blood Cross had been run through my shirt like a needle, keeping it in place. I pulled the sliver with my left hand and hefted the two weapons in my hands as if measuring their weights, sliver in one fist, glistening diamond in the other.

Near the fire was a shotgun and a pistol and a knife I recognized. *Edoda*'s knife, the bone hilt crosshatched for a good grip. Beside that knife was another knife I knew, the curved blade sheathed in the red velvet. Bruiser's gift. I was surprised to see it there. And then again, I wasn't. Were my father's weapons part of the decision I had to make? Was Bruiser part of it? Clothes of a War Woman. Weapons of a warrior from my father's time. Arcane weapons from my own time. A killing weapon from Bruiser. What else?

I looked up from the weapons lit by the steady flames into the arc of the smooth cavern roof with its hanging stalactites, and down where the ceiling curved into the walls. Shadows moved where the stalagmites rose from the floor, wet and glistening. But the stone that composed my soul home was different. Where it was once pale, it was now dark.

My cavern was damaged, as if fire—or lightning—had left soot and char all over it, black and gray and dirty, with the undamaged wall showing through in places, white and palest of greens and creamy grays in what looked like strange symbols, nonpatterns that I didn't recognize right at first. I tilted my head and walked around the pit, studying the shapes, and they resolved into hundreds of representations of the Blood Cross scorched into the walls at every angle, as if the lightning and the cross had been spinning around, engaged in a dance—or some arcane form of combat.

I held my right fist up to the wall. The crosses covered and overlapped the tracery image of veins left from the injury I had suffered to my hand, the injury of the *wyrd* spell Santana had thrown at me. I'd never been completely healed of it, and, perhaps the wound had made my spirit and my soul home susceptible to further damage.

Directly overhead was more white and dark, this time in

the shape of wings, white wings and dark wings, as if a snowy owl and a crow fought there.

From the far wall, I saw a flash of light and felt a burning shiver as if from the lightning, smelled again the odd scent, strong for a moment, inorganic and acidic. Though I had never smelled it before, I identified the smell. *Limestone burning.* My cave walls were being burned by the lightning. I understood what I was seeing and smelling. The sliver of the Blood Cross, the diamond, and the lightning were doing ... something ... in reality, and it was affecting me there, in the Gray Between. And perhaps in yet another reality where light and dark, chaos and order, were fighting for supremacy. Or maybe in another time, another moment.

Lightning flashed again, a sear I felt on my skin, hot and burning and then gone.

The shape the lightning left behind was of the cross itself, not the sliver that I carried, but the portion that Sabina kept safe in her lair. I remembered the cross, the way it had felt in my hand, the wood unshaped, tightly grained, the two pieces not much more than rough stakes, splintered ends smoothed and oiled. The wire that wrapped the two pieces, shaping them into a cross, was metal, green with verdigris. The cross had been weighty, much heavier than it appeared, and old. Ancient. It had been made from the three broken crosses that the sons of Ioudas Issachar had used to bring their father—dead and buried—back to a semblance of life. And thereby they created the first vampire.

Another flash of light burst, this almost directly overhead, near the imprint of the wings, leaving behind the stronger scent of scorched limestone. As it burst, my face burned, a flash of heat. The stink of burning hair and skin overlaid the smell of burning rock.

I understood that my body was under attack in reality, and my soul home was under attack in the Gray Between, but I wasn't certain if the lightning was my enemy, or the blood diamond, or the Blood Cross. Or Santana. Of if the spell had gone horribly awry. Or maybe all of them.

It was possible that I had been pricked by the cross in real time, real life; Sabina had warned me that if I was wounded by it, the weapon might kill me. But it wasn't as if she'd been certain. And I'd wielded the sliver of the cross before. So if the *cross* wasn't my enemy, then that made the diamond my enemy. And maybe the *lightning* had provided the power to whatever was going on in a battle between light and dark, chaos and order.

Two more flashes lit the roof of my cavern in bright light. Sooo ... who directed the lightning? And if my soul home was ruined, would I be dead in the human world too? Or, conversely, could I survive if I was there, in my soul home, when my body died in the other reality?

There were too many metaphysical questions and not a single answer. I had no idea what any of it might mean in my current state of spiritual darkness. Or maybe spiritual wandering. Whatever. What really mattered was that ... I hadn't blessed or warded my soul home in ... ever. I wasn't even sure how to do that. Until now, I hadn't considered that I might need to do that. It—the spiritual heart of me— wasn't purified or strong. I had left it weak and unshielded in my neglect and my wandering.

Decide, Beast thought at me. *Decide whether you will be War Woman or killer.*

"Aren't they the same thing?" I asked, surprised.

There was another flash, another pain, a second. A third. These coming much sooner than the last. Much closer to me. And much more agonizing. Burns always are. I hissed as the pain spread. Real time was speeding up again. I was almost out of nontime. Which was kinda funny on the face of it. I didn't have long to figure out what to do in a choice where both sides seemed to be the same thing.

Except ...

A War Woman always fought *for* something. For family. Clan. Land. Tribe. Honor. Justice. Important things.

Killers just killed. For sport. Money. Without thought or caring. Killers killed without ... spiritual purpose. Except that my grandmother was a War Woman. She had tortured the two men who killed my father and raped my mother. How did vengeance fit into the paradigm?

I had killed sentient beings of multiple species. Were-wolves. Vampires who were in the devoveo. But they might have been able to return to sanity with enough time and the proper blood to drink. Brute and I had discussed that once, but no answer had been forthcoming. I had killed humans. In every case of killing, they were trying to kill me at the time, but I had never tried to save them. Never tried to find another, nonlethal way to stop them. Never tried to give them a chance at . . . What? Redemption? Change? A different life? And if I had given them a chance to change, I'd probably be dead now because, honestly, people didn't often change.

Except the taxi driver. Zareb. He had changed. Turned his life around. Sooo. Had I therefore sent people into the next life unprepared for the light, worthy only of the darkness and chaos? Had I deprived them of the opportunity to transform? To find redemption?

I had perhaps even been seeking the darkness and chaos myself, depending on things and people instead of on the spiritual. Had that weakened me, allowed my soul to be damaged? *Crap.* I had been stupid. This wasn't good. Not at all.

Choose, Beast said.

"War Woman," I said.

A light so bright it stole all my vision engulfed me. I was in the air, hanging in the midst of a lightning bolt. Pain shook me. I burned. I was on fire. My body caught in the fiery lightning, unable to move. My skin blackening and falling off my muscles, exposing my bones. But unlike in my soul home, there was blood.

Forcing my muscles to obey, I brought my hands together, the sliver of the cross, the glowing-white blood diamond, and my blood, what little hadn't boiled away, meeting. Touching. I made a double fist around the weapons and gripped tight with hands that were on fire. My entire body spasmed in a seizure as some new magic, some new power, met the lightning. Together they seared into me.

The lightning bolt swatted me the rest of the way out of the witch circle. Over Molly's and Sabina's heads. Through the magics of the middle circle. Through the wards of the outer circle. Smashed me against the earth. Bowled me over and over in a sickening rush of melting skin and clacking bones. As I rolled, the fire was snuffed out. Pain continued to explode on and through me. I *was* pain, as if the sensation were a sentient being, alive and seething.

The Gray Between took me again. A different kind of pain ripped through me, colder, icy. Pelt sprouted through the burned flesh. I came to rest on the grass, in the dark, against the front wheel of a vehicle.

The last echo of thunder shook the earth. Rain strafed the ground. Hard, drumming rain.

A shot rang out. Reverberating through the beating downpour.

Women screamed.

My bones twisted and snapped. My ribs wouldn't expand and I couldn't breathe, couldn't move, couldn't even die. The pain was beyond my own comprehension. I was in the midst of the shift into . . . something. But I was burned, burned, *burned*. Bruiser lifted me. I knew by the feel of him in the Gray Between. My body twisted in his arms, writhing in agony. *Let me die.* But the words didn't form. My mouth wasn't shaped right for speech.

But, oddly, I could still hear.

Rain decreasing. Slamming of doors. Engine starting. Sound of tires over something.

"Hospital?"

"What good would that do us?"

"Vet?" That was Eli, worry underlying the snark.

"Church?"

"Alex? Closest church?"

A tinny voice said, "Closest is upriver. Eight miles."

"I say back to the French Quarter. The St. Louis Cathedral. I mean, if you want a church, that's a big-assed church."

"Do it."

My body lurched and rocked and I finally inhaled, the breath so painful it felt like I was still breathing lightning. I tried to scream, tried to flail against the pain. I couldn't. Every slightest movement sent pain rocketing through me, slicing through me. "Can't get in the church," I managed. "Will burn." But it came out as "'An' 'eeen urk. Iu urn."

"Can you get the weapons and clothes off her?" Eli asked.

I felt pressure here and there on my body. "They're burned into her flesh," Bruiser said. "They'll have to be cut out unless we get her to shift."

I felt wetness on my back, the backs of my thighs. The only part of me that wasn't screaming in pain. "Jane? She's awake. Can you shift, Jane? Can you shift?!"

I reached into me. Nothing happened. Nothing. Something was wrong. "No," I managed to say, but it came out, "Nuh." My mouth was broken. "Nuh."

"Hang on, Janie," Bruiser whispered. "Hang on." My consciousness slipped away in a haze of agony.

Much later I whispered, "KitKit?" the sound guttural and hoarse. I had no idea where that question came from, among all the ones I should have asked.

Bruiser laughed, though it sounded more like tears. "A little singed. Last time I saw her, she was in Molly's arms."

That was when I realized that Beast had asked. *Beast.* Speaking in English through my mouth. Or . . . maybe my mouth. Maybe something else.

"Flesh of Joses/Joseph?" I asked, sounding a bit more human.

"Gone. Burned to ashes by the lightning."

Maybe that was a good thing, I thought. Or maybe not. Because there was still a way to call the SoD. Using the three hairs that Bruiser carried. Maybe we didn't need the witches at all.

Once again, everything went black.

CHAPTER 27

Medium-Well-Cooked Meat

When Bruiser picked me up, I came to again. It was the altering level of pain that woke me. My eyes were open, slitted to see down along my body. I was in half-Beast form, but burned. *Crispy critter.* The phrase came to me, uttered once by a firefighter, back in the mountains, when he thought no one was listening. My blackened hands were clasped, half-human, half-paw, and were fused together, as if the muscles and juices had cooked them into that shape. Though I couldn't feel them, I could see the glow of the white diamond through my flesh, and I knew I was holding the two magical items in a double fist sealed by burned flesh.

We were illegally parked directly in front of the St. Louis Cathedral, in the area marked off for foot traffic only. Bruiser was carrying me up the short flight of steps, through a downpour that rivaled Noah's flood.

"Nuh. Nuh!" I shouted. But it came out in a whisper. The light in my hands exploded. I croaked out a scream. Writhed in Bruiser's arms. He whirled and raced away from the front doors, back to the SUV, trailing a wisp of smoke. The light died. The pain that had spiraled up into some new height of agony died back down with the distance. But now, I felt cold, so cold.

"I'm such an ass!" Eli shouted, frustration and fear in his voice. "Janie tried once before to take the diamond into a holy place. It's black magic. It burns."

The sound of his fear made me reach out for the Gray Between. Nothing happened. I tried again. And again. Nothing worked. *Beast?* She didn't answer. It was getting to be a bad habit. And now I was afraid too.

"What are our options?" Bruiser answered Eli, his voice thick with fear. "It's seared into her body. Suggestions?"

"Leo? One of the priestesses?" Alex asked over the open cell's speaker.

"I don't—" Bruiser stopped. I could feel his breathing, hear his heartbeat. "I don't think Leo can help. Not with this. Bethany would as soon kill Jane as heal her, and this would be beyond even her talents. Sabina is hurt from the lightning strike. But if we can't find another way, then the Master of the City would be our last resort."

"Aggie One Feather? Alex, see if they're home."

"Already tried. No answer, bro," the tinny voice said. "I left a message on Aggie's cell, but there's a powwow in North Carolina this coming weekend. They may have left for that already."

Car doors closed and the engine started. The tires rolled over something and Bruiser shifted on the seat. I couldn't help the sound that wrenched from my lungs, a groan-moan-sob-croak.

"Sorry, sweetheart," he whispered. "So sorry."

I thought I felt something touch my forehead, and I remembered the blessing he had given me before the witch circle, the feel of his Onorio magics skittering over my skin. Hadn't helped much then. Didn't help now.

We hit another bump and pain pummeled me. I went blissfully unconscious again. Sometime later, pain woke me. "Alex. Send me directions to something. *Any*thing," Eli said. "Yeah? Got it. Let's go."

Bruiser murmured through my own personal hell of pain, reminding me, "Find the Gray Between, love. Find the Gray Between." This time I didn't go unconscious but was alert through the drive, trying to follow Bruiser's orders,

trying to open the Gray Between, to become calm enough
to sink deep inside, to the well of my own power, and shift
and heal. But every breath was agony. Every heartbeat was
torture. And the magical implements cooked into my palms/
paws were the problem.

My pelt was scorched and my skin was blistered and
breaking and draining in places, blackened and crisp in others. My burned muscles were contracted into knots of charley horses. On the drive, I started shivering as my body went
into shock. I was losing fluids so fast that I'd die soon if we
didn't figure out something.

"Where are we?" Bruiser asked.

"Coliseum Place Baptist Church on Camp Street," Alex
said over speakerphone, just as the SUV came to a stop. "It
was burned sometime after Hurricane Katrina. It's sacred
ground but not a place of worship anymore. It's slated to be
torn down because it's unstable and likely to fall apart, but
the historical society is trying to save it, and so there's an
injunction."

Eli said, "This may work. Good thinking, Alex." His
voice got louder as he spoke over his shoulder to Bruiser.
"Janie was partially healed when she landed in a baptismal
pool at The Church. And once before, I saw Janie enter a
sacred place in Natchez, the foundation of an old church. It
was only an outline of the foundations, the rest burned to
the ground. But when Jane walked through the front door,
she disappeared into a mist and met with a woman. An Elder of the Choctaws, I think."

I remembered that. I remembered how to do that, to enter sacred ground. But that time I'd had a coin to call the
Elder to me, and an invitation to do so. This time I had . . .
dangerous stuff gripped in the medium-well-cooked meat
of my hands. And something just as dangerous—under the
right circumstance—in my pocket. Something that had
been part of that previous night, that previous journey into
a different place and time, a place of dreams and the past
and an old, old power.

Bruiser got us out of the backseat, and I managed not to
scream too much, but my shivering was worse, much worse,
even with the heat of an Onorio holding me. "Get the iron
out of my pocket," I said. Or nonsense syllables close to
that. Mind-reading, Eli knelt and rummaged in what was left

of my pocket, coming up with the fused iron discs. "Take me into the church grounds and lay me down." The tremors of each footstep jolted through me as Bruiser, even with his Onorio grace, walked across the uneven ground toward the church. It was raining again, far harder. I could feel the cold as it seeped into me, even if I couldn't feel the raindrops hit.

Beast? I called, sounding desperate. She didn't answer.

To distract myself from the pain, I went over the formula I had once used to call a holy woman to me. This time I wasn't calling a holy woman. I was trying to heal myself. The words had been ... *Long years past was cold iron, blood, three cursed trees, and lightning. Red iron will set you free.* Followed by: *Shadow and blood are a dark light, buried beneath the ground.*

Maybe it had been ... a prophecy of sorts?

Red iron and trees. I had determined the *tree* part to refer to the three cursed trees of Calvary that the Sons of Darkness, the witch sons of Judas Iscariot, had used to bring their father back to life. According to vamp-myth, the wood from the three crosses had been mixed with human sacrifice, witch blood, and black magic to create the first immortal, and when the sons ate the reanimated flesh of their father, they became the first two blood drinkers and fathers of all the vampires who followed. I had a piece of that in the cooked meat of my fused fists. The *red iron* had been iron from the spikes used to attach the three men crucified that night to the trees. According to vamp legend, the new vamps had melted them down and created a single massive spike, which had become a weapon to control vamps. *Got that too.*

Shadow and blood are a dark light. Once again there was shadow and my blood, in this place, just as there had been shadow and blood on Golgotha the evening the Christ died. There had been his blood on the tree. And on the cold iron that pierced his flesh, holding him there. The same cold iron that Eli had pulled from my pocket. In Natchez, I had figured out that the crosses and melted-down iron had been used for transformative black magic, magic that had turned Naturaleza vamps into spidey vamps—vampires that had transmogrified into *things* that were genetic amalgamations of insects, reptiles, and ... and ... horrid *things*. And the iron had given the things control over time.

I went over the whole saying again, trying to decide how

much to use, how much to alter, knowing that I was crafting a spell I couldn't use because I wasn't a witch. *Long years past was cold iron, blood, three cursed trees, and lightning. Red iron will set you free.* Then: *Shadow and blood are a dark light, buried beneath the ground.*

I had everything I needed. I had a sliver of the crosses and pieces of the iron, blood. I had a soul home, also beneath the ground. And I had the blood diamond, which was a dark light if there had ever been one.

Lightning cracked in the distance and thunder rumbled. The rain warmed. Or maybe I was just getting colder. Dying. Yeah. That.

Bruiser and I passed through one of the arched doorways and into the center of what must have been the sanctuary. He stumbled over the fallen rafters and knelt inside the charred walls. The brick still smelled of soot and fire and wounded earth, which felt perfect for me.

Rain grew harder. Bruiser set me down on the wet earth and lay me over on my side. My body was frozen in the position in which he had been carrying me, a semi-fetal position. As he eased back, away from me, on his knees, I could feel the rain on that side of my face. It felt heated. Where the rain hit into the mud, droplets shot up in the air and landed on me, adding mud to the burns and the clothing that was melted into my skin.

Eli spread one of his metallic, heat-retaining blankets over me, and I heard him say, "Molly called. I'm going to get her."

"Are you sure that's wise?" Bruiser asked.

"She says the lightning bolt did something to her magic. She says she can help. I don't think we can turn down any help that's offered. Back in a bit. Keep her alive." I heard him jog back to the street, his boots loud in the mud and standing water.

The lightning bolt did something to her magic? I remembered the vision of wings, white and black, snowy owl and crow, fighting. Had the lightning offered *everyone* in the witch circles a choice? Had the triple circles and the *wyrds* done something unexpected with us? Something planned and used by . . . someone?

Darkness found me again, and I slept beneath the metallic blanket, watched over by Bruiser. In the shadows of uneasy sleep, I dreamed and remembered dreams. I saw the cavern of my soul home, as if from the outside, the wings fighting, light and dark. Lightning flashed again and again, in dreams and in reality, rousing me, but I was only pulled under into dreams again. The pain came in waves and spikes, as if I were still in the midst of the lightning strike, hanging between heaven and earth.

I woke when the rain slowed, to see Bruiser kneeling in the mud beside me, his eyes closed and lips moving. I wasn't sure, but it looked like he might be praying. For me. My heart stuttered and paused and stuttered back into some kind of rhythm again, but not a normal rhythm. This one hurt and rambled and stumbled. Time was out.

I struggled to find breath to speak. "You got a knife?" I asked him, my voice an ugly croak.

Somehow he heard me over the pattering rain and bent over me, his knees in the mud, a small blade in his hand. "Do you want me to cut some of your clothing loose? It's . . . tight."

Swollen. He meant that I was swollen and leaking and ruined. "No," I managed. And lifted my hands to his in a fast move that sent pain rocketing through me. And impaled my hands on his knife.

"Jane!" He jerked back and away.

I chuckled, a sound more sob-like than humorous. "Poke the iron discs into the wound," I ordered. Lightning flashed and thundered down. Close, like a punctuation to my command. Rain followed, hard and pelting once again.

There was a long hesitation; then Bruiser was holding my crusted-together fists in both of his. He bent his head over mine, his mouth at my ear, and said, "Love, are you sure?"

I smiled and felt, for the first time, my tusks. I was still in my half-beast form and my canines were shaped like tusks. Weird. And he still called me love. "Yeah. Blood and iron. Do it. Please." I couldn't feel it when he pressed the iron discs into my flesh, but I saw it. The moment it was done I closed my eyes.

My words mangled by my puma mouth, I called, "Creator God." Lightning struck close by and I felt the tingle of electricity as it flashed through the ground and through the standing water. I spoke on, stumbling on the words, finding the right phrases, "Cold iron, the iron spike of Golgotha, three cursed trees, a once-black-magic diamond that now glows white and pure, my blood, my skinwalker flesh, and lightning are all in the same place." I had to stop to breathe, to give my heart a chance to catch up. "An angel of light and an angel of death fight in the space between worlds, fight in the Gray Between that is within me and in the shadows of my soul home." While I breathed again, I searched through my fractured Cherokee memories and my childhood memories for prayers and finally came up with, "Creator God, El Roi—the god who sees me. Yehovah." I paused, panting, remembering the fragment of a dream from days ago. Remembered that the *Tsalagi* had words for the Almighty. I said, *"Yehowa, Edoda,"* and two words for Great Spirit came to me: *"unequa, adanvdo."* And words for angels: *"Anidawehi—"* I stopped again, to catch my breath. My heart was stuttering inside and the pain was building. I had to finish it right then. "All that is good and all that *was* evil, or had been used for evil, are now inside my body, surrounded by my blood, my . . ." I searched for the right words and settled on: "my sacrifice of pain. *Unequa, anidawehi,* let me die or help me. Help me and set me free as War Woman." The words were soft, half growling.

Once again, lightning struck, slamming into the ground only yards away. The power of it sent electric shivers through me. Bruiser yelped and rolled back. My loose hair stood on end despite the rain, and my skin crackled with the pain of electricity, but it seemed to help, and the Gray Between finally opened.

Beast?

Change. Now! she thought at me.

I reached inside, down into the marrow of my/our bones, searching for the snake that lies within each cell of the body, the twined snakes of DNA that make each of us what we are. Beast's and my genetic material, our DNA strands, were twisted together in places, into tripled strands that looked like nothing on this earth. My heart skipped a beat. Sped fast and skipped several. Heart pain spread through me, adding to my anguish. I was dying. Seemed I was doing that an awful lot lately. It meant I didn't have time to separate the strands. I had to use what I was offered. I took the tripled strands in my mind.

Somewhere close by, I heard shouting. A scream of pain.

Wings fluttered over me, feathers white and black, the roar of battle, of swords clashing, of the stink of old blood and ozone. A vision of black shadows and bright light flashed past, interwoven and forever divided. My choices caused this battle. Or not. Maybe they just contributed to it. Or maybe the fight had been going on for eons, in the spaces between worlds, and I was no more than a single grain of sand on the shores of war.

I yanked on the strands.

My heart stopped. The sounds of battle were sharp, bright, and painful on my ears.

Change! Beast snarled at me.

I *changed*. I pulled the merged genetic material over me, over us, taking on the half-human, half-puma warrior shape of the War Woman of my clan. Taking it on fully, healing even as I sprouted pelt, as my toes spread and flexed. Retractable claws unsheathed and ripped away burned boot leather, clawed, tore my hands apart. My fingers separated and fisted, healed in front of my eyes, fully formed into the knobby-knuckled, long-fingered shape of my stronger-than-skinwalker hands. Hips and knees and shoulders were bigger, rounder boned. My waist was tiny and solid muscle. I rolled to a sitting position, rain splattering down on me, warm and wet and slick.

I took a breath and it didn't hurt. "Oh." *It didn't hurt.*

I felt the *things* in my left hand, warm and tingling and full of power. Holding the fist up, I saw the glow of—

"Jane! Down!"

I ducked a sword cut and rolled through the mud. A smooth, clean cut. The blade smelling of blood. Bruiser's blood. I rolled out of the way, my weapons clanking and grinding on my misshaped body, up against a wall that stank of old fire. Lightning struck close, rattling the brick of the burned church. A wall nearby, weakened by fire and storm and time, crumbled and fell in a crash. I wiped my hand across my half-human face, focusing on the battle taking place in front of me. In the midst of a rainstorm, a brutal punishing lightning storm, Bruiser and the Son of Darkness were fighting. With swords. The dual swords of the *Duel Sang*, the blood duel.

How did Joseph find us? The gobbet of his flesh had been burned to ashes by the lightning bolt.

But . . . I looked at my left fist. He could track me through the blood diamond. And perhaps through his own flesh, the hairs in Bruiser's pocket. I opened the fist, my fingers stretching out, my claws sliding free, gleaming in the wet dark.

In my paw/palm was a new thing. A new weapon? Or something else, something that had never been before. The metal from the iron spike of Golgotha had melted when I shifted and had re-formed around the blood diamond and the sliver of the Blood Cross. The diamond, now glowing with a white light, humming with power, was touching the sliver of ancient wood, the two weapons touching, held in place by hardened iron. It wasn't the weapon or the shape that Sabina had suggested, but it was . . . curious. Unexpected. Remarkable in so many ways.

It had made itself.

I looked from my hand to the fighting and took a quick breath that flowed in through my nose and mouth, over the scent receptors in flehmen response, smelling, tasting, seeing Bruiser's blood flow, looking black in the darkness, red in the lightning flashes, hearing the crash of steel and the grunts of pain.

Joseph Santana was uncut, his body looking whole and healed, but as he moved and cut, I caught the stink of burning flesh. He was still injured, still on fire, somewhere deep inside, the reek smelling of pain and fury. I could risk using the weapon in my fist on him, risk a result I couldn't predict. Or I could—

I reached over my shoulder and hunted for the butt of the Benelli Super 90. It was way around to the side, hanging at a strange angle, one strap too loose on my body, the other too tight. I got my right hand around the stock and tried to draw it.

The new shotgun-shell holder, mounted on the left side of the receiver, caught. The leather had shrunk and tightened in fire and lightning and rain. I twisted and jerked the weapon, trying to free it.

Bruiser took a cut to his left shoulder and fell to one knee. He got his weapon up to block a sword strike. I yanked on the shotgun, and the damaged leather of the spine holster parted. I rolled to my feet and ran, screaming, "Hey, suckhead! Take on someone your own size!" Bruiser fell flat. Joseph Santana whirled to me as I fired. He took the full blast into his chest cavity. The second blast took him in the belly. The third took off part of his right shoulder.

He whipped up his arm. The bracelet on his wrist shot out a silver light. Santana vanished.

I dropped to my knees beside Bruiser. He looked up at me, his eyes too wide with shock and adrenaline. "Hey, gorgeous," he said, his voice tight with the pain. "What took you so long?"

CHAPTER 28

I Smelled Onorio Blood

"I was busy figuring out stuff," I said through my half-human mouth. The sounds were odd and distorted, but Bruiser seemed to have no trouble understanding. I ripped open what was left of my med-kit and handed him a slightly scorched sanitary pad, part of Eli's medic gear, for battlefield wounds. Bruiser slipped the pad under his ruined leather and placed it over his bleeding shoulder. "How fast will you heal?" I asked.

"Fast enough." He hissed in a breath, held it, released it on a gasp, and asked, "Why?"

"You still got the hairs you took out of Pinkie's neck?"

Bruiser smiled slowly, the skin around his eyes crinkling. "Yes. What do you have in mind?"

"Let's hold hands, call his name, click our heels together, and see if this will take us to him. Or bring him to us. Whichever." I held out the new weapon, part iron, part diamond, part wood sliver. "He's wounded. The diamond is connected to the bracelet he's wearing, and to me. And there's fresh blood on the ground from where I shot him. It might be now or never to finish him."

Bruiser lifted a hand and curled his fingers around my jaw, a hairy, pelted jaw. "Whatever my lady desires."

I chuckled and tried to holster the shotgun, but the leather was ruined. All my gear was ruined. I was wearing tatters but managed to find a vamp-killer that was in fairly good shape despite the lightning strike and held the shotgun and the knife in my left hand. I lowered the new weapon—it had to be a weapon, because I'd had to choose to become War Woman to use it—to the ground and smeared it through a splatter of Santana's blood and sooty mud from the church. I gripped it in my right palm, along with the three hairs Bruiser pulled from an envelope. I closed my knobby pawed fingers around it. "If this works, I'll shoot him a few times and then cut out his heart."

"I'll try to stay out of the way." Bruiser was laughing at me, that kind of loving laughter that . . . that I'd never experienced before and that sent warm bubbles of happiness dancing through my bloodstream.

I hooked my right arm through Bruiser's left, noting that he held a long sword in his right. And his bleeding had stopped. Onorio magic.

Silently, I asked, *Beast?*

Beast is here.

Do you know where Santana is?

No. Angel Hayyel knows. Santana kills and eats his prey.

I thought about that for a moment, not quite sure what to do about the fact that Beast knew what an angel knew. *Okay, that's scary.* And worse, Santana was eating his prey. Like skinwalkers did when they went insane and became *u'tlun'ta.* And Santana had tasted Immanuel's blood—Immanuel, whom I had killed, who had been *u'tlun'ta.* And whom Leo had not drunk from. Leo'd had no idea his son had been eaten and replaced by a different being.

Diamond is yours for now, Beast thought at me. *Will take you to vampire killer.*

"Joses son of Judas Iscariot," I said, pronouncing it *Yosace, son of Ioudas Issachar.* "Joses Bar-Judas." *Yosace Bar-Ioudas.* "Joseph Santana."

Nothing happened. Bruiser lifted one brow, Leo-like, and asked, "Blood?"

"It's always blood, to you people."

"To Mithrans. You are my people now."

We might be about to go into battle with angel oversight and me in pelt instead of skin, but my heart warmed and the bubbles of happiness sizzled through me. I lifted the vamp-killer and nicked my padded fingertip, letting the blood dribble on the weapon, the three hairs, and Santana's blood. "Joses, son of —"

The world exploded in white light and gray energies and we entered the Gray Between. My gut roiled and twisted and the nausea that hit was fiery. Seconds passed in the Gray as my abdomen kinked and coiled.

We came out of the Gray Between, propelled over a puddle of muddy goo and blood and part of a vampire, blond and broken. *Dominique*. Her throat ripped out. Santana's face buried in her abdomen. Eating. Like an *u'tlun'ta*.

We hit, splashing through the thick mud, and rolled apart, facing the Son of Darkness.

Faster than the lightning that nearly killed me, Santana rose and unsheathed a sword. He was mostly healed but still missing part of one shoulder, that arm dangling, useless. With the single sword, he attacked. Bruiser blocked the strike with two swords and danced through the room, forcing Santana to follow him. Away from me. Swords clanged and rang on the night air. Steel flashed.

I lay propped against the wall and vomited blood. Brick wall, old brick. Heaving was horrible, but when it let up, I felt marginally better. Well enough to wonder why I was tossing cookies. I hadn't bent time. I had just . . . *utilized the blood diamond*. Like a witch. Or it had used me . . . I vomited again, the stink of stomach acid and blood, foul. I wasn't designed to use magic. Using magic was killing me little by little in ways that my skinwalker magics couldn't fix.

I wiped my mouth and took in the smell of mold and vamp blood and vomit on the humid air. Light came from candles lit throughout the room. Old furniture, half-rotted and broken. No floor. The walls had been spray-painted by vandals. Roaches scuttled everywhere. Two dead humans were piled in the corner. Santana's and Bruiser's shadows swayed and gamboled in the flickering light. Through the broken-out window I saw the Royal Mojo Blues Company, and I knew that we were at one of Santana's old properties, one we had eliminated early on in our search for the SoD.

Bruiser took a hit to his already damaged shoulder and dropped, rolled through the water and away. Using the brick, he shoved off with one leg and engaged Santana again. One sword to one sword.

I tucked the diamond into what was left of my bra and managed to get the M4 shotgun up and in place, against my shoulder, trying to find balance where I lay propped against the wall. Bruiser took a sword strike into his torso, through and through. Santana whipped the sword out, slashing. I stared, breathless, as Bruiser fell. I smelled Onorio blood and bowel and I pulled the trigger. Again. I hadn't reloaded, and the rounds were gone, but Santana was on his knees. He might have been growling through his fangs, but I was deaf from the shotgun. Using the expensive weapon as a crutch, I levered myself up to a standing position and dropped the gun. I took the vamp-killer in both hands and stalked close. I took a steady backhand and swung at his neck, putting muscle into the strike. The blade caught in the cervical spine and the SoD fell over, taking the weapon with him, jerking it from my hands; his head was still attached. There was life in his eyes, but even vamps have spinal columns. I'd severed Santana's.

"You alive?" I asked Bruiser, not looking. I couldn't bear to see.

He chuckled without humor, graveyard comedy, the sound barely heard over the ringing in my ears. "I'll live. But the recovery will mean a lot of time in bed."

"Silver lining," I said. Leaving the vamp-killer buried in Santana, I stumbled back to my M4 and reloaded, knobby fingers shaking. Bruiser laughed again, sounding more alive.

At the edges of the ringing in my ears, I heard sirens, the sound of traffic, and music. And voices, growing closer. "I like the new look," he said.

"Yeah? No mirror handy. I'll admire myself later." I went back to Santana and leaned over him. I removed the bracelet from his wrist and stuck it into the other side of my bra, where it wouldn't accidently touch the new weapon. I went back to Santana and aimed down at his body. I fired. Kept firing. Until I stood over the Son of Darkness, empty weapon pointed down onto a macerated pile of blood and meat simmering in silver on the ground. Head still attached. Heart still beating. Not dead. It was messy.

I tucked the M4 under an arm, and with my fully healed hands, I yanked up on a broken rib, exposing what might once have been a lung. It had the right shape but was deflated, full of silver-fléchette holes and blood. Beside it, something pulsed. *Can anything survive without a heart?* Leo had asked me. I put a foot on Santana's shoulder and yanked the vamp-killer out of his spine, feeling, hearing, the crunch of bone. I'd done it before. It felt familiar, and maybe that was a bad thing, because I didn't feel any guilt at the sensation. No guilt at all. Yeah. A bad thing.

Bare-handed, I shoved the lung aside and gathered up the heart in one hand. Using the vamp-killer like a filleting knife, I cut it out, a cold, gooey mess of silver-chewed muscle that stank of silver-charred-vamp. "Ick," I muttered, letting blood drip through my fingers back into the goo that had once been Joses Bar-Judas / Joseph Santana. There wasn't life in his eyes anymore, but I didn't delude myself that he was dead. Not yet. I swished my bloody hand in a puddle. "Ick and yuck and eww." I stood and slung my hand in the rain to finish the cleaning. I looked up and discovered that the building had no roof. From the hole I'd made in Santana's flesh, a coil of silver-stinking smoke curled into the rain.

"What do we do with this?" I indicated the silver-charred pulp. "He's still on fire."

"Put out the fire?" Bruiser looked up at the sky, turning his face to the rain, which washed away his spreading blood. He'd taken a cut to his face, across his eyebrow and up into the widow's peak of his hairline. He was holding his gut together with both hands, but already the flesh was knitting together. He might have some dandy scars, but he'd heal. Onorios—whatever they are—are hard to kill. Which looked to be a really good thing. He looked back at the body. "The rain doesn't seem to be having a great effect on the fire."

"Holy water might work."

Bruiser chuckled, the sound exhausted and beaten.

He was staring at me, taking in my face, and a spark of something unknown lit his warm brown eyes. Something tender. An answering something turned over in me and murmured *Ours . . .*

Behind me I heard a growl and turned, lifting the vamp-killer, but it was only Brute. The white werewolf stood in the doorway, his hackles high, his canines glistening in the candlelight. He was wet and stank like dog.

"Too late, Brute."

The white wolf walked slowly into the ruined house, his nose on the ground, sniffing. He stopped at the body of Joses Bar-Judas / Joseph Santana and sniffed. When he was convinced Santana wasn't going to get up and do anything, he sat in the mud and looked up at me. His pale eyes seemed to be satisfied.

Thinking, I pulled out the diamond/sliver/iron thingamajig. I wondered if the doohickey would turn Brute back to human. Or maybe just kill him. I remembered the dream where someone—Me? Brute?—asked to be set free. Not worth the risk to prick either one of us, I guessed.

Humor stronger in his voice, Bruiser said, "What are you going to call your new toy?"

"I was going for Glob. What do you think?" I held it up.

"Simple. Catchy." From his position in the mud, Bruiser kicked at Joseph's left hand. It flopped before it fell motionless, blood and rain pooling in the palm. "I don't know, Jane. It might make things worse for him."

"Yeah?" I tracked the smoke that was coming from the body of Joses Bar-Judas and shoved the tip of the Glob inside the cold, bloody mass. All around the weapon I felt a frisson of something heated and icy as it passed from the weapon into the flesh of the Son of Darkness, but I saw absolutely nothing. Smelled nothing. And then there was a soft sizzle and the smoke died away. "Huh. It worked. How 'bout that?"

Bruiser shook his head in what looked like amused affection.

"Janie?" Eli called from the dark. "Janie, where are you?"

Had he tracked me via the cell? I touched a pocket. It had once held a cell phone, but it was gone now. Reading my mind, Bruiser said, "They used mine. I felt it vibrate during the fight."

"I have Molly," Eli shouted.

I tucked the Glob back into my bra, which was uncomfortable, but I didn't have much choice, and shouted, "Over here! Bruiser's hurt. He needs vamp blood."

"And we need to haul a bleeding mass of meat to the

Master of the City," Bruiser added, softly, "before he heals enough to get away."

Eli and Molly trudged through the softening rain, passed through the empty doorway, and walked inside the walls of the burned house. When they reached us, Molly's mouth fell open. Eli's eyes took in me, Bruiser, and the thing at my feet. "Looks like I missed all the fun. Not bad, Janie," he said. "Not bad at all."

"Got a plastic zip bag?" I asked, holding out the heart.

"Son of a witch on a switch," Molly cursed.

Hours later, back at the house, Molly took a shower while I stared at myself in the mirror. I didn't quite look like me anymore. Or Beast. Or even the half me, half Beast of my previous form. I didn't have tusks in this form. My face had my human bone structure but was lightly pelted, with glowing gold eyes and longer-than-human canines. Very pointy canines.

I had rounded ears, perched too high on my head, ears that I could move to catch sounds better. And I had Jane hair, still wet, flowing down my back, long and lustrous black.

"I like it," Bruiser said. I smelled truth coming off him. "But I think we'll eat in tonight."

"Afraid I'd scare the other diners?"

He grinned, his eyes resting lightly on me. "I couldn't care less what anyone else thinks. But you might want to try eating in private first."

I touched my tongue to my pointy teeth. "Eh. Maybe so. Could be messy."

His face went serious. "Thank you for returning the body to Leo. He's already sent word to the Europeans that he has recovered a wounded Son of Darkness and is *healing him* in his lair. If they were planning anything, they will stop now. At least for a time."

"Before they show up here, I need to know how to make Leo fall in love."

Bruiser's eyebrow rose, just the uninjured one. The other had a new, sexy scar bisecting it. "With you?"

"No. Either Del or Katie. Or both."

"I'll get right on that," he said, his tone wry. "Where's the heart of the Son of Darkness?"

"In my fridge. Jodi will be here to pick it up in an hour or so. I also need to know what happened to Immanuel's scions and blood-servants."

"They were absorbed into Leo's clan a century ago."

"I need to talk to them."

"That can be arranged. I think the new look will make them all talkative."

"I don't plan on keeping it," I said. "Gimme a minute." I sat on the floor and thought about my Jane-form. And changed.

When I was human again, I turned on the shower, twisting the knob to nearly scalding, stripped, set all my handy-dandy new magical thingamabobs on the sink rim, and stepped in. Bruiser wasn't far behind me.

CHAPTER 29

I Don't Give a Rat's Ass Who's Getting Pampered

Beast crouched on limb over edge of bayou, where slow stream curved like snake and doubled back on itself. Staring down at good, stinky water full of big fish. Jane called them cat-fish, but fish are not cats. Fish are food for cats. Fish are good to eat. Fish with whiskers like cat and spines to stick, like claws of cat. Jane was smart. Cat-fish was good to hunt and good to fight and good to eat. Like cat-fight, with fish-meat after.

Cat-fish are sneaky like cat too. Cat-fish were not always where they looked to be, when Beast stared from above. Sometimes were to the side. Or deeper. Fish moved fast. Had to study fish. Had to take time to be sure where they were. Would only have one chance to catch fish. When Beast dove into water, fish would flee, sliding through water like snake, and would be gone.

Beast does not like water. Alli-gator live in water. Some much bigger than Beast. But did not see any alli-gator in bayou. Was safe.

Stared at water. Stared at fish, longer than Beast tail, bigger around than Beast head, full of good, stinky fish-meat. Good food. Licked jaw with coarse, rough tongue, thinking about fish-taste. Wanted fish to eat.

Stared. Was more than five cat-fish. Beast could count to five. Was more than five.

Studied water. Water flowed from there to there, from upstream to downstream, like wind flowed from upwind to downwind. If Beast landed wrong, fish would flee from below Beast to there and Beast would have to hunt again.

Pulled paws in tight. Inched out on limb, pawpawpaw. Slow, so cat-fish would not see movement reflected in water. Beast was beautiful in surface of water. Big-cat. Beast hunter. Beast picked place where three cat-fish lay unmoving in water, nose to nose to nose. Slowly stretched out back legs and lifted hips into air. Slowly, slowly, slowly pulled paws close to fish-side of limb.

Snarled and closed mouth. Dropped. Hit water, nose first. Water shot up nose, into head. Opened mouth and spread claws wide. Before tail hit water, Beast brought front paws together in fast move.

Claws hooked into fish. Cat-fish wriggled and fought. Pulled cat-fish to mouth. Bit down on head. Caught cat-fish! Held cat-fish in mouth and swam to surface. Other cat-fish were gone. Sneaky cat-fish.

Swam to shore with cat-fish struggling like . . . like fish. Bit down harder and walked from bank of bayou, dripping, shaking pelt and loose skin free of bayou water. Lay belly down in cool mud and put paw on catfish, holding fish in mud. Bit off fish head and chewed. Fish stopped fighting. Was dead. Was good cat-fish. Was good fish-meat. Ate and ate. Beast belly was full and stretched. Beast lay on side in cool mud and snorted with laughter. Would change here. Would let Jane wake in muddy place, stinking of dead fish. Snorted with laughter again.

Entered Gray Between. And changed.

"I don't freaking believe it. *Mud?* Beast, you are dead meat!" I slipped and slid to my knees and then to my feet. I was slathered in mud, as if I'd gone to a spa and had them do a total-body mud bath. But this mud was rank and fishy and . . . I saw something on my thigh and pulled off a fish fin. Tossed it to the water. "Oh, you are in so much trouble," I muttered.

Inside, Beast chuffed with laughter.

I pulled off my gobag, tossed it into a low tree limb, and dove into the water. A trail of mud followed me as I swam off the muck and then paddled to the low-hanging limb where the gobag was resting in the branches. Using the limber branches, I pulled myself out of the water and up into the tree. And got dressed. I stank, but at least I wasn't muddy. Two hours later I was back home, in the shower, and smelled less like rotting fish. Gag.

Deep inside, Beast was still amused and snorting with laughter from time to time. Dang cat.

We stood in sub-five, staring at the thing on the wall. It had some vaguely humanoid features—left hand, mouth, throat, two feet. The rest looked like hamburger, including his skull. The body smelled like sickness, like the way vamps smelled when the plague ravaged them, and slightly scorched, the way vamp blood smelled when it came in contact with sterling silver. As we watched, a small, discolored, bloody blob was expelled from the mass and fell to the clay floor. A silver fléchette, ruined by vamp blood and then extruded from the mass of muscle and bone as if by peristalsis. That had been Bruiser's word. I had looked it up, as it hadn't been part of my EMT training so long ago. It meant the fléchette had been pooped out on the floor.

If Santana was conscious, there was no way to tell. Leo had seen to it that vamps came by several times a day, always under guard, and fed it from their torn wrists. Humans came by too, two or three handpicked by Leo, and gave a few drops.

Jodi asked, "What's the werewolf doing here?" She indicated the floor in front of the thing on the wall.

"Brute lies there twelve hours a day. He refuses to be sent away. You try getting a three-hundred-pound wolf to move."

Jodi narrowed her eyes and looked from the bizarre thing on the wall to me. "I said, 'What's the werewolf doing here?' A werewolf. In the city. Without one of those green things that kill them when they try to get out of hand."

"Oh." Lately I had begun to forget about Brute as a source of were-taint contagion and started thinking about him as a big dog. Not the smartest thing I'd ever done. "He lies there staring at the artwork while it quivers and drinks and occasionally pulses with some bizarre form of life. When that happens, Brute sniffs and growls and snarls. That's about it. No grindylow has come by to check on him, but he also doesn't seem interested in biting people."

I didn't add that at night the wolf appeared at my side door scratching to be let in. I had no idea how he got from vamp central to my house, but Alex had done a preliminary sweep of security cameras and found no trace of the wolf on the streets trotting, running, lumbering, or riding in a car to get there. He just appeared, scratched, demanded a steak on a plate, and went to sleep. He slept on a small twin mattress Alex bought him the morning after the Kid woke buried beneath three hundred pounds of dog.

"I'm satisfied," Jodi said. "For now. But if he bites a human I'll shoot him." Brute raised his head to us and chuffed. Jodi frowned.

"Questions. What did you do with the heart of the vamp?" I nodded to the wall. "And is it decomposing?"

Jodi's lips twisted into something that was nothing like amusement. More like satisfaction and vengeance and something darker than I'd ever seen on her face before. "Lachish has it. She's . . . working with it."

She turned on a heel and walked to the elevator. Just before the doors closed, she said, "Don't forget girls' day out this Thursday."

"I haven't. Del will be joining us."

"Long as I get pampered, I don't give a rat's ass who's getting pampered with me." She lifted a shoulder as if she thought her words were a tad too strong. "I like Del. She's good people." The doors closed and the elevator took the local law up to the public floors. I was looking forward to a massage and maybe a facial. Maybe a little time in a steam room.

I heard a snort and looked at Brute. He had risen while Jodi walked away and was standing at my thigh. I tensed. Brute still didn't like me, and I had been inattentive long enough for him to get from the feet of the SoD to me. Not my smartest moment for distraction. "What?" I asked him mildly.

He put his nose at my hand, where it hung by my side, and snuffled me. Tentatively, he opened his mouth and his large tongue licked out and . . . tasted my hand. Then he shoved his big head under my palm and nudged me. I took the hint and scratched him behind his ears. "Don't get used to this," I warned. "I am not a dog person."

Brute snorted slightly in clear disbelief. I stayed with Brute for a while, scratching his ears, neck, chest, and shoulders, studying the Son of Darkness. He was a problem I had no idea how to deal with. I should have killed him. If killing him was even possible. But if I had succeeded, the Euro-Vamps would have declared war, descended on the U.S., and . . . That would have been bad.

Leaving him semi-alive was better than us at war. Maybe.

Leo had informed the vamp world that Santana was "currently abiding as my guest," refusing to add any details.

The Europeans had screamed and wailed about Santana, sent long letters and even e-mails full of promises and threats, demanding their Dark Heir be returned to them. Then they had sent notice that the negotiation and visit by senior vamps was back on, according to the previous schedule. And they went silent again. We knew they were plotting. Planning. We knew they would come eventually, looking for vengeance and justice, looking for a return of their creator, but mostly looking to steal land and territory.

We'd be ready.

I turned on a booted foot and left the subbasement for the morning skies and an overheated summer day.

Entering from the back, I stepped into my garden. The morning light softened the broken stone of the boulders I'd had put there and sparkled off pooled rainwater.

Molly sat on the ground beside the fountain, her clothes rain damp, her hands pressed into the soil, fingers curled around what looked like a stick. Her eyes were closed, her face turned up to the sun. I stopped and studied her, watching and wondering. I could see her magics sparkling around her, not the new death magics but the old earth magic that had been hers before she embraced death to save her sisters, her daughter, and herself. Silvery and greenish and full of life.

I didn't know what it meant, but Molly looked almost

peaceful. Almost normal. Except for the stick. It was the root and branch of the dead rosemary plant she used in workings. It had once been alive, but her death magics had killed it, and I didn't know why she still kept it. It had to be painful to constantly see proof of one's magic gone awry.

Molly lowered her face and opened her eyes, staring at the deadwood. *"Vivo. Coalesco,"* she said in Latin, instead of her usual Gaelic. Her power swirled and shot down to the dead stick. Hesitantly, she raised one hand and held it over the dead root and branch of rosemary resting near her knees, and . . . it sprouted. Pale green leaves sprang from the branch, growing to half an inch long. The root spread rootlets that crawled over the ground and dug into the earth. Molly gasped and made a soft, surprised, questing sound.

My mouth fell open.

My best friend ever looked up at me, her eyes practically glowing with happiness. "Life. There was life in it still." Her eyes spilled over and tears ran down her cheeks.

And maybe that was what I'd learned through all this, through dealing with the undead. That even in the midst of death, there was often a spark of life left. That life went on even in the heart of mortality. And that perhaps that was something the undead had forgotten—the beauty of simply being alive.

I walked to Mol and sat on the wet ground, the rosemary plant between us, its fresh scent filling the small garden.

ABOUT THE AUTHOR

Faith Hunter was born in Louisiana and raised all over the South. She writes full-time, tries to keep house, and is a workaholic with a passion for travel, jewelry making, orchids, skulls, Class II and III white-water kayaking, and writing.

Many of the orchid pics on her Facebook fan page show skulls juxtaposed with orchid blooms; the bones are from roadkill prepared by taxidermists or a pal named Mud. In her collection are a fox skull, a cat skull, a dog skull, a goat skull (that is, unfortunately, falling apart), a cow skull, the jawbone of an ass, and a wild boar skull, complete with tusks. She recently purchased a mountain lion skull and would love to have the thighbone and skull of an African lion (one that died of old age, of course).

She and her husband own thirteen kayaks at last count and love to RV, as they travel with their dogs to white-water rivers all over the Southeast.

Read on for a special preview of the
first book in Faith Hunter's Soulwood series,

BLOOD OF THE EARTH

Coming October 2015 from Roc

Edgy and not sure why, I twisted the water out of the
laundry and carried the basket off the back porch. I hung
my T-shirts and overalls on the front wire, my two long
skirts on the outer wire, and what my mama had called my
intimate attire on the wire between, where no one could see
them. I didn't want another visit from Brother Ephraim or
Elder Ebenezer because of my wanton ways. Or even
another courting attempt from Joshua Purdy. Or worse, a
visit from Ernest Jackson, Jr., the preacher. So far I'd kept
him out of my house, but there would come a time when
he'd bring help and try to force his way in. It was getting
tiresome having to chase churchmen off my land at the
business end of a shotgun, and at some point God's Cloud
of Glory Church would bring enough reinforcements that I
couldn't stand against them. It was a battle I was preparing
for, one I knew I'd likely lose, but I would go down fighting
one way or another.

The breeze freshened, sending my wet skirts rippling on
the line as if they were alive. Red, gold, and brown leaves
skittered across the three acres of freshly cut grass. Branches
overhead cracked, clacked, and groaned with the wind,
leaves rustling as if whispering some dread tiding. The chill

fall air had been perfect for birdsong; squirrels had been racing up and down the trees, stealing nuts and hiding them for the coming winter. I'd seen a big black bear this morning, chewing on nuts, halfway up the hill.

Standing in the cool breeze, I studied my woods, listening, feeling, tasting the unease that had prickled at my flesh for the past few months, ever since Jane Yellowrock had come visiting and turned my life upside down. She was the one responsible for the repeated visits by the churchmen. She was the one who had brought all the changes, even if it wasn't intentional. Maybe it had been worth it all—saving all the children—but I was the one paying the price, not her. She was long gone and I was alone in the fight for my life. Even the woods knew things were different.

Sunlight dappled the earth, and cabbages, gourds, pumpkins, and winter squash burst with color in the garden. A muscadine vine running up the nearest tree, tangling in the branches, had started dropping ripe fruit. I smelled my wood fire on the breeze, and hints of that apple-crisp chill that meant a change of seasons, the sliding into fall. I tilted my head, listening to the wind, smelling the breeze, feeling the forest through the soles of my bare feet. There was no one on my land except the wild critters, nothing wrong that I could sense, but the hundred and fifty acres of woods bordering the flatland around the house, up the steep hill and down into the gorge, had been whispering all day. Something was not right.

In the distance I heard a crow call a warning, sharp with distress. The squirrels ducked into hiding, suddenly invisible. The feral cat I had been feeding darted under the shrubs, her black head and multicolored body fading into the shadows. The trees murmured restlessly.

I didn't know what it meant. It wasn't an omen or a portent, as there were no such things according to my mawmaw. But I listened anyway. I always listened to my woods and the gnawing, whispering sense of *danger*, *injury*, *damage* was like sandpaper abrading my skin, making me jumpy, disturbing my sleep. Something was *wrong* even if I didn't know what it was.

I reached out to it, to the woods, reached with my mind. Silently I asked it, *What? What is it?*

There was no answer. There never was. But as if the forest

knew that it had my attention, the wind died and the whispering leaves fell still. I caught my breath at the strange hush, not daring even to blink. But nothing happened. No sound, no movement. I lifted the empty wash basket and stepped away from my old-fashioned solar clothes dryer—turning and turning—my feet on the cool grass, my gaze cast up and inward, but I could sense no direct threat. Yet chill bumps rose on my skin. *What?* I asked. An eerie fear grew in me, racing up my spine like spiders with sharp, tiny feet. Something was coming. Something similar to Jane but subtly different. Something was coming that might hurt me. Again.

From down the hill I heard the sound of a vehicle climbing the mountain's narrow, single-lane, rutted road. It wasn't Ebenezer's rattletrap Ford truck, or Joshua's newer Toyota long bed. It wasn't the high-pitched motor of a hunter's all-terrain vehicle. It was a car, straining up the twisty Deer Creek Mountain.

My house was the last one, just below the crest of the hill. No one came up here. No one but trouble. The wind whooshed down again, icy and cutting, a downdraft that bowed the trees. They swayed in the wind, branches scrubbing. Sighing. Muttering, too low to hear.

I raced back inside my cabin, dropping the empty basket, placing John's old single-shot, bolt-action shotgun near the stove under a pile of folded blankets. His lever-action carbine .30-30 Winchester went near the front window. I shoved the small Smith & Wesson .32 into the bib of my coveralls, hoping I didn't shoot myself if I had to draw it fast. I picked up the double-barrel break-action shotgun and checked the ammo. Both barrels held three-inch shells. The contact area of the latch was worn and needed to be replaced, but at close distance I wasn't going to miss. I might dislocate my shoulder, but the strangers would be a while in healing too.

I debated for a second whether I should switch out the standard shot rounds for salt or birdshot, but the woods' disharmony seemed to be growing, causing a particular and abrasive itch under my skin. I snapped the gun closed and peeked out the blinds to see a four-door sedan coming to a stop beside John's old Chevy C10 truck. Two people inside, a man and a woman.

Strangers, I thought. Not from God's Cloud of Glory

Church, the cult I'd grown up in. Not a local vehicle. And no dogs to check them out for me with noses and senses humans no longer had. Just three small graves at the edge of the woods.

A black-haired, dark-eyed man stepped out of the driver's side. Maybe Cherokee or Creek if he was a mountain native, though his features didn't seem tribal. I'd never seen a French man or a Spaniard, so maybe one of those Mediterranean countries. He was tall, like the churchmen, maybe six feet, but he wasn't dressed like a local. More citified, in black pants, starched shirt, tie, and jacket. He had a cell phone in his pocket, sticking out just a little. Western boots, old and well cared for. There was something about the way he moved, feline and graceful. Not a farmer or a God's Cloud preacher. Not enough bulk for the first one, not enough righteous determination in his expression or bearing for the other. City clothes.

He opened the passenger door for the other occupant, and a woman stepped out. Petite, with black skin and curly black hair. Her clothes billowed in the cool breeze and she put her face into the wind as if sniffing. Like the man, she moved all catlike. Feral. As if she had never been tamed, though I couldn't have said why I got that impression.

Around the house, my woods moaned in the freshening wind, branches clattering like old bones, anxious, but I could see nothing about the couple that would indicate danger. They looked like any other city folk who might come looking for my herbal teas. As they approached the house, they passed the tall length of flagpole in the middle of the raised beds of the front yard, and started up the seven steps to the porch. And then I realized why they moved and felt all wrong. They weren't human. And I saw the weapon bulge at the man's shoulder, beneath his jacket. In a single smooth motion, I braced the break-action shotgun against my shoulder, slammed open the door, and pointed the business end of the gun at the strangers.

"Whaddya want?" I demanded in my childhood God's Cloud of Glory Church dialect. They came to a halt at the third step, too close for me to miss, too far away for them to disarm me safely. The man raised his hands as if he was asking for peace, but the little woman hissed. She drew back her lips in a snarl and growled at me. I knew cats. This was a cat. A cat in human form. A devil, according to the church. I trained the barrel on her midsection, just like John had showed me the first time he'd put the gun in my hands. As I aimed, I took a single step backward so my back was against the doorjamb, to keep me from getting bowled over or from breaking a shoulder when I fired.

"Paka, no," the man said. The words were gentle, the touch to her arm tender. I had never seen a man touch a woman like that and my hands jiggled the shotgun in surprise before I caught myself. The woman's snarl subsided and she leaned in to the man, just like one of my cats might. His arm went around her and he smoothed her hair back, watching me as I watched them. Alert, taking in everything about me and my home, the man lifted his nose in the air to sniff the scents of my land, his nose widening and contracting. Alien. All so alien, these two.

"What do you want?" I asked again, this time with no church accent, and with the grammar I'd learned from reading my once-forbidden and much-loved library books.

"I'm Special Agent Rick LaFleur, with PsyLED, and this is Paka. Jane Yellowrock sent us," the man said.

Of *course* this new problem was related to Jane. Nothing in my whole life had gone right since she had darkened my door. The Cherokee vampire hunter who worked for vampires might as well have brought a curse on my home. She had a strange job, wore clothes and guns and knives like a man, and I had known from the beginning that she would be trouble. But I had liked her. So had my woods. She moved like these two, willowy and slinky. Alert.

She had come to my house asking questions about God's Cloud of Glory. She had wanted a way onto the church's property, which bordered mine, to rescue a blood-sucker. Because John and I had left the church, Jane had figured that I'd be willing to help her. And, God help me, I had.

I'd paid the price for helping her and wished now that I'd left well enough alone.

"Prove it," I said, resettling the gun against my shoulder. The man slowly lowered his hand and removed a wallet from his pocket, displaying an identification card and badge. "Not good enough. Tell me something about Jane that no one but her knows."

Paka leaned away from the man and sniffed the wind,

her mouth open and lips pulled back, then leaned toward me and sniffed again with a sucking *scree* of sound. It was the way cats scented the world around them.

"Jane is not a human, though she apes it better than some," Paka said, her words strangely accented, her voice scratchy and hoarse. "She was once mated to my mate. He is mine now." She placed a possessive hand on his arm.

Well. That was more than I had expected. When I'd talked to Jane she had told me that the man she would send would break my heart if I let him, as he'd broken Jane's. This Rick was what the romance novels I'd read called tall, dark, and handsome, a grim, distant man with too many secrets. A heartbreaker for sure. I wondered whether Paka would cut out his heart when he got around to breaking hers.

Rick pulled out his cell phone and tapped and swiped it a few times with his thumb. He read from the screen. "Jane quoted you as saying, 'Woman, I been in trouble from God's Cloud of Glory and the colonel ever since I turned twelve and he tried to marry me. Anything you can do to piss him off will just make my day.' She also said you make the best chicken and dumplings she ever tasted. That about right?"

That was it exactly. I frowned. Around me the forest rustled, expectant and uneasy. "I was doing just fine until Jane came along. She made my problems a lot worse. But yeah, that sums it up." I broke open the shotgun, leaving it draped over my arm, and backed into my home, standing aside as they mounted the last of the steps.

My black cat, Jezzie, raced out of the house and Paka caught her. The two hissed and batted at each other, and Jezzie left scratches on Paka's arms. Scratches that bled, yet Paka didn't seem to notice. The tiny woman laughed, the sound as odd and scratchy as her words. And the strangest thing happened—Jezzie rolled over, lay belly-up in Paka's arms, and closed her eyes. Instantly, she was asleep. Jezzie didn't like people; she barely tolerated me in her house, and let me live here because I brought canned food. From the corner of the doorway, Cello peeked, the meek and terrified cat staring up at Paka, her tail twitching. Paka extended her other arm and Cello leapt up, sprang along Paka's arm to stop on the woman's shoulder. The cat's eyes looked excited, maybe a little too focused, the way they got when she spotted something that might be fun to chase.

Around the grassy property, the woods quieted, as if waiting for a storm that would break soon, bringing them rain to feed their roots.

"Come on in," I said, backing farther into my house.

I watched the two strangers enter. I wondered what was about to happen to my once sheltered and isolated life. I wondered what the churchmen watching my house with binoculars from the next property would have to say about it. What they would do about it. Maybe this time they'd kill my cats too, the way they had shot my dogs. More graves to feed the earth. Grief welled up in me and I tamped it down where no one could see it, concentrating on the here and now and what I knew about the couple.

Paka seemed less human than Rick, more cat. Not necessarily unstable, but all claws and instinct, with a taste for games and blood. Rick was with PsyLED. I'd looked up the paranormal department of Homeland Security and discovered that PsyLED stood for Psychometric Law Enforcement Department of Homeland Security, and they investigated and solved paranormal crimes—crimes involving magic, blood-suckers, were-creatures, and witches. So why were they here, except to cause me more trouble?

Warily, keeping my body turned toward them, I backed into the main room of the house, sliding my feet on the wood floor into the great room that was the living space, with the eating area and the kitchen at the back. I jutted my chin toward the far end of the old table and mismatched chairs that had been John's maw-maw's. "Sit a spell. I've got some hot tea steeping on the Waterford."

The man pulled the woman's chair out for her and they sat. *Solicitous*—that's what the romance books called it. Stupid books that had nothing to do with the life of a mountain woman. City women, maybe. But never the wives and women of God's Cloud of Glory Church. When I was sure the visitors were in positions that would require them to make two or three moves before they could attack, I set the shotgun on the table and got out three pottery mugs. I wasn't using John's maw-maw's good china for strangers who I might have to shoot later. That seemed deceitful, and though John was dead and gone, I'd still want him to be proud of me.

With a pot holder, I moved the teapot to the right of the

woodstove, where the hob was cooler, and removed the tea strainer. I could have made some coffee—the man looked like a coffee-drinking type—but I didn't want to encourage them to stay. I poured the spice tea into the mugs and put them on an old carved oak tray, with cloth napkins and fresh cream and sugar. I added three spoons and placed the tea tray on the table.

"Welcome to my home. Hospitality and safety while you're here," I said, hearing the reluctance in my tone. It was an old God's Cloud saying, and though the church and I had parted ways a long time ago, some things stayed with a woman. Guests should be safe so long as they acted right.

The nonhumans took the tea, the woman adding an inch of the real cream to the top and wrapping her hands around the mug as though she felt the chill of winter coming. The man held his mug one-handed, shooting surreptitious glances at my stuff. I noticed that his gun hand stayed empty, where he could get to his weapon fast.

I narrowed my eyes at him. "I asked you once, and I'll ask again: What do you want?" And knowing . . . knowing . . . it would be nothing but trouble.